Antman

by

Robert V. Adams

'Antman' is the copyright of the author, Robert V. Adams, 2005 - 2012.

All rights reserved. No part of this book may be reproduced or transmitted in any form or by any means, electronic or mechanical, including photocopying, recording, or by any information storage and retrieval system, without permission in writing from the copyright owner.

    ISBN   1477656170
    EAN   978-1477656174

'Antman' is published by Taylor Street Publishing LLC, who can be contacted at:

http://www.taylorstreetbooks.com
http://ninwriters.ning.com

The book cover illustration is by Millie Hine. The book cover design is by Peril of http://www.perilstudio.co.uk. All rights are reserved.

All characters are fictional, and any resemblance to anyone living or dead is accidental.

'A "supercolony" of the ant Formica yessensis on the Ishikari Coast of Hokkaido was reported to be composed of 306 million workers and 1,080,000 queens living in 45,000 interconnected nests across a territory of 2.7 square kilometres.'

Holldobler, Bert and Wilson, Edward O. (1990) The Ants Springer-Verlage, Berlin p. 1

'Ants are waiting to become the next weapon of the serial killer, the terrorist. We can probably say that in the early history of peoples, in the beginning was the fear of attack by plagues, swarms or armies, whether of other people, locusts, cockroaches or ants. Plagues of insects have biblical associations. Armies have a militaristic, almost humanised, image, whereas hordes evoke something huge and out of control. Ants regularly become swarms, armies and hordes and it is hordes which contribute to myths of transformation, throughout the life course. In myth and reality, ant hordes are prominent among the gatekeepers to rituals of life or death. In the face of almost every natural disaster or human agency, including nuclear war, along with termites and cockroaches, their powers of organisation and adaptability make them virtually indestructible. They are apparently immune to nuclear radiation sickness. In contrast with termites and cockroaches, their open-air habits and hardiness mean that in the hands of a criminal with even a modicum of scientific knowledge, they are capable of wielding with equal vigour and deadliness the twin-edged sword of extreme terror and destruction.'

Fortius, Tom (1999) 'Ants: Allies, Terrorists or Instruments of Terror?' Conference Paper. Northern Colloquium of Entomological Research, Hull, Hull Wilberforce University p. 15

Part One

Genesis

Chapter 1

From the night they'd taken his whimpering brother, wearing the little red romper suit, to that place from which he'd never returned, Graver always saw red against the black of darkness as the colour of fear. You could hide the signs of fear behind a curtain of anger, but you could never do away with the feeling itself. It was one more task beyond all the practical problems of every day: how to avoid being swamped by that fear.

He got dressed but not washed, dressed up so he wouldn't be recognised, and prepared to drive to town and go walkabout.

Two words flew from the ether and lodged themselves in his head, becoming a mantra: kill-ing-pi-gs-kill-ing-pi-gs-kill-ing ...

He let the sounds float, now as ever finding their repetition reassuring. They created a song-line independent of the meaning of the words. He hummed them, fitting them to the rhythm of that introduction to the third movement of the Bruckner seventh.

Di-di-dum-dum-dum-dum-dum-dum-dum-dum-dum-duuuuuum.
Strong rhythm. Over and over. Most of the time the music obliterated the reverberating tinnitus caused by the movements of the slimy maggots which, like those parasitic flesh-boring insects he'd read about, had crawled in through his ears while he slept and slithered towards the tunnels of his brain. They were microscopic in size and few in number as yet though, and he'd seen and read enough to know they could be lost for twenty years if they explored every route in that maze of the outer brain, before they came upon his queen.

On the other hand, they could find her in a single year, or less. He couldn't take the chance. He had to act now.

* * *

Graver experienced one of those moods of great lucidity. He found himself outside the central branch of the library in town. He walked casually in. Between five and six there were plenty of empty chairs at the tables in the reading area. He went straight to the shelves he invariably visited and took down the reference work on the social insects. He flicked the well-thumbed pages to a passage he knew almost off by heart and read: 'The collective power of the ant should not be underestimated. The African colonies of the driver ants of the genus Dorylus can contain more than twenty million ants. These are different from South American army ants in that they tend to have a much more permanent base nest, excavated to a depth of up to four metres, from which they carry out raids on an almost daily basis. Raiding swarms of these ants can devour with frightening rapidity any prey which for one reason or another is unable to move out of their path. There are accounts of tethered horses being reduced to skeletons within hours.'

* * *

Graver was not entirely sure when he became the executioner.

'It was probably when the urge to conduct the performances became realisable. You rehearse some things in your head so many times that when they happen you hardly notice the slide from thought to action. I daydreamed a good deal about the past. I had wanted for some time to reach into my past and tell people – especially Marg from down the road, a couple of hundred miles away, who, when I was a child, leaned over me and patted my head with "what a nice boy" – that they were utterly mistaken. After a while, because the appearance of niceness couldn't exist indefinitely on top of the nastiness, it wouldn't matter one way or the other. Yet (this is the bit that messes you up) I wanted both of them. When I had one I wanted the other. And vice versa. You can only do this by splitting your mind in two or three or four, or any number you care to imagine.

'I put the trouble down to being in the Homes. At primary school the Homes children were picked out by everyone. At register on Monday mornings, Miss Clock – we called her this; I can't remember her real name but recall the sentence which carried her through most days: "I'll clock you if you don't stop that." – used to call out "Homes children to the front". We all filed out and stood in a line facing the rest of the class, while she collected the dinner money from everyone else. It went on from there, all day, every school day, every week of term, the picking out of the Homes children.

'I could cope with the attempts to bully me at school, since in any case the Homes children stuck together at school and this made other pupils sufficiently hesitant about attacking us to ward off the worst intimidation or violence. But the real threats came from within the Homes. School was a minor dread, compared to the fear which yawned in the pit of my stomach as I walked back from school every afternoon. And it wasn't all the children by any means.

'As a consequence of what happened to me in the Homes, the main target of my anger was that dried up, crackleskin, leather-faced prune of a reverend mother whom I hated as anything but reverend and as the antithesis of the mother I couldn't have, as neither could most of the other children in the orphanage. But after it happened, I was stricken with guilt about those thoughts, as though I'd actually done it.'

***

Graver scraped his gnawed forefinger over the pages till he reached a later chapter of the book. The page was well-thumbed. He almost knew it by heart. "Ants are the inheritors of the earth. They survive in conditions which would defeat most other living organisms. They can survive in heavily polluted environments. Species such as the common red ants and black ants on many British lawns, Myrmica Ruginodis and Acanthomyops Niger, actually seem able to activate micro-organisms which reduce the level of nitrate concentrations in the atmosphere. Ants seem virtually unaffected by radiation. Along with a small number of other insects they would probably survive a nuclear war." He experienced a tremor in the lower abdomen as he read the words, his lips mouthing key phrases. He wouldn't have known it as such, but he was near orgasm, as near as when the ants were carrying out his gruesome wishes.

Graver turned back to the beginning of the book. He read passages from the introductory chapter, skipping to pages he'd marked with Stick-its, revisiting particularly familiar paragraphs:

"There are somewhere over 8,700 species of ants in the world and once the entire planet has been explored this total may rise to 10,000. Ants are found almost everywhere, from Alaska to the Equator, with the exception of a few remote Pacific islands and the ice-covered continents around the North and South Poles.

"Ants, along with spiders, cockroaches and centipedes, are the stuff of nightmares. They are the crawling beings which while we sleep inhabit our dreaming brains, clogging them with fears and fantasies, reducing our daytime confidence to palpitating night time fears under the bedclothes.

"When you sit on the lawn with your bare feet in sandals, six legs which make your flesh creep make their way from slivers of grass bent over the lip of your sandal onto the naked bulb of your ankle, up through the fine hairs of your calf, behind your knee, before injecting venom through the softer skin in response to your hand reaching down to scratch the itch."

***

Graver rose suddenly from the table, looking up as though someone had called him. Leaving the open book on the table, he walked rapidly from the building. He was talking to himself, using two quite distinct voices.

'It's rubbish to assert the past is a foreign country. It's always with us.'

'Of course it is. The sound of voices is the echo left by our ancestors. They leaned over us when we were children, fixing themselves in our memory before their frail bodies crumbled into coffin shapes.'

* * *

As if he could forget those rows, the beatings, his cries of terror as his father's hand raised the strap once, twice, again and again. As if he could forget the defiling of his body, the violation of his privacy under the sheets. Or the loneliness, the intense self-loathing, the guilt, the anger.

* * *

Here was a memory with a tolerable lead-in. He remembered Mother Bernadette. She attended to the children. Oh she attended all right. She had the power. She ruled the Home with the awesome power of the dictator, backed by her punishing God.

* * *

Graver, down in the park, staring at the ducks, walking along by the waterside, appealing to the spirit of Mother Bernadette.
  'I never meant to trip you. I was sad to see you bleeding when you fell. I heard you call out as you lay there, blood hissing from your ear and nose, reaching towards me: "Bring me a glass of somet'ing, little one, a little glass of somet'ing. Oh, my poor head. Fetch a doctor for my poor head."
  'I nodded and nearly let you reach me with your hand which still held the cane. It was a lifetime before you stopped calling out. I felt easier when you called me Thomas because then I knew you couldn't see me, or if you could, you couldn't recognise me and take my name with you to that place beyond death, from which to return and haunt me. When you died I watched your body for ages, hypnotised by the sounds still coming from it as the organs within it slowly came to rest. No one had ever told me how noisy a newly dead person's body is. It's like a steam engine when the heat's removed from the firebox. But even then, no earthly power would move my feet or let me lean towards you. I got up, walked towards the door, closed it and ran away. If I had known a single line of a hymn you hadn't corrupted, I'd have sung it for joy.
  'I would have got away with it because no one in that place would have suspected a small boy of doing in Reverend Mother. Any more than outsiders would have believed the injuries she inflicted on the children in her care. The sisters knew of course, and the other children.

Which was why nobody breathed a word till about thirty years later, when it became quite all right to sprag on staff who on the whole were too old and decrepit to beat you. Three of the girls grassed Mother Bernadette then, but it was too late because she had been under the sod for almost a quarter of a century.'

* * *

Years later, the turning point, the first time he became aware of the possibility of evening up the score. Remember, he kept saying to himself: in order to be a successful experimenter you have to be very, very clever.

* * *

The experiment. He would remember this first experiment.
People stared curiously, walking away, or if it was too late, trying to avoid his glance. Graver wandered through the park, debating endlessly with the voices, the crowd multiplying in his head, jostling for space to express themselves.
'What does she want?'
'She wants to come out, sir.'
'Out of what?'
'She wants to come out of the killing machine, sir.'
Graver shook his head.
'No, can't do that.'
He turned, faced his invisible audience, challenging them to debate the matter.
'What? No reason to do it.'
'What did you say your name was?'
'Shbiggesdrywauk, sir.'
'Whassat? Never heard of it.'
'Remember what I said: in order to succeed you have to be very, very clever.'

Chapter 2

Less than twenty-five miles from Coldharbour as the crow flies, Laura Fortius shepherded her two children, Matthew aged nine and Sarah aged eight, through the early spring crowds of Kingston upon Hull, Yorkshire, England, down King Edward Street, past the Town Docks Museum and the Ferens Art Gallery, and into the Old Town at Whitefriargate. She turned to the shop window and caught sight of her reflection – tall, slender to the point of thinness, her aquiline nose accentuated by her short hair. Auburn was an exaggeration, she thought. Mousey, more like. The overall effect was of neatness rather than beauty. Her irritation at the hairdresser boiled up again. The problem with some hairdressers was their pre-formed view of what she needed. It didn't matter what she said, they followed their own plan regardless. Fancy styling it to make me look so pinched and mean, she said to herself as she led the children through the Victorian arcade, crossed the road and walked the short distance to the car park.

Laura let out a long, involuntary sigh as she unlocked the battered old Volvo estate. The car had seen them through more than a decade since before her husband Tom obtained his tenured post at the University. The reliability of the car annoyed her. Its appearance reminded her of stuffy, intellectual husbands, sinking into safe middle age. Bloody reliable Volvos. She had a premonition that at this rate the car would outlast their marriage. This was slightly contradictory. Why shouldn't I be contradictory, she thought. All these intellectual men, so damned logical all the time. She installed the two children in their seat belts in the back. She went round to the driver's side and inserted the ignition key. As she turned it slightly, the radio was in mid-flow: "... absconded forty-eight hours ago from Cortham Hall secure mental health unit near Goole. Police are warning members of the public not to approach him. He could be dangerous." She turned the key back and the radio clicked into silence.

'I'm thirsty,' said Sarah.

'I want an ice cream,' said Matthew.

'When we've dropped the shopping off at the car, we're going to meet Helen at the coffee shop,' said Laura. 'Stay here, cherubs, while Mummy pops back to the corner of the road. Don't worry, you'll be able to see me waving. I only want to look up and down the road for one sec. Keep your hands on the boot of the car, like this. Look Matthew, copy Sarah.'

Matthew, like his father in appearance as well as personality would always be less reliable than his sister, she thought. Sarah was the image of her mother, tall for her age and built like a coat hanger. "For Heaven's sake, feed the child," Laura's mother had said when they visited her recently. It was her self-appointed mission to stuff both the children with sweets and cakes at all opportunities, which was why Laura's visits had tailed off since her father's death. Sarah already looks as though she'll be running an office, Laura thought. She desperately wanted not to pass her mistake on to her daughter. If we split up, I'll keep Sarah, he can have Matthew. Only this morning she'd let the thought fall like a stone into the puddle of her over-busy brain. The ripples spread, merging into all the other thoughts, losing definition, flattening out till they almost disappeared.

A noise near at hand brought her back to reality with a jolt. She couldn't place it, then she saw Matthew had a handful of small pebbles and was tossing them into the air, one at a time, trying to catch them. She immediately was able to place the metallic sound she now realised she had heard. One of the stones must have hit the bodywork of a car. Laura hoped fervently that it was her car.

'For goodness sake, Matthew, put those stones down. What do you think you're doing?'

Matthew did not reply, pulled a face and slowly opened his hand, letting the stones drop to the ground, one by one.

* * *

Laura wondered how different life would be if she acted on her intuitions immediately. Was it only minutes earlier – it might as well have been a lifetime – when she was listening to Matthew and Sarah giggling about the funny man as she walked with them back to the car park? It had dawned on her it would be ironic, if in the middle of an unseasonably warm and sunny morning in Hull, it took a couple of kids only two minutes to spot a seriously disturbed man the police hadn't found in as many days. These were stray thoughts. Like the wisps of cloud in the blue sky above, they came and blew away in moments in the strong, warm breeze.

She was back at the car in two minutes.

'Is that what Helen can't face,' she exclaimed to herself out loud, 'the chance that Detlev didn't commit suicide but was killed by such a man?'

'What did you say, Mummy?'

'Nothing darling. Mummy thought she'd lost her purse.'

'It's in your hand already, Mummy.'

'Yes, it is.'

'Silly Mummy.'

'That's right. Too silly for words.'

Laura's mind had jumped wildly from the strange man to the inquest.

She was still puzzled at how Detlev's death had occurred. She had her own reasons for wondering what the verdict of the inquest might be.

* * *

One minute to ten o'clock. Professor Tom Fortius from the Centre for Entomological Research at Hull Wilberforce University, shuffled uncomfortably on the tiny island of his chair. Big framed and, apart from his spreading waistline, muscular rather than fat, he often had difficulty accommodating his six foot six body in spaces built for more average people. His pet aversion was being given lifts in tiny cars designed for under-size people to drive about town.

Tom looked round the courtroom, his brilliant blue eyes almost hidden under a mass of near jet-black wavy hair, which as he leaned forward threatened to cascade down his forehead and prevent him seeing anything. He had too much on his mind to focus properly on the proceedings. It reminded him of a crematorium – not the kind of place you'd ever anticipate attending unless you had to. The usher had disappeared a few minutes ago through the door behind the coroner's bench. Those left in that sombre courtroom in Beverley, ten miles from Hull, sat in a silence strongly reminiscent of a religious ceremony.

Tom had worries over and above his questions about Detlev's untimely death, about ten months ago. The funeral, a few days later, had taken place too close to the shock of his death and the immediate grieving, for considered reflection. It was different now. This occasion created that uniquely dramatic atmosphere, through the deliberate concentration of many hearts and minds on the circumstances surrounding the death.

The courtroom was modestly small, with a raised desk and seats at the front facing a line of tables and chairs in the centre, and along each side two rows of chairs facing inwards. It was barely formal enough to serve its sombre purpose. The square seats in the courtroom, like the decor, were comfortable at a minimal level.

When the usher returned, he didn't have to raise his voice to be heard clearly by the fifteen people present: witnesses, relatives, two police officers and two press reporters.

The uniforms of the two police officers contrasted with the everyday clothes of most of the relatives and other witnesses. Constable Tebbutt displayed his nervousness at his first time giving evidence to a coroner's court by standing at the front table in the courtroom from soon after half past nine, whilst sorting and re-sorting his papers. Constable Birch, Scenes of Crime Officer, and very experienced at appearing in coroners' courts, was there as well, sitting down, more relaxed and conversational than her colleague.

The rear table was occupied by the two press reporters, who came in at the last minute and kept themselves to themselves. Witnesses, including Detlev's friends and family who had flown over from Wolfach, their home village in the Schwarz Wald of Germany, were sitting to the left of the coroner, next to the usher.

The usher, Frederick Blunt, his face as grey and his suit as plain and off-the-peg as his name, came in and stood, grey and bald like the butler in an old-style drama. He intoned in his sepulchral voice: 'The Court will stand.'

James Wilkes, coroner, followed and then Faith Wistow, the clerk who for the past six years had taken a shorthand record of these proceedings. Wilkes appeared embarrassed at even this minimal ritual and spoke almost to one side as though he couldn't abide that people still stood there while he sat down first:

'Please sit down.'

* * *

Robin Lovelace was lying on the unmade bed browsing through the pile of uninteresting morning mail. His eye caught an unwelcome view of the pudgy roll of fat round his waist which normally, because it was out of sight under his shirt, he could ignore. His bulging midriff apart, Robin had the undeveloped physique of the intellectual. Fair hair in his case meant almost devoid of body hair as well, a characteristic he thought might put women off. Perhaps his insecurity about his appearance was one reason for his repeated searching for reassurance through extra-marital relationships.

His wife Helen, still as slim at thirty-five as she had been fifteen years ago, shushed the dryer over her long blonde hair, before dressing.

'I'll fetch breakfast,' said Robin. He had intended to go into the University for nine-thirty. Impulsively he scrubbed that plan.

'When I watch you,' he said, 'I think rude thoughts.'

'You'd be better off working them out at the gym.'

A thought struck her.

'Didn't you have to be at work early?'

'No one'll miss me for an hour. Tom's away at the inquest.'

'Right.' Helen felt stupid. She paused. She changed the subject and hoped he didn't notice her hesitation. 'I wasn't joking about Rosie. You've had more than your nine lives with me. One more slip and we'll be going our separate ways.'

'I'm desperately sorry, darling. You have my word, on my life, that I will always be true to you till the day I die. I don't know what came over me. It must have been the effect of the drink and the tiredness.'

'And the hormones,' she said acidly. 'Perhaps you've been going through the male menopause.'

He pulled a face. He was sensitive about being on the brink of fifty. 'Truly, darling, it was you I was thinking about that night. You really are the most beautiful woman in the whole world. You're the only one for me.'

'I wish you'd give me compliments like that in the normal course of events, rather than only when you want something.'

'I love you, utterly, completely.'

She laughed, trying to act dismissively:

'You're a flatterer.' And an emotional child, she thought.

'Are we friends again?'

'I suppose so.'

'And lovers?'

'You'll have to wait and see. I'm about to leap out of the house to keep a date with a very patient hairdresser.'

He looked hurt now.

'Please, Helen, darling.'

She came round to his side of the bed, bent over and kissed him. 'I'm keeping your behaviour under review. I may give you an appointment later this evening, Dr Lovelace, when things have quietened down?'

Robin smiled. His mood changed abruptly and he sniggered.

'What is it?'

'It can wait,' he said.

'Come on,' she said impatiently.

'I realised just then when I was watching you, how bees make love with their fingers.'

'I didn't know bees had fingers. I'm surprised at such an elementary mistake from a University Reader in entomology.'

'They don't. It's poetic licence.'

'That's not fair,' she said crossly. 'Now you're a Reader you can make anything up. If I'd written that in an exam you'd have failed me. Reader? Why do they promote you and give you such a daft title? I mean, every primary school pupil learns to read.'

Robin refused to be put off.

'I wish I'd only just met you and you'd asked me what I did. I'd say I'm researching lovemaking with flowers, instead of boring insects.'

'Rule one,' she said. 'Never bite the hand that feeds you. You're only saying they're boring. I know you find them far more fascinating than us mere humans.'

Robin nodded absently.

'You're not meant to agree with that,' she complained. 'Anyway, insects aren't boring. Their lives interlock so closely with every other living organism. Without them to pollinate plants, for instance, there'd be no seeds to produce the next generation.'

'True, but there's hardly romance attached to them.'

'I don't believe this,' she said. 'You've switched sides and now I'm defending your subject.'

She looked quizzically at him from the stool in front of the dressing table:

'Are you trying to achieve an outside view for some paper you're writing?'

Robin seemed to ignore this as he accelerated into his argument.

'If the alternative is your average male in wellies, with beer gut and boxing gloves, give me a twelve hour love-making session between a pair of hermaphroditic giant snails any day.'

'Why hermaphroditic for goodness sake?'

'Basically because until they've explored each other's bodies they don't decide which is to be the man and which the woman. He sticks his love dart into her side and injects her with a massive dose of calcium carbonate plus various aphrodisiacs.'

'Robin, is this true?'

'Well the love dart and the calcium carbonate are, but the rest is speculative.'

'As usual,' she said, 'accurate on the pedestrian bits, while indulging wildly on the male fantasy front. Men!'

'Come back to bed.'

'No, I'm meeting Laura at ten-thirty and I have to do some shopping after the hairdresser.'

'You never said earlier you had to be anywhere.'

'You never listen.'

'That gives us at least half an hour.'

'Five minutes.'

'Pessimist.'

'You're incorrigible. You'll have to cut the description and forget the slowness of those snails.'

'My love dart is already quivering.'

'What makes you think it's your stab. It could be mine. Fancy snails having solved the problem of liberating women. Simply exchange genders.'

'Tease.' He was standing behind her, sliding his hand round to unbutton her blouse.

Helen was in that matter-of-fact mode he didn't fancy. 'Hurry, or I'll be late. You'll have to drop me in town before going to work.'

* * *

Laura had planned to be in town shopping with the children. She knew Helen was intending to pop into Marks and Spencer's that morning to try to change a skirt which she now felt was too short. Of all mornings, this day of the resumed inquest was the one to be out of the house, and hopefully distracted. So they had arranged to meet for coffee and a chat at Quenchers opposite Princes Quay between nine forty-five and ten. Normally, when their paths crossed casually on the street, Laura couldn't have a proper conversation with Helen for more than a minute or two. There was always some interruption, or a reason for not stopping longer. She thought about congratulating Helen. Tom had found out late last night about Robin's successful grant for the expedition to equatorial Africa. That would be a relatively safe topic of conversation. Tom was going to leave a message for Robin first thing. Helen would know by now. On another tack, it wasn't the occasion to ask about whether the inquest brought back all that emotion associated with Detlev's shocking death. Helen probably wouldn't have talked in any case. Perhaps it would release feelings which would somehow make too public her affair with the most senior research fellow in the tightly-knit Research Centre in which Robin and Tom were deputy director and director respectively. Helen had always said to Laura what a disaster it would be if Robin found out about her and Detlev.

'He'll use it to justify going for anyone he fancies,' she confided.

Laura had got the children up early, breakfasted, braved the early morning traffic jams and driven into town with them for nine o'clock. She parked in the long-stay park in the Old Town, but having arrived couldn't settle to shopping. Instead, she irritated herself and the children by passing in quick succession through several department stores without a clear notion about what style of summer outfit she was looking for and where she might find it. The kids grew increasingly restive. Sarah wanted the toilet and Matthew a drink. This took more time and chipped further away at her patience. She was able to change the skirt at M&S on the way. She finished up hunting through children's clothes stores for bargains and impulse buying one or two totally unsatisfactory items which neither Sarah nor Matthew liked. By ten o'clock she'd dropped the shopping back at the car and was already hanging about with the kids near the Ferens Art Gallery, but it was ten-fifteen before Helen turned up. They walked across Castle Street and sat outside the cafe at one of the tables by the yachts in the Marina. Ocean-going craft with half a dozen busy crew berthed side by side with tiny boats for sculling up and down the Humber. The breeze ruffled the water, jangling riggings on a hundred masts. Seagulls swooped and called raucously.

Helen was hardly aware of the colourful scene. It was earlier than she was used to stopping for coffee, but because it was later than she'd anticipated, she had that irritated sense of being late herself. Normally, she would have enjoyed the feeling of indulgence, but today she was angry and frustrated. She was mad with Robin for being so matter of fact about it, mad with herself for weakening and going to bed with him this morning. She was also very upset and not a little guilty about the tragedy of Detlev, but she couldn't take that on board at this moment. The frustration in her voice wasn't far from tears.

'Hell, Robin! First you were going, then you said you definitely weren't going. Now you are.'

'I wasn't,' he said sorrowfully.

'Just as I hoped we were moving onto an even keel you change the rules again. I can't believe it.'

'It's hardly me changing the rules. These research bodies are a law unto themselves, part of the uncertainty of academic life.'

'It can't be the Science Research Council. You told me the grants took ages to sort out.'

'No, it isn't,' he said hastily. 'It's our partner university. Someone's had to drop out.'

'Your wife has to suffer so you can fill the gap at the drop of a hat. Meanwhile another academic changes his mind and prefers to put his feet up.'

'It isn't like that. He's ill.'

'We have all this upheaval because one of your colleagues has the flu.'

'He hasn't got flu. He was told yesterday he's dying of cancer. He may only last a month.'

'Love it, don't you. Seeing me dig a pit for myself.'

Robin waved a hand: 'I didn't mean –'

'I thought the trip wasn't for another month.'

'They leave in less than a week.'

'You could follow on, presumably.'

'Unfortunately there's no chance of that. Either I go with them or we lose the tickets. That means we lose the place in the research team and possibly put the entire expedition, and the grant, in jeopardy.'

'So, suddenly, from not going at all, you're leaving immediately.'

'Well,' he said lamely, 'not exactly immediately.'

'Come on, Robin, within the next day or so.'

'I was due to go to the meeting in London anyway and the Oxford conference afterwards has been arranged for ages. It seems logical to return to Heathrow after that and hop on a plane.'

'That's all it is,' she said sarcastically, 'hopping on a plane.'

'That's the bad news.' He looked embarrassed and added brightly, 'The good news is, the man I'm replacing was taking his wife.'

'You'll be travelling with his wife?' Helen's heart went into a panic fluttering. 'Is she young and attractive?' She regretted the question as soon as she'd uttered it. But these were anxieties never far from the surface when you lived with Robin.

'No, silly. There's a place for another person. But he was paying. We'd have to pay for you to go. And it's full fare, no special deals.'

'You mean I could go, but we can't afford it,' Helen said bitterly.

'I could try the bank, but the University is a no-go area. Times are hard.'

'Forget it,' said Helen, knowing their overdraft and credit card debts piled higher each month. Another thought occurred to her:

'Is money the only reason you won't?'

'Won't what?'

'Won't want me being with you.'

'Of course I only want you, my angel.'

'Tell that to your biological equipment.'

She snorted. That old joke between them reminded her of the gulf between Robin's intellectual brilliance and his incorrigible immaturity in relationships.

'I hate the thought of you leaving me and jetting off five thousand miles to jump into bed with some beautiful young African woman.'

'Darling, I promise you, never. You are, you always have been, the only woman for me.'

'What about Rosie?'

Robin pulled a face.

'You're getting this out of proportion.'

Five years ago, his sporadic affair with Rosie, a temporary laboratory assistant had ended. But it had sputtered on for several months after he and Helen had got together. Helen couldn't quite come to terms with his explanation that this was purely at Rosie's insistence during the closure of their relationship when he was trying to let her down lightly. Helen was then an undergraduate mature student, at a time when he was making the transition from being the star graduate student to appointment as a research assistant.

Rosie had suddenly re-emerged as a bone of contention between them, appearing last month as part of the host team at an international conference Robin was attending at the University of Manchester. Robin had drunk too much and, according to him, she'd turned up outside his hotel room in a thunderstorm in the middle of the night, in hysterics. One thing had led to another.

'It was never more than a physical aberration on my part. She threw herself at me. I was vulnerable, semi-conscious. It's no consolation, I realise, but I was in no fit state to do it when push came to shove.'

'Don't insult my intelligence. God knows why I put up with you, Robin Lovelace. Most women would give you your marching orders.'

* * *

The atmosphere between Robin and Helen was decidedly edgy as he drove her to town.

'You don't want me to come with you,' she said.

'No, I thought you wouldn't want to come. Of course I don't mind if you do intend to come with me. I'm just surprised, that's all. You'll be fine at the airport but when we reach the forest you'll need rain clothes,' said Robin.

The struggle between them was like a verbal game. Once he could shift the discussion onto the discomforts of camping in a tropical rain forest, Helen's response was predictable.

'You must be joking. If I knew I had to take a raincoat I wouldn't go in the first place.'

'It's not that awful,' he offered tentatively. 'It may rain every day but it's so hot you'll dry off quickly.'

'Warm showers? You make it sound idyllic. But what does that say about the creepy crawlies – apart from your ant friends of course – that go with the steaming jungle? Mosquitos?'

'Probably. But you can use nets at night.'

'Stay in during daylight, avoid going out at night, I suppose,' she said sarcastically. 'What about snakes?'

'Very few will bite, and even fewer are fatal.'

'Brilliant. Germs?'

'There's some dysentery and even nastier infections, though provided you take precautions it's rare to be caught out. There are plenty of minor parasites like fleas. In the region where we'll be staying, the people keep them out of their huts by mixing the earth from ant heaps with cow dung and smearing it over the floor every week or so.'

Helen shuddered: 'Spare me the details.'

'Then there are bed bugs,' he continued. 'They like warmer climates, which stimulate them to breed rather more prolifically. They also produce a very oily secretion which stinks so much that most predators, birds for instance, won't touch them. These days there are very effective chemical controls, but if they run out, there's a small black ant which is said to clear every bed bug from a house within a day or two.'

'Very reassuring. And how do I get hold of this ant?'

'Er, in Portugal. Though I believe it's also found in other parts of the world,' he added hastily. 'Don't worry though; when we're on safari we're comparatively safe. They're quite rare in the huts of natives. They seem to prefer a certain level of comfort. Have you heard the old rhyme: "The lightning-bug has wings of gold, the June-bug wings of flame, the bed-bug has no wings at all, but it gets there all the same!" It does like to move with people as they migrate from dwelling to dwelling, along pipes and drains and so on. Some say they arrived with boat loads of emigrants from Europe. So you see, we can't blame all these minor horrors on the natives. We exported more than Christianity to these warmer countries.'

She gave him a withering look: 'Wonderful. Someone should tell the World Health Organisation to base their next strategy on this newly discovered formula for abolishing global disease – non-stop air tickets.'

'It's not quite that simple,' he admitted.

'Nothing bloody is with you. I can tell from this catalogue of horrors you don't want me to go anyway.'

'Yes I do,' he protested weakly.

'We can't afford it. Anyway, I'd cramp your style.'

'That's ridiculous.'

'You can stuff your African bug hunt right where you sit. I'm staying here. I'll stick to coffee shops, shopping and the odd night out. Better than shivering with malaria or finding reptiles in the bed.'

'Isn't that rather an extreme reaction?'

He stopped the car and backed into an alley near the river, at the end of George Street.

'I'll drop you here.'

As Helen got out, she was still responding to his earlier remark:

'Rather extreme,' she mimicked as she got out. 'I'd say it's very controlled, given the stimulus. Isn't that what you scientists say?'

* * *

Laura and Helen sat outside the coffee shop in silence for a while. Pedestrians trickled past in skeins and tentatively prodded dockside capstans, remnants of Hull's massive fishing fleet, now consigned to tourist history. Helen used the spoon to play with the frothy milk on the surface of her coffee. It seemed as though they were the only still point and the entire world was passing by in a hurry to be somewhere. Increasing tourism meant Hull's indigenous population was swelled by visitors to the Old Town and mementos of its great fishing history.

'I'll have even less time now,' said Helen, 'with Robin being up to his eyes in the University.'

'I was going to ask you how all that's going,' said Laura.

'The African field trip, or Robin being deputy director?'

'Africa.'

Helen eyed her curiously.

'You knew about it?'

'I thought about you last night, when Tom told me about the grant. Tom was quite upset at losing Robin, having only just secured him as full-time deputy of the Research Centre. I nearly rang. But I had to wait until now. I didn't want to be the first person to break the news.'

'You mean you thought Robin might not tell me last night?'

'Not quite. But I didn't know when. And then I couldn't think of an excuse to ring you very late at night.'

Helen seemed to find this reassuring.

Laura giggled. 'All those well-endowed Africans.'

'That's not a very p.c. remark – surprising, coming from you. Anyway, more than half the families of university staff where they're going have at least one member with HIV AIDS. It's the enemy of promiscuity.'

With characteristic suddenness Laura's flippancy fell away. She was full of regret.

'A thousand apols. I hope I haven't offended you.'

Helen waved her hand. She was one of those women whose gestures conveyed her meaning graphically.

'Forget it, darling. I'll slaughter Robin if he ever takes me for granted again. One thing Robin and I still share though – typical Scots – is we're well balanced. A chip on each shoulder.'

They both laughed. Laura stirred her coffee. She'd anticipated trouble between Robin and Helen for ages. She wished she didn't know so much. It was difficult, hearing snippets from Tom about Robin's flings and being supportive over the past month while Helen went through the trauma of ending her affair with Detlev and what Helen saw as the aftermath of her actions.

'How are you feeling about it?'

'I was pissed off when Robin first told me. I shouted at him.'

'Naturally.'

Helen saw Laura's smile. She returned a somewhat wan smile.

'I've calmed down now.'

Laura licked her spoon reflectively.

'You know, living with an academic at worst is living with a person who isn't there.'

'Tell me about it.'

'At best it's like living with the rest of the research team,' she said. 'You get the body now and again, usually at the wrong time of the month. As for the mind, only between grants.'

'Grunts? You make them sound like animals.'

'I said grants, research grants, darling. But grunts is about right.'

'You said body and mind. What about the heart?'

'What about the heart? Do they have them?'

Since the waiter had brought Helen a glass of fruit juice with ice, she had perked up considerably, despite the warmth. Somehow, this warm, muggy weather in Hull drained her in ways which a far hotter but drier Mediterranean or tropical climate never had.

'You're all right with Tom,' Helen continued. 'He's more reliable than

Robin.'

Laura's face displayed her scepticism. At that moment though, she wasn't ready to talk about herself. Helen giggled unexpectedly.

'I'm not at all keen on anything wriggly unless it's chocolate covered. That goes for ants as well.'

'If it's a choice between pleasure and righteousness, go for the pleasure.'

'Every time.' Helen nodded vigorously, slipping off a shoe and wriggling her legs. 'The big ones with the most sweet and genetically modified ingredients are much more fun than the pale, laboratory-bred ones. That goes for people as well.' They both laughed.

That was why you fell for Detlev, Laura thought. He was tall and well-built, in contrast with Robin's more portly, if ardent, sensuousness.

Helen continued. 'I should be so lucky.'

'Seriously though, it'll be an amazing experience I'm sure. But I don't envy you having to face all those creepy crawlies.'

'Robin won't exactly be living in a tent. I've some pictures of the University at home.'

Laura hadn't the heart to share her private thoughts about the venture. On past form, she doubted whether Helen would even get as far as the airport.

* * *

Day in day out, Wilkes hardly varied his introduction to different inquests by a single word:

'This is not like a trial court, though there are some similarities. It doesn't have rules of evidence of sufficient rigour to support an investigation into who was responsible for a particular outcome. The purpose of an inquest is not to apportion blame, but merely to find out the facts. The coroner's court attends to four questions: who died, where, when and how the person came by death. As you might expect, the last of these questions takes up most of the time. At the end of these proceedings, I am required to give a verdict, so phrased that it does not determine criminal or civil liability. In the process, a number of witnesses will be called to give evidence. Normally they will have submitted statements. They may read these, or I may simply go through the statement, highlighting the main points and asking questions here and there. There are some statements submitted to be read in the court by people not attending and under Rule 37 of the Coroner's Rules I am required to tell you who these are.'

Tom found his mind wandering. He gazed at those present, trying to imagine what they were thinking and feeling as the coroner listed those giving statements. He was jolted back as Wilkes began to summarise the case.

'Dr Detlev Brandt was a research fellow from the Centre for Entomological Studies at the Hull Wilberforce University, and until a year before his death, a special constable in the East Yorkshire constabulary. On November 17 last, he took the train from Hull to Beverley, and then a taxi to the Beverley Motel, a three-star hotel on the outskirts of this market town in East Yorkshire, about ten miles from Hull. He was due to attend a meeting with scientists from the Cawood agricultural research establishment the following morning. When he did not arrive at 9:00 hours, they telephoned the hotel, to find he had not yet appeared for breakfast. The hotel is one of those where the rooms are single-storey, detached from the main hotel block. Dr Brandt's room was the end one in the block and the adjacent room had been unoccupied the previous night. An investigation began: the hotel manager entered his room at 9:15 hours and found it empty. The bed, apparently, had not been slept in. Meanwhile, at about that time a body was discovered by Mr Alderson, farmer at Lowfield Farm, immediately adjacent to the hotel. This was subsequently confirmed as being that of Dr Brandt. Dr Edna Williams, consultant histopathologist, you carried out the post-mortem.'

'Yes, sir.'

'Please take us through your report.'

'Yes, sir. We normally begin the post-mortem by an external examination of the body and then carry out an internal examination.'

'If I may interrupt,' said Wilkes hastily as though realising he'd forgotten, 'I'll ask Dr Williams to summarise the report, omitting the unnecessary medical details for the sake of those members present.

'Of course,' said Dr Williams. 'In this case, the body lay on its back with the head facing upwards. A wound in the upper palate was visible in the open mouth. A shotgun lay between the legs. On measuring, the length of the shotgun from the trigger to the end of the barrel was found to be significantly shorter than the distance from the finger of the person to the mouth. This confirmed that it was physically possible for the person to have fired the fatal shot.'

'The second part of the necropsy consists of an internal examination, including all organs. The injuries confirmed the cause of death as from a shotgun wound to the head. There was massive damage to the skull and the brain, which would have led to instantaneous loss of consciousness and death within seconds through loss of blood. In carrying out further examination, it was evident that there was no significant disease or injury present which would have had a bearing on this death. Samples of blood and urine were retained for analysis. The blood showed an alcohol concentration of 185 milligrams per 100 millilitres and the urine showed 290. This greatly exceeds the legal maximum in the UK of 80 milligrams per 100 millilitres. It indicates a marked degree of intoxication which would be likely significantly to impair cognition, physical co-ordination and emotional responses.'

'Thank you, Doctor.'

'If the Court permits,' said Dr Williams, 'I should appreciate it if I could be excused, once I have dealt with any questions.'

'I understand. Does anyone have any questions?'

An expectant silence followed this question. But nobody spoke. The coroner nodded his assent and the consultant left the court.

The words special constable still echoed round Tom's head. He was staggered. There was no reason why he should have known, of course. He hadn't been a member of the interviewing panel when Detlev was appointed. But it was more than that. The information added to the intangible suspicion, already fed by occasional remarks from Laura. It lay out of focus and was un-addressed; so as time went by, it was increasingly threatening to his precise mind. He'd come to the coroner's court, hoping the process of the inquest would resolve his uncertainties. He particularly wanted to be dissuaded from the suspicion that there could be more to Detlev's former life, and so to his death, than a simple suicide – if suicide could ever be called simple.

* * *

'I'm sure you'll make the best of it, whether in Africa or at home,' said Laura, well aware of how adept Helen was at turning the conversation away from herself.

Laura thought Helen was avoiding eye contact under the guise of spooning the froth on her cappuccino.

'I'd rather not talk about it any more,' said Helen. 'How are you?'

'Oh, business as usual I guess,' replied Laura with false jollity. 'The department and the Research Centre will go on having their crises of survival.'

'But that's not you. You're good at turning the conversation onto other topics rather than talking about yourself. You haven't told me how you are.'

'No, I haven't.' Laura bit her lip pensively.

'So?'

'Tom and I? We'll work it out, I suppose.'

Laura didn't want to talk about it. She saw Helen looking at her with a mixture of puzzlement and concern.

'I don't need sympathy,' she said sharply. 'We're doing what married people do after a few years of – whatever. It's okay. Anyway, if it's not, that's too bad. Plenty of other couples manage. We've been managing for years. We're experts at it by now.'

* * *

Coroner Wilkes had taken statements from relatives and other witnesses and was speaking again.

'Now we shall hear the statements from the police. You are Constable Tebbutt, Number 149?'

'Yes, sir.' Tebbutt looked nervously round the courtroom.

'Please read the court your statement.'

'Yes, sir. At approximately 9:10 hours on the Monday morning of 17 November 1997, I was on patrol in the village of Nesterton near Beverley, when I received instructions to proceed in response to a 999 call from Mr Alderson, a farmer from Lowfield Farm, Beverley Lane. On arrival, I found Mr Alderson, the farmer at Lowfield Farm, erecting some temporary fencing to prevent his cattle wandering into the immediate vicinity of the barn. Mr Alderson told me that he had heard a shot at about 8:45 and on going outside to search the farm outbuildings, had found the deceased lying in the barn. I walked with Mr Alderson to the barn fifty metres to the rear of Lowfield Farm. There I viewed the body of the deceased lying on a pile of hay beside a stack of hay bales. I directed Mr Alderson to wait while I confirmed that the deceased could not be resuscitated. I then contacted headquarters at 9:48 hours and arranged for them to call out the Scenes of Crime officer, ambulance and duty doctor. Meanwhile, I observed that a shotgun lay between the legs of the deceased, pointing upwards. The shotgun was the up and over type. I first made the weapon safe. Then I inspected the inside of the weapon and found a spent cartridge in the top barrel and that the bottom barrel contained an intact cartridge. The ambulance arrived at 10:15 and two paramedics checked the body and confirmed the death.'

'You knew and worked with the deceased in his capacity as Special Constable?'

'Yes, sir.'

'Did you have any reason to suspect Dr Brandt might take his own life?'

'None at all, sir.'

'Thank you, Constable Tebbutt. Has anyone any questions? You may step down. I shall now take the statement of Constable Birch, the Scenes of Crime officer.'

Constable Birch stepped up, took the oath, sat next to the coroner and read her statement:

'I was on duty at about 9:30 hours on the morning of 17th November, when I received a radio message from headquarters directing me to attend a reported incident at Lowfield Farm, Beverley. I approached a group of people standing on the driveway. Following their directions, I approached the body, which lay in the barn, adjacent to some stacked hay bales. I observed a large pool of blood under and around the head of the deceased. I could see a shotgun between the legs of the deceased. I took photographs. The negatives of these are held at Central Police Station, Beverley, East Yorkshire. Prints PS one to nineteen from these photographs labelled HDS1 can be viewed at Central Police Station, Beverley, East Yorkshire. I searched the barn in the immediate vicinity of the body. I was unable to locate the spent cartridge from the shotgun in the loose hay surrounding the body. I also searched the hotel room occupied by the deceased. I took away a note book which was lying on the bedside cabinet. This item was entered in police property at Beverley Central Police Station and is available for inspection there as police item DS 1.'

'Am I right, Constable, that the writing on this notepad has been confirmed as that of the deceased?' Wilkes asked.

'Yes, sir. The handwriting has been identified by Professor Fortius, a colleague of the deceased in the Centre for Entomological Research at the Hull Wilberforce University, as that of Dr Brandt.'

'And am I right that there was not any definite message in the writing? It was just scribbled notes.'

'Yes, sir. The content was not specific and was not of any interest or relevance to the death.'

'Thank you,' said Wilkes. 'Has anyone any questions to ask the witness? No? That completes all the evidence. Is there any further statement that anyone wishes to make? It is my responsibility, therefore, to summarise these proceedings and finally to give a verdict.'

* * *

'I'm sorry, Helen. I didn't mean to loose off at you.'

'Forget it.' Helen waved her hand. 'I'm an insensitive clod-hopper. I should have kept my nose out and my mouth shut.'

'Don't say that. I appreciate you like mad.'

'Mummy, Mummy, come and look at the insects in the window,' called Sarah.

'Wait, darling. Mummy's finishing her coffee.'

'Perhaps it would help if you had some space away from the kids,' observed Helen.

'Please, Mummy.'

Laura nodded. 'It might, but it's not a very practicable idea.'

'Too much going on.'

'Like life, for instance.'

Matthew now joined the chorus, with the one-liner he had found to be most effective in shops and at market stalls alike, whenever he was taken shopping:

'I really need it. Please, Mummy.'

Laura shook her head: 'I can't even think about it any more at the moment, Helen.' She couldn't cope with making serious decisions when she was out like this with the kids.

'I'm coming, Matthew. But I haven't the money for any more presents.'

At the centre of the display in the corner of the charity shop window was an old plastic container accompanied by a faded poster proclaiming "Ant Farm. Kids: Keep your own colony of ants and watch them lay eggs, feed their young and milk their ant cows."

'Listen, you two, I've no money to buy any toys today.'

The chorus from the children died away. Laura stood up, went over to the shop window and peered in. It was full of second-hand junk.

'I don't believe it. I bring my kids to town and the only things they show any interest in buying are the most common items of equipment in Tom's labs at the Uni. They also have an instinct for the most awkward items in every shop.'

Laura sat down again.

'At least yours have other interests. All my nephews want to do is surf the net and play on computer games ...' said Helen. Her voice tailed off and she stared at the cup.

'Are you thinking about the inquest?' asked Laura. It was an inspired guess.

Helen nodded, lips pursed and eyes filling up.

'It was a bad accident,' said Laura. 'But he wouldn't have suffered. He'd have died instantaneously.'

Helen shook her head: 'Don't even try to soften it. I've seen the photographs. I happened to be there when Tom shared them with Robin.'

She sat staring at the table. Laura fidgeted, not knowing how best to help.

'He didn't do it. He would never have killed himself.' The words burst from Helen. She pressed her hands flat against her face, as though to shut herself off from the reality. She took a deep breath before removing her hands, composing herself.

'I'm so sorry, love,' said Laura, putting her hand on Helen's shoulder. They leaned together and hugged.

* * *

Coroner Wilkes was speaking again.

'Finally, I come to the verdict. In considering the possibility that the deceased took his own life, I have to bear in mind that whilst most verdicts are given on the basis of the balance of probabilities, this doesn't apply to the taking of one's own life. For this verdict to be given, the level of evidence used to prove it has to be far higher than for other verdicts. That is, it has to be clear beyond all reasonable doubt that all other possible explanations have been ruled out.

'In this case, no overwhelming and unambiguous motive for suicide is evident. There is evidence that the judgement of the deceased may have been clouded by the consumption of alcohol. There is further evidence of factors which could have led to the deceased being depressed. There is also evidence he was recovering from the particular trauma of the death of his father, four years earlier. There is no evidence he was suicidal over this. My conclusion, therefore, is that the evidence is not sufficient to support the verdict of taking his own life. I am giving an open verdict. This is a final verdict, but it leaves open the question of what caused the death. I should like, finally, to offer my condolences to you for this sad event and to thank you all for attending today.'

Tom was in a daze. Was that it? He'd given up a day's work for this ritualistic nod in the direction of truth. He hadn't realised the proceedings would come to a climax and end as suddenly as this. The clerk froze with bowed head and both hands pressing on her temples. The usher stood up and stepped forward:

'The Court will rise.' They stood while the coroner left the courtroom, followed by the clerk and the usher.

* * *

Laura looked across the wide pavement, with its scattering of tourists, shoppers and others, to where the two children had stood till a moment ago, noses more or less glued to the shop window. But now, the equilibrium, always delicate between these two strong, outgoing personalities, was disturbed. Sarah said something to Matthew and he pouted and pushed her.

While this was going on, unnoticed by the two adults, across the pavement, standing lopsidedly and gazing intently at both children and shop window, was a stockily built man. He was dressed oddly out of harmony with the brilliant sunshine, in orange anorak, bright blue hiking trousers and boots. He carried a large frame rucksack on his back. His face, too, was at odds with the outdoor gear. Instead of weather-beaten features, the puffy flesh of his cheeks and jowls was waxy and pallid, as though he'd been fed on some unsavoury fatty substances and had spent a long period away from daylight.

There was a moment when Matthew, sensing a sinister presence, stopped arguing and looked across the pavement. Afterwards, the eyes of the stranger, the silence which surrounded him and the chill of being near him, were what the little boy remembered.

The altercation between the children quickly became more public as the volume increased. The last sentence reached Laura's ears with the clarity of children's voices floating over a hundred adult conversations which also must have been within earshot.

'Shut up, Sarah, or I'll call Mummy.'

Laura made a sudden decision.

'I'll tell you about our last trip to Africa,' she said, 'but not when I'm shopping with these two.'

She pushed back her chair and made for the children, just arriving in time to prevent a full-scale eruption.

'Now, you two.'

'Mummy, who was that man?' asked Matthew.

'Which man, darling? I can't see any man.'

'Over there. He was staring at us.'

'What's the matter?' Laura asked Helen.

'He had a horrid face.'

'What does that mean?' Laura was getting no answers, which wasn't unusual, given the leapfrog imaginations of her two little ones.

'He walked funny.'

'The kids are on about a man watching them.'

Helen's mind wasn't on what was happening. 'When?'

'Just now.'

'I didn't see any man.'

'They see too much on their cousins' computer games. All those surreal situations with horribly realistic videos embedded in them.'

'He was dizzy.'

'Drunk, silly. Like Auntie Vera.'

'He smelt,' said Matthew.

'It's rude to say that,' said Sarah.

'He smelt of dog-meat.'

Laura was embarrassed by the children's loud voices. This is why I never get the chance to have a proper conversation with my friends, she thought. She was suddenly angry. It was doubly frustrating though, because Tom had sworn her to secrecy about the uncertainty hanging over the future of the Centre. She absolutely hated being a party to secrets at work and objected strenuously: 'How do you expect me to act naturally with the partners of your colleagues when you're constantly passing me these little time-bombs of confidential information? "Don't tell so-and-so, but ... Don't say anything to anybody, but ..."' She felt inhibited from talking about her relationship with Tom, particularly on this day when Helen was likely to be vulnerable.

Suddenly Laura was feeling physically sickened by the whole

situation. She couldn't escape from it quickly enough. She went back to the table, pulled out her purse from her handbag, extracted a five pound note and shoved it into Helen's hand.

'Pay for the drinks with this, there's a love. Come on, kids, time to go.'

Sometimes Laura hated Hull; the appalling deprivation, the downtrodden people wandering through the streets. She was trying to shelve this and reassure herself about the man.

'Probably a squaddy. Gulf war syndrome, makes them go dizzy.'

'That was years ago. Anyway, I thought they'd found no evidence that GWS exists.'

'Whatever you call it, as my doctor says, there's a lot of them about. Plenty of them still can't find jobs. Anyway –' Laura gathered up the children, who'd sensed the end of the game. She was showing signs of agitation. She leaned forward and kissed Helen on the cheek. 'See you later. Sorry about the –' She was already moving away and mouthed the word 'kids' and threw her hands up in a gesture of hopelessness.

'Don't worry,' Helen mimed. Then she waved to the kids and out loud called 'Byee.'

* * *

Tom was shaking his head as he walked out of the courtroom into the warm summer's day:

'It's all wrong,' he muttered, 'all so terribly wrong.'

Despite his general feeling of dissatisfaction, he struggled to put his finger on any specific failing in the verdict on the gruesome account of Detlev Brandt's last day on earth. It was incomprehensible that Detlev should have killed himself.

'Watch out!'

The warning came from an old man pushing a bicycle across his path. Before Tom could stop himself, he'd cannoned into the machine. The man lost his grip and it fell over. Vegetables piled loosely in the basket on the handle bars spilled all over the pavement. Tom bent and scrabbled frantically to recover onions, potatoes and carrots before they rolled onto the road, or other pedestrians came along. He pulled the cycle upright and piled the rescued items back in the basket. The man went on his way to the mantra of Tom's profuse apologies.

Get a grip, Tom chided himself as he took a deep breath before walking off. You're becoming neurotic over a tragedy beyond anyone's control.

Chapter 3

'Damn, damn, damn,' said Tom to himself. His conversation with Roger Hedley, professor of legal studies, grew out of Roger's concern for him. He sat in the senior common room with a coffee, well before nine on the morning after the inquest.

'What are you doing in so early?' asked Roger. He reminded Tom of a used-car salesman, short, rotund, dapper, a few straggling silver hairs slicked across his scalp.

'I could ask you the same thing.'

'Touché. A hundred examination scripts to moderate in my role as external examiner. What about you? A bit tetchy for the time of day. Come on, Tommy, what's bugging you?'

Tom could take even this hated corruption of his name from Roger, his long-standing colleague. They were contemporaries, having been in the University so long, side by side in dissimilar, yet parallel situations. He gave Roger the gist of the previous day's events.

'Why didn't you set to at the time, old chap, and tell the police what you thought?' asked Roger.

'I didn't think it was significant at the time.'

'That's what our students say.'

Tom was so preoccupied that he missed the force of this remark.

'I'm kicking myself. It was only today I realised the limited scope of the coroner's court proceedings.'

'Most people never realise it, because they never have reason to come into contact with an inquest.'

'Even then, I had no inkling he would return an open verdict.'

'Things have changed since the old days.'

'How do you mean?'

'There's a lot at stake for families. Stigma and that sort of thing, to say nothing of the insurance. There's every incentive for the relatives to challenge what they view as an unjustified verdict of suicide. The coroner can't bung in a verdict of suicide without cast-iron evidence.'

'People aren't meant to benefit financially as a result of an inquest verdict.'

'They aren't. But you can't stop insurance companies including certain conditions in their rules. Many life policies exclude payment in the event of a person taking their own life.'

'I wasn't thinking so much of suicide as the other extreme of –'

'You think he was murdered?'

'I believe he was.'

'Good God. Why didn't this come out in the inquest? You made a statement.'

'That was months ago.'

'You've changed your mind?'

'Not exactly. I've reconsidered and am prepared now to examine the possibility that Detlev was killed.'

'You're prepared to examine the possibility. Sounds a bit wishy washy and typically academic to me, if you don't mind me saying so. A minute ago you said he definitely was killed.'

'Correction. I think he may have been murdered.'

'Have you any evidence for this remarkable assertion?'

'I could have, eventually.'

'In my world, Tommy, could have is never. It's nearly a year on. In my line, we say every year later is evidence lost. My advice is, if you don't know, keep your trap shut and stay out of it. Nothing you do will bring him back. It's over. Forget it.'

Roger was right about the difficulties of evidence, but wrong to say it was over. It had hardly begun.

* * *

It was mid-morning. After an early start, Tom already had been at work for almost five hours, when the phone rang.

'Tom Fortius.'

'Hi Tom, Robin here. Are you busy?'

'No more than usual.'

'Does that mean you haven't a few minutes to spare?'

'Quite the reverse. I could do with a break from this bloody job. I was about to brew up.'

'Beaten you to it. Come to my office. It'll give me the chance to run some ideas past you.'

* * *

Tom found Robin blithely unaffected by the chaos of boxes and files around him in his office, spilling into the departmental office. In all their years as neighbours, he had never known it to be much different. If their research interests had coincided, they would have gone to war, for they were almost incompatible. When Robin had particular concerns, they merged into the blur of items they discussed. Then came the perennial issue whenever a member of departmental staff went away on fieldwork leaving colleagues behind working in related fields.

'It would help to know what we might look out for, on your behalf,' said Robin.

Tom's long, tried and tested relationship with Robin enabled him to set aside the traditional hesitance of the academic about sharing his newest research preoccupations with another person.

'Let's think,' he said. 'As you might expect, it has to be the impact of various insect migrations on human settlement and agriculture in particular, and also I guess we'll find time for patterns of predation and communication. Probably most of all among the driver ants of course. We're building up quite a body of experience with them, and an ever longer list of questions. I'll make some notes on these. When are you and Helen off?'

There was a pause.

'Helen's seeing me off, not going with me.'

'Right.' Tom sounded surprised.

Robin found himself waffling an explanation. 'It's a host of things. The house, Helen's father's health, leaving the house empty.'

'There's nothing else? I thought Helen would be dead set on going.'

Tom knew Robin's restless temperament. Robin could not abide staying in college term after term. He had to be on the move. His relationships were like that too. Over the years, he had acquired a legendary reputation for slipping rapidly from one woman to another. Tom had been taken aback when Robin moved in with Helen, and he was surprised now at the realisation they had been living together for nearly seven years:

'Nothing to do with me. She decided. To be honest, she was doubtful as soon as I mentioned it. We have to think about so many factors.'

'It's none of my business so tell me to take a running jump. There's nothing wrong between you and Helen?'

Robin glanced at Tom, but obliquely as though avoiding looking him in the eye:

'Between me and Helen?' He laughed. 'You must be joking. Helen and I are secure as a rock, safe as houses. How do you want your coffee?'

'Black with no sugar.'

'You sounded pretty uptight on the phone.'

'It's the laboratory. No it's not. Why should I shelter him? It's one of the technicians. If we could hire and fire laboratory technicians purely on the quality of their day to day work that man would be out of here today. Also, more generally, we'd have far fewer hiccups with the experimental work.'

'Flog-em and sack-em? Not you, I think.'

'No dammit, it isn't.'

Tom couldn't hide the weariness in his voice.

'What's the man done?'

'It makes me so mad. I won't bore you with the why's and wherefore's. To cut a long story short, I asked him on Friday to prepare the equipment for me to replicate with the postgrad students the communications experiments we did with the slave-making sanguineas. I turned up Monday morning five minutes before my session to find he'd installed a colony of Myrmica Rubra in a maze, to test very basic patterns of communication in locating food sources. Then, to cap it all, we've lost, he's lost, or at least he can't track down, the equipment we used to carry out those first communication experiments with ants. I don't know if you remember that work we did with the Nuffield grant three or four years ago.'

'It rings a bell. I probably do. At the moment, my head's a shed with all this packing.'

'Sorry, Robin. I shouldn't load all this onto you.'

'No, it's me that feels guilty leaving you with all this.'

'Think nothing of it. It isn't your problem. It started as one of those days and in my experience it'll go on that way. Get out of this place and do your fieldwork. That's where the real world is. Hopefully, in the process you'll make new contacts and generate the extra income we need to survive.'

'That's a big responsibility.'

'I'm not laying it on you like that. Just pack up and go.'

'There must be more to it,' said Robin. 'I haven't seen you this uptight for years.'

Tom shook his head, as though to dislodge a persistent thought.

'I suppose this inquest has got to me. I'd never been to one before. I can't believe the coroner didn't pursue the investigation further. I also felt powerless. I'm not used to not being able to resolve queries and to explore possibilities till questions are answered. I can't see why the coroner was so uninterested in reaching a full explanation beyond a verdict on the immediate physical cause of death. How could such a puzzling incident be simply left as "open verdict"?'

* * *

Tom felt guilty after leaving Robin. He'd dumped onto him many of the questions humming round in his head. Robin had enough to contend with. They hadn't got round to looking at the notes he'd made. He always did this. "The jottings of an obsessive mind," Laura had once called them, pages of reminders about building contacts with other universities and developing research opportunities.

Tom transferred his irritation for the time being to the task in hand – hunting through the untidy mess in the storeroom at the rear of Lab One in the laboratory block. Why is it, he thought, that you find all kinds of lost items except the one you're actually seeking? It was partly his own untidiness which was responsible for this situation. He also realised the error of leaving the lab technicians to sort it. Discarded apparatus and surplus office furniture tended to find their way here, in a haphazard fashion. No one person had ultimate responsibility, so the various stacks of boxes had grown more impenetrable over the past four or five years. Now the prototype apparatus used for the communication experiments with ants was not to hand. He did not even know whether it had been thrown out. That really would be a criminal waste of resources. On the other hand, he could recall over the years seeing some near-mint items of furniture in skips around the campus.

Where had he put the inventory? Perhaps that would have shed some light on the mystery. There was no great urgency and the inventory itself didn't matter. Tom felt more than a touch of that obsessiveness about detail which sustained him through his experimental work. By next week when he gave his "state of the Research Centre" address to the staff and post-graduate students, he wanted to be able to satisfy himself about particular points of departmental housekeeping, setting out future priorities and targets.

'Nothing much in the post,' said Jean. 'There's only one message on the voice-mail – from Hugh Mackintosh. He must speak to you.'

'What does he want?' Tom muttered.

Several stacked boxes of envelopes fell into the last clear space on the floor.

'Can I help, Professor Fortius?'

'No, please ignore me. I'm trying to find something.'

She did not pursue this. Tom was exercised over the possible reasons for Hugh's call. It was unusual. Hugh didn't normally leave messages like that. He rang at home over the weekend, or if it was a trivial matter, left it till Monday morning. It could be his concern over Tom's state of mind after the inquest. It isn't every day a key member of staff dies unexpectedly under mysterious circumstances. That was a possibility. He had to admit it was a very un-Hugh possibility.

'He asks you to ring as soon as you arrive at the office.'

'Odder and odder,' said Tom, shaking his head.

Hugh's secretary, Margaret, answered the phone.

'Hullo, Margaret,' said Tom. 'Is Hugh in?'

'No, he's popped out to see someone. He'll only be five minutes.'

'I'll ring back.'

'Wait a moment. He asked me to book an appointment for you when you rang.'

'Oh.' This was definitely not Hugh the minimalist manager. The awful feeling grew ever stronger that this wasn't sparked by the aftermath of Detlev's inquest.

'Have you some time this morning? He was particularly anxious to meet you before lunch.'

'Is eleven any good?'

'Yes, he should be back by then. I'll put you in the diary for eleven.'

Tom hoped once the funeral was well in the past and the police and other people had stopped asking questions, Hugh would settle back into his normal pattern of non-intervention. This amounted to virtual non-participation in the affairs of the Research Centre.

Before meeting Hugh, Tom had a further task. He looked at his watch. Nine-thirty, probably about right to make this particular telephone call. A mission only now had surfaced from his submerged memory of the inquest.

Seated to one side of his desk in the easy chair he called his thinking chair, he dialled Directory Enquiries for the number of the coroner's court. Afterwards, he looked at his watch – still sufficiently early – and dialled.

'Hello, is that the coroner's office? Could I speak to the clerk please – yes, it is urgent – I can't pass on a message, no – hello, are you the clerk who was present at yesterday's inquest? Good, my name is Professor Tom Fortius, Hull Wilberforce University – yes that's right, from my Department, yes – that's right, I was there, sitting near the door on the right – yes, with the black suit and, er, hair. This is a little difficult, but I need the opportunity to ask you something. At the point the verdict was announced, I noticed, were you feeling, that is – oh, please, don't ring off. I didn't mean – no, all I wanted to know was whether you'd meet me for lunch tomorrow – I don't know, I only just – yes – no, I promise, it's purely a professional matter – say, a quarter to one in the front lounge at the Beverley Arms – no, it won't compromise your professional role in any way. I can guarantee that. I considered being a magistrate you know, before this job became so time-consuming.'

On his way back through the office, Tom stopped by his secretary's desk.

'Excuse me, Jean. You haven't any idea where the prototype equipment we used for the social insect communication experiments is stored?'

'I'm sorry, Professor Fortius. You've already asked me.'

'I'm losing track. With you having been with us so many years, I've never had anything to do with the laboratories. I wouldn't know one end of a Bunsen burner from the other.' She smiled.

'No, of course not.'

'The technicians should be able to put their finger on it for you.'

'Yes,' he responded, unconvinced. 'The problem is our current staff haven't been with us long enough to know what I'm referring to.'

'Oh dear, that's difficult.'

Ever the diplomat. One of the reasons people found Jean so reassuring and calming in the stressed atmosphere of academic research, was her refusal to engage in any sort of banter or sniping. She rarely made any comment, or even hinted at a judgement on other people's work. Tom found it an occasionally irritating, but ultimately reassuring characteristic. He set off across the quadrangle towards Hugh's office, in a thoughtful frame of mind.

'Come in, Tom.' With his distinctive Sandhurst accent, Hugh always came across as the aristocratic English gentleman, which meant he cut an eccentric figure in the University. Five-foot nine in height and rather portly, he invariably wore a Harris tweed, or a brightly checked sports jacket. Typically, his trousers were immaculately pressed cavalry twill of the off-duty army officer, hanging perfect length over brown leather shoes so carefully polished you could imagine using them as mirrors. His moustache and upright posture, whether seated or standing, completed the picture.

Tom was sure Hugh's cultivation of the image of the retired brigadier or colonel who had taken up country pursuits on his small farm between Hull and Malton, was one reason why, despite many critics of his laid-back approach to working with people, he'd survived for so long in his job as Dean. With his confident manner, he tended to cast opponents, especially younger ones, in the role of junior officers, or in the case of some new staff and students, in the role of apprentices, from which it was difficult for them to challenge him.

Hugh's days were numbered, though. It wasn't so much that colleagues saw his old-fashioned manners as inherently bad. He was such an obvious anachronism in the increasingly robust, even brutal, contemporary world of higher education.

On the rare occasions when Hugh came straight to the point – as now – it was a very bad sign:

'I've just had the VC's latest pronouncements on targets for the coming round of income generation.'

'We used to call them research grants,' said Tom drily.

'Yes,' said Hugh absently. He wasn't renowned for his political subtlety.

'Depressing reading. Look at these figures for the professional courses – nurses, teachers, social work – far below our expected income.'

'You mean their student numbers, especially postgrad figures, are sky high,' said Tom. 'So the pressure's off them.'

'You can say that again,' Hugh agreed. 'Anyway, they're not our problem. The good news is that as far as sciences as a whole are concerned, we have an across-the-board agreement that in the next financial year, there will be no compulsory redundancies among academic staff on permanent contracts.'

Tom nodded without enthusiasm.

'Incidentally, Tom, I should have said at the outset how much I enjoyed your lecture the other day. That was a good write-up in the University Blah. If I may say, you did yourself no harm with senior management and from the point of view of your own career prospects that's no bad thing. There were people listening very carefully to your comments about forensic entomology, by the way. I have that on the best authority.'

'They were almost off the top of my head,' said Tom.

Hugh smiled. 'Don't say that, you'll tarnish your halo.'

'What about our work on insect predation?'

'Ah,' said Hugh. Tom knew immediately what this meant. 'Marvellous, but –' The parliamentary compliment, before the rapier thrust. He should have known.

All he could do was to wait for the sting in the tail – it was Hugh's style.

'So, on some fronts the future appears rosy,' said Hugh. 'Our research profile in entomology looks very respectable. However, in the immediate future we have to be careful, and ensure that we cut our cloth to suit our pocket. For the time being, and I emphasise it's probably only for the time being, we have to look on the debit side and reduce costs.'

Tom was seething. Damning with faint praise. 'Very respectable,' he ground through clenched teeth. 'Do you realise how we've sweated to bring extra contracts in.'

'The bad news,' said Hugh, 'is that our research centres have to meet even more stringent performance standards if they are to survive. Specifically, Tom, I'm afraid without an increase on your last year's income, you'll have to lose staff.'

'You mean we've no chance of replacing Detlev?'

'Well, you've appointed Robin Lovelace.'

'That's something and nothing. I've lost him to this externally funded expedition. So I'm back with no deputy.'

'I realise that. Lovelace's field trip is short-term as well, but I'm afraid this is over and above the Detlev and Lovelace situation.'

'So the message is you're doing great work and here's a kick in the teeth,' said Tom. 'The question is, by how much will we have to raise our threshold of income?'

'Significantly, I think, given the quantity of down-sizing we're doing in other areas.'

'For God's sake, Hugh, you sound like the chairman of ICI.'

'Sorry old chap,' Hugh said softly, 'I know it hurts.'

'Not as much as it will hurt the University in four years time,' said Tom, 'when their entomological research goes down the pan.'

'There's more, I'm afraid. Let me put the issue in a broader context.

The University is suggesting you boost the Centre's revenue from research by shifting the balance of its work from research into communication and predation among the social insects – to pathology.'

'For goodness' sake, Hugh. Who has the right to dictate this?'

'Senior management have every right, I'm afraid. University priorities rule in that area. We can anticipate as a strategic goal moving into competition with some of the established centres which shall be nameless. They've already pushed ahead with research into forensic entomology.'

'So the future will be based upon more lucrative areas for research.'

'I didn't say those words.'

'Curse my big mouth. You didn't need to.'

'Why curse?'

'Because you've lifted my words from the lecture. I should have kept quiet.'

'I have to say, Tom, this has been on the cards for some time. A number of other voices have been convergent on your own views. You should feel flattered. Perhaps the word is relevance. Take forensic entomology, for example. It seems to me to be indisputable that if you were to develop the work of the Centre in that direction, the applications would be of more direct use to the agencies in this region, such as the police.'

'Rather than working on insect predation with developing countries who have less money to pay our vast overheads.'

'Rather than spreading your meagre resources halfway across the globe, yes. The loaded meaning is your own. Look Tom, I realise you must be very bitter,' said Hugh, 'seeing the fruits of all your years of hard work being eroded by the winds of free market competition.'

You're mixing your metaphors a little, thought Tom, and it doesn't suit you. He responded out loud more softly for fear of antagonising Hugh and reducing the scope for negotiation:

'Give me the bad news in hard cash so we know what we're talking about.'

'Two and a half million, gross,' said Hugh. 'Earn that per year over the next three years, plus inflation and we'll call it all square.'

'Grief, man,' Tom exclaimed. 'That's nearly twice what we're earning now.'

Hugh spread his palms wide in a gesture of hopelessness.

'I tried to argue your case, but – what can I do?'

'This is ridiculous,' Tom said, lost for words in the face of such crassness on the part of his employers.

'What I'm giving you is only preliminary. It still has to go through committee and Senate,' said Hugh, trying to soften the blow. 'There'll be plenty of opportunity to argue your case.'

'Yes, and with Detlev dead, it will be even more against the tide than usual,' said Tom bitterly.

At the mention of Detlev's death, Hugh stiffened visibly. He was clearly unable to deal with that aspect of the situation. In contrast, Tom's inclination towards a softly-softly approach had melted away at the mention of the ludicrous financial target. His anger at the unfairness of it won out over other feelings. He recalled the last time his research base had nearly been wiped out, five years ago, when the Government pulled the plug on a wide range of biological, horticultural and oceanographic projects.

Tom walked to the door, opened it and turned. Hugh shrugged, rather pathetically he thought.

'I'll leave you with this thought, Hugh. If the grant goes, the Research Centre goes. If the Research Centre goes, then I go. The entire Department may be eclipsed by other departments – scientists, or professions allied to medicine – and two years from now you too will be nothing more than a memory.'

Chapter 4

Helen was seeing Robin off.

'Byeee, darling,' she said. 'Sorry about yesterday. I didn't mean all those horrid remarks.'

'All?'

'Robin, you've a gift for not responding the way I want.'

'Sorry.'

'And for pity's sake stop saying sorry.'

She saw his face. He suddenly looked so sad, like a little boy lost. 'Give me a hug,' she said.

He clutched her to him. Close, he thought, but not intimate, affectionate, not loving. That summed up their relationship.

Helen was nestled into Robin's coat, thinking, if only. There was so much she couldn't put into words. She didn't want him to go, because she'd miss him, but that was only part of it. She was scared of what would happen while he was away.

She drew away so she could see his face again. 'I'm going to walk straight away without waving you off,' she said. Robin thought he knew what lay behind this. Helen couldn't stand goodbyes. They were too upsetting and drove her distracted.

I wish I could reciprocate, he thought as he hugged her.

The embrace was short and cursory, she thought as they parted, and she turned and imagined him walking away. It was ironic that in this farewell embrace they were no longer in eye contact. She was thinking and hoping. This would give her the space she desperately needed, after all this time, finally to exorcise Detlev from her heart and life.

* * *

Tom's departmental meeting had dragged on rather longer than expected. He resolved to apologise to Laura as soon as he walked in for being late and for everything else that had gone wrong between them. Perhaps it would heal matters sufficiently till they could find time to talk properly, away from the children. Somehow though, as he walked in, he knew this wouldn't happen; the meal was burnt, the kids were scrapping, and there was an urgent message from a colleague. He rang straight away. Laura was shaking with rage as soon as he came off the phone. 'I've a bunch of very anxious research staff,' he tried to explain. 'There's a budgetary crisis in higher education.'

'You're bloody telling me on top of everything else I'm spending too much,' she shouted.

'I am not telling you anything. I've only just walked in,' he shouted back.

'Two hours late.'

'I'm sorry.' His voice lowered in tone.

'You don't want me to buy that coat and the shoes to attend that reception at Hugh's next week. Well I shan't go without them and I shan't go in any case. I can't stand their stuck-up narrow ways.'

'Darling, I'm not exactly on the verge of being sacked.'

'But –'

'There isn't a "but".'

'Don't play your bloody academic games with me. You aren't in one of your meetings now.'

'Listen, darling, there may be redundancies, but it won't affect us.'

'That makes me feel great. The wives I mix with daily may be soon living with bankrupt husbands from your Centre, but I'm not to be concerned about it.'

'Okay, we're putting together a package to stave this off. It's whether we can deliver in the next few weeks.'

'Package, deliver? You make it sound like the bloody Post Office,' she shouted, unable to curb her anger.

'There's no need to shout. It's a consequence of the global uncertainties affecting the sector.'

'I hate you when you speak like that.'

Tom shrugged: 'I can only tell you the situation.'

'I won't put up with any more of this, Tom. I am not one of your bloody staff,' Laura blurted out between clenched teeth.

The truce between them had held briefly last winter, from Detlev's death to just after the funeral; now it was falling apart, sentence by sentence:

'Not in front of the children,' he said very quietly.

'Mum,' called Matthew from the corner of the L-shaped lounge, screened off by a small group of bookshelves in a rectangular U shape.

'You and your bloody smooth phrases,' she shouted. 'Why should I keep quiet to protect your lies about the happily married university professor and this stuffy campus? They want to get real and come into the late twentieth century. People balance careers against families in the real world, they have rows and sometimes' – she was crying now – 'they're unhappy and they split up.'

'You shouldn't say these things,' he said quietly.

'Mum, I want to tell you something.'

'Don't counsel me,' said Laura defiantly. 'I'll say what I like.'

'Mum,' said Matthew, more insistently than ever. 'Why do you always ignore me when you're arguing with Daddy?'

'I am not arguing, Matthew. We're having a discussion. All parents discuss and sometimes they disagree.'

'Michael's parents don't. They aren't always cross like you and Daddy.'

'How can you be sure?'

'Because they aren't when I go to tea with Michael.'

'How do you know they don't when you leave?'

'I've slept at Michael's and they don't then either.'

'Bully for them,' Tom said and regretted it immediately.

The mobile in his pocket played an insistent jingle. He pulled it out and put it to his ear. He stood by the front door and stepped outside so he could hear. When he returned he was agitated. 'Got to go,' he said hastily.

'Will we see you again tonight?'

'I won't be too late. Don't stay up for me. My colleagues are having a crisis. It's a late shift meeting about our strategy to resist the budget cuts.'

'It's always a late shift these days,' she said as he disappeared towards the car.

The children were undressed and having supper in the loft extension upstairs which doubled as spare bedroom and playroom. Matthew picked up the paper Laura had been reading.

'This is a picture of the funny man we saw today in town.'

'Mmmm,' said Laura without looking.

'I'm getting really really mad,' exclaimed Matthew.

'What, darling?'

'The man,' said Matthew. 'This is his picture in the paper.'

'It can't be, darling,' said Laura, hearing him for the first time.

'It is, Mum,' insisted Matthew. 'Grown-ups don't ever believe children but they believe each other even when they're wrong.'

Laura came back from her reverie with a bump as she knocked her head on the corner of the sloping roof with the velux window in it:

'I do believe you, darlings.' She was slightly relieved to find the children pointing to a rather poor print in the TV guide of a third-rank actor in a spaghetti Western. 'But there isn't a lot we can do about it. This man in the picture most likely lives in America, thousands of miles away. But the man you saw was probably very like him.'

She gabbled on, partly to relieve her nerves.

'You can't be sure, because these tiny pictures in papers like this are often not very clear. Mind you, if he looked like this, he might not be very nice.' She shivered. 'Ow, Mummy must get a flannel.' She clutched the bump on her head 'There'll be a bruise here if she doesn't put something on it to relieve the pain and the swelling. Snuggle down, there's a love. Mummy's so shattered, she's off to bed in a couple of minutes.'

'Daddy said he'd kiss us good night.'

'Daddy's at work and won't be back till you're both asleep.'

She suppressed her anger at Tom and bent over Matthew and Sarah in turn, kissing them as they lay in their beds.

Chapter 5

The coroner's office received a phone call early the following morning.

'This is the University. Is that Ms Wistow?'

'Yes.' Faith Wistow presumed the job of altering the arrangements had been left to a male administrative assistant.

'Professor Fortius apologises for inconveniencing you. His arrangements have had to change. He wants to bring the meeting forward an hour. Is it possible? He'll be driving. He'll pick you up at the entrance to the industrial estate on Grove Park Road. He has a call to make there. He suggests 11:45. Is that acceptable?'

Because of her background and experience, Faith was a confident young woman. The Grove Park Road area was run down and some way from the shopping centre, but perhaps the professor was short of time. He might even have an eating place in mind, perhaps a short car journey away at pubs in the villages of Tickton or Dunswell. To be fair, the coroner's office had quite difficult parking unless you knew your way about. Late at night, she'd have hesitated to walk there alone, but in the daytime it was different. She could handle herself, and men. She had travelled alone quite extensively in Western Europe whilst in her previous job.

She was there at the pre-arranged time. The car drew up. She leaned over and bent forward to greet the professor through the open window on the passenger side. She couldn't see into the interior properly. The window wasn't opened far enough. He wore sunglasses.

'Professor Fortius?

'Hi, Faith Wistow? Please get in. We must drive. I saw a traffic warden hovering round the corner.'

Faith felt pressured to act quickly. He was in a hurry to move off the double yellow lines.

She hadn't a clear recollection of the professor from the day of the inquest, but she quickly realised this was not professor Fortius. He lacked an air of authority. He just didn't act the part.

'Are you the professor's chauffeur?' she asked, going for the next most plausible explanation.

'He doesn't have one, but I'm his driver for today,' the man replied.

She relaxed a little, but still sat towards the front edge of the rear seat.

Graver drove the woman out onto the ring road, to the east side of town. After a couple of junctions, instead of turning to follow the main road, he veered off, turning left at a very minor junction before driving into a wood where the road was nothing more than a muddy bridle path.

The car stopped.

It was too late, far later than Faith realised. She scrabbled for the door handle but it had been removed. At her first intimation that any minute she might be fighting for her life, the driver's right arm shot across, and while his left hand suddenly gripped her right forearm, he slipped her sleeve up and slid under her skin the hypodermic which had appeared in his right hand. It was done in two seconds, with great slickness which capitalised on the element of surprise. Even in the few seconds before her head nodded forward, she noticed in puzzlement that the front windscreen was already misting over. She slumped sideways on the seat.

* * *

Faith regained consciousness, aware only of being completely unable to move her limbs. It was dark. She was uncomfortably hot and itchy, frightened of she knew not what. Her eyes hadn't adjusted to the faint glimmer of light. She had another go at wriggling free, flexing every muscle in her arms and legs. It was no good. Secure straps she couldn't even see held her body and limbs tightly.

She panted in the heat and the perspiration ran down her face and neck, and dripped off her nose. Her head was immobilised by the improvised wooden collar Graver had fastened round her neck. She repeatedly turned her head from side to side to try to catch her chin under her blouse and mop up the wetness dribbling down. It was the only movement she could make. Was it sweat or was it from her mouth?

The sweat bathing her head caused intolerable patches of itching; it irritated her eyes and made her shiver.

It was only when she stopped to rest that she became aware of something over and above the quiet – the silky smooth sound of a quadrillion tiny legs moving. A motion so seamless and unerring it lapped every crevice like the incoming tide of a totally becalmed sea, moving upward yet almost without any movement. The slight rustling was the nearest she could come to appreciating the ticking time-bomb of impending attack. For now, the hidden presence only rustled. She sensed something dreadful was about to happen. She couldn't possibly have anticipated the truth. Phalanx upon phalanx of skeletal forms advanced, chained together by the invisible bonding of tapping antennae and interlocking legs.

* * *

Faith struggled fiercely against the gag and chains, sweating and shaking. She heard the sound of a voice. It was counting. An invisible man, counting down from sixty. She didn't know why. He was counting while hordes of insects ran out from a hole.

Faith's eyes were running.

The invisible person wielded a long pole, shoved it through a hessian sleeve covered in a protective plastic envelope into which he thrust his arm. With this he manipulated a mirror a little above and in front of her. He turned the mirror so she could see her face clearly reflected. The image was so clear she could see the sweat trickling down her face.

'This mirror.'

Faith started at the intrusion of the voice.

'I surprised you. Look up and leftwards, Miss Wistow. Where you see a flash of metallic light, that's the mirror. Here, I'm turning it so you can see your little visitors.'

Faith gave another jump, this time of pure revulsion.

The voice came again:

'I have to alter your hair Miss Wistow and make a tiny scratch on your neck here, like this, only to give a smidgeon of blood. You understand why. They're energetic little bastards but they need a hint of what's on offer.

'Now, Miss Wistow, a person has at least the veneer of socialisation, which helps create the impression of masses cooperating in an orderly society. But a worker ant is' – he opened the viewing slit a little further, but with the mesh slid across so that not a single insect could escape and make physical contact with his body – 'a savage individual in a crowd of savages. He, or I should say she – the workers are all neutered females, not males, an interesting reversal of the human condition where it is the male who is more violent and homicidal – is a potential anarchist. She shows no emotion, Miss Wistow. She is pitiless.'

Tens of thousands of them were in place, so many that they bowed every branch down, and couldn't shift their places on the ground without stepping over each other. As if by mental powers alone, they stopped. In fact, it was the almost simultaneous waves of feelers briskly stroking on other feelers and bodies, in an indescribably delicate ballet of intention, which ordered their stillness and made it inevitable. The lack of movement was complete, as devastating as the waves of motion had been. It was the silence of armies holding their breath.

Like a single slow transpiration, the entire horde advanced. Each occupied only the antenna-space in front; only the gap behind was filled, no less, no more. It was the merest shiver, a trickle of life. But when that slight adjustment multiplies a billion times and is repeated over and over again, its impact becomes gross, devastating, irresistible.

She was aghast, paralysed by the shock of it. She realised the ants were all over her. Then she moved. Arms flailing like sails on a windmill.

But they were pouring off the high branches which overhung her, like thick streams of sticky black treacle. Faster than she could brush and shake them off, fresh lumps of the black crawling masses of insects landed on her, hissing and crackling as they dispersed to find a hold anywhere on her skin or clothing. With mandibles and hooked feet they clung on, resisting with all means the force of her wild movements.

She screamed. She went on screaming for some minutes after she had nearly lost her mind. Until they had completely filled her mouth, crawling, softly nipping, sucking and stickily suffocating her with blood and saliva, secretions of her own nose and mouth which she was unable to cough completely out. Revolted, she crunched and spat ... until her last breath.

Chapter 6

E-mail Robin to Tom:

Meeting at Research Council very productive, had some v. positive responses. Have met up with people who've just returned from where we're going. Incidentally, they've identified new species coleoptera which cd have value in cosmetics. And some parasites which affect people as well as cattle, so the government out there may be willing to pay to pulverise. What do you think about a bid? Attaching bid and abstracts of research into Dorylus for you as promised. Don't suppose there is much you haven't already seen or heard of.

R.

E-mail Tom to Robin:

Thanks for welcome message. Keep up the good work. You always were great on the PR front, for our unit and for the University! Anyone with sense would make you Ambassador. Pl. send details of those possible research bids. Haven't had time to go through the abstracts in detail yet, but will look forward to them. At first glance some useful stuff. Haven't seen it all before.

TF.

E-mail Tom to Robin:

PS. By the way, problems over budgets. Review of Centre's future role. Such is life.

Forgot to ask – You remember I mentioned apparatus used in first communication experiments, when we met that day in your office. I still can't track it down. Have you any idea when you last saw it?

TF.

Underneath Tom's casual manner there was a seriousness reflecting the make or break situation of the department.

E-mail Robin to Tom:

> *Ambassador, no chance. I'd rather be director of external affairs (not my own though. Only punning!) Sorry to hear about financial probs. Bad luck! Can't change our senior managers – more's the pity – they're the root of our problems! Can't help over apparatus. No precise recollections at all. Old age creeping on I expect, though don't mention pre-senile – what is it? My grandfather died of that. Hereditary I believe. Do ask if there's anything else I can do. Good luck. Pl. bear in mind leaving for Heathrow tomorrow. Will be at least 3 days before arrive destination. Till then no news is good news.*
>
> *Ciaow!*
>
> *R.*

* * *

Tom crossed the road from the Station. He looked at his watch. Twelve o'clock. He was in good time as he headed for the homely atmosphere of the Beverley Arms where he was due to meet Mrs or Ms Wistow. He wondered which. He allowed himself the thought that she was an attractive young woman.

* * *

Sergeant Brill was venting his feelings. PC Paul Morrison was on the receiving end.
'You say it arrived through the post this morning? That's five bloody hours. I'm telling you, Constable, another delay like this and you'll be looking for another job. Is that clear?'
'Sorry, sir. I didn't think it was serious. Written by a nutter.'
'It's not your job to judge seriousness. It's your job to bring material to the attention of a more senior officer. Plenty of serious crimes are committed by so-called nutters. Now get lost doing something useful.'
'Sir.'
Brill took the close-written sheets of paper down the corridor and knocked on Detective Inspector Dave Berringham's half-open door:
'Don't knock, the door's open.'

'Sir, if you have a minute I think you'll find this interesting.'

After Berringham had conveyed to Sergeant Brill the unsatisfactory state of affairs which had led to the note taking several hours to reach his desk, he spent a good twenty minutes reading it. From time to time, he winced as the pains came more sharply, further down in his abdomen and more to his right side than before. He'd tried ignoring them and using anti-acid remedies from the local pharmacy. He was approaching the point where denial wouldn't work any longer.

"Killing is dead serious. If you get more than one chance and if you're a perfectionist, practice makes perfect. Close the door, take off the mask and allow space to breathe.

"How you get to the killing bit. It's like lots of things, one step at a time. I know this thought so well, it's become a part of me, rather than a suggestion coming from my brain, or from somewhere else, inside or outside of me. (The organs of my body are different regions of the colony, all linked by living streams of workers. So I won't be likely to dissolve into component limbs and organs. I have to keep control.)

"Here's another thought: Despite my meticulous memory, and the diary of course (which must never fall into their hands), I'm not entirely sure at which moment I became the conductor. It was probably when the urge to conduct the performances of other colonies apart from the colony I am, became realisable.

"I rehearsed some things in my head so many times that when they happened I hardly noticed the slide from thought to action. I went into the kitchen and sat on a stool from which I could reach the controls of the video recorder and the television. Then it was back to the hi-fi, CD player, record and cassette players, all precariously perched on that raffia-woven stool, the one auntie used to sit on when messing about with her calliper. (She had them too, but if I ever asked if it was in the family, with me having some leg trouble, mother would bad mouth and cuff me.) The music on its own couldn't work the magic for me this time. I was too tense – I can't tell you why, not this early in the game. I haven't primed you yet with any of the crucial details about what makes me tick, turns me on, as they say. But, cursing at the bad connections to the speakers balanced on cardboard boxes in the corridor linking the farmhouse to the old dairy, now the ground floor lab. Which would it be – the fourth movement of the Bruckner seventh symphony or the last passages of the Mahler fourth symphony? No, not the Mahler. Too much public exposure means too many stray memories and associations. (I'm very honest and open, so don't go pigeon-holing me as like the rest.) I'll go for the Bruckner tonight.

"I was feeling unsettled and I didn't know how to calm myself. I felt like watching the film I'd made of the experiment in the barn.

"I turned on the video. The camera was placed in the rear corner, below the spotlight. It was primitive but it worked for my purposes. The pig was jittery from the moment I pulled aside the bale of straw and shoved it across the sheet of chipboard I used as a bridge across the moat. The island was about six metres square. It had taken months to dig out the ditch round it and line it with butyl rubber, but I was quite pleased with the result.

"(I'm nearly there. Push me, push me and I'll do it.) I'd gone to such trouble to produce an imitation of a corner of the rain forest on the island, with reasonable accuracy. There were shortcomings in the tree department, but the undergrowth surrounding the small clearing, some at a much higher level over a rocky outcrop, was pretty convincing. The lean-to conservatory enclosing the whole was pitched up against one wall of the barn. It was of plain design with panels of double-glazing down to within a metre or so of floor level. It was the largest building project I'd ever undertaken and had taken some assembling. I had to do it on my own, though. I didn't want strangers prying.

"Below the surface of the soil, of course, was where the conditions had to be absolutely ideal. Here the detailed planning followed everything I'd learnt over years of keeping ant colonies in the laboratory. Not too cool, not too dry, not too moist. Above all, not too warm, or they race so fast in confined conditions they overheat and die. To achieve the right climatic conditions, I installed a mister which automatically sprayed very fine droplets of warm water in infrequent but regular bursts from a strip along the inside of the roof of the conservatory. The final two touches of which I was particularly proud were first, the connection between the activator for this and a humidity tester. Second, there was the little windscreen wiper I had taken from the front headlight of an upmarket car at the scrap-yard and installed at the front of the camera, after some early attempts at filming which only gave me a few seconds before the lens steamed up.

"Take deep breaths to regain control. (You see how candid I can be. With such insight and self-awareness, I can't be insane.) The pig stood still, not squealing any more, but panting slightly from the exertion of resisting his prodding towards the barn housing this contraption. It was the size of a large Labrador dog, not fully grown but by no means a piglet either. It weighed a good thirty kilos. I had to keep glancing back at the screen while leaning over to switch on the kettle at the other side of the kitchen worktop. I could just about reach the coffee jar and a mug without moving from my stool. There wouldn't be much happening for a while, I knew that. But then the action would move quickly, and I wanted to be ready. My stomach was wobbling, my head slightly woozy – sometimes the stuff helps. I can't say what, in case this record goes astray.

"Can't keep this up. Body won't take it. Got to though. Deep breaths now, so as not to be sick at the crucial moment. (You won't believe this, but watching anything die excites me, but cuts me up rotten. I feel so physically sick I could die myself.) There was a rustling in the thick carpeting of leaves on the island. My pulse quickened. I knew where to watch. It was the shadowy patch half hidden from view by a large-leafed pitcher plant growing over a rotting log. I rubbed my hands together unconsciously and then gripped them tightly together at a flicker of movement from the shadow. It was a tiny flickering body, no larger than a blow-fly or large earwig, scuttling so fast from the shadows that he lost sight of it immediately under some leaves. Then another and another, till half a dozen of the darting insects had emerged. One or two stopped, clearly sensing the slight movements made by the pig. The animal scuffed up leaves as it moved nervously. The tiny insects were too small though, to make any impression on it. They couldn't even climb up its shiny hooves to gain a purchase on the coarse hairs of its slender legs.

"Despite this apparent stand-off between beast and insects, the effect on the small number of wandering ants was surprisingly uniform. Three or four of them immediately became very excited, running round in circles, waving their heads and exercising their considerable mandibles as though willing to bite any object within range. Several times it looked as though they were about to bite each other. Then they made off at great speed towards the prone tree trunk, continually criss-crossing each other's path.

"I leaned forward in anticipation. I knew that the shadow where they had disappeared was really an elliptically shaped object like a giant rugby ball which hung from the underside of the tree trunk. It was made up of hundreds of thousands of army ants clinging to each other's legs to form a protective ball around the young ants, brood and queen within. This was their bivouac whilst on the march. The few ants which had emerged were foragers with particular sensitivity to possible sites of food, acting as scouts on behalf of the main body of ants in their temporary nest.

"I took a deep breath as the ball of ants literally began to drip onto the earth, each drip hissing as it landed, like hot, black pitch. This is the only way I can describe the combined effect of the clattering of myriads of tiny legs and mandibles. It reminds me of when I once dreamt of the sound a giant made when he shook up a handful of bones. Great clumps of insects fell off the nest as the excitement of the scouts spread rapidly through to its interior. Within minutes, a thick living lava of ants flowed across the forest floor. One stream took a path up onto a rocky outcrop from which bushes and creepers were arranged so that they overhung the clearing beneath. The pig, still unaware of the coming catastrophe, still stood hesitantly, facing the other way. By the time the ants were piling up against its hooves so that those on top had easy access to run up its legs, those on the overhang were already falling in thousands onto its neck and back. Ten thousand simultaneous bites threw the animal into a squealing convulsion from which it landed on its back and in its terror, never succeeded in rising to its feet again. (Red. Red on black. Can't bear it. Can't stop this shaking.) It was steadily reduced over the next ten minutes to a suppurating mass of wounds, the blood from which was never allowed to congeal but was sucked up eagerly by crowds of workers, each replaced by another as soon as one was replete. By this time the animal was so weakened by shock and loss of blood that it was unable to resist the macabre carving up of its living flesh which accelerated. After thirty minutes it was at its last gasp and three hours later most of the flesh had been removed by its remorseless and utterly tireless assailants.

"It's over. Head shaking and retching. I sat and watched with tears (If you don't believe me, you can get lost now) running down my cheeks, cupping my mug of cocoa in both hands.

"There is a further step. The thinking part takes over the rest of the body. This is found out through killing the pig first, before the next stage. One step at a time.

"The hypothesis to test now is whether the equipment will significantly speed up the interaction between the excitement centre ants and the rest, thereby hastening communication and hence the death of the victim. Thinking about it, I will wind the tape back and press PLAY to watch my little drama all over again. This time I will have the bucket and towel ready. I hate the smell of stale vomit, especially my own. G"

'*Killing the pig before the next stage,*' quoted Berringham out loud when he'd read this document twice through. 'Jesus, we're going to need some help with this one.'

He picked up the phone and dialled the number of Detective Superintendent Bradshaw, who happened to be the last person in the world with whom he wanted to share any information, speculation, thoughts or feelings. But he was Berringham's immediate boss while he was working at Wawne Road and as such was his first point of reference. As he waited for him to reply, Berringham was trying to suppress his intuition that like a geyser, the situation was about to blow sky high and scalding hot, right in their faces.

It was while Berringham was in Bradshaw's office, waiting for his reaction to the document, that the pain stabbed him in waves whose intensity increased alarmingly beyond what he'd thought was possible. The pain catapulted him out of the seat, leaving him grey-faced and sweating profusely, in a doubled up contortion on the floor. He couldn't speak. He thought he could see Bradshaw dialling. By the time the ambulance came, he'd rather have been dead.

After they'd shipped Berringham off to the Infirmary and Brill had done the necessary with his family, Bradshaw was in touch with Assistant Chief Constable Jack Deerbolt.

'I must have a replacement – I don't know. The paramedics wouldn't make a diagnosis – but they agree with me he's not coming back in a few days. Reading between the lines, it could be a duodenal but appendicitis is more likely. I've rung the Infirmary. They've done an ECG or whatever and ruled out a heart attack.'

Ten minutes later, the ACC rang back:

'I've a recently promoted detective chief inspector you can have on an open-ended basis, until Berringham's back. Experience includes time in the Met. fraud, some vice, murder squad, that sort of thing.'

'Sounds like a good all-rounder. Starting when, sir?'

'With immediate effect, give or take tidying up a few loose ends. Winchester. Chris Winchester. I'll do the necessary at this end. Ask your office to liaise with Personnel.'

Bradshaw was highly relieved. He'd been operating below strength as it was. At least he now had a man to put straight in charge of this team who would take responsibility for the rest of Berringham's work and the latest investigation – which was probably a storm in a tea-cup.

* * *

Tom walked briskly across the cobbled square of Saturday Market in Beverley. He stood still, looking around for a minute or two before heading for the bar and restaurant on the far side.

He didn't worry too much when his visitor was ten minutes late. By twenty minutes, he was becoming slightly fidgety. After thirty minutes, he was wondering if he had the right time and place. Forty-five minutes after first sitting down in the restaurant, he went to the payphone next to the entrance to the toilets and phoned the coroner's office. No reply, just the answerphone: "The office is now closed until Wednesday 16 March. If you wish to leave a message ..."

Tom went back to the counter, ordered a scone and another coffee, went back to his table and spent another twenty minutes eating it. His mind was numbed, as though a crucial thinking process was blocked. Nothing could be done now. He'd have to wait and phone the office in the morning.

There wasn't much point in waiting any longer. He got up and left the restaurant. The train wasn't due for another forty minutes, so he took a longer route back towards the Station. He needed time to think, or rather, to try to jog his mind from its paralysis back into reflective mode.

Habit took over. Tom was an inveterate walker, especially in unknown territory, whether town or country. His return route involved two or three side streets. Reaching the end of one street and turning into the next, he had the rather odd sensation that someone was following him. 'I'm imagining this,' he told himself out loud and didn't look round. But at the next street turn, it happened again. 'You're watching too many late night films,' he murmured. This time, he half turned his head and was in time to catch a glimpse of a figure far behind, probably too far away to be in pursuit and certainly too far away for him to be able to pick out features for later recognition. By the time he reached the cavernous redbrick shelter of the Station building, he had other more practical preoccupations – confirming the train time, crossing to the platform, choosing a drink from the snack-bar retailing various unappealing liquids, and facing the prospect of the journey home.

Chapter 7

Bradshaw called Brill into the office. 'I'm not asking for a response to this, Sergeant.'
'No, sir.'
'I haven't finished yet.'
'Sorry, sir.'
'This note –'
'From the nutter. Yes, sir, we're onto it.'
'I'm not sure what that means, Sergeant.'
'Well, sir, it means – it means we're onto it, sir.'
'Quite. Well, Sergeant, there are several possibilities when we receive a note like this. It could be a complete nutter. In that case we'd best put it away in a drawer and forget about it. On the other hand, it could be a communication from a criminal we're already investigating. I don't think that's the case.'
'No, sir. Is that all, sir?'
'It isn't, Sergeant. There is another possibility. It could be from a particular type of dangerous person, who has a need to communicate with the authorities whilst committing extreme crimes. You see what I'm driving at.'
'You're saying the person has written us a note saying he's about to commit a crime.'
Bradshaw sighed. 'Something like that, yes, Sergeant. You'd better return to your duties.'
Brill leapt to his feet and almost ran out of the door.
'There goes the reason for our low detection rates,' Bradshaw muttered.
Brill stopped and turning back, stuck his head round the door.
'Did you say something, sir?'
'No, Sergeant, nothing of importance. Thanks for the thought.'
'Yes, sir. Thank you, sir. I'll be off then.'
'Good idea, Sergeant.'

* * *

Graver sat reading, this time from a book he'd kept at home since he was eleven:
'Ant society is almost exclusively female. The requirements of queens dominate the nuptial phase, whilst the entire economy of the colony rests on the labours of the neutered females, commonly called workers. Males live less longer than females. In many species, their

sole function and purpose in life is to fertilise a queen, which they do in a single nuptial flight, after which they are unceremoniously ejected from the nest. Sometimes the neutered females, the workers, turn on the males, attacking them, injuring or even killing them. Unable to feed or defend themselves, one way or another the males inevitably die within a short time.'

He spoke, in his head at first, to the hordes inhabiting it. At the first syllable of his voice, they turned their heads, waving antennae towards him. He was King, the Emperor, an anomaly in their matriarchy.

Chapter 8

'Reason to believe, sir, it isn't a human body but the remains of a pig,' local PC George Tenant stated in his pedantic way.

Dr Lonsdale, the pathologist on call, vented the tiniest sliver of his annoyance:

'A pig? Speak up, officer.'

'That's correct, sir. A pig.'

'Let me get this straight. You've called me out on a weekend to carry out a preliminary examination on the body of a pig?'

'Not a weekend, sir, it's Friday night.'

'I've started my weekend, I don't know about you.'

'Yes, sir. I didn't know it was an animal before I called you.'

'But you did by the time you rang?'

'Not absolutely definitely, sir.'

'I don't believe this.'

'If it helps I'll say I didn't, sir.'

'It doesn't help one little bit, Sergeant.'

'I'm not a sergeant, sir, only a constable.'

'Show me the way, officer.' Lonsdale's irritation was boiling over. Constable Tenant took him to where the body lay. Lonsdale knelt down, opened his bag and looked round in suppressed fury. Tenant withdrew several yards, to what he judged a safe distance.

Detective Chief Inspector Chris Winchester had parked her car a distance down the road in the lay-by, walked up and witnessed this exchange:

'Am I hearing right? No body, just a pig?'

Tenant looked round in surprise. She held out her identification. He glanced at it and raised his eyebrows. 'No, ma'am.'

'It isn't a code word for copper, or –?'

Watch your step, Constable, Tenant thought. You don't know her. There's humour within limits and there's pushing it too far. He restricted himself to muttering under his breath, 'It isn't my fault it's only a bloody pig.' Out loud he added, 'It is the genuine, four-footed specimen, ma'am.'

There was the sound of a motor cycle approaching round the bend, seemingly from nowhere. It roared straight up, not far from where they stood, died to silence and the rider switched off all the lights. Another constable, motor cycle patrol Bob Mander, appeared out of the darkness:

'Bloody Norah, someone's cracking up here.'

'As long as you make sure it isn't you, Constable,' offered Chris.

'Yes, sir, er, ma'am.'

'Let me know as soon as the scenes of crime officer arrives,' said Chris.

'Who the hell was that?' asked Tenant as Chris left the scene.

'DCI Winchester, apparently. Bloody confident. I thought you knew her.'

'Where's she from?'

'I'll find out. Hang on.'

He went to the patrol car and made a call to base. He was back in a couple of minutes.

'That's your replacement for Dave Berringham.'

'It can't be. Bradshaw says we've got a bloke – Chris somebody.'

'She said that. Chris Winchester. First name's Chris.'

'Bloody hell, Bradshaw will go potty. Doesn't mind women in the Force as long as he doesn't have to work with them.'

A sudden afterthought struck him.

'Unless –' He pulled a face and mouthed a kiss in the air.

Late that evening at Wawne Road Police Station, information trickled through. The mood was edgy.

'Strange,' said Sergeant Brill, 'we've a body, but no reported disappearances.'

'Am I right in thinking it's definitely pork, sir?'

Brill was on guard. 'Meaning what?'

'Meaning this isn't a Kosher or Halal job?'

'As opposed to human, perhaps as well,' DC Mander interjected.

Brill gave him the evil eye. Mander put his head down to the report he was writing.

'What's so odd about not reporting a pig missing, sir?' Morrison asked.

Brill turned his icy stare on him in case he was having a dig, but Morrison didn't flinch.

'We receive plenty of other reports of disappearances and no correlated crimes,' he continued. 'There was an article in the Police Journal this month about how to use the Internet to match one up with the other.'

Brill pounced on this remark.

'I don't see the World Wide Web as an alternative to the hard graft of positive detective work. Do you, Constable?'

'Only thinking aloud, sir.'

'Then I suggest you keep your thoughts private and restrain your tongue from flapping about like a fart in a gale. If you don't use your brain before opening your mouth, there'll be an advert on the data-match page of the World Wide Web offering a supernumerary constable in exchange for some useful information. Got that?'

'Sir.'

After he had left the room, Brill jumped as though a horsefly had bitten him.

'Good God, the note.'

He picked up the phone and dialled Bradshaw's extension. As the phone rang without a reply, he replaced the receiver, hesitated, then dialled Bradshaw's home number.

* * *

Chris chewed the situation over as she set off back home in the car. She couldn't believe it. Driving a dozen miles from her cottage in Kelvinthorpe village to a God-forsaken corner of nowhere land near Wawne Road, for a half-gutted pig. No clues or explanations, nothing.

Any bright lights on the horizon? None. Except perhaps that the lads didn't seem any more laddish than where she'd been for two years. They were just the infantry, of course. The cavalry and officers would be waiting in the office. That was always the litmus test of the culture – office banter. Sex, sex, sex, police politics and sex again. Having to inhale all that testosterone. There was plenty to make a woman feel superior – men, for example. Why are you bothered now? she asked herself. You've survived fourteen years, including the Met.

* * *

Constable Bob Mander came into the office first thing: 'Am I interrupting?'

'Be my guest,' said Brill.

After a pause, Morrison tried again: 'This phone call. I'm sorry, sir, I feel quite –'

Morrison slid his chair back and shot from the room. He could be heard charging down the corridor to the toilet.

'I was interrupting,' said Mander.

Brill shook his head: 'That man should consider his position seriously.'

Five minutes later, Morrison was back. He sat down and picked up the telephone receiver.

'Put that down, Morrison.'

'Sir.'

'Before you do another thing, I want to know what this is all about.'

'Nothing, sir.'

'Nothing, my arse.'

'Sir.'

'You were upset.'

'Sir.'

'Why?'

'The state of the pig, sir. Forensics have been trying to get you. Their preliminary report. They said some of the corpse was in pieces – more like mincemeat than identifiable parts.'

'Yes. Not very nice, I admit. Go on.'

'That's it, sir.'

'What do you take me for, Morrison?'

'Signs of being eaten.'

'Well, what by? Rats, people even. Come on, man.'

'No, sir. Insects.'

'Down off your cloud, Morrison.'

'It's true, sir. The doctor found some traces of insects' legs and wings on the body.'

'First rule, Morrison, stick to your own job, then you might have a chance of becoming a half-decent police officer. Second rule, don't second-guess Forensics. They'll come up with their own analysis in the fullness of time. Anyway, how the hell can flies eat pigs?'

'Grubs can, sir, when they're dead. But I never said flies, sir. Flying ants some were, and the rest were those big ones with huge teeth.'

'Mandibles, Morrison.'

'Sir?'

'For God's sake, Morrison, use the correct term. Not teeth. You've been watching too many of those late night science fiction films. Stop getting wound up and, more important, stop wasting my time.'

'I'm not wound up and I'm not winding you up, sir. The doctor didn't say anything about the cause of death. Apparently the ants had crawled into every body orifice, sir –'

'Morrison! Cut it out.'

'Including the mouth. Sir, do you think that was after the death or was the death caused by choking?'

'It's not your job to speculate.'

'Not very pleasant, sir, asphyxia from insect congestion in the mouth. And the partial dismemberment was due to ant attack as well.'

'Look, Morrison, if you get pleasure from revelling in the gory details, transfer to Forensics and reduce my problems a hundred percent.'

'I haven't got the background, sir.'

'The man's a genius. Right, Morrison, if you're staying here, remember this isn't science fiction fortnight. This is Yorkshire.' He banged his fist on the table. 'We Yorkshiremen keep our feet on the ground, in the here and now. I've told you before. Wait for the report from Forensics. You can safely ignore any other speculation.'

'I agree, sir.'

Brill shook his head: 'God help us, if we carry on recruiting cloud-niners from University.'

'Hull Grammar School, sir. I only registered in higher education recently, as a mature student.'

'Registered! Mature! Is that what they call it? God help the Force, that's all I can say. I'm going for a slash, Morrison. When I come back, I want you to have a list of all pig farmers within a ten-mile radius of here. Find out whether any of them have missed an animal or two in the past week or so. Look snappy man, get practical. I expect to have a normal conversation with you. No fantastic fiction, no surrealism, no academic argy-bargy. Understood?'

'Sir.'

Brill left the room. Morrison added under his breath: 'Silly old git. Wouldn't know a surrealist painting if it was tattooed on his –'

Brill must have heard him speak without being able to make out the words:

'Did you say something, Constable?'

'No, sir.' Morrison lied with conviction.

* * *

At the very moment Chris stepped through the doorway and slammed the door shut before setting off for work, the phone rang. She had overslept and was late. She sighed and waited a few seconds for the ringing to stop. It went on. With an even longer sigh, she inserted the key, walked back into the hall and picked up the receiver.

'Hullo, 49789,' she said without enthusiasm.

'Is that Inspector Winchester?'

'Speaking.'

'This is Sergeant Brill. We've found another body, or rather a retired army chap found it. He's an officer, Major Ransley. He was walking his Labrador and spotted it in the bracken on Beverley Common. The dog chased off the path and started barking. He followed it and saw some light-coloured clothing in the undergrowth. The major sees a body in a right state, goes to the other side of the path and starts throwing up. You wouldn't have thought it of a major, I mean, with being in the army. By the time the major's finished throwing up, the dog is playing fetch with certain essential body parts which don't affect identification but –'

'Thank you, Sergeant.'

'I was going to say when you come in –'

'I'm not in today,' she answered.

'I didn't know you were on leave, Inspector. I don't know if Superintendent Bradshaw will like that,' said Brill, embarrassed. 'I was ringing to let you know the Superintendent is looking for you, in a hurry.'

'Thank you,' said Chris. 'For the record, Sergeant, I am not on leave.

I'll be clearing up the last of my former duties. I'm technically off today but on duty at Bramwell, clearing my desk in my last office. This was arranged when my secondment was agreed. Please inform Superintendent Bradshaw I may be in later, depending on the situation at Bramwell.'

Chris drove off, seething at this unreasonable pressure. How dare they squeeze her from her previous role and into her present one, without allowing sufficient time and space for her to clear up necessary business.

* * *

At the Police Station, the tension was rising. Bradshaw knew his competence was on the line. He had to demonstrate to top management he could manage the investigation. He was determined it would go like clockwork. He wanted to put DCI Winchester in charge immediately.

'Where is that woman?' he seethed down the phone.

'Having a day at her previous post, clearing up, sir,' said Deerbolt's secretary. 'She'll be with you shortly.'

'Shortly! What use is that?'

'Tomorrow morning at the latest.'

Bradshaw tried to distract himself. He walked down the corridor to the office. Morrison and Livesey stood poring over some papers with Brill.

'Sergeant Brill, I'm off to this scene of crime. I'll take another officer with me. Who have you got?'

Brill thought quickly. 'DC Livesey, sir.'

'Excellent. If DCI Winchester calls – no, on second thoughts it can wait.'

After they had left, Morrison spoke up.

'I've an idea I know of a number one suspect for that pig, sir.'

'Let's hear it,' said Brill.

'That absconder from the secure unit, not the young offender one but the regional mental health unit.'

'What makes you think that?'

'The dates, sir. He was in for violence.'

'Good thinking, Morrison. You may even have the makings of a half-decent copper when we drum that criminology out and inject some practical policing.'

'Thank you, sir.'

'Another thing.'

'Sir?'

'I've seen enough of you for one day. Take yourself off. Bugger off and pester your wife and kids.'

'Haven't got any kids, sir.'

'Have an early night and your luck might change.'

A little later, a voice was heard in the office: 'Sir, goodnight, sir.'

'What's it take to become a creep-arse,' muttered Mander as Morrison walked past the office.

Morrison stopped and stuck his head round the door. 'You say something?'

'Not me, mate,' said Mander. He kept his eyes down on the report he was writing.

Chapter 9

'Ouch', said Laura. She slapped her ankle. 'These damned red ants. I'm sure they know you're an ant person. Our garden seems to have masses more than any others round here. They bite like mad.'

'Sting,' Tom corrected. 'The small black ones, Anthomyops Niger, can nip but rarely do. They have no stings. The others are Myrmeca ruginodis, I expect. They rely on their stings whether they're on the defensive or the attack.'

'I don't care what they rely on. There are times when I wish you were a Dalek.'

'I can believe that,' muttered Tom.

She peered at him askance. 'You look a bit like Dr Who, with your wild hair and eccentric scientist manner.' She imitated the metallic Dalek voice. 'Exterminate the ants on the lawn, exterminate. This is an ultimatum. Wife and kids to professor of antomology.'

'Entomology,' said Tom.

Annoyance welled up from deep inside her. 'Stop correcting me, as though I was one of your students. I find it very irritating. Either you exterminate those biters, stingers or whatever they are from those parts of the gardens we humans wish to use, or I shall attack and I shan't care who's in the way. Bleach or bulldozers, I'm not fussy. Is the car usable? I want to take the kids into town.'

'Yes. How long will you be?'

'I'll come back when the garden's habitable.'

'Darling, I am rather busy today.'

'Don't condescend, you're always busy.'

'I wasn't,' he rapped, uncharacteristically of him, but entirely in keeping with their interactions of late.

She looked at his face. She hadn't the energy to fight over every word, but the impulse was there. That alone was serious. She shrugged.

'You're damned snappy, but what's new? Anyway, we're meeting Helen. We'll probably have a walk in the Old Town or by the Marina and finish up with a drink and ices, at say four-ish. You might deign to take a break around then from whatever's preoccupying you.'

* * *

As Tom turned the car towards the outskirts of town he addressed passers-by as though they were passengers. So clear was his enunciation that at the traffic lights on Cottingham Road the man driving the car which pulled up alongside him looked extremely puzzled to see Tom talking volubly to empty passenger seats.

'You can't talk love into existence. And you can protest too much about it,' he announced in the intonation of a great conclusion, as the lights turned green and both cars accelerated. He turned onto the ring road whilst the other driver sped southwards. 'I know there are poems. But love can't be spoken, not adequately. It can be made, but even that is imperfect. It can only truly be felt'. As he said this, he knew that in Laura's case, he didn't feel it. He had done once, but didn't any longer.

* * *

Tom hummed the tune of the song on the car radio. The voice of the DJ broke in as the music faded.

'There we are, a lovely song about love. As the poet says, love is a many splendoured thing. Ring us or e-mail us if you know which poet. John Donne spent time sharing his lover's thoughts with the rest of the world, good for us. I wonder what his parishioners thought about the wicked wonderings of the Dean of St Paul's Cathedral, in the City of London. What was it? *When lying on this bank with you, We fix our gaze with eyebeams two. I am the page, the book you read, You are the food my soul does need.* First person who can ring us to correct me, we'll give you a free book of –'

Tom snapped the radio off. 'For pity's sake, we all know what love is,' he muttered. 'The problem is finding and keeping it.' He drove on in silence.

* * *

Tom reached his office in a flat mood.

He picked up the phone and dialled. 'Hullo, is that the coroner's court?'

'It is, sir.'

'Could I speak to the coroner's clerk, please?'

'Speaking.'

'Is Mrs –'

'This is Miss Cannock. 'The regular clerk is still away, sir. Can I ask who is speaking?'

There was a knock at Tom's door and it opened a fraction. Jean put her head round it. 'The missing equipment,' she mouthed.

'It doesn't matter,' said Tom and put the phone down.

'Sorry,' said Jean. 'Was I interrupting?'

'No, no,' said Tom, 'only the library. They can wait. Do come in.'

'I've been making a few enquiries,' said Jean. 'It's quite interesting.

When you start asking questions and looking for equipment, all kinds of other objects which had gone missing start to turn up.'

'Amazing what the fear of the auditor and charges of stealing from work will do,' said Tom. 'And I never even mentioned them.'

'You didn't have to,' said Jean. 'As usual, you left it to your faithful female secretary. Another prime example of men leaving the dirty work to women. From the nappy to the bedpan, it never stops.'

Tom held up his hand. 'I agree,' he said. 'I surrender to the overwhelming combined forces of feminism and equal opportunity.'

'If you try sarcasm,' said Jean, 'I shan't tell you what I found.'

Tom made a further gesture of compliance.

'Right,' she said, 'Item one: you didn't lose the equipment. Item two: it was loaned to, or rather borrowed by, the Department of Oceanography nearly fifteen months ago. Item three: it's never been returned.'

'I'll be damned,' he exclaimed. 'What have they to say for themselves?'

'Hang on,' said Jean. 'I haven't finished. I contacted Oceanography to ask for its return. Guess what?'

'They sold it to pay for the Christmas dinner?'

'It was never received.'

'How can they tell?'

'They're adamant. I spoke to the administrative officer who registers the movement of all equipment. They're far more rigorous about it than we are. They have to be, remember, because they work with so many outside bodies. Some of the marine exploration equipment they use costs as much as our entire laboratory.'

'Where is this going?'

'What is more, they never requested this equipment.'

'In other words –'

'In other words, someone probably half-inched it and laid a false trail, relying on the fact that nobody follows up most of these items in any case.'

'Why would somebody do that?'

'I don't know,' Jean said. That's your department.'

'Jean, you're a wonder. You'd put Sherlock Holmes to shame. Take the rest of the day off.'

'It's four o'clock already,' said Jean, 'Having spent time sorting this out, I've still the post to do. But thanks for the thought.'

'And you,' said Tom thoughtfully. 'Thanks for the thought, Jean. Something's going on here. I'll get to the bottom of it.'

'Even if it means swimming into dirty water,' said Jean.

'That too. I really don't care, as long as the reason for the dirt becomes clear. I'll start by asking the technical staff. They're the ones who really know what goes on in this place.'

She smiled at him as she left. Her smile said, I know you, Tom Fortius. Something else will overtake you. You're too busy to concern yourself with every detail of what goes on in your department.

Chapter 10

'Weather's turned cold.'

'Super's boiling hot, though. That temporary transfer's arrived to replace Dave Berringham,' said Paul Morrison.

'How is he?' asked Bob Mander.

'The new guy? We haven't met yet.'

'Piss-ant! I meant Dave.'

'Dave? He was in intensive care for a while. But they've taken his appendix out. It was knackered. He's back on the ward now.'

'His missus will be relieved. Who's the replacement? Do I know him?'

'Her. An inspector on temporary duty, from out of county, just been appointed in this Force to chief inspector.'

'Did you say she?'

'Yep.'

'Old news. I've already met her at the dead pig fiasco,' said Mander.

Sergeant Brill was passing the doorway and looked in. 'By the way, you two bloody washerwomen, the incident room is now the murder investigation room, with DCI Winchester in charge.'

'When was that decided?'

'Don't ask me,' said Mander. 'I'm looking forward to a long weekend in my caravan at sunny Runswick Bay, watching frets rolling in off the North Sea.

Brill put both hands on the desk. 'Rumour has it that somebody leaned on Bradshaw and said this is how it's bloody gonna be. So I advise you to watch yourselves with her. She's probably got friends in even higher places than the bloody Masons.'

'That's not funny. You wanna be careful where you make that kind of remark,' said Mander.

'Yeah, watch Bradshaw's left trouser leg when he's next in. It's always at half mast,' said Morrison.

'Come to think of it, your handshake's a bit suspect, Morrison,' said Mander.

'See what you've missed. Serves you right for taking leave during a busy period. That woman eh?'

'Yes. What about it?'

'In this Station. With him?'

He motioned next door.

'Morrison!' Bradshaw bellowed from the adjacent office, as if on cue. Bradshaw's office was like himself, large and lean. It was almost bare of furniture apart from his own desk and chair, offering no place for the visitor to feel relaxed.

'Sir?'

'Bring me those expense claims, pronto.'

Any doubts about whether Bradshaw's intervention was coincidental were settled in the next minute. The Superintendent scrutinised each sheet of paper before signing it grudgingly. He leaned across the desk, rising slightly off his seat with his weight carried on his outstretched arms, palms down on its polished surface, like a spider about to leap forward on its prey. Morrison returned to the main office. Brill spoke slowly and deliberately to him:

'Now Superintendent Bradshaw has finished with you, I want to say I've heard quite enough about caravanning exploits to last me the rest of your possibly quite short career. I want this Station to be known for its efficient work, not for the quality of its caravanning holidays. Is that understood?'

'Yes, sir,' Morrison answered obediently.

'Get on then, man. And wash your mouth out. We've a woman DCI working in this Station and I want no more sodding language fouling this effing place up.'

'We've WPC's. Why the song and dance about this one?'

'Because she's new, because she's joining us temporarily so she's taking her impressions back to another Force, because she's a good bit higher in rank than you. Three reasons enough?'

'Definitely, sir.'

'So watch your bloody ps and qs. I'm off to lunch now. I want a full report on any developments as soon as I return.'

'Yes, sir.' Morrison looked round and there was Mander dancing a miniature jig behind Brill's back as he left the general office, mouthing 'This is bloody pot calling bloody kettle black, over and out.'

* * *

Detective Constables Andy Dobbs and Bob Livesey were in the locker room, coming on duty for the first time that week.

'Winchester,' said Livesey

'Rifle or cathedral?' Dobbs asked.

'Keep your witty remarks to yourself. Neither. It's her name. Christine Winchester.'

'I can tell you a bit about her,' said George Tenant, who'd come in to the room halfway through the conversation: 'I've heard she turned down accelerated promotion at one point. By coincidence, I think I've already met her.'

He wasn't put off by the 'Ooohs' this remark stimulated.

'At the scene of the dead pig fiasco, and in the car park at HQ. I helped her move some box files from her old office.'

'He's going to tell us he found out her back box files are seldom used.'

'You're a crude bastard. No wonder you never made it through the sergeant's exam.'

Tenant had unzipped his trousers to tuck in his shirt.

'Look at Mr bloody cocky, waving it about.'

'How is it other people know they've sent a woman to replace Dave Berringham and I don't.'

Tenant tapped the side of his nose. 'Not enough of this, lad. Keep your nose to her grindstone, eye on your balls.'

'You are a dirty bastard.'

'Fast mover, this lad.'

'Fancies his chances.'

'If it's the same one. I asked in the office afterwards and they gave me the gossip on her. Young, thirty-ish, extremely attractive, no current attachments, likes smart men and smart cars. First class degree from Oxford University so right out of your league.'

'Smart, high achiever. Sorry Andy, that rules you out as well,' said Bob.

'You'll have to do something about the rust on that old Vauxhall,' said Tenant.

'Shut it. Just because you're already smarming your way in with her, Georgie Porgie. Remember what happens when you kiss the girls.'

'Woah, guilty minds speak most.'

'Who said I'm even interested? I haven't got your one-track mind.'

* * *

It was three hours since the body had been found. Bradshaw was back in his office.

DC Morrison made a mistake. Mug of coffee in hand, he was peering out of the office window at a helicopter hovering over the streets to the rear of the car park.

'Ah, Morrison.' Bradshaw took a deep breath. 'Free and looking for something to occupy you?'

'Not exactly, sir.'

'A woman's body has been found.'

'Yes, sir. I know.'

Bradshaw rocked back on his heels. 'You know, sir?'

'Yes, sir.'

Bradshaw recovered quickly from his surprise. 'Bad news travels.'

'Sir.'

'Then you'll probably know she's thirty-ish. No ID yet. Suspected foul play.'

'No, sir.'

Bradshaw tried, and failed, not to let his satisfaction show.

'Is DCI Winchester on duty yet?'

'Haven't seen her, sir.'

'Phone headquarters. Ask them if they've any reports anywhere in the county in the last two weeks of bodies found in suspicious circumstances.'

'Who shall I report back to?' Morrison sensed the situation between Bradshaw and DCI Winchester was potential dynamite and had no wish to be around for any detonation.

'Sergeant Brill of course.'

'Sir.'

'On second thoughts ...'

Morrison's hopes of being let off the hook were raised momentarily then dashed.

'... make that the last month or so. Don't just ring Forensics. They've a locum in place of our regular. Check with the undertakers as well. You can't be too careful. Another nail in the coffin of quality, eh?'

'Yes, sir.' Morrison turned towards the doorway of the general office. He showed no sign that he'd recognised any witticism buried in this remark. Constables Tenant and Morrison, sitting opposite each other, looked sideways at him and exchanged glances and shrugs. They were used to not understanding what Bradshaw was on about.

Bradshaw's face didn't crack. Morrison was wondering why he should check with undertakers when the body had already been found.

'Yes, sir what? Don't speak unless you know what I am referring to.'

'I do, sir.'

Morrison should have known better. Whenever he was under pressure, Bradshaw turned out his hog on the softest ground. By that standard, Morrison was mud.

'What then?'

'Well, sir, we're having problems getting reports on substances in time.'

'Substances in time!' roared Bradshaw. 'What would they be? Clocks filled with smack? Ha!'

'Er, I may have put that rather badly, sir. I meant the reports from Forensics take rather longer than we would like.'

'How absolutely regrettable, old boy,' said Bradshaw in a sarcastic imitation of Morrison's verbal sophistication. 'Which substances would you say are particularly affected, old chap?'

If Morrison was affected, he gave no sign:

'All sorts really. Substances in plastic bags and that sort of thing.'

'Plastic bags! More drugs, in shopping bags perhaps. Your pushers go to Asda or would they prefer Sainsbury's, or maybe a few tabs from the quaint village shop, with toilets next door where they can wash their hands afterwards.'

'No, sir.'

'No sir what!'

'No shopping, sir. Drugs, syringes and so on.'

'Go back to your Open University degree Morrison and stop bothering your head with practical policing.'

Morrison was heartily sick of constantly being pulled down.

'Sir, it wasn't the OU but law and criminology at the local Uni. Can I check what you said just now, sir? Don't you trust Forensics?'

'Good lord, yes. With my life, as it were. Listen to me, Morrison. I'm not casting aspersions on the medical profession. We can rely on our regular people in the mortuary. They're part of our own forensic team as it were. But if one is sick, another is on holiday in the Bahamas and a third is out on another job, we remain hesitant about relying too heavily on the locum pulled in from another area. That's what I mean about questionable quality. *Comprendes*?'

Morrison nodded uncertainly.

'Don't forget, Morrison. Check the body!'

'Sir.'

* * *

Brill came into the office in a hurry.

'That body they found near Beverley. Preliminary forensic report's ready.'

The Station phone rang. Brill put the call through to Bradshaw, adding, 'Suspicious circumstances. Beverley Westwood. Some of the flesh had been removed.'

A collective groan spread rapidly among the other officers in the room.

'Spare us the gory details.'

'Forensics said somebody rang from this office.'

'Who rang?'

'I did,' said Morrison. 'Superintendent Bradshaw's orders.'

Brill pulled a face and walked out of the office, carrying a report he'd been writing.

'If it's another pig,' muttered Tenant, 'put me down for some chops for the freezer.'

'I'll have a pound of sausages,' a voice called from the other end of the office.

'You're sick,' said Morrison.

'There were signs of the flesh being eaten.'

'How can you tell?'

'We know what it's like to live with bloody piranhas.'

'Flown in from the Amazon, or swam across the Atlantic, round the channel and up the chuffin' Ouse?'

'Nothing so exotic. Young men round here getting hungry for it on their way home from the pub.'

'You're bizarre. Not lost your peculiar hangups about women.'

'Do not doubt the seriousness of the situation,' said Tenant pompously, in an exaggerated imitation of Bradshaw.

'For pity's sake give over,' said Morrison. 'A woman's been found dead.'

Silence fell. The other officers shuffled uneasily. Brill returned, having deposited the report with a typist. At that moment, Bradshaw called out from his office:

'DS Brill? Have you an officer free?'

Tenant grimaced and mimed Bradshaw's words again, raising a smile from the others.

'Always busy, sir. But I can release one,' said Brill, striking a judicious balance. He nodded to Morrison, who left the room. Tenant, behind his back, melodramatically acted out the horrified facial expression and struggles of the person being dragged by invisible forces to a dreadful fate.

Morrison took a deep breath and picked up his case.

'I'll be off.'

'Wait a moment, Constable. Wheel yourself down to where the action is. Beverley Westwood. You can give some relief to the team.'

'Too many chiefs here. Bradshaw says this, someone else says that,' muttered Morrison.

'What did you say?' Brill asked sharply.

'I said where's Beverley.'

'For God's sake, man. Have a look at the map and try walking ten yards to the other office. Do I have to spell out every detail? Contact the local team on the spot before you leave here and make yourself known to them.'

Brill was halfway out of the nearest door, when a woman's voice came clearly across from the doorway on the far side of the room:

'Before you go, Constable.'

Both men turned.

'Right,' said Brill, the wheels turning rather rapidly in his head, 'Inspector Winchester, is it?'

'I am Detective Chief Inspector Winchester, yes, Sergeant.'

'Detective Chief Inspector Winchester, well I never,' said Brill, 'and no one even informed me you were arriving today.'

'I actually started before today, at the scene of the pig incident.'

'Ah, the pig. What a shame you've just missed our Detective Superintendent Bradshaw. I was just saying to Morrison here –'

'I heard what you were saying, Sergeant. I suggest it will be advisable to leave, Constable – your name, Constable?'

'Morrison, ma'am.'

'– to leave Constable Morrison here a few minutes or until I've had a brief meeting with everybody.'

'Why yes, ma'am, absolutely. But if I may say, ma'am, there is some urgency. The world won't wait, etcetera etcetera.'

'That's fine, Sergeant, you can brief me on what Constable Morrison is doing. Morrison, you don't need to wait. Sergeant, bring all the relevant papers to me in my office, immediately. You can give me a verbal update on action taken so far. I shall want a meeting with everyone in the team as quickly as possible. We'll make that,' Chris looked at her watch, 'half an hour from now.'

'Which office, ma'am?' The question sounded innocent. He was stirring.

'I'm glad you mentioned that, Sergeant. That's another job for you before we meet. I'll be clearing my car out. I shall need some help to carry stuff in.'

Brill called out. 'Morrison, the lady needs help.'

'Sir.'

'Sergeant.'

'Ma'am?'

'I'm not used to being called a lady. We'll stick to normal conventions. Call me boss, or guv, I'm not fussy which.'

'Not bloody much,' someone muttered. Chris pretended not to hear.

'Yes, ma'am,' said Brill, standing as though paralysed.

'What is it, Sergeant? Have you any questions?'

'No, no, sir er – ma'am, er guv.'

'Good.'

'Bradshaw's going to love working with you,' Brill said under his breath as he busied himself at his desk.

'Sergeant,' Chris called.

'Ma'am, er guv?'

Chris appeared at the door.

'This was in my tray.'

'That's right, guv.'

'Will someone tell me what's going on?" complained an anonymous voice to nobody in particular.

* * *

Ten minutes later, Chris was in the makeshift incident investigation office, peering round a jumble of desks, tables, chairs, computers, boxes of stored stationery and filing cabinets. About a dozen police officers and clerical staff sat about, some working on PCs, others looking in files or doodling on notepads.

As she addressed her colleagues the talking continued at the back.

'I'll continue when you're all quiet,' said Chris. From that moment the silence would have cracked like an egg. She carried on as though nothing had happened. 'I'm Detective Chief Inspector Chris Winchester. Pleased to meet you. I'm heading this team while DI Berringham is off. First, this working environment. Who is admin here – hands up please. Right, who is in charge? Come on, who holds the highest grade? Fine, I want you – what's your name? Tracy? – to take responsibility for sorting out the layout of this investigation team's working space by tomorrow. I want all PC workstations which do not comply with EU regulations reported to me with a list of shortcomings and I'll do my best to have these rectified as quickly as possible. You need health and safety issues sorting so you can put your best effort into the job. Clear all unwanted stored items, including stationery, equipment and furniture from the room. Bring any problems to me. Don't liaise with anyone unless you're sure it's within your existing responsibilities to do so. Check with me and I'll do any necessary negotiating apart from this. If I can't, I'll tell you. You can cry on my shoulder and I'll cry on yours.'

'It's bloody liaise now, not talk,' said Bob in his own stage-whispered imitation of an Oxford University accent. Chris gave no sign of having heard him.

'The rest of this concerns everybody. As from this moment, I want every significant incoming report to be passed by me and every action that's part of this team's work to be cleared with me first. This is a short-term device to enable me to come to grips with the stage the inquiry has already reached. I'm not authoritarian, or a dictator by inclination or habit, but I am a newcomer and I carry the can from today if this investigation goes sour. So brief me as fully as you can. Is that clear? Any problems with anything I've said?'

The indistinct murmur which arose was profoundly ambiguous.

'I said, are we agreed?'

There was a ragged, but more recognisable chorus of assent. Heads were nodding. Towards the back of the room, two young men and a woman were whispering; one giggled.

'Can we share the information?' called Chris.

They looked up.

'The joke,' said Chris. 'Can we share it?'

One of them coughed.

'If you must know, miss, it was about you.'

'Don't be inhibited, man. Spit it out.'

'Someone found this writing on a piece of paper.'

Chris walked quickly to where they stood and held out her hand. Reluctantly, the officer handed it over. She read the words out loud.

'Winchester doesn't like grass, unless she likes your arse.'

A general snigger followed, then silence as everyone looked at Chris. She stared straight back, slowly surveying the room. She hadn't seen Superintendent Bradshaw come in behind her.

'Fair enough,' she said. 'I can take a joke, even a childish or smutty one. But I'm not tolerating indiscipline or indecency, harassment or any of those other fashionable features of police forces. I guess whoever passed that ditty on, knows how unpleasant I made it in my last team for people who treat others unfairly. I also reward openness with honesty, honest mistakes with my personal support and professional sincerity with my fullest backing. My idea of this team is that you cover me and I cover you. In return, I expect the highest standards of integrity, and I'll give you my commitment to the same high standards. Is that understood?'

There was an embarrassed silence.

'I'll make myself crystal clear,' said Chris. 'If you don't give your verbal agreement now, to each other and to me, I will be in to see your superintendent to ask to return whence I came. You can take pot-luck then who replaces me. So, your answer please.'

People looked at each other, then at Chris. Gradually the nods came, to each other and to her.

'Better the devil you know. That's all for today. Back to your duties,' she said. 'I want all those on duty back here tomorrow morning for a full run down at 8:00 a.m. Be prepared to give a verbal report on everything you've been doing to date. I gather today a woman's body has been found. I'll see the officers involved in finding this latest body, in my office in fifteen minutes time.'

* * *

Chris returned to the Station desk, unaware that Bradshaw had been in the doorway and witnessed the proceedings, withdrawing at the last minute to go to his own office.

'The Super's in,' said Brill.

'Thank you, Sergeant,' said Chris.

She knocked on Bradshaw's door.

'Come in. Ah, DCI Winchester. Close the door.'

'I took the liberty of introducing myself to the team,' said Chris.

'I know,' said Bradshaw, 'I was there.'

'I'm sorry, sir. I didn't mean – you could have introduced –'

'Introduced, nothing. If I'd spoken, you'd have been knocked off your perch till I chose to pick you back up and put you on it. Even if I hadn't spoken, you might have been put on the defensive by them. For reasons best known to them perhaps, they chose not to go onto the attack. This meeting between us is better held in private.'

Chris looked shocked.

'You took a chance there. You aren't heading this team by permission of your officers. You realise that.'

'Perfectly.'

'Why the hell create that impression?'

'To make a point.'

'I want you to understand your authority comes from the Police Force, through me, and not through your charisma, personality, charm or any other feminine or other personal qualities. As it happens, over and above heading the team, I'm appointing you to head this inquiry into the finding of the two bodies: the woman and the, er, pig. You haven't been voted in. You're seconded from another place, by higher authority. The other side of the equation is that you don't need to seek the approval or support of your colleagues. This is a disciplined service. You tell them what to do and they'll do it. Their job is to carry out orders. They're responsible for the work they do. Is that clear?'

'Yes, sir. Very.'

'I don't want any sarcasm or irony either, Miss Winchester. I know you're highly educated. Without doubt the most educated woman in this Station, and probably the person with the highest qualifications of anyone – men or women – as well. I don't doubt they've taught you well at Oxford, and at Bramshill. One word of warning. Don't misuse your gifts. The men here, and the women,' he added hastily, 'won't tolerate it and neither will I. Understood?'

'Understood.' She made as if to leave.

'Hang on. I've one final thing to say, before you rush out and start filling in complaints forms against me.'

Chris stared hard at him.

'I was impressed with your handling of that meeting. I admire your style, even if I don't agree with it. They're an awkward bunch. We haven't a lot of experience of women in charge, as leaders or managers. You've some good people there. To be frank, I despair of how to rescue them and stop them being sucked into the rather negative, cynical undercurrent in this Station. Your introduction could have gone either way. My hope is that if you play it straight with them, they'll give you their best. But there's no guarantee, even if you don't mess them about.'

'Thank you, sir.'

'Don't thank me. We'll wait and see and for your sake we'll hope for the best.'

* * *

'How's it going in there?'

'Bradshaw's still with her. Eleven minutes and he hasn't thrown her out yet.'

'Local record, going now for the Force record.'

'Fancies his chances with a woman after all these years being beaten by his old lady. Can't imagine anyone fancying him.'

'He'll be trying the look at me, the most eligible single man routine.'

'Silly bastard. That look in her eye. Like a spider. She'd shag him, eat him afterwards and spit out the rough bits.'

Chapter 11

After her meeting with Bradshaw, Chris drove to the scene of crime. She took DC Morrison with her. DC Livesey was already there when they arrived and briefed her.

'Female, guv. Young, signs of clothing being disturbed. We found this in the bushes near the body. Forensics haven't confirmed yet, but it could be that missing person from Beverley. We're checking the details in the driving licence.'

'So whoever it was doesn't mind us establishing the identity of the dead person,' Chris observed.

'We found this as well, ma'am.'

Chris took the transparent plastic wallet from him and held it up to the light, illuminating the single A4 sheet of paper it contained.

'Thank you, Constable. I assume this has been to Forensics.'

'To be strictly accurate, er, guv, I should have said the original is with Forensics. My best estimate is that their report won't be back for forty-eight hours. The one you have in your hand is a photocopy someone's just brought back. Superintendent Bradshaw's instructions. We had it delivered here, but he's returned to the Station.'

'Thank you, Constable. I'll see he receives it.'

'M – er, guv.'

Chris peered at the scribbled writing, most of it surprisingly legible despite the smudges.

'God, whoever wrote this has good eyesight.' The A4 sheet was covered in tiny scrawled writing in four vertical columns, the entire length of the page. She read out loud and shivered, not from the cold:

> *Miss Greenhill. She's one good reason I turned from performing to conducting at an early age. She used to stand too close and the breath from her mouldy body used to settle round me like a cloud. I imagined it infecting both of us, with her venomous impatience at my slowness to grasp the mechanics of playing the violin. Then when the rays of the sun came shafting through the window at a steep angle, I narrowed my eyes and saw the specks dancing in front of them. I realised they were bacteria from her breath, which teased me before diving towards my mouth and down into my throat. The realisation of all parts of my body as separate entities overwhelmed me. J*

Chris spoke to herself: 'What the hell is this? Recollections of a schizo?'

'Something like that I guess, guv.'

Chris continued to read out loud:

> *I used to giggle when Miss Greenhill said "your fingers have minds of their own." But I wasn't giggling inside. The thought made me shiver. "Are you cold, boy?" she asked, in a tone which said you can't be. (Nightmare: Lying in bed with a huge monstrous insect bearing down on me, unable to move my legs or arms to get out of the way. Screaming and screaming in terror, yet not able to escape.) The grip of her hand on my fingers hurt sometimes, as she clamped them onto the fingerboard of my little violin. Not that it made any difference to the notes. They never played in tune and the bow used to slide across the sweaty strings where I had held them with my own grimy hands. Once she caught sight of me picking it out of the case, lost her temper, which was bigger than the rest of her tiny body and swiped me with her arm. But even at nine I caught it and held on tight, so she lost her balance and cannoned into a desk. "You wicked boy!" she screamed. "You tried to hit me", I replied. Naturally, she ignored me and continued: "I'll see you punished. This is the last lesson you'll have from me." She did and it was, providing further evidence that what children say counts for nothing whilst what grown-ups say comes to pass, regardless of the truth. But I got my own back.*

'What's this?' The last column of writing was even smaller and much harder to read.

> *Music has the advantage of blanking out the sound of the maggots. I don't like to think of them advancing slowly, but always advancing. It's better not to be able to hear the low vibration of their rippling muscles against the tunnel walls.*

'This person's in serious trouble. Psychotic, would you say?'

The constable shrugged:

'Dunno, guv. Unless the author is this Miss what's-her-name music teacher. Head cases aren't my strong point.'

'Not mine either, thank God. Listen to this ending though, something,

something – I can't quite read – then *in a quiet, meditative way, infusing the music with emotion welling up I can't say where from. A first essay in the aesthetics of death, you might say.* The quicker we find this nutter the better.'

'It's different from the first.'

Chris was alerted. 'The first what?'

'The first letter, guv.'

Chris leaned towards him.

'There's been another of these?'

'Sorry, guv, I thought you knew.'

'When?'

'Just before they found the pig.'

'Come on, Constable, you'll have to explain. To whom was this letter sent?'

'I don't know, guv. It arrived. The sergeant had it, then the super.'

'Bradshaw?'

'Yes.'

'Thank you.'

* * *

Back at the Station, Chris was incandescent with rage. Heads turned as she marched down the corridor, straight to Bradshaw's and in without knocking. Bradshaw looked up in astonishment from the papers he was reading.

'Good day, Inspector, I didn't hear you knock.'

'I didn't knock, sir. Why didn't you tell me about the first note from our suspect, before the pig was found?'

'Ah the note. It wasn't germane to the case. Superseded by more important events, I'd say.'

'It's damned important, sir, if you hand me an investigation and don't brief me fully.'

Chris's raised voice was clearly audible down the corridor, and in the main office. Office staff exchanged meaningful glances. Then came the sound of the door slamming shut. Fifteen minutes passed.

Heads raised as the door opened and Chris's footsteps could be heard, rhythmic, confident, less angry now. She passed the door, head high, a slight smile on her face, reached her own office and went in.

* * *

Chris took Sergeant Brill with her when she visited the mortuary. It was a long time before anyone came to the door.

'I thought you were –' said Brill.

85

'Dead?' Rathbone smiled at his joke. 'No, I'm all alone at present, so it's difficult to break off. In the middle of a cut and paste job, so to speak.'

'Spare us the messy details,' said Brill.

'Nothing messy to it,' said Rathbone, 'no mess anyway. How's tricks?'

'We're nowhere on this one,' Brill continued. 'No suspects, no leads, no particular pointers. This is DCI Winchester, by the way.'

'How are you? Tim Rathbone. You can guess what I do. I won't shake hands.'

'That's why we've come to see you.'

'I should be flattered. Everybody always says Forensics will come up with something.'

'I wouldn't put it as crudely.'

'I would. You'll no doubt be wanting a full profile of the killer and to know whether this person has killed before and is likely to do it again.'

'I was wondering what sort of person would do this,' Chris said.

Rathbone gave her a grim look: 'A very disturbed one.'

'I wasn't expecting to put you on the spot. I realise it's more the kind of question for a forensic psychiatrist.'

'It is. Mary Threadgold was in earlier.'

'Dr Mary Threadgold?'

Rathbone nodded. 'You know her?'

'I worked with her on a case in East Yorkshire – a man who'd cut up his wife and run off with his mistress.'

'She's been reading the notes left at the scene of crime and sent through the post.'

'Both of them?'

Rathbone nodded.

'My impression is she's pretty worried about the risk.'

'It would help if she communicated with us direct.'

'You can say that to her yourself. She'll be back in a few minutes.'

* * *

Less than two minutes later, Mary Threadgold arrived. In response to Chris's query, she shrugged:

'I'm not into offender profiling as such, but I've had a look at what you have so far. It's a pity you didn't call me straight away. I like to visit the scene of the crime – in a case like this where the body was found at any rate.'

'I'll put you on the list for next time,' said Chris.

'Next time,' Mary exclaimed. 'What makes you think that?'

'I was going to ask *you* that question,' said Chris.

'Anybody in my line of work tends to be a hostage to fortune. No predictions can be made about a case like this. But subject to further analysis as we say, this person has a very out-of-the ordinary mind, in several senses. You've read the notes he or she – probably he – has been writing?'

'I've seen two.'

'Here are my thoughts to date. First, our killer may be working to a programme. We don't know what it is, but the notes indicate that the pig was killed as some kind of experiment and I wouldn't mind betting that the first body found after that was also part of an experiment. Unfortunately for us, and for the victim of course, this might mean she was selected opportunistically, which reduces our scope for inferring anything from that set of circumstances.

'Second, the killings contain a ritual or fetishist element. We don't have much to go on. I've asked around and my colleagues and I have no knowledge of any murderer past or present allowing insects to eat a body after death. The written material gives some clues but doesn't tell us why this person has done this. Nor does it give any real insight into what's going on in the mind of the killer.

'Third, we know from the notes the killer leaves that this person wants to communicate with us, or with somebody. This is even more unusual than moving the body from the scene of the crime, which only happens in a minority of murders. Perhaps the body was dumped on an ants' nest. The killings could be suicidal, not physically but in the sense that the killer wants to be caught. People do strange things.

'Fourth, the notes are signed with different initials, J and G, but at this stage I can't tell if this is significant.

'Finally – and this is what you're asking about – I believe the killer is likely to strike again, in pursuit of some personal agenda. We don't know what this is. It could be a vendetta of some sort against a person or family, selected for a reason the killer understands clearly but no one else is likely to.'

'You can say that again,' said Chris. 'All very interesting, but does it give you any ideas about where we should be looking?'

'Unfortunately not,' said Mary. 'Except the fairly obvious comment that there may be a strong link between the killer and the victims. This could apply to the experimental victim – the first one, or it might not. I can't say at this stage.'

'Anything else?'

'Only the thought that this is an intelligent killer. The way the notes are written – style, vocabulary and so on. I'd plump for a professional person. The emphasis on experiments could be a clue, or a deliberate red herring, to put us off the real scent. One way or another, I'd go for a person with a university background, even possibly someone who's employed as a researcher. This is pure speculation, but the obvious extreme case would be a person whose job involves experimenting on ants. If there are such people within travelling distance of Hull, I think it would be worth eliminating them from your inquiries. Unless our perpetrator really is wanting to be apprehended straight away, it's most unlikely this will produce anything.'

'One way or another, he sounds like an eccentric monster,' Chris observed.

'I tend to collect them,' said Mary.

'Eccentrics?'

'Monsters,' she replied with a bland smile.

* * *

Chris was back at the Station studying copies of the two documents found so far. She'd left Bradshaw a copy of the second note. He was out at a Rotary Club lunch. Forensics were still doing their stuff with the originals. There were similarities between them: the notepaper, the blue ink, the smudges. It was odd, though; now that she put them close together, the handwriting was distinctly different in each sample. The first, longer piece was written hastily, almost scribbled and sloping noticeably forward, the script marked by long straight lines for b, p, t, l and h. The second note was penned with large neatly formed, rounded letters. Had they even been written by the same person? Mary Threadgold clearly thought so. Chris doubted it, though she thought there was a chance she could be fooled by a careful counterfeiter. It was definitely a case for some expert advice.

'You busy, guv?'

'No, come in.'

DCs Mander and Lounds stepped into Chris's office to report on their preliminary inquiries at the coroner's office, Beverley.

'A Professor Fortius phoned the coroner's office a couple of times. The last occasion was just before Faith Wistow left the office on her last day alive,' said DC Lounds. 'I could find out where he's from and pay him a visit.'

'Good. In the meantime I want you here,' said Chris. 'Find me a handwriting expert. Get back to Forensics and see which of their own people is available. If not, ask their advice about who else to bring in. Don't give away the samples. Put them in touch with me.

'DC Mander, contact the University. Find out whether this professor is based there. If not, try Leeds, Hull, Bradford, Teesside, Sheffield.'

'What if he's not there either?'

'Check with me before you take off anywhere pretty, like Edinburgh

88

or Dublin. Otherwise, work your way round the country till you locate him. Don't talk to anyone who is likely to link your call with us. Come back to me. Then perhaps you and I can go to university. It'll do one of us some good, I reckon,' she added cryptically, keeping her face so straight he couldn't tell in which direction the irony was directed.

Morrison hung back. Chris noticed this.

'Are you waiting for someone? Sorry, I've forgotten your name.'

'Morrison, guv, waiting for yourself.'

'Here I am.'

'I think there's a suspect. We have a reported absconder from a mental health resource centre.'

'When was that?'

'Some uncertainty, guv. A day, possibly two, before the, er, pig was found.'

'Right. And where is this unit?'

'Cortham House.'

'Sorry, that means nothing.'

'It's about twenty miles west of Hull, nearest village Holme on Spalding Moor.'

'Where's this absconder from?'

'Home address Withernsea, ma'am. The most direct route home would be through Hull.'

'Sounds promising. It's your lead, Constable. I suggest you follow it up and let me know how you get on. If it doesn't go cold on you, come back quickly and we'll jack up resources for a search in that direction.'

Half an hour later, Forensics phoned. Dental records confirmed the woman's body was that of Faith Wistow.

Chapter 12

Tom Fortius grasped and released his spectacle case rhythmically and tried to take deep breaths as he walked into the general office in his department at the University. He had gleaned this technique from scanning a Readers Digest article in the doctor's surgery last month, which proposed twenty-four virtually undetectable ways to deal with stress.

'Any messages?' He wondered if his voice sounded normal. Jean was pretty psychic. Could she pick up how bad things were between him and Laura? Given the healthy state of the grapevine in this institution, it was odds on she already knew.

'No,' said Jean slowly, with an intonation he knew well.

'You don't sound too sure.'

'I had the police on half an hour ago. An inspector Chris Winchester.'

'That's all I need. What did he want? Tax disc out of date on the departmental bus?'

'She didn't say. She's ringing again any time now.'

'She!'

'Not you as well as Dr Mackintosh. They do have women in the higher ranks in the Police Force. There are even some women professors, priests, judges, doctors, and queens of our country.'

'Peace,' said Tom, holding up his hand. 'I heard Chris and assumed it was a man's name. Yes I know, stereotypes, equal opps. To be frank, it's hardly top of my list of priorities. Please don't put any calls through for half an hour or so. If that inspector calls, fend her off for me.'

'I spend my life fending people off for you. The elusive pimpernel, they seek him here, they seek him there. That's the job of a university professor's secretary.'

'And when you've a minute, try to get hold of Robin.'

'Have you a fax number?'

'No, he must be away from his PC because he hasn't responded to my last few e-mails. All I can tell you is that he's probably in the jungle somewhere within two hundred miles of the nearest town.'

'To think I didn't believe them when they told me you were difficult to work for,' said Jean with a wry smile.

Perhaps she doesn't know about Laura, Tom thought.

* * *

It was sod's law that when Chris Winchester rang, Jean was out of the office. The call came straight through to Tom. He picked up the phone without thinking:

'Hullo. Professor Fortius?'

'What can I do for you?'

'Chief Inspector Chris Winchester here.' Tom looked at his watch, pulled a face and cursed silently. 'We're investigating a couple of deaths, human and animal, in suspicious circumstances. We believe damage by insects may have occurred to the bodies, before or after death. In the case of the human – the death of the coroner's clerk at Beverley – we believe you've had some contact with the deceased.'

'Good grief.' Tom was shocked. 'I did have, yes. What happened? When was she found?'

'You knew her?'

The implications were sinking in. 'No, but I arranged to meet her. Dead? That's terrible.'

'And she didn't turn up?'

'No.'

'When did you arrange to meet her?'

'Yesterday. Was she –?'

'She was probably already dead. Probably died within the last twenty-four hours.'

'Ah, that explains it.'

'Where did you arrange to meet?'

'At the Beverley Arms.'

'I have to ask you this. Had you met before?'

Tom laughed.

'You mean, were we having an affair?'

'Not necessarily.'

'No, I'd seen her at the inquest and I wanted to talk about the proceedings.'

'What inquest was that?'

'I attended the inquest of a colleague, a researcher from my department who committed suicide – so it appears – last year. Dr Detlev Brandt.'

'There are several things going on here, Professor. I need to come and talk face to face.'

'Fine, it's a question of dates, so if you'll wait a second I'll call my secretary and we'll work something out.'

'Immediately, if possible.'

'I am extremely busy.'

'It's extremely important.'

'I can appreciate that.'

'Hang on,' said Tom, 'I've a meeting soon after two which I can't miss. I'll be finished by five, say five-thirty to be on the safe side.'

'That's fine. I've a job to clear up at my former post and an appointment I can't shift this afternoon. I should be finished by four-thirty. It'll take me a few minutes to drive through the rush hour traffic. It should be enough, allowing half an hour to be on the safe side.'

'Fine. Do you know where I am? The Research Centre is on the main University campus on Cottingham Road. Turn right off Beverley Road right on Cottingham Road and right down the second right turn into the campus itself. Ask for the Biological Sciences building and they'll direct you.'

* * *

Bradshaw's phone rang. It was the ACC. He spoke immediately, quickly, with the presumptiveness of the very senior officer of the old school.

'Bradshaw, some members of the police committee are becoming extremely fidgety about the lack of an outcome on that murder investigation.'

Bradshaw thought fast.

'You've caught me at a busy moment, sir. I'm about to leave for the University to set up a systematic trawl on everyone who might have the skills, or the bent shall we say, to carry out such gruesome crimes involving insects.'

'Glad to hear it. Can I give my members a positive message?'

'You can inform your members we're optimistic. We have some good leads and we should be in a position to give a positive update shortly.'

'Does that mean we have a suspect?'

'We're optimistic about that, sir.' When under pressure, Bradshaw was prone to exaggeration.

'Good, good, let me know as soon as you have some kind of result, preferably before the weekend.'

'We're pulling out all the stops, sir.'

* * *

Bradshaw's heart was thumping. He checked in the office to see who was available. Only DC Livesey was in, snatching a sandwich at his desk.

'Is DCI Winchester around?' asked Bradshaw.

'No, sir.'

'Strange how she's never around when she's wanted.'

'She's clearing up a job at her former station, sir, but she may be back later this afternoon.'

'I see.'

Livesey could see he wasn't best pleased.

'I've a job for you, Livesey. Come with me.'

Livesey stood up, leaving his half-eaten sandwich on the desk.
'No, finish your sandwich, then we'll go. Were you doing anything?'
'I've these files to check, sir.' Livesey nodded to the pile beside him.
'They'll wait till you return.'
'When will that be?'
'Difficult to say. How long's a piece of string?'

He replied that he didn't know. 'That's how long we'll be,' came the reply.

* * *

Two o'clock and there was a knock at the door of Professor Tom Fortius. His secretary had advised him the meeting was delayed till three and he'd only just sat down to some long-delayed paperwork.

'Come in,' Tom called. It opened and two men stood there. Seeing their cheap but smart suits and short haircuts, Tom's irreverent thought was they were either police or Mormon missionaries. He put his money on the former. When the more senior and older one spoke, his voice was as smooth as gravel dumped on the carpet.

'Superintendent Bradshaw, East Yorkshire police. This is my colleague, Detective Constable Livesey.'

Tom wondered momentarily whether he'd imagined the part of the conversation with Inspector Winchester where they'd put the interview off till late this afternoon.

'Mind if we have a few words?'

'Be my guest,' said Tom. 'I had a free slot now and originally – well, that doesn't matter, now you're here.'

'Strange', said Bradshaw, 'I was just saying to DC Livesey how every road keeps turning back in your direction, Mr Fortius.'

Tom shrugged. In the normal way, people who barged into his office without a by-your-leave would have received short shrift. But he presumed this was in some way linked with the phone call from Chief Inspector Winchester. Perhaps she'd decided her colleagues could do the interview. Or he'd mixed up the times – not unknown in Tom's experience. Primarily though, he didn't react because his preoccupations with many other matters made protesting about police inquiries low priority.

'First the body, or rather bodies,' said Bradshaw. 'Then the links between possible suspects and your previous employees. Now the questions about who has the know-how to advise us.'

Tom started. 'I'm not quite sure what you're referring to. Can you explain what this is about?'

'Of course,' said Bradshaw. 'We're investigating a mysterious incident involving the killing of a pig, possibly in some ritual or other, and the death of a woman.'

'Is this a formal interview, Superintendent?'

'No, sir, a purely informal discussion, which you can terminate at any time.'

'On that basis, I'm willing to continue, the only caveat being my other commitment, which is a meeting I'm attending at three. I'd like some time before that to prepare my papers. In response to your question, it's not really surprising that many roads in the field of insect experimentation lead to us. This University has almost the monopoly of research expertise in parts of this field in the UK, if not the rest of Europe. That's especially in the area of the hymenoptera, sorry, the social insects, particularly ants, rather than bees and wasps.'

'I gather modesty is another of your strong points.'

Tom curbed his anger at the man's impudence. 'There isn't much to be modest about. It's a simple matter of fact. Every laboratory and Research Centre in the country survives only by virtue of developing a reputation for its ability to focus on certain topics more than others. The problem comes, of course, when the particular specialism is no longer wanted, for one reason or another.'

'Hence the disappearance of certain technicians from your workforce, at certain times?'

'It isn't as simple as that. We have employed people on short term contracts. Researchers are commonly engaged on that basis. Although we have been fortunate in the past decade in that we've managed to re-engage most of our contracted researchers on successive projects. So, with a few exceptions, we have retained most of our technical staff associated with the major research programmes.'

'And the exceptions?'

'People are always coming and going at the margins, for a variety of reasons. I see that as part of the normality of life.'

'You haven't mentioned yourself and your senior colleagues.'

'No.'

'Is that because you regard yourselves as above suspicion?'

'It's because we're out in the open. We're here long-term and you can easily gain access to us, as you've just proved.'

'You haven't answered my question.'

Tom didn't care by this time how irritated Bradshaw became.

'You're the detective. I leave you to decide on the questions. I'll decide whether or not they warrant a response from me.'

'I'll be frank with you, Mr Fortius. Our killer is displaying a particular knowledge of ants. You happen to head up a research department specialising in ants, half a dozen miles away. It would be logical for us to interview you early on in our investigations, if only to eliminate you from our enquiries. You see the point.'

Tom replied, barely attempting to keep the irritation out of his voice:

'Only too plainly. I'll be frank with you, too, Mr Bradshaw. Pursue your enquiries into me as quickly as possible so as to leave us both free that much more quickly to get on with more productive activities.'

Then Tom threw in the final hand grenade.

'By the way, gentlemen, if part of your enquiries are about the missing clerk to the coroner at Beverley, you do know, I suppose, about the note I sent to your department in confirmation of my phone call, when she failed to turn up as arranged at our meeting the other week.'

'You telephoned us, and wrote subsequently?' Bradshaw looked at Livesey, who shrugged. 'I shall follow this up, Mr Fortius. I suppose it would be too much to ask whether you kept a copy of that letter.'

'It wouldn't at all. I typed it myself. The new technology has its uses, despite our grumbles about it. Just a moment while I bring it up on screen and print you out a copy. There.'

'You seem very well organised – a regular one-man office. Do you have any secretaries to monitor the administration?'

'If I was sensitive, Mr Bradshaw, I'd say that remark is downright patronising and insinuating. However, I'll content myself by observing that most academics work in resource-starved institutions and are used to spending a good deal of time working on admin tasks alongside their office-based colleagues.'

'How does that go down with the University?' asked Bradshaw.

'As long as we bring in the research income and support ourselves, it goes down very well.'

'You're a practical man.'

'My personal preference,' Tom said, 'has always been more to work in applied science. I don't mind writing research proposals and on the odd occasion getting up on my hind legs and performing. But my preference is to spend my time on applied projects. There's plenty of demand for my kind of science, Mr Bradshaw. And where there's a demand, there's money. Now, if you'll excuse me, my time is up. I must go.'

* * *

Tom was back in his office when Chris arrived at five-fifteen.

'Sorry,' she panted. 'The traffic's a swine.'

She saw his surprised expression.

'Don't I know it. Hull's visitors used to arrive in the summer. These days, tourism and industry clog the roads up all the year round.'

'Have you still time to talk?'

'To be frank, I haven't long,' said Tom apologetically. 'I only returned from my meeting ten minutes ago and I have to send some e-mails before going home tonight. I had been intending to finish them earlier, till your colleagues turned up.'

'Colleagues?'

'You should have warned me you were sending in the heavy artillery this afternoon, to soften me up.'

Chris looked puzzled. 'I don't understand.'

'Your police officer friends,' said Tom. 'I had an entertaining half hour with Superintendent Bradshaw and one of his accomplices in crime.'

Chris's face was a picture.

'Are you pulling my leg? Did he ring you to ask for information?'

'Nothing like that. He turned up. Fortunately, I'd offered you the space and Jean my secretary hadn't reallocated it. I couldn't get used to being a murder suspect though.'

'A what?' She was aghast. 'He didn't accuse you.'

'Not in so many words. But I gathered the gist.'

'This is so embarrassing. I'm apologising.'

'Do I presume the fur will fly back at the ranch?'

'You do. I'll be frank about this. I'm new to this locality and I've been put in charge of this investigation. But the words in charge seem to have a local meaning.'

'Like people can come in and tread over your patch.'

'Rather like that, yes.'

'I know how you must feel. There are academics like that.'

Chris looked at her watch. She was anxious to move the meeting on.

'Aha,' Tom exclaimed. He pulled a manilla envelope and an orange document file from the drawer of the filing cabinet. 'Found it. Now I can sit and can pay proper attention to you for half an hour or so.'

She looked relieved. He pushed the door closed and came and sat on the easy chair opposite hers.

'I'm all yours,' he said.

For some reason, Chris was embarrassed by this simple remark, apparently made with no intended double meaning.

'I've two things to ask you,' she said. 'First, our forensic people are suggesting we look at employees in research as possible suspects in this murder investigation.'

'You clearly thought earlier today I might have killed Ms Wistow.'

'We'll set that to one side,' said Chris.

'I still might.'

'I'll follow that up separately.' She was clearly embarrassed.

Tom returned to her earlier question. 'What kind of research?'

'I was hoping you could advise me.'

'People assume research only goes on in universities, but of course it happens everywhere: pharmaceuticals, computers, horticulture and in Hull, food processing, par excellence.'

'We think we may be looking for someone with a background or interest in insects, and possibly ants.'

'You're talking about entomological research. That narrows the field considerably.'

'How specific can you be about that?'

'Very. You're talking universities, almost exclusively. Right on your doorstep there's the department I work in, with my Research Centre and the people associated with us in the Centre, in full or part time research and teaching.'

'You say *my* Research Centre.'

'I direct it.'

'You feel a strong sense of ownership.'

'I more or less set up the Centre, a few years ago now. It's absorbed a good deal of my time, more than I care to think about.'

'If we went through that list of people currently linked with your Centre, would that exhaust the number of those who've been associated with it, say, in the past five years?'

'It depends what you mean by associated. We don't have any undergraduate courses. The department does, of course, but that's another story. The Centre only attracts postgraduate researchers. Although our graduate research programme is small – dwindling annually, thanks to fewer government grants – there is quite a large body of people floating around at any one time, say another thirty or forty – either post-doctoral or transitional to a doctoral programme. Then there are former staff. Is that what you mean?'

'That's exactly what I mean.'

'I'd say there's quite a large category of peripherally-involved people, in contrast with the relatively small number of full time registered research students. That's one of our problems, from the University's point of view, because they don't bring in any revenue. Last year we registered only ten new students. This year it was eight.'

'Do many drop out?'

'Ah, I see, you think this could be a disaffected student. Well, most of them complete the two-year Masters programme. Some register at the outset and transfer to the MPhil. Most doctoral students register first for the MPhil and then transfer to the PhD programme once we see they're on an acceptable track. The successful ones tend to be around for three or four years. The less successful often hang around for longer. That's one consequence of our examining system. It gives students the right to several bites at the cherry, short of the ultimate rejection of failure.'

'So a failing student could be on the books for five years or more?'

'Easily.'

'Tell me about staff in the Centre.'

'That's easy. There are so few. Myself, Robin Lovelace my deputy who's just gone off to Africa on a field expedition, Luis Deakin our senior research fellow, plus a handful of contract researchers on our different funded projects.'

'You mean only three of you are permanent full time academics.'

'Well, Luis isn't permanent but he's full time.'

'It's a lot of plates to have in the air. What happens if one of you goes sick.'

'We don't. The odd suicide maybe, but no sickness.'

'Meaning what?'

'Detlev Brandt, our research fellow.'

'Sorry?'

'According to the inquest the other day, he committed suicide.'

'I'm afraid I'm not familiar with this. You'll have to explain.'

'I thought you'd have known. Well, we had another permanent staff member, Dr Detlev Brandt. He took a shotgun to a hotel room near here, went out and shot himself.'

'When was this?'

'Last November.'

Tom saw her expression. 'Do you think there may be some link?'

'It's all new information. I can't tell at this stage,' said Chris.

There was silence for a few moments before Chris spoke again:

'How long would it take someone in your office to knock us up an address list of all these people?'

'Not long I guess. When do you want it? You're going to say yesterday.'

Chris laughed. 'That would be preferable.'

'Give me your fax number. We can probably have it with you tomorrow morning. I'll ask Jean, my secretary, to update copies of our current lists of academic staff and students.'

'Brilliant.'

'We'll probably need to go through the list subsequently, so I can fill you in on the details.'

'I'd appreciate that.'

'What about other people?'

'You tell me.'

'The whole army of people who work in the Department, not only full-timers in the Centre, but secretarial, clerical, administrative, computer support, laboratory technicians, porters, gardeners, domestic cleaners, canteen, it's endless.'

'As full as you can, would be my suggestion.'

'I can't speak with any authority about this aspect. Your best guarantee of completeness in that area is through Personnel. I'll give you the number to ring.'

'Thanks,' she said.

'One further query,' said Tom. 'Has Ms Wistow's family been contacted?'

'She lived alone. The only known relative is a brother in South Wales.'

At that moment Tom's phone rang. Someone knocked on the door, opened it and peeped round. He threw his hands up.

'I know,' Chris said. 'Time's up. It's been a great help. I'll ring you. We can have another chat?'

'Anything I can do,' said Tom.

* * *

Tom arrived home after ten, still preoccupied. Laura had turned to the flip side of arguing – denying any problems and not questioning him about where he had been:

'What's the matter?' she asked eventually. 'You were so quiet during tea, even the kids commented on it.'

He found himself going along with this novel game. As though it matters what we say, he thought. Nothing will bring back what we had.

'Oh, nothing,' he said.

'That's a classic. On your way to your first bout of stress counselling, or even a heart attack, are you? Not work? Pull the other one.'

'For goodness sake, I give in. Now shut up,' said Tom. 'It's a really stupid thing, hardly worth the time of day.'

'But it's still got to you.'

'I've agreed dammit, so give it a rest,' he almost shouted.

'Are you going to tell me, or leave us all in suspense.'

'For God's sake. If you must know, the dratted equipment we developed for the social insect communication experiments has gone missing.'

'You mean someone has walked off with it.'

'I didn't say that. It's missing.'

Her voice was rising. 'Why are you in such a stew then, if as you say, it's only missing?'

'Because I don't know. I can't bloody remember, can I? I could simply have mislaid it. That's why I'm so angry. I'm mad with myself really. It's several years since we used the prototype gear. I should have had it destroyed. For all I know that's what one of the technicians has done. You know what my memory is like, especially when I'm working under pressure. I think I'm getting worse each year that passes. I may have asked one of the staff to store it in a particular cupboard or cellar.'

'Why does it matter, if it's obsolete?'

'Like our marriage,' he said under his breath, but loud enough.

Her voice was lower, dangerously low. 'What did you say?'

'Nothing.'
'You said something about our marriage.'
'I did not.'
There was a pause.
They sat watching television. The silence went on. As it lengthened, Laura felt increasingly unable to break it. Neither had spoken for nearly an hour. Tom seemed totally abstracted. Laura gave a deep sigh, between frustration and resignation. She suddenly found herself speaking:
'Luis Deakin rang.'
'Oh?'
'He wanted to speak to you. I said you were already at work. He said you'd not been in all day.'
'Hm.'
'I wondered where you were.'
'I don't remember.'
'That's the kind of remark which really annoys me. A man of your intellect pretending to forget where he's been all day.'
'It happens.'
She tried to pursue this, but Tom was still immersed in his own worries.
'Where were you, Tom? You're insulting my intelligence. Who were you with?'
'You know what I'm like. I'm forgetful when I'm in research mode.'
'Don't treat me like an idiot. I'm so bloody angry with you. I can't predict what I might do.'
'It's like all these things. If the equipment goes to the wrong place, it could get into the hands of the wrong people. Time, and that includes equipment, is money. Someone could use it to duplicate the work we're doing and bang goes our lead, and with it a research grant or two worth one, three, five hundred thousand pounds.'
'Have you heard what I've been saying?'
'I was thinking about the lost equipment.'
'If it's so damned important, why not search systematically through all those places? Then perhaps people could live with you again. I could never work with you. I'd have to start at one end of the job and work through to the other. I would go through every storage area one by one, and turn everything out until I found it.'
'We can't do that. You're talking about six months work. We have equipment all over the building, in fact, all over the University. We simply can't spare anyone for that length of time. We shall have to hope it turns up.'
The equipment did, but not in the way he would have intended or wanted.

Some time later that evening, while she was soaking in the bath, Laura finally decided to leave Tom. The unspoken question was when to do it.

Chapter 13

Bradshaw was right about there being more to this story, but he was some hours late. While Brill was having a late breakfast, the telephone rang. It rang on and on in the CID office at Wawne Road Police Station. Eventually somebody heard it.

'I'm coming, I'm coming. DC Morrison speaking.' As Morrison listened, his frown deepened.

It was a short call. Morrison put the receiver down, picked it up immediately and dialled Bradshaw:

'DC Morrison here, sir. Another dead person, sir.'

Bradshaw couldn't resist a quip at Morrison's expense. 'Well? Happens all the time. People die, not in every Yorkshire village every weekend I'm pleased to say, but we've had our share over the years.'

'Sir.'

'Stop farting about, Brill. Either give me real information or don't waste my time.'

'Sir.'

'And stop sirring me.'

'Yes, sir, there's something else. It's the body.'

'Come on, man, where is it? Up a tree, down a sewer?'

'Not so much where is it as what was it, sir?'

'You mean it's too old for identification. It's been in the water too long.'

'Not underwater, sir. More a case of not much left.'

'The killer has dismembered it and scattered the parts.'

'Not scattered, sir, but a lot has gone.'

'Gone?'

'Yes, sir. It looks as though someone, or something, has eaten it.'

'God! As if I haven't enough problems with the staff. Now I've got a bloody anonymous cannibal running round the county. You're telling me our mystery carnivore has struck again.'

'I suppose so. Yes, sir.'

As soon as Bradshaw put his phone down it rang again.

'Bradshaw,' he intoned mechanically.

The voice at the other end was crisp and on the ball. 'ACC here. Is that Bradshaw?'

Bradshaw jumped to it. The last thing he wanted at this moment was a conversation with Assistant Chief Constable Jack Deerbolt.

'Yes, sir. I was intending to ring you.'

'Save your breath. I gather another body has been found.'

'Yes, sir, but everything is under control.'

'Correction, Bradshaw. Everything is bordering on out of control.'

'We're doing everything we can, sir. We have it all in hand. We're close to having a suspect.'

'All this time, all these bodies? You'll soon have half a football team in that mortuary. "Close to having a suspect?" I don't recognise the expression. Either you suspect a person or you don't.'

'We do, sir.' Bradshaw wriggled on his chair.

'Good. That confirms what I picked up on the grapevine. Who is it?'

'We're not revealing the identity of the person at present, sir. Media attention, cock-ups and so forth. *Comprendes*?'

'I'm not the bloody press for God's sake, I'm your line manager. Who the hell is it?'

'Nobody you know, sir. We think he absconded from Cortham RSU, the mental health one, not the children's secure unit at Cortham Grange.'

Deerbolt was irritated. 'I know the bloody difference. What's his name?'

'Er, I don't have the name. We're still checking.'

'I'm a busy man, Bradshaw. Don't play silly buggers. Ring me back ASAP with the details.'

'It will be soon, sir, but not immediate.'

He heard Deerbolt banging the desk. 'Don't split hairs with me. I say ASAP, that's what I mean. Nail this suspect. Another thing, when you make the arrest, make sure you inform me immediately. I don't want half the reporters in the county banging on my door with me unable to tell them a dickie bird. Got that?'

'Will do, sir.' Deerbolt didn't hear him. He had put the phone down.

Bradshaw picked up the phone and dialled. Morrison answered.

'I must have an ID done on that body. You had it sussed. Any confirmation? I need it, one way or the other.'

'Forensics say it'll be forty-eight hours, sir.'

'We haven't got forty-eight hours.' Bradshaw was almost shouting with impatience.

'I'll check with them and find out if they can speed it up. We'll be as quick as possible.'

'See you are. Deerbolt'll have our guts for garters if we can't find out today.'

* * *

When Brill returned, Morrison briefed him. Brill pulled a face. He knew DCI Winchester would not be back for two or three hours. After a couple of attempts, he was through to Forensics.

'Hi, it's me.'

'Who's me?'
'Don't play with me. You buggers don't answer the phone.'
'It's a bit difficult when you're up to your elbows in it.'
'Any luck on that ID?'
'Haven't the least idea, lad.'
'Stop arsing about.'
'We've a good set of dentures, but no other distinguishing features.'
'You could start by checking the records of all the dental surgeons in the district – say, within ten miles of Hull in every direction.'
'And you could start by appreciating we've no staff, not like you lot in CID, mob-handed.'
'Don't take your frustrations out on me, mate.'
The other man was unabashed. The banter was normal. 'Anyway, we're hoping for a stroke of luck with the prints, provided nobody interrupts us for the next couple of hours.'
'I'll see what I can do to restrain myself.'

* * *

Chris had made space to visit the University. The phone rang as Tom was preparing to go for some lunch. He was surprised to find how pleased he was to hear Chris Winchester's voice.
'I'm ringing partly to thank you for the list of names your secretary faxed me. I'd like to take up your offer to go through them with me, some time soon.'
'I'm about to have a bite to eat,' said Tom. 'How soon is soon?'
'Is that an invitation?'
'It could be. It depends how far away you are.'
'Not too far.'
'I could drive halfway.'
'Don't put yourself to any trouble. I'm the one causing the inconvenience. I'll be with you in ten minutes.'
'I'll wait in my office.'

* * *

Chris was a further half hour, but Tom didn't notice the time.
'We can pop across to the restaurant for a hot meal. Or I can ask Jean to bring us a sandwich from the senior common room.'
They walked into the University restaurant. Tom guided her to a table on the terrace overlooking the lake at the heart of the campus, where Chris sat and scanned the extensive menu. A thought occurred to her. She flashed a quick appraising glance at him and was almost relieved to confirm her initial judgement. He wasn't her type. Not only were

academics bad news; she could quote numerous scare stories from Oxford about their oddities. More immediately, he was so incredibly scruffy. His hair was too long, his clothes were a disgrace. He looked as though he could do with a good valet to go through his wardrobe and smarten up his –

Stop it, she said to herself. That's a dangerous road.

After the meal, they moved to an area of easy chairs, down steps near the water's edge.

'Why are university campuses so much more civilised than Police Force headquarters?' Chris asked.

'It's a veneer. It enables the academics to behave like animals without anyone noticing.'

She smiled. 'Give me a veneer any day, rather than crude reality. Is this how you eat all the time?'

'It's my main meal on days like this.'

'No meal waiting on the table at home.'

'Those days are over,' he replied cryptically.

Chris broke the awkwardness of the silence.

'First things first,' she said, with pen poised over the pad. 'What are you professor of?'

'Don't even ask. I have no desire to be pinned down on paper before I even start.'

'This isn't about pride or conceit. It's for the record. If you make a statement, you have to provide these details.'

* * *

Chris had worked through the preliminaries. She was warming to Tom, now that he was talking in a more relaxed way and less like the walking brains she was so prejudiced against.

'As a researcher I haven't found it easy to fit into a university environment. I'm not into the culture of the new universities, all those strange rituals and preoccupations, giving people who are basically administrators high academic titles like Dean and Professor.'

The political context Tom worked in was unexciting, with some fairly predictable personalities. He told her about his particularly abrasive relationship with Apthorpe, the rat professor as Tom called him, whose behaviourist inclinations clashed predictably with the entire trajectory of Tom's own work. As for Hugh Mackintosh, the Dean of Studies, he took the line of least resistance, being near retirement and a political appointment himself from after the late 1970s, when some genuflections towards the New Right seemed appropriate. So they offered the chair – he later became Dean – to an established economist with a preference for free markets. He'd outlasted his usefulness after

1997, when Labour swept into power with a huge majority, and pretty well everyone awaited his replacement. The new culture of devolved budgets for departments and research units brought with it a new vulnerability to the exigencies of the competition to win research grants. This made for an enhanced mutual dependence between academics in the department and emphasised the value of good administrative support.

Tom would have spent hours wandering through this territory. Chris moved him on.

'Okay, let's begin with the list of students. Do any of them stand out?'

'In what way?'

'Have any of them, for whatever reason, caused the University or the staff any trouble? Have you had any altercations with them? Have they failed because of your marking of exams or assignments?'

'We do have assessments of that kind. But the crunch point is the assessment of the student's research. It's the dissertation or thesis which decides pass or fail. We rely heavily on the supervisor and the external examiner to judge that, although technically the Examination Board, and ultimately the Board of Studies make the final decision.'

'And all academic staff supervise students?'

'To a greater or lesser extent. We aren't part of the little club of old universities. In an institution like this, the rule of thumb is you have to possess a PhD to supervise a PhD student. We draw in staff from the department as a whole to supervise. This is necessary, given the range of research topics.'

'Do you personally come into contact with any students, as their supervisor?'

'Only to a limited extent, in my specialist area of ant predation. But I do less than I used to, because of my other responsibilities – liaising with research bodies outside the University, pursuing my own research and running the Centre, of course.'

'I suggest you go down the list and comment on anything that comes to mind.'

'Right. Gemma Balkan – she's away doing fieldwork in Africa for the rest of the year.'

'You seem to have a significant pattern of overseas work.'

'It's one of our principles, to devote a proportion of our resources to projects which contribute to overseas development. For a couple of centuries Britain took everything and gave little back. Entomology is a key area for agricultural development.'

'Sounds altruistic and very noble.'

'Unfortunately, the University doesn't see it that way. Third world countries haven't the money to pay for expensive research. Here's another – Dalkeith, an interesting student. He's trying to establish an alternative to the behavioural paradigm as a way of understanding how the nests, particularly the larger nests, of social insects function.'

'Do you have any contact with him?'

'No, I've hardly seen him. Luis Deakin is the supervisor.'

Tom ran his finger down the remaining names on the list.

'No others here I have anything to say about.'

'Really?'

'You must understand I haven't had the contact with students, what with being away from that side of the work so much.'

'Anyone you've failed in the last year, perhaps?'

'No. Hang on, there was one, Mcnay. I wasn't the supervisor, but I was the second supervisor to Bill Hancock. I suppose my criticisms of his thesis have been the decisive factor in his referral to re-present next year. The external agreed with me, but the colleague who co-supervised with me was hesitant at first.'

Chris leaned over to underline the name. Tom became aware of the closeness of their two heads. He put the awareness to one side.

'Right. That's one to follow up. Any more? Anyone with a thing about you?'

Tom laughed:

'Nothing worth mentioning. Only dear Naomi.'

'Why *dear*?'

'She brings that out in everyone, I think. Naomi Waterson. Now there's a person with a problem.'

'In what way?'

'Excuse the epithet, but she has a bee in her bonnet about me.'

'That sounds ominous. The bee. Not the epithet.'

'It's not uncommon, believe me.'

'Don't I know it,' muttered Chris with feeling.

'Have I sparked off a memory?'

'Nothing much.'

'Don't be coy. I'm answering all your questions.'

'When I was an undergraduate one of my tutors pestered me.'

Tom reared up: 'I'll have you know – '

She waved a placatory hand. 'Okay, you don't go in for seducing students. I make no apologies. It's not unknown in the real world, you know.'

Tom changed tack abruptly. 'You didn't tell me you were at university.'

'You didn't ask.'

'Where were you, if I might ask?'

'Oxford.'

He couldn't detect a note of triumph, but it might have been there. She continued, sensing his unsated curiosity:

'You were telling me about Naomi. What was her name again?'

'Waterson. It sometimes happens that a student having problems with the research looks around for something or someone to blame. It could be the advice, or the lack of it, from the supervisor who becomes the scapegoat.'

'Are you the supervisor?'

'I was, but I transferred supervision last year to Professor Apthorpe.'

'Smart move, or not, in retrospect?'

'On balance not. We transferred it because the supervision wasn't working. Sometimes we counsel a student to stick it out, where, in our judgement, difficulties arise from issues relevant to the research being addressed through the interaction between the student and the supervisor. But in this case it was more a question of incompatible perspectives. In such a case, sometimes as the research focus clarifies, the student's theoretical orientation becomes firmer for the first time and the original choice of supervisor is reviewed. In Naomi's case there were personality factors as well.'

'You're referring to a personality clash?'

'Whatever that is. No, I wouldn't say that. Naomi might.'

'I don't think you're telling me the whole story. Is she beautiful?'

'An emotive word, beauty.'

'Is she?'

'Some people might say so.'

'Come off it, you're so wrapped up in your research you haven't noticed whether one of your young female students is physically attractive?'

'I can see her appealing to a particular type of man.'

'You sound like a typical academic fogey. Did Apthorpe go for her?'

Tom shrugged.

'You'll have to ask him that.'

'Or the Dean. He looks like he's ready for a second adolescence. Is his marriage on the rocks? Does his wife look the other way while he has affairs?'

'That's a quite improper suggestion.'

'Today's improper suggestions can be tomorrow's police business.'

'Hugh's even less likely than anybody.'

'Who's anybody?'

'The two students I mentioned. Okay, so that's two students to come back to. Any more students?'

Tom shook his head. 'From what point of view?'

'From the point of view of bearing a grudge against you.'

'I'm fairly sure that's the lot.'

'Let's look at the staff.'

'Even fewer, I'm afraid. We dealt with them last time we met.'

'Fewer doesn't mean less complicated. Either they do or don't hate you.'

'I can't think of anyone who would. It's a small unit. In a small research centre like this, we all depend on each other to keep it afloat. So even though you might not get on with each other, you have to keep up the pretence of working in various task groups on a variety of externally funded projects. That's what keeps the salaries paid. Not friends exactly, but definitely colleagues and team members.'

'Give me a brief snapshot of each of them.'

Tom picked up the list and sighed.

'I've done this once. I'll go down the list again. There's Robin, my deputy. He's out of it for six months. Luis Deakin is on a temporary contract. He's one of those professional short-term contract people. They're usually into the research so heavily that they go from temporary contract to temporary contract, throughout their careers. In Robin's absence I'm even more heavily dependant on Luis.'

'Where did he come from?'

'The usual route – a succession of short-term contracts in other universities.'

"I can't see any reference to links with other academics in other departments. You presumably have them.'

'Plenty, yes.'

'Why not add them to the list?'

'The problem is where to stop.'

'I'll need a full list, including support staff in other departments.'

'That's a massive task. You're talking about an ever-widening network of people, possibly hundreds. I restricted it to our department.'

'If only our killer was as considerate. It's horses for courses, Tom. You don't mind me calling you Tom, do you? You provide the list of people and leave it to us to judge how to use it. One other query. There's nobody here from higher up, you know, senior management?'

'Come off it. That load of bumbling – they don't even know what we're doing, let alone having a view about it.'

'There's Hugh, your Dean.'

'Exactly. That proves my point.'

'As bad as that?'

'Worse.'

'The most unlikely people have turned out to be hiding criminal propensities. Most murderers and serious sex offenders look fairly unassuming.'

'Is that a fact? Whatever, Hugh isn't among them. If he'd had the capacity, perhaps he'd have been a better advocate for our department and the Centre over the years – you know, university politics and that sort of thing.'

Tom saw her intransigent expression and capitulated.

'Okay, I'll organise the extra information through the Faculty Office. It may take a couple of days.'

* * *

They finished their meal. Tom suggested they walk back to his office.

'I'll take you through Jean's office.' He'd had an afterthought. 'She can give us the extra names so you can contact them yourself.'

'Sounds great.'

Chris hesitated before asking her next question.

'You said earlier no staff actually hate you. Are there any potential or actual points of tension between you and other staff?'

'None that particularly come to mind.'

'Any disagreements or feuds between staff?'

'It's not the kind of thing I would log on a daily basis.'

'Anything at all.'

'Nothing extraordinary comes to mind, the usual rivalries and politicking. They're part and parcel of any work group, I guess. Especially before Detlev Brandt died. That kind of damped everything down for a while.'

'Tell me about Dr Brandt.'

'He's been out of it since last year. Why rake all that up?'

Chris shrugged: 'Maybe I've got a tidy mind and I like to have every i dotted and every t crossed.'

'Nothing to say really. He was a bright young man.'

'Young? Was he good looking?'

'Smart and handsome.'

'Gay or straight?'

He gave her a bemused look.

'A routine question,' she said.

'Straight, I suppose.'

'Did he have any problems with women?'

'He never had a shortage of admirers when he first arrived. That was early on, though.'

'And later, what changed?'

'Robin's wife Helen changed things. From then on it was Helen all the way.'

'What did Robin think about that?'

'Robin didn't know, not officially. Anyway, if you knew Robin you'd realise he isn't the kind of man only to have one fish in the fryer at a time.'

They reached Jean's office and Tom introduced Chris. 'Could you bring us a coffee?' he asked.

They sat in his office. Chris was musing.

'Why do you think Dr Brandt committed suicide?'
'I don't think he did.'
'What?'
'Commit suicide.'
'What evidence do you have for that statement?'
'No hard evidence.'
'You said you attended the inquest.'
'I did.'
'You haven't much chance of convincing anyone without evidence.'
'I agree.'

Chris stared at him.

'What are you thinking?' Tom asked.
'I was thinking you're an eccentric man.'
'In what way?'
'In the sense of out-of-the-ordinary.'
'Is that all for today?' Tom asked innocently.
'There is one other small matter,' said Chris. 'Will you help us with this case?'
'I'm helping now.'

Chris hesitated.

'On a more formal basis, so we can have the benefit of your expertise. Will you act as entomological consultant to this murder inquiry?'

'Oh God. Poacher turned gamekeeper, eh? I always fear invitations like this. I'd love to help you. It isn't so much 'will I' as 'can I' and I fear the answer is 'not much'. Forensic entomology is a complex subject. I'm not in forensic work myself, but I know enough to withstand the temptation to dabble. I have one or two friends and colleagues in the field, though I'm sure you have your own contacts.'

'That's awkward,' said Chris, 'because I particularly approached you on the basis that you know about insects, especially ants. Also, you have an interest in forensic matters, though not necessarily claiming professional expertise in forensic entomology – the kind of people the police have on their books who specialise in post-mortem analysis – invasions of the body by blow flies and that sort of thing.'

'Forensic entomology is a very inexact science,' said Tom. 'I leave all that stuff about using evidence of invasions by various insects to determine the minimum time of death, to those who specialise in it.' He smiled grimly. 'To me they're strange people, messing about with dead bodies.'

'You're just as odd, publishing articles on attacks by ants on living animals,' Chris retorted.

'How do you know about that?'
'I've been doing my homework.'

'Bloody hell,' exclaimed Tom. He caught sight of the lunchtime mail on his desk. He reached over, opened an envelope and scanned a memo from Hugh. He pulled a face.

'I'm going in a minute,' she said. She saw his expression. 'What's up? Something I've said?'

'Not at all. The bastard. Excuse my French. A colleague has pulled off a deal.'

'Surely that's good for the University.'

'An internal deal. He wins, we lose. It's a game academics play. The cuts are slicing the ground from under my research department. He's in behavioural psychology and has just been granted special development status, immunity from the current budgetary cuts and a £900,000 development grant over the next three years for what they're calling flagship research for the university. That does it. Bugger it, of course I'll help you.'

'On the rebound?'

'Definitely, and proud of it. I'd love to act as consultant, or whatever you want to call it, to this case.'

'You knew what was in that envelope before you opened it.' This was an inspired guess. His face told her the answer before he spoke.

'Not in detail. When would this consulting start?' He grinned, a boyish grin. She saw a quality of excitement in him, bubbling up at the new challenge.

'I suppose we can start now. We already have, in a way.'

'I could do it as long as it's not full time.'

'Brilliant.'

'You're a manipulator on a Machiavellian scale, Inspector.'

'Oh dear,' she feigned, 'I wanted at least to give the appearance of free choice. But I couldn't take the risk you might turn me down.'

'You sound like a suitor rather than a professional contracting a consultant,' he said and laughed lightheartedly.

Her mobile bleeped. She scanned the tiny screen.

'I'll ring you when I get back to the office,' she said. 'We'll arrange another meeting as soon as possible, to go into the details.'

* * *

When had Graver decided to kill more than one person? He didn't know. What was previously an unlikely eventuality now became an urgent necessity. He spent days making the list, adding and deleting names. The list gave structure to his thoughts. It enabled him to focus and prioritise. He drew it up based on a number of different factors, mainly to do with the difficulty of carrying out the project in specific cases. Then he transferred each name to a separate piece of paper.

This took another week. In between, he changed his mind, deleted individuals, added them again, before he arrived at a list which satisfied him.

Then he began to differentiate them in other ways: whom to tackle first and how to conduct it. Because of all these complications, he couldn't reach a conclusion until he had tried virtually every possible permutation. All this time, he was making further amendments to the list itself, and finished up transferring all the names to filing cards. After many hours, a mood of desperation to put the difficulties beyond the scope of his own indecisiveness, he took the little pile of filing cards and quite surprisingly put them into alphabetical order. Then in some kind of spirit – he couldn't call it fairness, but it was something like that – he reversed the sequence, so that the name at the end of the alphabet now lay at the top. Finally, he abandoned the alphabet as his guide and fell back on the more fundamental principle of his own insatiable anger.

It dawned on him that ensuring they were dead was important, rather than the sequence in which they died. How they died – that was important too. He thought about that almost more than anything else.

* * *

Chris phoned early the following morning and arranged to call on Tom on her way to Leicester for a one-day course. When she arrived, he was in his office with the door open. He heard her sigh as she came down the corridor. She knocked and smiled brightly as she walked in.

He wasn't misled. 'We'll take a walk to the senior common room. The coffee's no better but the seats are comfier and there's less chance of the phone interrupting us,' said Tom. 'You look well brassed off.'

'It's nothing.'

'You could have fooled me. It's that lack of sunshine syndrome – what do they call it, LASS and the petfood to counteract it is Lassie?' Despite herself, she smiled, more convincing by this time.

'There's a good chance you've made that up as a diversion. Do you mean SAD, seasonal affective disorder?'

'No, sodding awful detective-work. Oops, I've put my foot in it again.'

Chris found herself laughing, not at the terrible jokes, but at his guileless efforts to be cooperative. This man was attractively naive.

'Not at all. You were trying to make me smile, which I appreciate. I can't expect you to be endlessly patient though, while I carry on behaving like this. It's Bradshaw. I'll swing for that man before I leave that Station.'

'Surprise surprise. And I thought Police Forces were so cohesive and team-minded. Has he been upsetting you? You surely aren't serious about the police as an ideal organisation?'

'Forget me for the moment. I'll tell you when you've told me your news. As for my comment about happy Police Forces, to be honest it was tongue-in-cheek. A cousin of Laura's married a copper and the tales he used to tell made it sound pretty dreadful – rather like the average University graduate common room.'

'Really?'

'Don't sound so surprised. Human nature is human nature. Change the social class, take off the uniforms and put a few letters after some people's names and you've changed nothing fundamental about their dealings with each other.'

'Point taken. Anyway, the gist of the Bradshaw situation is he's basically a sod. His approach to this case is to rule out anything that he hasn't already thought of. The only new details he will admit to his scheme of things have to be incorporated into his existing pattern first and then emerge in his chosen timescale as his own ideas.'

'From my brief contact with him I can confirm his star qualities,' exclaimed Tom with cheerful irony.

'I'll wring his bloody neck.'

'Unwise. You'd be detected.'

'Don't count on it with that crowd.'

'Is that it?' asked Tom.

'No, the remainder is a hundred and forty-nine ways in which Bradshaw refuses to acknowledge the danger posed by an extremely odd and perhaps thwarted man who has bottled it up for – who knows – ten, twenty, thirty years and may only now be starting to let it all out. That's our murderer.'

'There is one other item. I'm surprised you haven't mentioned it. You must know.'

'Go on.'

'I think Bradshaw still regards me as a possible murder suspect. That first time he came to see me, he covered pretty much the same ground you did. Only, I was one of his suspects. I could tell. Put it this way, he wouldn't exactly have been interested in asking me to act as adviser to any murder inquiries. We've had a few inquiries since – discreet ones. I wouldn't put it past him to have me followed.'

'You've no evidence of that.'

'Someone was following me that day I went to Branthorpe to meet Faith Wistow, the clerk to the coroner.'

'Bradshaw was having you followed? I'll see about this. Leave it with me.'

Tom waved her back into the chair.

'Forget it. I wouldn't waste your time. I'd rather have you here for a few minutes longer.'

She sat down. 'It couldn't have been Bradshaw. At that stage he wasn't that involved in the case.'

'It doesn't matter. Anyway, now I've a lecture to prepare.'

She paused, reflecting on what he'd said earlier.

'Did you mean what you said just now, about preferring to have me here.' Tom looked directly at her. There was a moment of complete eye contact.

'Yes,' he said. 'I meant every word of it.' Chris looked quite embarrassed. 'I tell you what,' said Tom, 'I'll make you another coffee. Have you time?'

'I've changed my mind about going to Leicester,' she said. 'There's too much going on here. I'll go into work as usual.'

Chapter 14

Bradshaw was fuming round the office, partly at the lack of movement on the case, partly at being kept at arm's length by Tom Fortius. Even more, because he sensed Chris Winchester was beyond his control.

'I've the chief breathing down my neck about the lack of progress on this murder inquiry. There'll be jobs on the line soon. What have we got from the scene of crime, Morrison?'

'They're still working on it, sir.'

'I want to know as soon as there's any development. Where's Inspector Winchester?'

'Out all day, sir.'

'Nice weather for a day's leave, if you can spare the time.'

'The DCI's on a course I believe, sir, at Leicester University.'

'Travelling halfway across the country at public expense to meet a load of cloud-niners.'

'They have that centre where they do research on riots and their control, sir. A few of us have been for conferences and short courses.'

'The last thing I want today is a conference or short course,' Bradshaw snapped. 'I want a result, PDQ.'

'Sir?'

'Pretty damn quick, unlike you, Morrison. I went to that Centre once. Strikes me they could do with some of that for their own students. I read about that sit-in last week. Can't even control them.'

'I think DCI Winchester is on a course in the forensic area, sir – I don't know the title – something to do with scenes of crime work and murder investigations. Sounded very relevant to me, sir.'

Bradshaw continued as though Morrison hadn't responded:

'Morrison, I need a report for ACC Deerbolt pronto. Summary of progress so far. Suspects, interviews, current lines of investigation. I'll be writing it, but you supply me with the info.'

'Sir, DCI Winchester – '

'Never mind her. She's out of the frame today. Unless I can reassure my paymasters we have this one in hand, Morrison, heads will be toppling. Understand?'

'Yes, sir.'

'By a quarter to nine.'

'I'll try, sir.'

'Never mind try.'

'I'll – I'll do it, sir.'

The way to the place where Bradshaw's heart would be if he had one, was by agreeing with him, unreservedly.

'Good man. You can trot round to headquarters when I've finished, so it's on the chief's desk when he walks in. Got your car with you?'

'Sir.'

'On second thoughts, have it ready by eight thirty. I'll deliver it myself on my way to my meeting. I want to bend the ear of the chief's secretary about that chief officers' trip to Copenhagen.'

Bradshaw was impressed by Morrison. He was a good officer, willing as well as bright.

* * *

At ten to nine, a lone driver stopped for a call of nature on the back road from Tickton past Weel, over the River Hull towards Beverley and found a man's body lying in a ditch, barely covered by loose brushwood. It was an hour before he decided to call the police.

* * *

Ten minutes later, Brill came into the office, looking flustered. 'Where's Bradshaw?'

'Left in a hurry in his shirtsleeves,' said Livesey.

'I asked where, not what was he wearing or doing?'

Livesey skipped a pirhouette and sang:

'I'm off to see the wizard, the wonderful wizard called Jack.'

Deerbolt had collected the nickname of wizard a few years back. In the face of pressure to cut the budget, he'd successfully used the threat of rising local crime and worsening clear-up rates to persuade everybody from the Police Committee, Chief Constable to the Home Office to abandon budget cuts and preserve existing ratios of officers on the streets to other staff.

Morrison spoke up. He explained what Bradshaw had instructed him to do. Brill shook his head.

'The man's no idea. This creates endless problems. He's by-passed me, to say nothing of DCI Winchester. She'll go ape-shit when she comes in.'

* * *

Bradshaw was back in his office by nine-fifty. He decided to hold a meeting with key members of Chris's team in the investigation room, which was marginally quieter. Chris walked in at ten fifteen to find the meeting taking place.

'Ah, Chief Inspector,' breezed Bradshaw, clearly embarrassed. 'I was going to call you, but I gathered you were out all day on a course.'

Chris gave him a blank stare, livid at being left out of she knew not what:

'I cancelled it, sir, because of this murder inquiry. I left a message on your voice-mail to say I'd be a little late in this morning because I was calling at the University on my way in, in connection with the investigation.'

Bradshaw tried to bluster his way through:

'I've had meetings so haven't had time to pick up the messages. I understand you've informed the ACC our suspect is already in the frame.'

'I certainly have not. That isn't my understanding of the situation at all. It sounds as though you men are managing quite well without me, so please excuse me. I've a phone call to make.'

She made for the doorway.

'Chief Inspector,' Bradshaw called.

'Did you wish to speak to me, sir?' she asked icily.

'I do yes, so come back in and close the door.'

'I will speak to you, alone, sir,' she said with emphasis, as she closed the outer door.

Bradshaw glared at Brill, Livesey and Morrison. Glancing meaningfully at each other, they exited through the connecting door to the main office.

'If we're to work together, Chief Inspector, I expect a high degree of co-operation and mutual respect between my officers.'

'My sentiments exactly, sir. But if co-operation and mutual respect are code-words for "come into line", I need to know first whether you intend to repeat this performance.'

'I'm being patient because you're new, Chief Inspector. Don't push me.'

Chris's voice was shaking with anger. 'I'm frustrated you've not informed me before going over my head to officers in my team carrying out the investigation for which you've made me responsible. I also object to you having interviewed Professor Fortius recently without informing me, while I was out on another call.'

'I won't have any of my officers acting the maverick.'

'It's hardly maverick of me to want to consult you before making key decisions about appointing an entomological adviser. Not so yourself. Is this your idea of delegation? Giving me a job to do then walking all over it. Could I request a transfer back to my former unit, sir?'

'With the loss of rank? Think carefully, Chief Inspector.'

'My professional integrity is worth more than a temporary promotion, with a kick in the teeth now and again.'

'If you carry on speaking to me like this, Chief Inspector, you'll be facing a disciplinary.'

Chris hesitated:
'I'm biting my tongue, sir, but I'm still waiting.'
'Waiting for what! You've got a bloody cheek.'
'If you want this investigation carried out by me, I carry the buck and I will be the first point of contact with my officers.'

Bradshaw took a deep breath.

'You're a lucky woman. Officers have been suspended for less. Let's be clear about this. If you run the show, you carry the can if it turns out to be full of worms.'

'I understand perfectly, sir.'

'Stick your understanding with your insolence. Do you agree?'

'It's all I ask.'

'Call them in,' he said without looking her in the eye.

'I need to share a conclusion with you first, sir, and make a request.'

'Spit it out.'

'Professor Fortius isn't our murderer, sir.'

Bradshaw looked up from his papers. 'Go on.'

'That's it, sir.'

'You came by this conclusion and happened to call in to share it with me.'

'I was in his office on other business, yes, sir.'

'I don't believe this. One of my key detective inspectors goes sick, they send me another and she goes soft on me. Next I know, she'll be running about with one of our suspects.'

'Professor Fortius has been eliminated from my inquiries, sir. I've called in to ask whether you'd agree to him acting as adviser to this investigation.'

'What! You can't have that man.'

'Can you suggest anyone better qualified?'

'No, but I daresay I could.'

'I hope it's quick. Our forensic psychiatrist says another murder is likely if we don't apprehend the killer within days, preferably hours.'

'You are pulling my leg now. No, you're about to tell me this professor is already a part-time special in this Force.'

'No, sir.'

'A private detective.'

'Not to my knowledge.'

'He reads Agatha Christie then.'

'He may do. I've no information on his reading habits. I'm making the suggestion having had sight of a preliminary forensic report on the latest body.'

Bradshaw leaned forward. Chris continued:

'They're still holding out on the cause of death, sir. But ante-mortem insect damage to the body is confirmed. The predators in this case are ants and Professor Fortius is one of this country's leading authorities on predation by ants.'

Bradshaw shrugged. He looked beaten.

'You've discussed this, er, ant business with Forensics, I take it.'

Chris nodded:

'The proposal that we approach someone with the reputation of Professor Fortius came from them.'

'I take it he's on their list of recognised forensic people.'

'You mean is he a forensic entomologist?'

'Whatever they call themselves.'

'No he isn't as it happens. You are aware, sir, of the view in Forensics that the success of a prosecution at the far end of an inquiry in a case where there are special circumstances in the deaths, can depend almost entirely on which forensic specialists you choose, their quality and credibility in court.'

'Of course I'm aware,' said Bradshaw irritably.

'Our usual person, Dr Blackledge, supports my recommendation. Apparently, her expertise, and that of her colleagues, lies in post-mortem damage, not ants. I'm picking up the vibes from Forensics that we need to focus on the possibility of ants being used as an aid to the killing.'

Bradshaw shook his head in apparent disbelief

'I don't know. What will they think of next? I'm getting too old for this kind of thing. I s'pose I don't watch enough late night TV. By the way, your colleagues are still waiting.'

'I have another request to make first, sir,' she said and Bradshaw missed the steel in her eye.

'Might as well spit it out now,' he said unsuspectingly.

'Sir, this team is adequate only as a core. We're doing very little and achieving almost nothing with this investigation. We aren't even running behind our killer, let alone keeping up. The high media profile we're likely to attract once people realise there's a multiple killer at large makes a larger scale police investigation a necessity.'

Shortly after, as Chris closed the door behind her, she heard with satisfaction Bradshaw's long exhaled breath and the thump of his beaten hand as it fell limply onto the desk. The officers in the nearby office heard Bradshaw's door open. Chris walked with a light step down the corridor. She had secured a slight but significant concession, subject to higher management approval, as was made apparent. Three groups of officers would be established, with their numbers still to be confirmed. After Forensics had checked the data and reported on each scene of crime, this group would carry out interviews and house to house searches in the vicinity of each crime, taking finger prints and hair, saliva and DNA samples. These would be tested against any swabs collected at each scene of crime, as well as against samples held in all Police Forces in the region – West Yorkshire, East Yorkshire, Northumbria and South Yorkshire. The second group would carry out a computer check on every adult male over seventeen within a fifty mile radius of Hull. All Schedule One offenders, anyone with an offence of sex or violence within the last ten years, would be followed up, anyone in a mental institution within the last five years and anyone escaping and still on the run, while serving a custodial sentence of more than five years. The third group would check for correlations, and irregularities, in the records of any employee of the universities and other educational institutions in those towns where there were facilities for teaching and/or research into biology and zoology.

Chapter 15

Within half a day, the headquarters of the investigation team was transformed. It now extended to three offices, having overflowed into two additional empty rooms further down the corridor. To give Bradshaw his due, he had bent Jack Deerbolt's ear and moved a few local mountains. Deerbolt had eighteen officers transferred from other duties and assigned to the murder investigation. Chris took it in her stride and behaved as if nothing had changed.

* * *

The call from Forensics came through to Brill's office about forty-five minutes later.

'Forensics here. About the ID of that body. We've had some good luck with the dental records. They're a match with a person we've been searching for. We're checking the prints now. Should have confirmation one way or the other within the hour.'

'Who is it?'

'We may have killed two birds with one stone. Sorry about the pun. A bit of an oddball, name of Martin John. Been in and out of various institutions – prisons, mental hospitals – for years. On this occasion, being treated in a unit for people with severe mental health problems.'

The other man clapped a hand to his forehead: 'Oh no! Not Cortham Hall.'

'How did you know?'

'A few of my friends have had dealings with it.'

'You must be psychic.'

'Never mind that. I'm devastated. Our unknown killer has probably murdered our main suspect.'

'Watch DCI Winchester,' whispered Livesey. 'They say she's a witch and she's cast a spell over Bradshaw. There's a rumour he's due to start behaving like a human being from next Monday. Careful she doesn't try her magic on you.'

'Piss off,' said Morrison.

'Constable Morrison, any problems?' Chris called from the door of the main office, holding the fax Brill had just passed her.

'No, guv,' said Morrison hastily.

'Good, you'd better see this.'

Livesey mimed her words, right in Morrison's face. Morrison pushed him away. 'Right, guv.'

Morrison disengaged from the gossiping group, got up, walked over, took the proffered slip of paper from her hand and read aloud:

'Report on ID of murder victim – sorry ma'am, body. Martin John, formerly of Landing Lane, Whitby, more recently Cortham Hall mental health unit. Oh, bloody hell.'

'The absconder? Yes.'

Knowing glances and comments crossed the room thick and fast.

'What was that about solving the murder investigation, Morrison?'

'I suppose that nutter killed the others and chopped himself up.'

'Bang goes your fast-track promotion and Bramshill, Morrison.'

'Have to rely on arse-licking.'

'Sorry, Morrison,' said Chris. 'We're still waiting for a full report from Forensics. First indications are he was already dead when the body was found at Beverley.'

Morrison looked downcast.

'Don't worry about it,' said Chris. 'Happens all the time. We'd never make progress if we didn't hypothesise.'

'It isn't much fun when the suspect becomes the victim.'

'Even less fun for him.'

'Feel anything on your hand when she gave you the paper?' whispered Andy Dobbs.

'Piss off,' muttered Morrison.

Morrison and Livesey exchanged glances. Both knew the investigation was back at square one.

* * *

'You look brassed off,' said Tom.

'Don't ask,' said Chris. 'Police politics.'

Chris was brassed off. Tom wanted to know the source of her mood and was not surprised when she told him it was Bradshaw.

Eventually he spoke.

'I've met Mr Bradshaw, interesting man.'

'Not how I'd describe him.'

'I find it quite hard to guess in what way he's got to you unless you tell me.'

'In plenty of ways. The latest was going over my head to the officers in my team, ignoring me just because I happened not to be in the building at the time.'

'Perhaps it wasn't intentional.'

'He does it all the time, in his way. You know what they say. Once is an accident, twice a coincidence, three times is bloody nasty.'

'Did you sort it with him?'

'No, well kind of. Oh I don't know. Let's talk about other things. Look at this,' said Chris. 'A copy of the latest note received.'

Chris opened her case and passed Tom a sheet of paper, its vertical columns filled with tiny, obsessively neat handwriting. He sat reading in silence for several minutes. Occasionally, he took a heavy breath, or clicked his tongue disapprovingly.

I don't know what triggered this latest dream. I recall the surging ant hordes around the Formica Rufa, wood ants' nest – a large conical heap about two metres across, consisting of pine needles, situated at the roadside adjacent to the woods near my home. Its edges were flattened by the weather and its great age and the newer, steeper pile of pine needles stood towards the southern edge of this larger construction. On the southern slope of this smaller conical heap was a twitching mass of ants that appeared to be sunning themselves. I remember picking up a stout piece of branch. I couldn't resist sticking it violently into the midst of this ant cauldron, which duly bubbled up and spewed angry bodies down the sides of the heap in great confusion. Spurts of the formic acid that wood ants deploy against predators came up from the mound a dozen centimetres or so, like miniature jets of water from hoses. Ants ran everywhere in frenzies of confusion.

Occasionally, among the hosts of smaller ants, a large, soldier-like ant stood out, like a sentinel from a higher order of authority. It reminded me of crowds of beleaguered peasants under aerial bombardment in some foreign war. I recalled TV and press images of the teeming communities of Vietnam in the 1960s – the streams of pedestrians filling every road – momentary film sequences in the films Platoon and The Deer Hunter, of agitated soldiers in armoured vehicles driving through masses of blank-eyed refugees.

I realise my place is in the driving seat, manipulating these crowds. Is that what you do when you've time on your hands – recreate the world after your own fashion? Can you imagine other people as you would have them be, invest in yourself the power to breed a total response to an encompassing problem?

At the cinema, I used to jump onto the screen to help

Superman out. Spreading oil over the water all round the stricken liner in the hurricane, diverting the flood from the threatened village with a mighty heave which threw rocks into the swollen river and changed its course, landing the aeroplane single-handed when the pilot had a heart attack.

After we've suppressed the strikes in St Petersburg, I act through the government to raise the bridges in the city. It's necessary to prevent people moving in large numbers from one part of the city to another. I ask the guards to take me out in my carriage to tour the city. I have to travel with care, of course. The populace are in a very disturbed state. One of the bridges – I don't know which one but it reminds me of one of the big bridges in London – is too big to lever upwards to the vertical position. As it slowly rises, a dead horse still harnessed to the shafts of its cart slips forward and it looks as though the entire load will fall into the river. But the cart jams against the ironwork and the horse is left hanging by its harness.

I returned to my spacious apartment. It wasn't long before the workers rose up and for two weeks they swarmed in thousands, looting and destroying any mementoes of the Tsar and his family, banners, flags, even huge statues – anything which reminded them of his years of tyrannical rule.

I talk to Lenin and his comrades. He listens to me. His speech-making voice is in my head. I worry about how to harness the massive power of the ant armies. The banners standing up from the masses of bodies on the film remind me of the occasional soldier ants running among their tiny comrades, on the march. The ultimate triumph of the workers over the middle class – as shortly before the middle class revolutionaries had themselves triumphed over the Czarate – was portrayed in their joyous faces, in the laughter of peasants and soldiers alike.

The ignorant bourgeoisie, they talk about me in corners. "Look at the boy, he never laughs. He spends all day watching those bloody insects." I shall show them. One day I shall rule this country and restore it to greatness.

The weather is unseasonably cold. As though Fate has stepped in, the very next day I wake to find the world completely white. The snow, they tell me, extends from St Petersburg to Moscow. This transformation impresses me very much. How clean every pavement and road looks. All the muck and rubbish from the fighting has been wiped away by the snow. It makes everywhere look new. That is how I see my life after the revolution, clean and white, the gold painted minarets of my dreams shining in the winter sun and this dreadful cough disappearing with the hard frost.

J

Tom finished reading and looked up.

'What do you make of the references to ants?' Chris asked.

'Not much I can say. Nothing particularly technical there. They're the kind of observations anyone could have made. That's the point. If it was written in the style of the professional entomologist, it would be recognisable as such.'

'What do you think about the way he writes? A cry for help perhaps?' Chris asked.

He shook his head. 'I'd say this man's articulate, but he's lost it in a big way. In this passage, look, he thinks he's some Russian leader. This reference to jumping onto the stage. He's at a cinema. These are films. I bet you this man sits watching videos.'

'Fancies himself as St George taming the dragon.'

'Unfortunately, it's more sinister than that. I once saw Eisenstein's film *Oktober* by accident, in one of those commemorative showings in October on late night television. That was at a time when I hardly knew anything about the Czar, the Bolsheviks, Lenin or the two revolutions of 1917 – the extermination of the Czar and his family and subsequently the overthrow of the democracy which replaced autocracy, and the establishment of Lenin's dictatorship of the proletariat. This man – I'm sure our killer is a man – is switching between his own personality and that of one of those Russian leaders, Lenin or Stalin, I don't know which.'

'I wonder if he's schizophrenic. They have delusions and imagine being under the influence of well-known figures,' said Chris.

'My knowledge of psychiatry and mental disorder doesn't go that far,' said Tom. 'I tell you what though, I'm positive he's remembered that anecdote about the horse caught in its harness and hanging from the bridge, from the film *Oktober*.'

'Look at that last sheet,' said Chris. 'Something bizarre happens. That short paragraph. The handwriting is different. The rest looks pretty well identical with that first note we found. That single line, not only is it in a different voice, from a different person as it were. But look at this. The writing is different.'

'I don't know. You're more into it than me. I can't comment on handwriting. Don't ask me to make an interpretation. I'm a scientist. I leave interpreting to someone else.'

'I can make more informed comments if I've actually seen what the ants have done,' said Tom – a fatal remark to make at that time.

Less than two hours later, Chris walked with Tom from the car park and towards the front door of the mortuary.

'Has her family been contacted?' he asked suddenly.

'Apparently she lived alone.' Chris sounded surprised. 'The only known relative is a brother in South Wales.'

Tom was silent, before adding, 'It's a bad situation.' He shuddered. 'I wouldn't have known where this was before, if you'd asked me.'

'Nor would ninety-nine per cent of the population,' said Chris. He'd taken some persuading. In one way, she was surprised he had agreed. Tim Rathbone, pathologist, opened the door and led them into the mortuary.

'I've some preliminary thoughts, Chris. You won't be too happy with them, I guess. I want to reserve judgement till we've had longer to gather our thoughts together and till we've some more results back on the tissue tests. We've a puzzling quantity of insect predation, with no ready explanation as to how it fits into the total picture. Look at this tissue. This is unusual. Crenation of the edges is indicative normally of insect teeth marks and bites, but it seems totally out of place here. It's usually associated with post-mortem attack. No bleeding is evident, apart from the tiny amount in the actual vessels of the damaged area of the wounds. Also there's no active haemorrhage into the edges of the wounds. There is some oedema or reddening of the edges, which indicates an insect attack – if that's what it is – was ante-mortem, that's before the death.'

Tom leaned on the door. His face was pale.

'Are you feeling all right? Please, feel free to go to the toilet if you need it. Straight through the door, first left.'

Tom came back and some of his normal colouring had returned. Tim carried on speaking. 'There are these abrasions to the neck, wrists and ankles, caused by ligatures. This person may have been bound and strangled, before being left in proximity to insects.'

'That seems possible,' said Chris. 'But what normal murderer would bother to do that?'

'I'm worried about you using the term *normal* in this context.'

'It's relative. There are murders and murders.'

'More seriously, from my experience of bee swarms, for instance, death could have been solely by asphyxiation without strangulation. For instance, a massive incursion of insects round the face and neck could have caused a panic attack, breathlessness and the inhalation of insects with each gasp. Whilst the victim would be retching and coughing these out again, there would be a tendency for insect traces to be left in the mouth, throat and windpipe. As for the marks on the neck, it was Shapiro, 1988 I think, who found linear lesions by insects can resemble ligature abrasions. In support of this, look at these tiny marks. They could be the beginnings of bites by insects. Small insects are likely to attack the softer parts of the head and extremities of the limbs where these are exposed – lips, eyelids and knuckles and so on.'

'I find the idea of asphyxia from a panic brought on by finding a few insects on your body rather far-fetched.'

'Okay, try this. The killer puts a polythene bag over the body, exposes the neck, dabs a sugar solution on it to start with. Unconsciousness follows as soon as the air supply in the bag is exhausted, death takes place within minutes. Meanwhile, the insects fill the bag as they are attracted to the sugar.'

'That's a new angle.'

'Only a tiny quantity of sweetener would suffice. They respond extremely quickly to minute quantities of liquid sugar.'

'There'd be traces.'

'Indeed, if they left any.'

'Then again, once we examine the abrasions closely, we can distinguish ant attack from injuries caused by a ligature. Insect bites often produce tiny wounds with scalloped, serpiginous margins.'

Chris looked puzzled. He explained: 'They aren't tidy eaters. They leave the marks of their mandibles along the edges of the wound.'

'You keep talking about insects. I'm not sure which insects you're on about. Grasshoppers, locusts, flies?'

'I'm talking about a coordinated attack by a swarm of ants.'

'You have to be joking. How many ants make a swarm in a case like this?'

'Difficult to say. Perhaps ten to fifty thousand.'

Chris shuddered.

'How long would it take – you know – how long would it take, if the victim was lying down?'

'Depends how securely he or she was bound. In optimum conditions, I'd say asphyxiation would be quite slow, anything between twenty minutes and half an hour.' He paused. 'That's if the shock didn't lead to death first.'

Chris gasped and squirmed as though her battle with the ants had already begun.

* * *

'Bloody chaos this investigation, chaos it bloody is,' said Livesey. 'The right hand doesn't know what the left is doing.'

'Correction,' said Morrison. 'The right hand knows bugger all and ignores the left; the left, meanwhile, ignores bugger all and knows what's right.'

Livesey pulled a face at this. 'Too profound for me lad. I'm for a coffee. What about you?'

'I'll have one,' said Morrison, 'but I'm washing the cup first.'

'Choosy bastard,' said Livesey. They walked out of the office towards the scullery.

Down the corridor, Chris was in her office, on the phone to Tom.

'I've been re-reading that message – if that's what it was – from our person.'

'And?'

'He leaves nothing to chance. It's a serious attempt to communicate. I thought at first he was hiding his diary from us. Despite what he says about, *it must never fall into their hands.*'

'I think this is a diary, or parts of it.'

'Our man likes to keep in touch,' said Morrison. 'More than that, he signs his letters.'

'Hardly a signature,' said Livesey.

'G, that's quite an unusual initial,' said Morrison.

'Plenty of surnames begin with G.'

'But not so many first names. George, Ginger. P'raps it's a surname.'

'Gormless,' said Livesey.

'Speak for yourself,' said Morrison.

Morrison jumped as though bitten. 'Hang on, the latest one was signed J.'

He rushed out of the office.

Morrison was in Chris's office.

'You're right,' said Chris. 'To be consistent, it should be G.' She picked up the phone. 'We'll see what Mary Threadgold thinks about this.'

Chapter 16

For a long time, I have wanted to control people, which meant restricting their ability to choose, and channelling their behaviour. The labyrinth. L-A-B-Y-R. Labyr, labile, labyrinthine. THE LAByrinth. Pigs can fly. Putrid pigs. Putrid pigs picking people's parts. Piles of Ponera perched on their petioles pecking at people's pubes. Peter Piper picked a petiole of pickled people. I hate people. Not all people but those picking at my brain. The larvae PUTRID LARVAE in my brain are responsible, not me. In the passages, in the remotest labyrinths of my brain. The maze of memory.

J

Maze was the key to it, as every behavioural scientist knows. The beautiful, convergent idea of the maze. Ever since my earliest games with the ants, the idea has cropped up. I followed the first attempts of Sir John Lubbock, later Lord Avebury, in the late nineteenth century – the inventor of bank holidays – to keep colonies between sheets of glass, with particles of soil. When my first crude attempts failed, the bodies of dead ants filled the passageways, bloated and spread mould through the sodden nest, I went to the garden centre. I experimented using nodules of soil-free compost as a way of warding off disease and moulds. The ants could arrange the soil and compost so as to create their complex patterns of tunnels and chambers. The maze became the stock image of this period. The significance of the imagery of the maze also grew for me, as I realised its other associations, notably with demeaning non-human life forms, by treating them wholly or largely as the objects of rigid laws governing behaviour. The maze symbolised for me the activities of the experiments with rats and other vulnerable animals of those scientists addicted to cruder, that is reductionist, versions of behaviourism.

G

* * *

On top of everything else, Tom had to prepare for his keynote lecture at Peterborough University. It was beginning to bug him. Thank God for Powerpoint. He'd burned the midnight oil and finished the draft, but wasn't happy with it. He walked through into Jean's office and left with her the notes to type up and a sheaf of stills to prepare.

Chris phoned five minutes later and caught Tom in his office. It was a bad moment. His head was in this lecture and he was impatient.

'I've been looking at this list of staff. You didn't go through them one by one with me. Tell me about Luis Deakin.'

'I told you, he's my deputy in Robin's absence. Surely you don't think he's anything to do with all this?'

'What more do you know about him?' she insisted.

Tom was stressed. His response was rapid, minimal. 'A very hard worker.'

Chris persisted. She was used to pursuing people for information. 'In what sense?'

'In the sense he does his job and more.'

'What about his private life?'

'I don't know.'

'You must know something.'

'Oh I don't know,' said Tom, more rattled. 'We don't employ people's families. He lives with his mother.'

'Have you met her?'

'Some time ago, a couple of years maybe. I dropped him off at home.'

'And?' Chris was aware she was scratching round in desperation.

'I went into the kitchen and met her. She seemed a normal mother to me.'

'Anything odd about him?'

'Nothing that comes to mind. By definition normality doesn't jump out at you. I can't be on intimate terms with all the staff. I simply don't know much about his personal life. I don't think there's much to know. He comes to work, goes home and looks after his mum. She's not too steady on her legs, from the little he's said. Spends all her time indoors. He's not talkative about it and I'm not inquisitive. That doesn't make him a criminal.'

'It doesn't,' Chris admitted. 'Who is Apthorpe? You have him down as an entomologist. What's his specialism?'

'Social insects.'

'You'll have to translate. Does it include ants?'

'Yes, but you must be joking. Apthorpe! If you met him. He's right out of it.'

'Does he have a motive? Is there anyone he doesn't get on with?'

'Apthorpe doesn't get on with anybody. He's a completely asocial being, works alone, lives alone.'

'We need to talk at more depth about that man.'

'This is stupid,' said Tom. He saw the slim window of opportunity to prepare for the lecture slipping away.

'What about Robin?'

'Now you're being ridiculous. He can't possibly be a suspect. He isn't even in the country. He was away when these latest killings took place.'

'I've told you before, leave the policing to me.'

After Chris rang off Tom dithered about while he turned the arguments of his Peterborough lecture over and over. All the time he was worrying away at the huge bank of his memories of Robin, from their many years of living and working close to each other. When Chris had gone the gaps in his knowledge began to eat away at him. When he arrived home later that night, he decided to contact Robin at the first opportunity.

* * *

The following day Tom was due to take an early train to attend a brief mid-morning research meeting at a hotel in central Newcastle. Instead of driving straight to the Station, he decided to call at the University at 8:00 a.m. and ask Jean to locate Robin while he was at his meeting.

It was seven fifty-nine when Tom reached the University. Jean was in on the dot of eight. Within a couple of minutes, she rang through from her office. 'Here's the number and address for where Robin's based. You don't need a local street map. He's linked with a local university and they will act as a conduit for messages during his fieldwork.' Tom didn't want the details. He left Jean with the task of chasing up Robin with a list of questions.

A couple of minutes later, there was a knock. Chris put her head round the door.

'I caught you. Your secretary predicted you'd call in early. I know you're busy. I'm in a hurry, too, on my way to work.'

Tom felt guilty about his impatience the previous day. 'I wanted to say –'

She held up a hand. 'Forget it.' She passed him a copied sheet. 'We've had this fresh note. I assume it's from our killer. It's strange but if all these notes have been written by the killer – and at present I'm reserving judgement on that – we know more about the killer than the victims.'

Tom studied the sheet. Chris continued: 'Morrison pointed out how the latest note is signed with a G rather than J.'

Tom shrugged. 'He could have two initials.' A thought struck him. 'I want to show you this in the first note from our mystery person.' He scrabbled for the file and pulled out the photocopied sheets.

'I've marked the lines.' He read in silence, making occasional marks with his pencil in a jabbing action. 'There,' he said, 'I've marked some phrases. " ... at which point I became the conductor". This man reached a turning point with the pig. We didn't find him before he killed again.'

'The notes were a cry for help? He wanted us to catch him in time?'

'Not quite or he'd have sent us a message about how to prevent him killing again. At present he only seems keen to inform us of his existence.'

'And his strange thoughts.'

'It's damn lonely, going mad on your own. Better to take the world with you, or that bit of it over which you can exercise total – life or death – control.'

'Hmm, could be.'

'Look at that line on the next sheet. "Don't pigeon-hole me." No, sorry, "Don't go pigeon-holing me as like the rest of them in here." Who are the rest? I don't think he means the office or the pub on the corner. More likely, he's been locked up – prison, mental hospital, special hospital perhaps?'

'Perhaps he's referring to a report someone wrote,' said Chris.

'Yes, a psychiatrist, could be. Someone's videoed this man during assessment, so now he's using video for his own purposes.'

'To get his own back.'

Tom shrugged. 'Who knows? Further down that same page, see where I've highlighted *laboratory*.'

'Can't be many of those.'

'Over the page. Makes him sick. See that? Look at the language. This isn't your average Alf. He's been where they observe and describe.'

'A research institute.'

'My thoughts exactly. Somewhere where they do research. He's either done it or watched people doing it. Turn over again. Bottom of the page. See where he talks about the next stage. Can't do more to a pig than kill it. The next stage was starting to kill other people.'

'This stuff about vomit.'

'So what?'

'He doesn't like what he's doing.'

'Put in for effect. Don't be fooled. This man shows no signs of any sensitivity to the feelings of others, including his victims. He's almost certainly a psychopath.'

Tom raced back from Newcastle on the 1:00 p.m. train. The rest of the day was blocked out with university work. He divided a typical week into research-development days and administration-catching-up days. This afternoon was meant to be an admin day. It should be an opportunity to clear the paperwork that was cluttering up his desk. He was anticipating the police work would eat into large chunks of whatever time he had at his disposal. Somehow he couldn't achieve the usual trick of cutting himself off from distractions and doing the mechanical job of clearing his desk.

At three-ish, Tom had a few minutes break. He took a walk round the campus, encountered Luis Deakin and chatted for a while, reviewing the latest run of experiments. These were being run under Dr Deakin's direct supervision, though Tom, as director, was grant holder.

Tom detected a mood of disgruntlement on Luis's part. He knew Luis was tense. It was rare for Luis's calm to be shaken. The strain of the investigation going on all around was beginning to affect all of them in the department.

He decided to take Luis into his confidence and show him a sheet he'd typed himself from one of the notes, without telling him where it was from.

Luis read out loud for several minutes.

> *The question is how do driver ants communicate. There has been a fair amount of work done on the fact that although they don't hear, ants tune into vibrations and are particularly reliant on scent. These senses make a major contribution to the psychological and social glue binding ant society together. I can recall reading rather off the wall speculations by the philosopher Maeterlinck about the so-called mental powers of ants, as well as termites. He is impressed perhaps by their creation of huge, columnar colonies as high as houses, from reconstituted soil cemented with bodily secretions so hard that it takes explosives to destroy them. He is more overawed by their ability to co-ordinate their efforts towards a common goal. The only way he can explain this success at achieving a unity of aim and function is by reference to the theory of the composite being, to consider the termitary as a single living organism made up of sixty million or so cells.*

'You're hesitating,' said Tom.

'I can't take any of his mysticism on board from that point on. He goes off into speculations about whether the termite has tapped into the vital force of life itself, what Schopenhauer refers to as the Will, Claude Bernard the Directing Idea, Providence, God or what have you. Anyway,

I'm not reading any more of this, I'm thirsty. I'll brew some more coffee.'

Tom changed the subject. There was a link between these ideas and the growing tally of bodies, but it bothered him he couldn't put his finger on it. He had a sudden thought. 'I found this article, hang on.' He crossed the room to the bureau by the window and rummaged through the pile of papers cluttering the available spaces round the word processor. 'It's here somewhere. In a recent copy of *Nature* I think. Or was it *New Scientist*. This is it.'

He handed the journal to Luis. The article was headed 'Composite Beings or Chaotic Individualists? What political scientists can learn from the social insects.'

Luis scanned the paper. 'Garbage.' He made a contemptuous sound.

'Why do you say that?'

'It's the kind of anthropomorphic nonsense that gives science a bad name.'

Luis tossed the journal onto the table, gulped his coffee down and left the room.

After Luis had gone, Tom sat in the easy chair in his office and brewed a further mug of tea. He regretted showing Luis now. The material was confidential to the inquiry. He was flustered, having just dropped the kettle, fortunately only full of cold water at the time, on the corridor floor on his way back to his office. It was a message, he told himself. 'You're stressed,' he said out loud to himself. The future of your Centre is on the line – down to the perennial struggle for funding; your marriage is on the rocks; and someone, somewhere may have purloined valuable, research-sensitive equipment from your department, enabling the pursuit of research which competes with yours. It could be one of the technicians or, heaven forbid, Robin, who had acquired it, intending to declare unilateral independence in some secret deal to become impresario of entomology at some South African university, in association with a well-endowed university-based research centre somewhere in the Western world.

* * *

Chris had gone to work after calling in on Tom. She walked in at nine-thirty a.m. The team was assembled, more or less. She decided to take no notice of the flurry of activity near the rear of the room.

'I've three items to bring to your attention. Has anyone else a constructive comment to contribute?'

Three hands went up, one after another.

'Depending on what you say,' someone muttered. She ignored this and began.

'First I want to share with you the stage we've reached with the forensic investigation of the bodies. Before I do that, any news from the checks on males in the region, Sergeant Brill?'

'Seven thousand completed. No positive news as yet.'

'As for the trawl at the University, I've been coordinating that,' said Chris. 'We've no result as yet. So, let's look at the bodies.' Her audience stirred. She picked up the wooden baton and indicated the several overlapping flip chart sheets pinned on the wall behind her, with their three columns, headed Body 1, Body 2, Body 3.

'We have the pigs and the young woman and another possible. There are similarities with this investigation, but we're not positive yet.'

Chris inwardly cursed the officers at the back of the room. She ploughed through her notes from the pathologists, leaving no detail untouched. At last there was silence. During the description of the injuries to the body orifices, someone at the back had a coughing fit and left the room. Got to you at last, Chris thought triumphantly.

'Any questions?'

She paused.

'Second, we've had a number of communications, if I can call them that, which are possibly from the killer, one or two roughly coincident with each of the deaths. The pile is growing daily. I've copied them.' Chris picked up an envelope folder. 'They're in here for anyone wishing to read them. Third, we have to work out a strategy and decide how to pursue it.'

'I'll start with the forensic reports on the bodies. We have reports on the first two. We're waiting for the results on the latest. I've persuaded a member of our pathology staff to attend this meeting and brief us about the delay, if that's what it is. Dr Tim Rathbone.'

'Bloody hell,' said Mander in a stage whisper, 'he's only a teenager.'

'We shall also have a report shortly from our regular forensic psychiatrist Dr Mary Threadgold whom some of you know already. I hesitate to use the term offender profiling because it's been so misused. However, Dr Threadgold's first task includes giving us a view on the significance of these killings, including any light they throw on the possible mental state of the killer and the likelihood that this person has killed previously and may kill again.

'It is rare for a killer to leave notes in this way. Sometimes murderers have been known to ring the police or contact the media. Doctors Rathbone and Threadgold have both suggested we have these notes analysed and after discussion with them we invited a graphologist, Angela Santer, to join us today and make some preliminary observations. I should point out that her formal report has been submitted to Dr Threadgold who has agreed that the unusual nature of this case necessitates you having the benefit of these comments at the earliest opportunity, hence Angela's presence at this meeting. Tim's going to begin.'

The youthful Rathbone began to speak. 'Not a lot I can say. Basically, we haven't had cases of insect damage like this before, so there's nothing in our local experience with which to compare the situation. We've been talking to DCI Winchester and to the head of pathology here and we've had advice from colleagues at the University. This also may be one for the forensic entomologists. We need new ideas about possible leads in a case like this. And quickly.'

'Thanks, Dr Rathbone. Any questions?'

'Okay, the path. Reports should be with us within forty-eight hours.'

'Hopefully,' added Dr Rathbone.

'I turn now —'

'Hang on, boss,' Mander interrupted. 'You're motoring a bit quick. I want to ask Dr Rathbone a question.'

'Go ahead,' said Chris.

'You mentioned forensic ento —'

'Entomologists,' said Rathbone.

'We seem to be in danger of being over-run by experts in this investigation.'

'Too many bloody chiefs,' came a voice from the middle of the room.

'Aye, thought you were the experts,' said somebody else.

Tim Rathbone nodded and replied disarmingly:

'These are understandable questions. In pathology, we have certain forensic knowledge and skills. But there's no way we can be experts in all fields. A murder investigation of this kind generates many questions and possibilities. At this stage, we have to follow up as many as possible. We can't afford to narrow down the inquiries because it's too early to be certain about the nature of the person we're looking for. We need the widest possible span of advice, from everyone. That includes friends, relatives, neighbours of the deceased, work colleagues, yourselves, all of us in pathology and anyone who we think can possibly throw any light on any aspects of our forensic investigations. It's all hands to the pumps I'm afraid at this early stage. As far as the entomologists are concerned, it's essential to ask for views about the role insects may have played in bringing the bodies to their present state.'

'You think they were killed by insects,' someone called out.

'Not killer insects, if that's what you mean. But it's possible insects contributed to these deaths in some way. Or that they attacked the bodies after death from other causes.'

Chris interrupted. 'We'll call a halt there and move on. Thanks, Tim. I'll deal now with the notes the killer, or someone, may have sent us in relation to the different bodies found so far.'

Tim Rathbone gathered his papers and left the room. Chris nodded to the administrative assistant who had come in bearing a pile of papers.

'Yes please, Vanessa.'

Vanessa started to work across the room, giving one sheaf of papers to each person.

'These are slightly edited, numbered copies. When you've read them, Vanessa will collect them again. They aren't to leave this room under any circumstances. Any infringement will be a major disciplinary offence. Is that clear?'

Chris looked round the room. One by one, as they felt her gaze settle on them, people nodded.

Ms Santer looked at least as young as Julian Rathbone and was slight and strikingly elegant. When she stood up, her quiet delivery had a presence which gave her instant command over the audience.

'Thank you. With two colleagues, I've had a good look at the documents from J, G, or whoever. That could be a ploy to confuse us. We are unanimous that most of them were written by one person. But we also suspect that in places they weren't. Our reasons for this observation are spelt out in detail in this report.' She held up a slim folder. 'We'll leave it with you, Chris. I could go on at length about our observations on the possible mental state of this person. Suffice it to say we believe he – we are pretty sure the writer is male – is neither a youth nor very old and may be suffering severe distortions of perception which affect his ability to record. These are typical of those experienced by people with severe psychoses, for example, though we aren't able to comment at all on the precise nature of any mental health problems in this case.'

'Thank you, Angela. Any questions about that?'

'Can you look at this letter from my girlfriend? I think she's two-timing me.'

A gale of laughter swept the back of the room.

'Come and see me after this session,' said Angela, keeping a straight face.

A muted ooohh rose from the back of the room.

'Anything else of relevance to this investigation?' asked Chris.

There was no response from anyone.

'Okay, our third task this morning is to address where we go from here,' she added. 'The main unknowns are who we're dealing with, what prompts him to kill, how likely it is that he'll kill again, if so, how soon, and how best we can catch him, preferably before he does any more damage. The priority, therefore, is to concentrate our resources on searching for him. I appreciate the reservations some of you feel about experts. But, like my colleagues here, I have no difficulty in admitting I can't do everything myself. I intend to enlist the continued help of the forensic and graphologist experts you've met today, to whom we can refer any further material. You've heard our pathologist suggest that the unusual circumstances of the deaths require advice from an entomologist, and I don't mean the forensic entomologist they'll be in touch with. I've been following this up locally as a matter of urgency. Because of the particular nature of the insect remains found with the bodies, we may need even more detailed help with the specific insect species we're facing. I shall be grateful if you can continue to maintain a complete embargo on discussing these details with any other person. And I mean anyone at all, including best friends, lovers and spouses. Unless anyone else has anything to raise – no? – that's it. We meet again tomorrow at 9:00 a.m., to review progress. Thank you, one and all.'

Chapter 17

My fascination with the maze was the high point of the behavioural approach. I saw in it the degradation of the species to the level of machines. Physiological organisms may be complex, but ultimately they are simply conditioned to respond to stimuli, biologically and chemically determined. Whereas what I strove towards was a way of transcending this view. To put a rat in a maze and observe its efforts to reach a solution, a way out, was a denial of the social dimension of its being. Likewise, ants were highly collective in their everyday patterns of living.

As I stared at the ants for hours every day, observing their comings and goings around their nests, the goal dawned on me. It became so blindingly obvious that once I'd realised it, I couldn't understand how I'd failed to realise it before. Their lives, the entire survival and prosperity of the nest, depended on interaction between individuals. I must find out what that interaction consisted of. Once having achieved that, of course, I would be well placed to move beyond the behaviourally-based assumptions of the biologists.

And, I hardly dared entertain the possibility, there was the goal of cracking the code, learning the language, actually entering into transactions, interacting with his ants with my with his who are they these crawling maggots in my head. Suppurating pores. This was my maze. The journey through it to the goal occupied me now and as far ahead as I could see.'

G

* * *

Laura was on the phone: 'Hullo Helen, yes, it was my message. It would be great. The kids get so bored. I thought you might be at a loose end with Robin being away. Tom? Don't ask. That's another story. Suffice to say he's still living here, physically, but I'm a free agent at pres. See you in town at the usual place. Elevenish? Fine.'

'Hurry up, kids. We're going to town.'
'Where are we going?'
'To town. We're meeting Helen.'
'Why did Auntie Helen call Uncle Robin a wasp, Mummy?'
'When? I never heard that.'
'The other day. When you were talking in the kitchen.'
'Oh that. She didn't mean it, darling. It was just one of those things people say.'
'Wasps sting. Does that mean they're horrid?'
'They are, but Uncle Robin isn't.'
'They have bright coloured coats, Mummy. Does that mean they show off?' said Matthew.'
'No, stupid. They're easily led,' said Sarah.
'What is measily led?' asked Matthew. 'Does it mean you can follow them because of the bright spots.'
'Stupid,' Sarah said, at which point a fight started between the two children. When Laura separated them the questions began again.
'Do the mummies have different coats to the daddies?'
'I think so. Don't talk so loud, Sarah. People will hear you. No, it's not quite like that.'
'Why is it then? Do they want everyone to see them and kill them?'
'Nearly right,' she said. 'They want to be noticed. But it's so their enemies will recognise them, associate this with their stings and leave them alone.'

* * *

Chris was seriously worried. With no fresh information coming in, the police investigation wasn't exactly grinding to a halt, but neither had it enough critical mass to develop its own momentum.

She came straight from a meeting with Mary Threadgold, determined to catch Bradshaw and ratchet up the scale of the investigation. Bradshaw was unimpressed. He was sceptical of experts in general and was particularly disinclined to invest in theories generated by forensic psychiatrists.

'Dr Threadgold believes this is the lull before the storm.'

Bradshaw looked quizzically at Chris.

'The storm before the lull, more likely.' He chortled at his joke.

'The likeliest scenario is that the killer will attack with increasing frequency and ferocity as his desperation at his own position increases.'

'How does Dr Threadgold know this?'

'I explained before, sir, it's her belief, having appraised all the available evidence.'

'Don't patronise me, Inspector. I've appraised the evidence too. I've taken advice from senior colleagues. We'll soon have the killer under lock and key, without the need to panic or do anything drastic.'

'I want to bring in a specialist on ants, as adviser, sir. And I want to increase the number of officers committed to the inquiries. We can't achieve anything at the present level of activity.'

'I can't agree to your request. It's resources in part. In part, it's my feeling you've flooded us with experts and we've damn all to show for it. There's a view at senior management level that these incidents are one-offs.'

'Sir, that's ridiculous. How can successive killings using similar quite eccentric methods be one-offs? We've not had anything like this for years, if ever.'

'Don't give me ridiculous. The informed view of senior management is there's no likelihood the killings will continue. They were a one-off. They may not be related to a couple of so-called letters from a so-called killer.'

'We've had three, possibly four notes now.'

'Which proves nothing. They could be part of a confidence trick, or wind-up.'

'I can't see how a member of the public could have found out about our four victims, sir.'

'Four! In your dreams, Inspector. Who are these four so-called victims?'

'The clerk to the coroner, sir.'

'The woman, yes.'

'Brandt, the university researcher.'

'You have no evidence linking that death to this inquiry.'

'The absconder from the mental health unit.'

'A quite unrelated incident.'

'The pig.'

'An animal! This is becoming a joke.'

'Brilliant. We have a management which puts murders in the same category as practical jokes.'

'You're treading near the line of insolence, Inspector.'

'Somebody needs to, in this Force. If we're to make progress, sir, I need you to confirm we're still conducting a murder inquiry. Otherwise we may as well pack up now.' Chris turned and walked towards the door.

Bradshaw must have realised he'd gone too far. He called out, 'Inspector.'

Chris stopped.

'All right, I may have over-played my scepticism.'

Chris turned to face him. He continued: 'I'm not suggesting we halt the investigation. But I'm not willing, the Force is not willing, to have the entire budget thrown into disarray at this point in the financial year, on an eccentric whim. As from this evening, I'm putting four fifths of the murder investigation team back onto regular duties.'

'You've been dying to do that ever since – well, the world's back in its place, me being the eccentric, presumably.'

'It's not about that. I value the work you and your colleagues have done.' Chris's expression was scepticial. 'I have to respond to a wide range of demands. Police responsibilities are wide-ranging. Bring me results and we'll have another look at the situation.'

This time Chris really was on her way to the door. She opened it. Bradshaw called after her:

'We're all part of the decision-making process.'

'That's why nothing will happen till too late,' she muttered as she left him alone.

* * *

It was nearly lunchtime. Tom's secretary Jean smiled almost imperceptibly.

'Thanks, Jean. Worth your weight in gold,' said Tom, as she brought him the stack of trays loaded with the various letters and packages which had arrived in his absence, sorted into action/no action and urgent/not urgent.

When Tom returned to his desk, the fax, e-mail and voicemail were all signalling urgently, seeming to conspire against him getting on with his own work. In a characteristic mood of rebellion, he showed his irritation at this concerted display of crass irrelevancies.

He caught sight of a folder containing his lecture notes for Peterborough and inspected it. She'd done a fantastic job. The disk and printouts of the stills were in the folder with the typescript.

Jean called through. 'People have been trying to contact you.'

'I'm out if anyone rings,' he said crossly.

'What do I do about Professor Apthorpe? He has been trying to reach you all morning.'

'Damn! Ring him back and say you just missed me. The vice-chancellor called me to an urgent meeting. No, say I've a conference in Stockholm for the rest of the week.'

Storms often blew around Jean at work. She coped with her job by keeping a cool head. 'Stockholm? Is there something on? He might ask.'

'No, yes, I mean no. Nothing of interest to him I suppose. No conferences or high profile ministerial meetings. Though you can say I'm spending time with our Swedish collaborating partners in the insect parasites project. I'm meeting a former colleague, and in the evening my aunt who married into the family of a prominent firm of Stockholm lawyers.'

'Are you actually going to Stockholm? I don't recall buying the tickets. I thought you were in Peterborough.'

'Don't ask,' said Tom. 'Then you won't be lying.'

* * *

Church bells pealed noisily in the Old Town of Hull. It would be somebody's celebration, probably a wedding, thought Laura, and sighed.

Helen and Laura sat at one of the tables on the fringe of the market place outside the cafe and sipped at cups of piping hot coffee.

'It's busy,' said Helen, not feeling able to respond adequately to Laura's sigh.

'Only till graduation week,' said Laura. 'It'll be just tourists then, for three months. Like a respectable English town with something to offer foreign visitors. Off season, in a way.'

'That's an unusual twist,' said Helen. 'Most people view the summer as the on-season.'

'It's an academic view,' said Laura. 'Tom's view. It rubs off on me. I can't help it.'

Helen topped up their coffees from the cafetière. 'So Tom was seeing that clerk to the coroner they found dead.'

'What do you mean?' Laura's heart was racing.

Helen peered at her. 'Darling, are you all right? I hope I'm not creating problems.'

'Fine, thank you.' Helen was silent while she digested the information. It was a shock, even though she tried to shrug it off.

'You can love a man without being in love with him,' said Laura casually.

'You can also love more than one man simultaneously.'

'That applies to men as well as women.'

'Unfortunately,' said Helen, thinking of Robin.

'You love your friends, but you're in love with your partner,' said Laura.

'I hate that word partner,' said Helen. 'It sounds as though living together is a business.'

'It can be, whichever way you use the word. Tom's been a good husband,' she added thoughtfully, à propos of nothing in particular. 'But he's also been a selfish, self-centred bastard.'

'Snap.'

'He's in the past tense, as well?'

'Afraid so.'

Helen leaned forward and put her arm round Laura. 'I'm so sorry.'

'Don't be, not for me. I passed that stage some time ago.' Laura remained sitting stiffly. She couldn't soften to emotions, not in public, not in front of the world.

Helen leaned back slightly. Laura continued. 'There are compensations.'

'In Robin's case, tell me about them.'

'I thought things had improved.'

'In theory yes, but now he's abroad I can see more clearly. He's become bad news for me, in a big way.'

'You don't think –'

'With Robin, you don't think. That's it. What I mean is it's quite difficult to repair your relationship at a distance of a few thousand miles.'

'Looking on the bright side, distance sharpens desire,' said Laura.

'Or extinguishes it.'

'I bet when he returns he'll be all over you again. I'm the one with the burnt-out marriage.'

'Why say that? I see you as one of life's winners, whatever the defects in your marriage. Married to one of the most eminent academics in the field.'

'Unfortunately,' said Laura, 'you can't have a relationship with a research grant, or make love by e-mail.'

'Some academics seem to manage it,' said Helen.

'That's precisely the problem. They live in their bloody heads all the time.'

'Virtual reality.'

'Virtual death.'

Talking about Helen's situation chewed Laura up. There was so much she couldn't share with Helen, not least that she, too, had fancied Robin for some time. It was terrible to feel a conflict of loyalties. There was one question she had to ask, to help her resolve a particular uncertainty.

'Would you be devastated if Robin did stray again?'

Helen considered. 'In some ways I'd be relieved another woman had taken the decision out of my hands.'

'That's what I felt about Tom,' said Laura, 'though the situation has gone beyond that.'

Laura dropped Helen off on her own way home. She was mopping her eyes with a tissue as she drove up to the front of their own garage and parked.

'Why are you crying, Mummy,' asked Matthew.

'Mummy isn't crying,' said Laura. 'She's got a fly in her eye.'

'Hmm! Both eyes, I suppose,' snorted Matthew.

'Shut up, Matthew,' said Sarah, assuming the role of protector.

'I must have a cold coming as well,' explained Laura, vainly seeking an escape from further inquiry. I'll look such a terrible mess now, she thought. Please don't let there be any phone calls or visitors, certainly for the next hour, but preferably for the next two or three years, till this is sorted out. What am I thinking of, she chided herself. Then she was annoyed. It only took a few remarks by Helen to bring on a severe attack of self-pity.

* * *

Laura picked up the phone. Before she met Helen she had no intention of contacting Tom. Now she dialled his number. She had to clear the air.

'What is going on, Tom? You didn't tell me you were seeing the murdered woman.'

'Who's that?' Tom was astonished, playing for time.

'The clerk to the coroner.'

'Who told you that?'

'Helen told me.'

'How does she know?' He regretted the words. They sounded like an admission. He tried to recover the ground. 'I had a bad feeling about Detlev. I arranged to meet her. The meeting never took place.'

For an air-clearing conversation, this is going averagely badly, she thought grimly.

'Someone's circling round, doing people in,' Tom explained. 'I wonder if it's connected with me and my Research Centre in some way I can't fathom at present.'

'You're having an affair.'

'I'm not.'

'You were at the time, even if you've finished it.'

'I wasn't, I never was.'

'You didn't tell me you were seeing her.'

'I wasn't seeing her, not that way. I had an odd feeling about Detlev's death, that was all. After the inquest, I rang her.'

'I fail to see why.'

'To see whether my doubt was shared among the court officers, I suppose.'

'I can't believe you'd be so naïve as to expect they'd be prepared to comment to a complete stranger on such a delicate matter.'

'I wasn't a complete stranger.'

'So you did know her.'

'I didn't.'

'But you'd spoken to her.'

'Yes.'

'When?'
'When I phoned.'
'Why did you phone?'
'To ask her to meet me.'
'You fancied her?'
'No.'
'Don't try to bluff me. I know you. What did her husband think?'
'I've no idea whether she even had one.'
'She'd have worn a wedding ring.'
'I wouldn't notice that day in the courtroom, would I?'
'It's the kind of detail women notice all the time. She was married.' Laura was thinking, why shouldn't I lie? She wanted to make Tom squirm. 'I've seen the husband on the telly. He's completely devastated, be in no doubt about that.'

'You think I don't feel guilty about it.'
'What time are you back for tea?'
Tom cursed inwardly. 'I won't be back till later this evening. I forgot to tell you I'm giving a lecture at Peterborough University.'

Laura slammed the phone down.

Chapter 18

> *Graver's looking across the table at the person opposite.*
> *Can't see who it is.*
> *It may be the Queen.*
> *She's replicating herself in my head*
> *nonsense says the larva.*
> *nonsense says the voice in my head.*
> *Is it a voice or a suppurating spore*

He's repeating 'no' and deliberately not turning his head. But he can see his old man moving round behind and he knows what's coming, but this is part of the escape from the trap. You have to build up sufficient pressure, he tells himself, to break through. It's like the kids shaking those fizzy bottles, the big ones, and then unscrewing the tops real quick. Whoosh! Except that now he's said the word there's a further bunch of hurdles which weren't all there before, or at least some were, but weren't visible.

Even what you've rehearsed many times never turns out quite how you expect. 'No', he says, and looks around in amazement, as in the total silence which follows, all the clocks don't stop and the gas goes on making the pans on the stove bubble and as far as he can tell his heart is still beating, only now it's more like a massive drum. And his father's face, the cause of this global pause, is draining slowly from red to white and then back to purple as the blood pounds back, attempting to break through every vessel and failing by the whisker which would save Graver even now from the beating of his life.

He lay on the floor where mother Mary had pushed him and moaned and protested at first, while the blows kept falling on his legs, back and head. He dared not lift his head to see which of them was hitting him at any particular time. It was a funny thing to be trying to guess. He risked peeping a couple of times and was surprised – though relieved because it justified his hating her as well – to see her wielding the switch on one side of his body and him on the other. Later, as though his body realised there was a behavioural consequence, an increase in pain every time he made a movement or a sound, he stopped. So, through degrees of pain he learned to stay quiet, or quieter, since sometimes the pain was so wicked you couldn't help the sounds coming out, even when grinding your teeth together like brake blocks on the bicycle's rusty wheel.

Unpleasant he was, and old looking round the chins, to the point where Graver thought *isn't it about time you died, old man?* This was just the stray thought of a child in an idle moment. But it repeated itself in daydreams as such thoughts have a habit of doing.

The Bakery. Not Jerson's, Smithson's, Palmerston's or any such distinguishing label. It was known as The Bakery to everyone. And it provided Graver with his first experience of employment. And something else as well. There was a handful of young ones, among an army of women whose children were at school and who could work part-time through the day, and a smaller force mostly of men, who baked through the early hours of each night. The younger ones, with fewer domestic commitments so it seemed, covered from 7:00 a.m. when the night shift went off. It was the breaks which were educational for him. There was Betty and her twin sister Leila and a couple of lads, and him. At first he had no idea what the girls were giggling about and why, during morning and afternoon breaks, when they were in this giggly mood, one or another of them was always going off to the sheds with one of the lads.

* * *

I spent hours in the villa observing the ceaseless activity of the tiny Pharaoh's ant, with which the building apparently was infested.

I watched the endless files of ants moving like strips of dark material, escalator-style, night and day, along the floors, up the walls, along the ceilings, usually tucked into the edges and corners, but breaking out across open areas in order to reach their goal. This would invariably be some food source. It didn't seem to matter how small.

The ants had amazing powers of concentration in large numbers around their target. Even when only an occasional ant every few centimetres scurried along, I would suddenly come upon several hundred around some unfortunate grub, or perhaps a morsel of food – a scrap of bread, or the sugar bowl – I'd thoughtlessly left on the kitchen worktop the night before.

Greasy, suppurating spores invading the brain. Lost control of the brain to the invaders. I told the doctor I could feel them. He took no notice.

Now I had encountered Pharaoh's ant, I wanted to try out various methods of testing their powers. I was impatient to proceed, yet knew I had to hold myself in check. It was going to be difficult, summoning patience and devoting my energies to scientific patterns of inquiry I'd turned my back on when abandoning my career.

I wanted to put Pharaoh's ant – the little formicas as I called them – to the test. They were little formicas to me because they reminded me of the diminutive specimens of Acanthomyops Niger which result from the queen's first brood and which she rears in total isolation. They are small because she founds a new colony by feeding the dozen or so larvae from the first eggs she lays, from her own regurgitated body juices, as her wing muscles waste after the once-in-a-lifetime mating flight. The formicas resembled niger only from a distance. Close up, they were less black and less wooden. They had an endearing habit of bending their abdomens upwards when they stopped walking, as though questing or stretching. It made me smile, this gesture. It seemed almost human, though with my scientific hat on I wondered what purpose it served. I surmised it was functional in some basic way, since they did it so often. Perhaps it was a form of scenting, to enable and encourage other ants to follow them. Or – at this stage I had neither read about them nor dissected one – maybe their olfactory glands were located in the abdomen and functioned more effectively when raised.

J

* * *

By 3:00 p.m. Tom was delivering his public lecture as Visiting Professor of Entomology to a couple of hundred staff and students in the main science lecture theatre at Peterborough University. He'd accepted the invitation on the basis that it would give a boost to the setting up of the University's new Centre for Insect Studies, headed by his former colleague, Dr Moses Livingstone.

'Ant, the word was probably amte in middle English, from the Anglo-Saxon aemelte or emmet, not exactly a term of endearment. It wasn't hard then and it isn't hard now for people to look down on ants. They're considered too small to have decent-sized brains. Instead they rely on a few clumps of ganglia or nerves, distributed in different parts of the soft tissues inside their chitinous exterior skeletons. The commonest response to an ants' nest on the path or by the house is to pour a kettleful of boiling water down the holes. Cornish people used to call English people emmets or foreigners, a term of disdain. It was common in my father's time, when you could still hear the Cornish language spoken in remote villages.

In reality, for beings so allegedly tied to instinctive drives, ants possess a remarkable facility for ecological matching – that is, responding quickly to environmental changes and seeking new food sources when existing ones become depleted.'

A stout, red-faced man near the front of the hall made a remark about his own Cornish ancestry which caused several people nearby to titter. Tom continued unchecked, as though lost in his own train of thought.

'Some species, Lasius Aalienus for example, change their nest sites frequently: they may do this on an almost daily basis, or at the slightest stimulus, such as interference by a potential predator. The so-called fire ant Solenopsis Invicta which has invaded much of the southern USA, when the water rises on flood plains forms a large raft with the queen and brood in the Centre, and at the coming of flash floods floats to safety, and may survive by anchoring the raft to bushes or other stable objects sticking out of the water. Pheidole Cephalica, which lives in tropical forests, relies on as few as one or two workers rushing through the nest in so-called alarm runs, to stimulate the entire colony to evacuate. This can save them from flash flooding, for example, where a couple of foragers return in front of advancing water.

Other species such as army ants are naturally nomadic. The predatory power of army ants is enormous. An entire colony of, say, 500,000 ants plus brood on the march can cover two hundred metres on a typical marching day, in a two – or three-week cycle of marching. Then, for a similar period, they stop in one place and consume small mammals and insects over up to three hundred square metres of forest trees and undergrowth in a single twenty-four hour period. The genus Dorylus, however, contrasts with Eciton. In the latter, whole colonies living, for example, in sub-Saharan Africa, march whereas the former send out daily raids from their huge nests of many millions of workers, and can overwhelm slow moving or immobilised animals of any size in their path. They have been known, for example, to kill pythons which are sluggish from having eaten recently, or young animals or children left while their parents are busy elsewhere. They can sting but they tend to bite their victims to death, which gives you some idea of the huge numbers which concentrate in one place to force prey to succumb. There are instances, notably quoted by Bates, the Amazon explorer, of ants tunnelling under reservoirs so the water breaks through the constraining walls. Thus, ants either may contribute significantly towards, or literally undermine, agriculture and rural development.'

Tom brought the lecture to a close soon after this example.

'Thank you, Professor Fortius. We have a few minutes for questions. Yes, that young woman in the middle.'

An earnest young woman from the Department's group of visiting research students stood up:

'I am interested in the acquisition and demonstration of language among chimpanzees. You will appreciate there are many genetic and cultural similarities between humans and animals. However, would you say that only humans have the capacity to use language?'

'There are some obvious differences between chimpanzees and ants,' said Tom and this produced a ripple of mirth among some of his audience. 'I'm not qualified to comment on chimpanzees. However, I would say in general that it would be hard for any other non-human species to rival the range and sophistication of our interaction using non-verbal body language as well as spoken words. I wouldn't put it as strongly as humans are the only beings to use language. Many species of animals communicate between themselves in one way or another. Sometimes, as with chimpanzees, there is a sign language or a vocal language of a sort, with some limited verbal signals through the voice box, or gestures. Humans who are deaf use sign language rather than sounds so there are parallels. Among the social insects, there are examples of communication, the problem being that we don't have too many details, beyond the obvious case of the dancing bees.

'Incidentally, I'm not ruling out the fact that ants may excite each other by more than one means at once. For instance, they may use pheromones as a way of speeding up the responses of other ants in the vicinity. To return to the dancing bees, in 1934, Maeterlinck's book *The Life of the Bee* referred to communication between bees of a food source, but it was von Hirsch who specified how precisely the forager returning to the nest signalled the distance, direction and possibly the size of the food source. The point I would make is that in the social insects, as I guess among chimpanzees, there is a sign language or a vocal language of a sort, but a very restricted form of language, limited to communication about what is happening now. Humans, on the other hand, can discuss what happened in the distant past and what may happen in the immediate and distant future.

'That gentleman at the back.'

'I have a question. Dr Fortius, would you regard the many predatory activities army ants engage in, which contribute to this extremely rigid regime, as a purely mechanical response to physiological stimuli determined by the cycle of egg-laying larval growth and hatching, or as made possible by the resourcefulness, initiative and learning powers of individuals and groups of ants?'

'A mixture of the two, I guess.'

Tom felt a growing unease. He didn't know who the questioner was, or where he was coming from, but there was something vaguely familiar about the man's voice. He couldn't see to the back of the hall, though, so had no chance of ascertaining whether he recognised him. He'd had some unpleasant brushes in the past with researchers and others angered by his critiques of the socio-biological perspective. Normally, he would wade in and damn the consequences, but this time something made him hesitate.

Another question came from the back of the hall. Tom couldn't see, but he guessed from the voice the questioner was the same man.

'Professor, I'd like to ask about your critical writing on the notion of the selfish gene. You have some rather harsh things to say about physicists, which as a physicist myself I'd like to exempt myself from. We aren't all as dogmatic as the person you describe, though I admit some of my colleagues do regard their physics in much the same way as the priest holds religious views, but I suggest we rise above sparring between the disciplines, whether through physics envy – I like your use of this term – or not, and focus on how to use our current knowledge of genes to contribute to our understanding of people. Do I take it that your main point is that genes, like physics, provide important routes to that understanding, but aren't the means of understanding everything?'

'Basically, yes.'

There was a ripple of laughter and some applause, which Tom put down to the brevity of his reply. He started to speak again, but slowly, partly out of a natural reticence, but impelled by the sudden wish to justify the content of his lecture.

'I don't think it's helpful to use analogies such as the brain as a computer to develop a view of how people think. It seems to me to be a denial of the social factors which contribute to human societies, that some scientists have tried to reduce complex, multi-factor explanations to the makeup of the individual.'

'But professor, research at the Centre for Psychiatry at the University of London indicates that individual genes as well as gene clusters influence children's behaviour such as shyness and adult proneness to alcoholism. Environmental experiences can either reinforce or undermine such tendencies but we can't assume a clear-cut division between nature and nurture.'

Despite himself, Tom found his argument pushing him along. 'If you're saying we need to recognise that a complex web of factors contribute to our thoughts, emotions and actions, I've got no problems with that. But I can't go along with the simplistic, reductionist view that genes for virtually every aspect of human behaviour lie waiting to be discovered by researchers. More generally, I'm not impressed by people who assume that physics is at the top of the scientific tree, that there has to be a theory of everything, that everything biological can be simplified to its physiological, chemical and physical determinants, or that human personality and behaviour are determined by the DNA and genes of the individual. Genes are important, but they need to be put in their place. Unfortunately for the genetic determinists, the entire pattern of people's lives is not locked into their DNA and genes at the moment of conception, to be unpacked in predictable behaviour throughout subsequent years. The genetic make-up of individuals cannot be held responsible for family problems, individual pre-dispositions to criminality, sexual abuse or alcoholism. Individuals who murder, and serial killers, are the products of their upbringing as well as their inheritance. It is unhelpful to polarise the debate between nature and nurture, as though all the causes have to be found either on one side or the other. People develop, and age, as a result of the ways they construct their being and their lives.'

'That's quite a mouthful, Professor. I wonder if I can pick you up on one thing you mentioned. Could you explain what you mean by reductionism?'

'Willingly, yes. People are not simply the sum total of the physical – notably biological and chemical – ingredients of which they are composed. I prefer explanations of how and why people are as they are and act as they do to be preserved in their full complexity rather than reduced to simplistic generalisations, however attractive these are to tabloid scientists.'

Tom had a sudden recollection of where he had heard these views. They reminded him of Apthorpe.

'Tabloid scientists, I like it. Have you borrowed the expression from somewhere? I don't remember seeing it.'

'Not as far as I know,' said Tom irritably, looking at his watch. He was suddenly very resentful of these questions and comments which intruded into his private world. He wanted the session to end and looked at Dr Pearson, his chairperson, for permission to escape. But if Pearson did realise, he didn't respond very quickly and the zealous questioner had time to land another.

'Would you describe yourself as something of a heretic, among your colleagues in biology?'

'I'm committed to my subject, if that's what you mean. If at times my work in the laboratory leads me to ask critical questions, so be it. What other people call me is their own affair. I don't really feel in a position to comment on that.'

At last Dr Pearson woke up to the situation and intervened. 'Thank you, Professor. I'm afraid that was the last question we had time for.'

Within a couple of minutes, with the "it only remains routine", he wound up the entire event.

* * *

At about 7:00 p.m., Chris was driving back from Hessle on the Clive Sullivan Way through soft, persistent drizzle. For some reason, she decided to stick to the main road and branch north after crossing the River Hull. On the bridge, she was surprised to see Tom to her right, leaning over the railing, staring out past the spectacular shiplike profile of the marine aquarium tourist attraction, The Deep, into the darkness of the Humber. She turned off, parked the car and made her way back to the spot. He hadn't seen her. She sidled alongside him and peered over the railings.

'How did it go?' she asked.

Tom gave a start. His words piled out. 'Where the hell did you come from? Don't get me wrong. Nice surprise.'

'You look very preoccupied.'

He tried to shrug off his mood.

'Oh that. I gave one of our research students a lift back to East Hull and thought I'd take a breather before plunging back in at the University.'

'Which is a way of avoiding my question. I was wondering how it went.'

'The lecture or the day as a whole?'

'Both, but especially the lecture, I suppose.'

'All right.'

'A man of few words.'

'Sometimes.'

'All right covers such a multitude of sins,' she persisted. 'You aren't really that British – stiff upper lip and don't talk about your feelings, like some of these hard-boiled coppers I work with. Or have I misjudged you?'

'Okay. I was happy with the lecture. But there was a persistent questioner. I couldn't see him at the back of the hall. I had a feeling I knew him – something about his voice. Or perhaps it was his views. They reminded me of a conversation I'd had, the arguments over the years with Apthorpe, you remember, our so-called rat professor. But I can't place who it was.'

'Did the questions bother you?'

'Yes.'

'Couldn't you answer them?'

'It wasn't that. They're standard debates between scientists studying the animal world – about whether there's more to non-human behaviour than behaviour. Are we the only beings with consciousness, that sort of territory. No, it's more the uneasiness I've described – déjà vu. If I'm honest, I was reminded of a period last year, when I became rather paranoid about the questions from one of my students.'

'Who is he?'

'She. Naomi Waterson, the student I mentioned before and the lad she goes about with. I saw them both. You remember, I said she has had a thing about me in the past and she went through a period of following me about.'

'And the lad, where does he fit in?'

Tom shrugged.

'I couldn't say.'

Side by side, they stared across at the opaque water.

'The river looks forbidding.'

'That's Hull. All the accumulated muck from half a million lives, from more than a thousand years of excretion and chucking rubbish away, concentrated in one filthy stream,' said Tom.

'How to spoil my illusions in a sentence. I was going to say trying to penetrate through those murky depths to what's in the river is like trying to guess what's in your mind.'

'I'm sorry,' said Tom. 'I'm so wrapped up in myself. I should have asked, what about you? You look as though you've had a basinful.'

'Don't talk about it. I'm recovering from a meeting with Dr Threadgold, our forensic psychiatrist. Any comments could tip me towards saying something I'll regret,' said Chris moodily.

'She was rude?'

'Nothing like that. We get on very well as it happens. But the phone kept ringing, people came in and out, her bleeper went off half a dozen times. It doesn't make for productive discussion.'

'Where did you meet her?' asked Tom, trying to turn the conversation in a less fraught direction.

'Her office is at Castle Hill Hospital, almost next to the psychologists. That's only a base, of course. She works all over the place. They don't have a forensic psychiatry department as such.'

'So no progress as far as profiling suspects is concerned.'

'That word profiling! I'm sick of hearing it. Mary Threadgold is very good, but apart from confirming that she has suspicions about what we suspect already – nothing.'

'What did she say?'

'Her advice was to look for someone suffering from schizophrenia. The chaotic thoughts in among the philosophical and scientific details in the notes, apparently. For starters, we're left with the task of checking about ten thousand current and former psychiatric patients in Yorkshire and Teesside. Beyond that her comments could apply to any case. They don't provide us with the kinds of specific factors which could be incorporated into a computer programme to enable us to eliminate people from the investigation. That's on the assumption this person is already known to the authorities. What if he's a recent arrival in the area?'

It was Tom's turn again to stare reflectively into the muddy water.

'They're all victims really.'

'Who exactly?'

'I was reading this article in a criminology journal – some psychiatrist writing about the triangle of victimology – to do with the common bonds between a murderer, the people who victimise him and his own murder victim or victims.'

'Geometrically neat but so what? He could be anybody.'

'Or she.'

'I meant to say that.'

'What did Mary say about gender?'

'It was on the lines of that argument about most abusers and bullies having been abused and bullied themselves.'

'Sounds like the old record which ignores the reality that for every one person who's been abused who goes on to do it to others, there are many who don't.'

'Record! Thanks, Chris, you've broken my block. I had an idea but couldn't recall it later. There's a link between those of us who have stayed on in the laboratory and our suspect who left. Two links actually, or more than two, who knows?'

'Why is it that men don't listen to women, but women are expected to listen to every wittering sentence of every wittering man?'

'The more obvious link first. The aspiring but failed scientist who becomes the frustrated technician working alongside the successful researchers he did not equal, in whatever way. You understand I'm not talking about merit here. He may have been equally deserving, but for whatever reason, we know he didn't make the grade.'

'You don't even know he would have wanted it,' Chris interposed, before she even knew who Tom was talking about.

'True, but every hypothesis has to start somewhere.'

'You said two links.'

'The other link is less obvious but more interesting. Probably also, it's unknown to anyone apart from myself and our suspect.'

'I wish you'd stop applying your pseudo-scientific jargon to the plain speaking world of detection. Not suspect, murderer. Forget the innocent till proved guilty. We're failing to find a murderer here.'

He stayed silent.

'I can't see where this is leading,' said Chris.

'You keep interrupting.'

'Don't push me,' she said grimly. 'We're on a bridge over a fast-flowing river. I'm beginning to see why he became frustrated enough to commit murder.'

He smiled. She was pleased.

'That's good, your face has cracked.' He laughed a little this time and continued.

'The less visible thread linking us is the music. Our suspect, sorry, murderer, mentions music and conducting. I think he's a failed performer. I'm not saying he wasn't good, but for some reason he didn't make the grade. Perhaps he had an accident and became disabled.'

'How do you know this?'

'Little scraps here and there, odd comments he's made about his early life. As a rather mediocre musician myself, I can recognise the signs.'

Chris didn't pick up on this remark. She was impressed, and was preoccupied with this new line of investigation.

Tom was following his own train of thought.

'The core of the conundrum is how these various barriers to conventional success have affected him and their relationship with the content of his scientific interests.'

'It's straightforward enough. He's a frustrated scientist.'

'It's a little more complicated than that. The theory is that our person – okay, our murderer – is driven to each further crime partly by an intensified anger – an urge to destroy, if you like – after each previous killing. At the same time, those same feelings of frustration, failure and anger which feed into this cycle of aggressive acts also fuel ever increasing guilt and self-disgust. The means by which our murderer chooses to commit each crime will relate closely to the themes which link him with his setting – the scientific focus, the music, or whatever – and the series of killings into which he is apparently locked becomes ultimately self-destructive. He's a sort of black hole in our universe, at an individual level, the alter-ego – probably the unacceptable side – of the people with whom he's interacted and at the group or social level, the negation of basic values of decency and humanity.'

'I hope he does kill himself if that's what you're working up to.'

'On the way, he's becoming an angrier person and the incidents have the potential to be more destructive.'

'You could be describing a mass murderer, in the right circumstances, rather than a serial killer.'

'I'm afraid so.'

'And we still haven't the remotest idea who he is.'

'That's why we have forensic psychiatrists.'

'Dr Threadgold probably wouldn't agree with you.'

'The problem is we have loads of information but no leads,' said Chris.

'So what's the next step?'

'My lords and masters are baying for blood. But the investigation is – it's at a dead end. All we can do is review all the evidence.'

'Where are you off to?' Tom asked.

'Back to the office, to start all over again.'

'Before you go, I've had a look at those insect remains your pathologist passed on. They're not run of the mill. Army or driver ants from the genus Dorylus not found anywhere in this country, or in Europe. They're found in parts of Africa.'

'Africa. Does that include rain forests?'

'The sub-Saharan regions, savannah and tropical rain forests, would be among their main habitats.'

'Presumably some zoos here will have them.'

'I doubt it. Someone would need the expertise to manage them. They need so much attention. It wouldn't be worth it, when you can set up an observation colony of harvesting ants for so much less trouble.'

'The implication of this is – what?'

'The only place you're likely to find them is a laboratory where such ants are being used for research.'

'Which is where?'

'There aren't many. Ours certainly. It could be the only one.'

'Right.'

'Who's working on these fellows? That's the question.'

'The person best placed has just left.'

'Perhaps we should have a word with him, or her.'

'It's a him. Robin Lovelace. It will be difficult. He's abroad.'

'Let me guess where. Sub-Saharan Africa.'

'Come on, Robin can't be a suspect. He's halfway across the world.'

'You're asking me to treat this as pure coincidence.'

'It has to be.'

'Even if not, I suppose there isn't enough to justify chasing after him to interview him. When did he go?'

'A few days ago.'

Chris pulled a face. 'Would you regard him as potentially homicidal?'

Tom laughed. 'We're back to that. Robin wouldn't hurt a fly.'

'How would you describe him?'

'An argumentative but otherwise harmless womaniser.'

'A crisp case study if ever I heard one.'

'Robin's not complicated, nor violent, nor even aggressive. Immoral, untrustworthy in matters of matrimony and the heart, disorganised, emotionally unstable even. But first and last, a harmless intellectual with the libido of an adolescent.'

Chris ruminated. 'People do kill for love, you know, eighty percent of the time. Most murders are by spouses or cohabitees. There could be a connection.'

'Even if he was implicated in the earlier killings, which would be ludicrous, he's hardly carried out this last one, not at several thousand miles distance.'

Chapter 19

The police investigation had ground to a halt. Bradshaw called Chris in. Even before he spoke, she anticipated what might be in prospect.

'We don't need to waste time pussyfooting about.' He paused and gave her a long look.

She shrugged as non-committally as possible.

'If there had been any significant developments in the past twelve hours, you would have informed me.'

She nodded.

'Look at these headlines.' He shoved lurid page one spreads in two tabloid papers across the desk.

Chris stared in silence.

'Well?' asked Bradshaw, abrasive as ever.

'Do you expect me to say I approve of these?' she asked.

'Good gracious no, Inspector. Perhaps the time has come for you to gain more varied experience of this Force.'

'You're sending me back.'

'Don't jump the gun.'

'It's tantamount to sacking me.'

'That's rather over-dramatic, before you've even heard my decision.'

'You're drafting me to other duties.'

'You've called in all these experts. Despite this, it could be argued that the investigation is going nowhere.'

Chris was aghast. 'You can't say that.'

'I haven't said that. I said it could be argued.'

'This is necessary preliminary work in an investigation where the circumstances are eccentric.'

'That's where you're wrong. In an investigation like this, the one thing we can't afford is eccentricity. The media will accuse us of dabbling in fringe sciences. They'll make us a laughing stock.'

'You're referring to consulting the graphologist.'

'And the rest.'

'Forensic psychiatry is a well-respected branch of Forensics. So is forensic entomology.'

'Bloody mind-readers and palm-readers. And as for insect men, people will accuse you of having let them into your brain.'

'I'm taking over the investigation myself,' said Bradshaw. 'Aspects of it need someone of my rank to head it up.'

'You can't do that. It doesn't make sense. On one hand you're telling me the investigation should be lower down our priorities. On the other, you're implying it's become too high profile for me to direct.'

Bradshaw waved a hand. 'No, no, Inspector. You're misrepresenting the situation. We've a difficult situation here, politically sensitive. Another aspect I'm unhappy with is the involvement of that fellow from the University.'

'You want Professor Fortius off the case as well, sir?'

Bradshaw stared at her and nodded. He can't even bring himself to say it, thought Chris. Her eyes narrowed. 'Are you being pushed, sir?'

'If you mean Jack Deerbolt, this view resonates with that held at the top, yes. You may as well know it, although at this moment the decision is mine.'

'You've already consulted the ACC?'

'Not specifically, but in general terms. The detail is irrelevant.'

Chris guessed Bradshaw was retreating to incomprehensibility when under pressure, as now.

'We need these experts to advise us, sir, in a case as bizarre as this.'

Bradshaw ignored her and continued his train of thought.

'Let's look at it positively. I thought it would be an opportunity for you to see at first hand some of our other work, before going back to your ivory tower.'

'I am not an academic, sir. I am a police officer.'

'Yes I know. But you have to admit, your background isn't exactly average.'

'At times like this I wish I'd left school from a secondary modern at sixteen and never gone back.'

'In that case, we wouldn't be having this conversation,' Bradshaw breezed urbanely.

'You no doubt would be highly relieved.'

'That's a presumption.'

'It's a conclusion in the light of experience.'

'Inspector, you're a talented woman and I'd hate anything to happen here which blighted the prospect of a long, successful career.'

'But you'd be obliged if I'd go quietly. I tell you, I won't.'

'You're putting me in an extremely awkward position.'

'Between the two of us, sir, I intend to. I want the extra time on this case. I assessed the situation, came to you with my plan to set up three teams of investigating officers so as once and for all to eliminate all but our main suspect from our inquiries. You were around at the time of the Yorkshire Ripper and Barwell inquiries. You must know that if the police had completed their systematic checks against the forensic profile, the criminals in these cases would have been apprehended more quickly. You owe it to me to allow this phase of the investigation to take place and, until it's run its course, to head off the media and your bosses. We both know it's complex and there are no prizes for this kind of slogging detective work. There are no short cuts to doing a quality job on the checks either, and there isn't anybody who could have done any better than us, faced with what we're up against in this case. That isn't to say we won't, if you give us more time.'

'We, Inspector?'

'Yes, we. I've got the team behind me.'

'You hope.'

'Ask them.'

The phone rang. Bradshaw ignored it and waited. It rang on and on, insistently. He picked it up.

'Bradshaw. Yes.'

Bradshaw's face became sombre. He listened for three or four minutes. He pulled a notepad towards him and scribbled quickly. Then he spoke, one eye on Chris.

'Give out nothing. I'll ring you back, in two minutes.'

He put the receiver down and spoke to Chris. 'That was our press officer. Arnold Westrop wants to interview me in connection with a feature he's running in the Yorkshire Post on unsolved murders.'

Fifteen minutes later, Bradshaw rang Chris.

'I'm giving you more time.'

'How long, sir?'

'A few days.'

'Days,' she exclaimed.

'A week at the most. I'm giving you time, Inspector, totally against my better judgement.'

'Five working days.'

Chris snorted. 'That's impossible, sir. Two weeks.'

'A week.'

'Ten days.'

'This is ridiculous. We're in an office of the Police Force, not bargaining at a market stall, Inspector. I'll have you remember that.'

'Yes, sir.'

'I haven't finished. Keep Westrop and his rat pack out of it.'

Chris raised her eyebrows.

He continued: 'Two weeks. Not an hour more. Not one single hour.'

Chris was relieved at the extra time, but didn't want to give Bradshaw any credit. She guessed he was under pressure from top management and politicians to produce results and she was his best bet.

'Right, sir.'

'I'm watching you. One foot over the line and I'll make sure one of us never visits Bramshill again. This part of the conversation never took place. Understand me?'

She forced a nod. He continued to watch her from under the dark arch of hooded eyebrows.

'Understood, Inspector?'

'I understand only too well, sir.'

'Keep me fully briefed from now on. Retain that University fellow on for the time being. It looks as though he may be needed for this one, but keep an eye on him. I'm not convinced all this insect business isn't a red herring. I don't like outside people trampling all over police affairs.'

Bradshaw tore the top sheet off the notepad. 'Here's the number. Liaise with Inspector Gowthorpe.'

Bradshaw didn't look up as Chris left the office. She was spitting blood, only constraining her tongue by the certainty it would play into his hands. That was the illusion people like him clung to, she thought.

Power held by custom rather than competence, less a Police Force, more scouting for boys.

* * *

Tom was in his office. He sat at his desk, full of thoughts and able for the first time in a couple of days to apply his mind to the day to day business of running the department. His eye fell on his notepad. The word apparatus was scribbled there, with the word *lost* beside it. He leapt to his feet.

He picked up the phone and dialled Chris's direct number.

'The bugger! He's got my lab equipment.'

'What?'

'The social insect communication experiments. We lost some of the back-up equipment some while ago.'

'So our suspect works with you?'

'Or did do till recently.'

'Yes!' Chris clenched her fists in triumph. This was the break-through she'd desperately needed in this case.

She picked up her mobile and pressed a button.

'Hullo, Chris Winchester here. I'd like to speak to Superintendent Bradshaw.'

* * *

Tom suspected a link between the deaths and insect research at the University, but beyond that couldn't specify what it might be. He took his suspicions that Detlev was murdered to Chris and tried to convince her Detlev's body should be exhumed. She put it to him it would be difficult without fresh evidence to challenge the verdict of the coroner at the inquest.

'Absurd! You can't have a body exhumed immediately after the inquest,' said Bradshaw.

'What about where there is doubt?' asked Chris.

'It'll cause a furore.'

This was how Chris imagined Bradshaw would react. He appeared preoccupied not with pursuing a possible murder but with avoiding rocking the boat.

'On what grounds will we make the request for an exhumation?'

'On the grounds of new evidence.'

Bradshaw stood up and walked round his desk, standing close to Chris. His voice was low; he hated being put on the spot. 'This is the last time I indulge any of your eccentricities. If I give you your way, you must come up with results, and quickly.'

Once the order was granted, the procedure was straightforward. The pathologist proposed exhuming the body early in the morning.

Quite apart from minimising the effects on decomposition of warming by ambient temperatures, there were fewer people about. There was less likelihood of attracting attention.

The exhumation was carried out at six o'clock, as the sky was lightening from the east. Dark clouds hung forlorn and grey over the coffin and its attendants.

Chris was shaking her head over a piece of paper, as Tom walked into her office. 'Problems?' she asked him.

'The post-mortem report on Dr Brandt.'

'That was quick.'

'They say there's no fresh evidence proving unlawful killing.'

Tom's expression showed his disappointment.

'And there's no evidence that he killed himself.'

'So the original open verdict is confirmed?'

She held up her hand. 'Hold on, they haven't closed the investigation yet. There is one unresolved matter. They found a fragment in the oesophagus. Only a fragment, you understand. Not much thicker or longer than a hair.'

'What's so special about that? Hardly enough to affect the hypothesis as to the cause of death.'

'We've just received the results from Forensics. It was a fragment of an insect. It's been identified as part of the mandible of an ant.'

Part Two

Generation

Chapter 20

Graver was back home. Safe in his home territory, the superficiality, the outer persona, fell away. Everything Graver felt and thought came down to the single word *hate*. He hated all those he saw as contributing to the injustices, the indignities, of his life: his parents, school, the town and at this moment the entire world. His general loathing extended in every direction and reflected back on himself. It drove him then; more and more it drove him now. He hated himself.

He couldn't cope with the complexity of himself as a composite animal. He jumped back in horror when he thought about or touched the mirror of his own reflections, his image fractured into the twenty million fragments of the photo cells at the back of his retina. This person was no more. In his place was the composite inhabited by the million fibres of the optic nerve, along which the pulses of the image travelled to different parts of his brain.

* * *

Tom parked in the public area on the street to the rear of Wawne Road Police Station. As he walked ruminatively towards the entrance to the offices, his reverie was rudely interrupted. Superintendent Bradshaw, walking just ahead of him, stopped and turned so Tom would catch up with him. 'Strange, Professor,' said Bradshaw, 'how every road keeps turning back in your direction.'

'Good morning, Superintendent,' said Tom with what little enthusiasm he could muster.

'A fortnight ago nobody ever talked about ants. Now I can't get away from them. I gather one of your little friends found their way into the windpipe of your ex-colleague Dr Brandt.'

'One of your ex-special constables.'

Bradshaw nodded. Apparently, he didn't like being reminded of this.

'I can't understand how it was missed.'

'It was only a small part of an ant's jaw,' said Tom. 'People, even specialists, see what they look for and they look for what they expect to find. Scientists have done it throughout the history of science. It happens to us all, all the time.'

Bradshaw changed the subject. He couldn't work up any enthusiasm for the history of science.

'I thought you'd be using our car park.'

'I wouldn't presume, not being a police officer.'

'True.'

Bradshaw didn't ask Tom's destination. Tom assumed he anticipated the reply. They walked side by side towards the building in tense silence. Tom was preoccupied with many other matters at this moment; police inquiries were rather low on his list of priorities.

'You're a difficult man to miss, Professor. You seem to be everywhere,' said Bradshaw. 'First the body, or rather bodies, the links between possible suspects and your previous employees and now the questions about who has the know-how to advise us.'

Tom started as he belatedly registered what Bradshaw was saying. 'It doesn't surprise me,' he said. 'In this field the University has almost the monopoly of research expertise in this part of the country.'

'The world has changed since I was a lad,' said Bradshaw. 'In those days we were expected to leave secondary modern school as soon as possible and earn a living. I was working in a factory before I was sixteen and it never did me any harm.'

Tom steeled himself. He wasn't in the mood to listen to nostalgic reflections from the man who from Chris's vantage point was adding to the difficulties of the investigation.

'I suppose you went to one of those grammar schools, Professor?'

'I did.'

'How does one become a professor? It must feel strange, sitting in that ivory tower on Cottingham Road looking out at all the people scurrying about far below'

'I don't work in an ivory tower. Most of our research is very practical, to do with helping farmers control insect pests, for instance.'

'People crowded together, they're a bit like ants.'

Tom was taken aback at this. 'I suppose crowds of people are rather similar in appearance to crowds of ants, but there are very big differences.'

Bradshaw returned to his former tack. 'My nephew wants to go to university to study music and my niece is studying for her PhD. Can you credit it, Professor? Me a complete ignoramus and the next generation are complete brainboxes. They'll be taking jobs in places where they're waiting for old codgers like me to retire. That's the way of the world. And now we have Professor Fortius coming into the Police Force to tell us how to do our detective work.'

'Correction,' said Tom, irritated. 'You're the detective and I'm just the biologist.'

Bradshaw left Tom waiting at the reception desk while he stomped off down the corridor to his own office.

A couple of minutes later, Chris walked briskly down that same corridor. She saw Tom, indicated with a nod and he followed her from the foyer out into the rear car park.

She looked extremely fed up. Tom turned away from his own

problems. 'How is police work?'

She pulled a long face. 'Police work isn't brilliant at present. In fact it's crap.'

She walked fast across the car park and he had to increase his speed to keep up.

'We aren't making visible headway with this investigation and Bradshaw's being a royal pain in the backside.'

'Are you sure you want me to help out?'

'You aren't having second thoughts?'

'It isn't that. I don't want to tread where it wouldn't help.'

'We need allies, more voices like yours, from the outside, to counteract this attitude that Bradshaw exemplifies, this kind of "we used to manage without all these experts" view. We need more, not less voices like yours, from the real world out there.'

'Bradshaw's just been telling me that he lives in the real world and I don't.'

'That's typical. The cheek of the man. Where would he and all his narrow-minded colleagues be without people like you, willing to come and share your expertise with us on particular investigations?'

'I'm flattered, but don't build me up. We aren't magicians at the University.'

'Bradshaw carries a lot of baggage. It gets in the way of our work.'

They reached Chris's car and climbed in. 'We have a problem persuading Bradshaw to widen the scope of this investigation beyond his own preconceptions.' She drove towards the exit of the car park. 'He likes to keep control of his staff. Take a look at the fourth window from the right, on the first floor. Tell me who you see.'

Tom looked up and saw Bradshaw's unmistakable figure, framed by the window, staring down at them.

'You don't even need to tell me,' she said. 'That's my problem – a boss who won't let us get on and do our job. If he could he'd do all our policing for us.'

* * *

Tom had to call home to collect some papers.

'I may be late tonight,' he said apologetically as he walked through the kitchen on his way out. Laura was mixing a cake for the children's tea.

'What do you expect me to say?' She laughed ironically, showing her slightly crooked eye teeth in that way Tom had once found so endearing when they were first together. Her open laughter had signified a welcome escape from the intensity of his laboratory work. He found himself trying vainly to recall when it had stopped being that way.

'I'm past the stage of becoming uptight over a member of your faculty staff flipping his lid. You do your thing and I'll continue to do mine. Are you bothered?'

'Bothered? Never. The only thing that I worry about is you and the kids.'

He saw Laura grimace. They're only words, he thought. What do they mean? They're what I'm expected to say, so I say it. Like a drama on television. Someone else's life being acted out in front of me by other people. Or rather, I'm there, but as one of the actors, not as me. Where did he belong in this family, this relationship? Tom fervently wished he could answer the question.

* * *

Graver was agitated.

> *This is wrong.*
> *Wrong, wrong, WRONG*
> *Bad*
> *Wrong.*
> *Let me start again.*
> *I am so frightened.*
> *I don't know what is out there.*
> *Who am I?*
> *There is a hole in the middle of me.*
> *It is called terror.*
> *An infinity of terror at the heart of me.*
> *Nobody can reach it.*
> *Nobody can reach it.*
>
> *I saw Charles Darwin today. I always know him by the stabbing eyes under the hood of that long black coat. He wanted to speak but I looked straight ahead and crossed the road. It was an effort. I had to be at work. I couldn't afford the time to argue the evolution of insect species and in particular to puzzle over the confinement of army ants to the Southern continents.*
>
> *J*

* * *

Graver had anger about teachers. He was confused. Where was his anger directed? He didn't know the endpoint but wanted to right something which was very wrong. He'd started with the aim of lancing those abscesses from the past. Not all of them were apparent any more. He would continue with the present.

The affinity between Graver and one of his teachers, Mr Regel, was inexplicable. It bridged some uncomfortable differences of role, age and race. In the stratified and narrow-minded atmosphere of the grammar school, Graver, the pupil, was victimised and so was Mr Regel, each in his way. Their common experience was more binding than the massive gulf between them.

As for making the science plain to Graver, that was something else. Regel had a rapport with him. It was quite unusual for Graver to have a rapport with anybody; few people established any kind of personal relationship with Graver. He was reckoned in the staff room to be a pretty impenetrable pupil. Insofar as Graver took anything from school apart from the scars of bullying by other pupils, it was Mr Regel who taught him pretty well everything he knew. It was an odd relationship, more leading by example than verbal. It felt like forced feeding, with plenty of the forced: a most unusually mixed diet of zoology, biology, history of science, music and even a little philosophy, until Graver's mind could absorb no more. Taking it all in became a panic and an obsession. Could he take it all in and how could he gather even more knowledge? He cried at night with the frustration of not being able to stay at his desk any longer and keep on reading. Regel's obsession with German Romantic composers of the late nineteenth and early twentieth centuries gradually seeped into Graver's consciousness. He imagined resemblances between the lives of Bruckner and Mahler and his own life. Regel lent him records of their symphonies. He borrowed biographical studies of both composers and spent hours transported into their world, creating scenarios in which he faced and surmounted the difficulties of Bruckner's childhood. He empathised with Bruckner's loneliness and disappointments. Mahler in adulthood exemplified to him the heroic tyrant whom he admired and pretended he could emulate. He furnished first a bedroom, then a complete downstairs room in the farmhouse with icons associated with these two composers. The bedroom became the theatre for his intimate fantasies. The drawing room took on the character of a concert hall, with a podium and conductor's lectern as its dominant feature.

The laboratory, in contrast, was a Spartan place, compared with many. Most of the tables were bare, a few contained drawers or shelves, some looking as though they had never been opened. There were no chairs, just a couple of tall stools at the bench to the rear of the lab, under the bookshelves. These, too, were an apology for proper furnishing. They looked like someone's cast-offs rather than a well-used resource. A pile of dusty journals, some loose-leaf reports, untidily stacked, a desultory row of old works of scientific reference, a few copies of New Scientist. Across the lab, under the window was the single exception to its atmosphere of disuse – some piled cardboard boxes, apparently containing equipment of an unspecified nature. To the side of one of these, on the bench top lay a large, opened box, with a pile of packaging, some plastic and glass tubes and tubing.

* * *

The Senate sub-committee was urbane, scrupulously polite. Tom wouldn't have expected anything else of an upper middle-class Inquisition. The outcome was inevitable.

In the loo after the meeting, Tom let rip out loud with the bitterness of years of struggling to keep his Research Centre going. 'Bloody rationalisation, down-sizing, out-sourcing and all the rest.' The young lecturer from physics who emerged from an adjacent cubicle a few seconds later gave him a wary look as he washed his hands. Tom looked the other way. He had thought the toilet was empty.

Tom called at Hugh's office for the inevitable debrief. 'I'm sorry,' said Hugh, who was browsing through a copy of Nature. 'I'll do what I can to help. You can draft a letter for me to send to the Senate.' This was typical Hugh. It was what Tom called passive management, or management by default. Hugh wasn't one to act assertively on his own behalf. He relied on others to take the initiative. 'We can appeal to the research committee.'

Hugh became aware of Tom's irritated expression. 'I say, Tom, are you feeling off colour?'

'No, absolutely brilliant,' said Tom tonelessly. 'I love this game called work harder while we try to destroy what you're doing. The recommendation to put my unit on the line must have come from the research committee in the first place. If you haven't any more suggestions, I'll be going. I've some urgent tasks, postponed because of your sub-committee meeting.'

'I see.' Hugh's embarrassment and guilt was a wall between the two men. 'I want you to know, Tom, that this isn't my doing, or even my wish.'

Hugh's phone rang. He turned his head and picked up the receiver. At moments of stress, it didn't take much to distract him: 'Mackintosh, hullo, yes, ring you back in a couple of minutes.' He continued, as though they were still discussing the subcommittee.

'Good, good. So speculation apart we haven't anything further to add at this point.'

Tom looked puzzled, but Hugh continued. 'There's no mad rush. I suggest we take a break and you pop in after lunch with any further ideas.'

Tom, inwardly fuming, stood up and walked to the door: He knew further discussion was useless. Hugh's mind had moved on to whoever had phoned.

'I'll see you later,' said Hugh. Even before Tom reached the door, Hugh was picking up the phone.

Tom's anger blotted out rational thought as he walked through the gloomy lobby, past the Epstein bust of a previous professor of biology, out into the bright sunshine.

Chapter 21

Bradshaw was prepared to resource a blanket approach – screening every potential suspect in a thirty-mile radius of where the last two bodies were found. He pointedly ignored Chris's efforts to restrict the search initially to people connected with insects in some way, based on Tom's advice and the forensic evidence of insect predation.

'We have to scrutinise all University staff, past and present,' said Bradshaw. 'They're all privileged and they're all potentially corruptible.'

'They're all suspects in your book.' Chris had lost patience with his attitude. She was furious with his constant digs at Tom.

Bradshaw refused to answer but nodded sagely as though reserving some private information for later revelation to prove his point.

Chris was disappointed, though not fazed, by the lack of obvious progress in the general sweeps of groups of suspects. One of her colleagues once described this approach as building haystacks and then looking for needles in them. She had set aside time to trawl through the University herself and today was meeting the deputy chief administrative officer for Tom's department, Stella Lunik. She was the longest serving member of staff in the department, having been involved in every staff appointment for the past seventeen years, so clearly was a better source of information than the recently appointed head of administration, a Mr Coxwold. Stella was a wiry, silver-haired woman, always immaculately dressed in a tweed suit, one of those stalwarts of the organisation who has made it the centre of her life. They spent half an hour working systematically through past and present lists, with Chris taking copious notes.

After leaving Stella, Chris rang Tom on the off-chance they could meet.

'It won't take long,' she said. 'We've been talking about various technical and ancillary staff at the University, past and present, well, mostly past.'

'Anyone in particular?'

Chris consulted her notepad. 'A few in your department. Tomkins, Macmillan, Donaldson.' She paused and looked at Tom.

He looked non-committal.

'Walters, do you remember him?'

'Yes, in a manner of speaking.'

'What did he do here?'

'He was just a technician.'

'Not a very memorable staff member?'

'We have quite a turnover of ancillary and technical staff.'

'So I've noticed. You must make quite an impression. What did Walters do here?'

'What they all tend to do, supply general help in the labs.'

'And was he – did you notice anything distinctive about him?'

'Now you're asking. It's such a long time ago. I don't think so. We are probably all odd in a way, wanting to work with insects all day long.'

'In a manner of speaking.' She mimicked him. 'Your words, not mine. So he was a run of the mill employee?'

'I remember he could be obsessive. We all are about our research, you understand. It goes with the job. But he had particular hang-ups which seemed inappropriate.'

'In what way?'

Tom hesitated. 'He was over-interested in aspects of the work.'

'In what sense?'

'I don't know, really.' He screwed up his eyes as if peering into the past. 'His attitude to the ants, I suppose. He was completely obsessed.'

'With just the ants? No other insects or animals?'

'We don't have any animals, just insects.'

'Any other insects then?'

'No, it was ants. That was what stood out about him.'

'Nothing else, no grievances, no grudges?'

'Not so you'd notice.'

'What does that mean?'

'We do have technicians from time to time who have bees in their bonnets about their status.'

'That's a good metaphor, in this department.'

'Sorry.' He shrugged. 'Why the big interest in this man?'

'I've been looking at the people our trawl at the Station has turned up. This man's details may correspond with those of a man with a record for serious personal violence including at least two stretches inside.'

'You don't say.'

'I haven't had the time to check yet. I've just come from a very constructive meeting with your administrative officer.'

'Not Tim Coxwold?' Tom's tone indicated what a waste of time this was likely to be.

'Miss Lunik.'

Tom nodded approvingly. Good for Stella, he thought. What she didn't know about the University could be written on the back of a postage stamp.

'One last thing,' said Chris. 'Our check of tattooists may have turned up trumps. A tattoo parlour in Bridlington has a record of a man who wanted a tattoo of an ant on his chest.'

'What species?'

Chris snorted. 'Does it matter? I can't believe you scientists. The most important thing is who it was.'

'Who was it then?'

'We don't know. They don't keep a record of names or addresses.'

It was Tom's turn to snort and he took full advantage.

* * *

Tom and Luis Deakin were sitting in the office adjacent to the laboratory. It was late in the day, the hour when normally they'd wind down before one or both of them went home, or if the work demanded it, at least went to tea before returning for a late session.

'Am I keeping you?' asked Tom.

'No, filling in time,' said Luis, 'before the drama group.'

This was a side of Luis Tom hadn't appreciated. 'You're an actor.'

'Only in a very amateur sense. It's relaxation. Takes me totally away from work.' Deakin changed the subject. 'You're not convinced about the forensic analysis,' he observed.

'There's something not quite right about the police theory,' said Tom. 'I don't agree that the state of that body is simply the result of decomposition and rodent attack.'

'I can't comment, not having seen it.'

'I can't help thinking about a body I saw when we were on that South American trip.'

'The Departmental jamboree?"

'Not the big expedition, too dominated by taxonomists for me. I mean the small one, when we were trying to find out what made the army ant Eciton so successful as a mobile predator, above ant species with more static nests. Do you remember seeing the corpses of those two prisoners in the jail at St – what was it? I can't recall the name of the place now. They were left tethered to the wall and the ants got them.'

'I saw the photographs. Pretty gruesome. Manaus unless I'm thinking of somewhere else.'

'I can't get that story out of my mind,' said Tom, 'the one by H.G. Wells, about the empire of the ants. I know it's only a schoolboy fantasy. But there's something about the idea of the use of ants as a weapon.'

Thank goodness for colleagues like Luis, Tom thought afterwards. Undemanding, flexible yet reliable, always around when he wanted to relax and float a few ideas, or simply let off steam.

* * *

Helen and Laura stood outside the school waiting for the children to come out.

'We humans have missed our way somewhere,' said Helen. 'Queen ants have it made. The males are expendable after they've sown their oats; after that the queens don't lift a leg without a crowd of adoring workers rushing forward to attend to every need.'

'You really are into your husband's work,' said Helen.

'It's a general comment.' Laura's irritation showed. Helen backed off and dealt straightforwardly with her comment.

'It is a somewhat anthropomorphic view,' said Helen. 'I agree with the thrust of what you're saying. You're not one of those man-haters, though.'

Helen giggled. 'Not exactly. In my day, I was quite a man-eater really.' She put her head on one side, looking mischievous. 'Or even a man-chewer.'

Laura gave her a wry glance. 'Painful.'

'Can be fun when you're in the mood.'

Laura wriggled. She suddenly felt middle-aged and, difficult to admit, slightly disgusted. She was relieved the train of conversation at that moment was broken by the sound of the bell. Silence was transformed into a quake of footsteps and noise, which magnified second by second. Flashes of movement streaked along corridors on all sides. Then two doors burst open simultaneously from the buildings looking onto different sides of the playground and children ran out excitedly, yelling to each other like released prisoners.

'They're like bloody ants!' muttered Laura.

'Pardon? I didn't quite catch that.'

'Oh nothing. I was just thinking about how similar the children are to Tom's ants when something disturbs the nest. How they all come rushing out when they've been disturbed.'

'But the school hasn't been disturbed.'

'No, it hasn't,' Laura mused half to herself.

'The bell.'

'What?'

'It's the bell,' said Helen. 'A signal. They respond to the signal.'

'Yes, the bell. Of course, I see. The bell has gone.'

'Laura, are you sure you're all right.'

Laura came back to the present with a bump, as there was a combined shout of 'Hi, Mum!' and a couple of small bodies cannoned into her.

* * *

Graver planned so carefully. On the outside he held his life together quite easily. He put on the disguise which gave him the safety to develop a nodding association with Helen and the children, from the most casual of bases. It was easy to wait until most of the students had gone down in the summer, trawl the agencies without giving a real address, and identify some property available in the locality of the Lovelace household for a reasonably short term let. Although they occupied a large semi-detached Edwardian house in Victoria Avenue, a street of similar houses in the Avenues conservation area of town, an increasing number were divided into flats. The surrounding streets both towards and away from town contained much smaller, terraced houses. After a good deal of hunting around, he found what he was looking for; a tiny, two up two down terrace off Ella Street, literally in the next street from the Lovelaces. Pretending to be an occasional local visitor, away from his family, he paid three months rent in advance for the house. He used it on odd occasions, well disguised so that nobody who knew him in his other life could guess his identity.

From the window of the tiny rear bedroom, the boxroom, he looked out casually. Sarah and Matthew played on the wide strip of grass bordering the ten-foot area to the rear of the houses in the avenue. Nobody was around who would overlook his vantage point and raise suspicions.

Graver took a garden seat and magazines and sat near the thin hedge to one side of the garden. Now he was less than a dozen feet from the two children. He played it slowly. It would take time to build up trust.

* * *

Tom wondered how Chris was progressing with her inquiries. He was browsing through the rows of social insects books on the shelves in his office. It was difficult to envisage, but he supposed there was a precedent. The link with the present circumstances was tenuous. He had tried the memoirs of Bates on his explorations of the Amazon. He had an idea the nineteenth century explorer Paul Du Chaillu referred to army ants being used as a form of execution. The problem was how to source the reference.

Tom was walking down the corridor away from his office when the student buttonholed him. He didn't recognise her at first. He was preoccupied with many things, not least the chief inspector and the police investigation, but despite the fact that he was overdue for another appointment, he gave in to her request for a few minutes of his time.

'I shan't take up more than five minutes of your time, Professor Fortius,' she said.

'I'm all right for a few minutes, go ahead. I'm sorry, I can't place our last meeting.'

'Naomi Waterson. You may recall our meeting some time ago, when

I applied to register for a PhD on theoretical aspects of evolution in the social insects.'

Once she started talking, he recalled her distinctive accent – strongly Texas or thereabouts, overlaid on what could be rural East Anglian dialect – and much of the background. She had applied in the first place to do research on debates between adaptationism and structuralism in insect evolution. Tom wasn't keen to take on research students, particularly in areas that diverted him from his main interest, and even more so when there wasn't the obvious prospect of research money trailing behind in addition to the personal bursary or scholarship. He'd referred her to Luis and then lost track of her. That must have been a couple of years ago.

'Since I first contacted you and you referred me to your colleague Dr Deakin, I've been away to the States and back again, for domestic and employment reasons. But all the time I've continued to read round the subject I originally proffered in my application and I'm even more committed to continuing with my PhD. One of the things I've done is to search the literature. Explorers from Darwin onwards, including Henry Walter Bates in the Amazon and Thomas Belt in Nicaragua, through to our contemporaries such as Edward Ilson, have considered ant communication and the question of whether ants have the power to reason. I see this as irrelevant. I'd like to rewrite the history of science of the social insects around the thesis that ants are physiologically programmed and their behaviour, genetically and chemically, is determined by this programming.'

'I'm sure this is interesting,' admitted Tom, 'but it isn't for me at this time. I'm sure there are many fascinating issues to be explored. You might even build your doctorate round it, though I have to say that there would be some formidable barriers to grapple with in the literature, because you'd be writing entirely theoretically. I tend to stick to working with research students who are carrying out experimental work, collecting data empirically and reflecting on that.'

'Look, Dr Fortius, I get the message. If I don't toe the methodological line in your department, no PhD.'

'I didn't say that.'

'You don't have to. All that crap in your publicity for the Research Centre and in your lectures, about encouraging broader and more imaginative ways of looking at research into the social insects. I have to tell you, Dr Fortius that – that – rather than succumb to your authoritarian ways of thought and research, I'd rather terminate my studies in your department and seek a more sympathetic university environment.'

'Anywhere in particular?'

'Professor Apthorpe thinks my work is very interesting.'

'I guess he would.' Tom couldn't keep the acid out of his voice. He and Apthorpe were at polar extremes of most debates about animal and insect communication and behaviour.

She was a free agent and could do what she liked. She sounded as oppressive as she was accusing him of being. As she marched off, Tom was thinking half-heartedly he should have been more positive, but his head was full of other matters. He shrugged as she pushed the swing door open and disappeared from view.

* * *

Graver recalled how he'd first been impressed by a tattoo when he saw that big lad who held them all to ransom in the children's home, seeing him so fearless and hard, with the tattooed emblem across his forehead. It was no guarantee, but the chance that a skilfully chosen and well executed design – not like some of those self-inflicted lash-ups you saw on lads' knuckles and arms, and the necklace round their necks – would confer on him some of those qualities of confidence and influence he most envied in boys who were bigger and stronger. It was years later, when he had money in his pocket, that he set out to find a tattooist, not immediately in the vicinity of his job, but a good hour away.

It was easier to decide to go to the tattoo shop than to go in when he arrived. He paced up and down the pavement, like many before him though he did not know it. Of course, that was only the beginning of the problems. When he finally plucked up courage to push open the strange, star-studded and otherwise decorated door, he entered a half-light world with the quality of a cavern, at the far end of which was the little semicircle of chairs where the waiting began. This gave him ample time to ponder and brood over all the options: whether to, where to, what to have, how large to have it, how much it would cost, how to do it the way he'd read in a magazine at the hairdresser's, which was so that each time you could have a bit more added to the motif.

As for the motif, he already knew what it would be, how the six legs would be arranged, the head, the attitude of the head, pointing forward, out of his chest, the jaws opened to their fullest extent, the fearsome mandibles of the soldier ant.

Graver felt tension. He had to relieve it. He had a purpose and was turning the possibilities over in his mind. His target in the present was the University. There were some technical problems he was still grappling with. He wasn't quite ready to cope with the two children, running about outside. The subjects of his experiments – that was how he regarded them at the moment – needed to be contained. But it was time to try two at once. He had enough anger to overcome his other less trustworthy feelings. It was necessary to remain strong once he'd started. So a more emotionally distant, but more accessible target must be taken next, the Dean of Biological Sciences at the University, Hugh Mackintosh, and his wife. An interesting duo. They should prove a suitable test of his resources.

Chapter 22

Janie wasn't in when Hugh arrived home. She had a huge network of people whom she constantly e-mailed, phoned and met up with. 'Probably visiting friends,' said Hugh out loud to himself. He was distracted by the task of pouring himself a whisky. It had been a stressful day at the University.

An hour passed, two hours. Hugh was increasingly concerned. Three hours later, there was still no word from Janie. Hugh was worried. It wasn't like her. He paced about the house for a further hour, at the end of which Tom rang from the office, about a detail of the budget which was niggling him. Hugh was clearly so distracted that Tom asked what the matter was.

Tom drove straight to Hugh's house, where he found Hugh wandering in a daze. After letting Tom in, Hugh tripped over the coal scuttle and nearly measured his length on the hearth; he was within a couple of centimetres of knocking himself out on the marble surround. He balanced precariously on one knee on the hearth, risking sparks landing on his trousers from the spitting log fire on the open grate.

Tom helped him over to the nearest armchair. 'Come and sit down,' said Tom, very concerned. 'I'll make you a cup of tea.'

Thunder prowled over the distant Wolds like a pack of wild dogs, hungry for prey. Tom went off to boil the kettle. The phone rang. Hugh pounced on the receiver.

'Hullo, thank God it's you, Janie. Where have you been?'

Tom stuck his head round the kitchen door and waved to attract Hugh's attention. 'Keep her talking,' he mouthed. 'I'll ring the police from the line in your study. Hopefully they'll trace the number.'

Janie's voice sounded faint. 'Hugh, can you hear me?'

'Janie, darling, are you all right?'

Another voice came onto the line and spoke quietly into Hugh's ear. 'Please, don't let anything happen to her,' Hugh begged.

'I'm giving you five seconds,' said the voice.

'Don't! Wait.'

There was rustling at the other end of the phone.

'Hullo, hullo!'

'Hugh.' The voice was weak. 'Is that you?'

'This is me, Janie.'

'You won't ever leave me, darling.'

'No, of course not.'

The tears flowed silently down his crumpled face.

'Come and take me home.'

'I will.'
'Tell me you're coming now.'
Tom was back in the room. Hugh covered the phone with his hand.
'For God's sake, what can I say?'
'Tell her you'll be there,' said Tom.
He took his hand off the mouthpiece.
'I'm on my way, darling.'
The phone clicked.
'Janie, Janie.'
The line was dead. Hugh's eyes were moist. He bit his lip and turned to Tom.
'What can I do? Did they trace the call?'
Tom shrugged. 'They'll ring and let us know.'
At that moment the phone rang. Tom walked to the hall and picked it up. There was a brief exchange. He replaced the receiver and came back.
'Damn.'
Hugh was beside himself with anxiety. 'Didn't they do it?'
'Not enough time, apparently.'
'But surely – I thought that was the idea of all this technology.'
The police are setting up a tap on this number. You're to let them know if you have any other further contact with this person.'

Chris faced Bradshaw in his office.
'Why did you leave Hugh Mackintosh like that?'
'I said we'll do the tap. All calls will be recorded.'
'You treated him like a suspect. The man's a victim, anyone can see that.'
'I did not say he's a suspect.'
'Something else for your little academic coterie to consider, Chief Inspector.' Bradshaw tossed a folder across the desk. 'When you've a minute spare from drinking coffees in the senior common room at the University, let me have your opinion on where these came from.' Chris opened the folder and peered in. They appeared to be faxes to Tom's Centre from an unnamed person, dated five years ago.
'Who gave you these?'
'You aren't the only repository of information in this Station. These were given to one of our DCs on a routine trawl of University staff.'
'I thought we'd agreed all information would be passed through me.'
'I'm passing it. Anything more?'
Back in her office, Chris had time to study the faxes. They were sent on the same day. Each was in the same tone, a vitriolic attack on the integrity of Tom's work, the reputation of the Centre and, in particular, the procedures for selecting staff.

She was on the phone to Tom. 'I've had it up to here with Bradshaw,' she said.

'The question is, does he do the business?'

'Yes, but in the face, rather than on the basis of respect for people.'

'Your superintendent sounds rather like Dr Dollent,' said Tom.

Chris looked icily at him. 'Whose side are you on? He isn't my superintendent.'

Tom put up a placating hand. 'I didn't mean it like that. Let me tell you about Dr Dollent. He was George Simenon's creation. Very successful too, for his author, although by no means as well known as Inspector Maigret. He also had a habit of approaching cases in an unorthodox way.'

'Did Dr Dollent make a mess of things?'

'No, he was rather successful, despite his eccentricities.'

'Forget him, there isn't much resemblance.'

* * *

Hugh crouched at the wheel of his car and drove through the gathering dusk. He'd received another phone message, less than ten minutes after Tom had left and fifteen minutes before the phone tap was in place.

'I'm coming, Janie darling. Soon you won't need to worry any more.'

* * *

Tom was musing on the implication of the faxes. He'd asked Jean to confirm with Stella the names of candidates for all departmental vacancies for the previous six months.

He called into one of the insect laboratories and found a trio of research students poring over one of the observation nests.

'Watch out,' said Tom. 'One's going into the nest.'

There was a pause. Then half a dozen ants rushed excitedly from the entrance, casting about on all sides as though searching for something.

'What are they doing?' asked Colin Nixon, a new student whose research topic was parasitic cuckoo bees in bumble bee nests.

'Keep watching,' said Roger Farriday, a potentially brilliant student of communication between the social insects and currently the boyfriend of Naomi Waterson.

After a few seconds, four of the ants struck out in the same direction as the incoming one. The other two were still milling about. One of the four seemed to hesitate and turned back towards the next. But the other three persisted.

'Hmm, not bad,' mused Tom. 'Some inefficiencies I'd say, but given large enough numbers it gets the job done.'

'How do they do it?' asked Nixon. 'Is it memory?'

'Donisthorpe's pyramid, from way back in 1924,' said Farriday.

'How do they remember?'

Farriday answered again. 'Whether or not you call it memory is a moot point. In any case, whether it is memory or physiological responses from what Wragge Morley called excitement centre ants to the rest, is immaterial. The fact is that great numbers overcome the inevitable inefficiencies of insect error and ensure overwhelming success most of the time, in a pyramid of communication. Or a chain reaction. Make the calculation. Assuming one ant communicates with another in a tenth of a second, that's up to 500 in the first second and up to half a million in the next. Even allowing for a fifty per cent drop out, that's one huge geometric progression. Just think, in less than half an hour every ant on the planet would be on line.'

'The pyramid sounds a powerful explanation, but surely it's too elementary to be real.'

'Remember this rule of Nature. The simpler the mechanism the more powerful its effects. It's the key to success among the social insects.'

Tom intervened. 'Ants communicate with each other. They signal using their antennae. Whether we call this a language or a series of behavioural cues and responses is debatable. It is a highly effective form of communication.' As he spoke he was thinking with irritation of the whereabouts of the antennation equipment. All that effort to develop the technology to stimulate ants' antennae. Other priorities, with appropriate funding which was the driving force, had taken over. He continued: 'In this department we've been carrying out a number of research projects into how ants use their antennae to communicate. Communication is the means by which ant societies capitalise on individual gains. The continuance of the colony as a competitive collective depends on the richness of interaction between individual ants, and, specifically, on the effectiveness of communication, in terms of the speed with which messages from one ant are relayed to more or less the entire affected population. Communication does not have to be absolutely one hundred per cent efficient, but it has to reach a critical mass in ten thousand daily situations requiring a mass response – whether defending or repairing the nest, or overwhelming rapidly moving prey – in order to meet the necessities of their collective life. 'Do you know what marks out ants from many other insects and even animals, birds and fish?'

'They're social,' said Nixon.

'Be more specific. What does that entail?'

'They can jump, swim and play.'

'I admit they are qualities of some species. But more broadly than that, give me an attribute of ants in general.'

'You've got me.'

'As I was saying, apart from communicating with their antennae, they leave scent trails with their abdomens, which gives them the power to retrace their steps and encourage other ants to follow them. So they can negotiate mazes.'

Nixon looked incredulous. Tom continued. 'Their ability to do this is far superior to that of rats.'

'I don't see that as too useful. Surely they don't encounter many mazes in everyday life.'

'Quite the contrary. A worker ant's entire life relies heavily upon the negotiation of labyrinths – above and below ground. Think about their nests. Mostly in complete darkness. Hundreds, thousands of metres of tunnels and galleries, each with different functions. The larger ant cities consisting of more tunnels than there are alleys in Bombay or Glasgow. If you watch them under infra-red bulbs – you can see them but as far as they're concerned it's pitch dark – they move round the nest with a confidence and speed which makes it impossible to regard them as mindless. Without a doubt they store a map in their memory of at least part of that complexity. How do they do it with such allegedly primitive brain cells?'

'Maurice Maeterlinck the philosopher studied cooperation between ants in building walls. He referred to examples of this kind in discussions about the boundary between instinct and intelligence. I think he was attempting to prevent the ant world on one hand being compared too closely with human societies, and on the other being dismissed as having no links at all with other social forms of living. At different times he considered whether the nest was an example of pure harmony – whether of autocracy, democracy or instinctively based – or a kind of organised chaos with the survival of ant societies resulting purely from their overwhelming numbers. He considered other issues too, such as whether ants felt and demonstrated affection for their brood and altruism in sacrificing themselves to protect their fellows, and the queen in particular.'

'One moment.' Tom walked to the office at one end of the laboratory. He pulled an old and well used book off the shelf and returned to where the students stood. He patted the book, as though welcoming a colleague to their discussion. 'Maeterlinck's Life of the Ant. Let's see if I can find the quote. Ah yes.' He thumbed the book open at one of many bookmarks. 'Here we are, page thirty-five. "The ant is one of the noblest, most courageous, most charitable, most devoted, most generous, and most altruistic creatures on earth." Although Maeterlinck raised the charge of anthropomorphism against some of the cruder comparisons made between human and ant societies, he didn't fundamentally challenge such a view. What is significant is that Maeterlinck's work in the 1930s on the life of the ant which followed his publications on the life of the bee and the life of the white ant, showed remarkable similarity with the work of Eugene Marais, the South African writer, who from 1928 switched his attention from publications on *the soul of the baboon* to theorising about the analogy between the individual nest of termites and the animal as an organism. He has a place alongside the great names of the natural history of the social insects and ants in particular Rene-Antoine Ferchault de Reaumur, William Morton Wheeler of Harvard, Pierre Huber, Auguste Forel and Emery the taxonomist of myrmecology.'

At this point, Farriday entered the discussion. 'But wasn't Maeterlinck remiss in not acknowledging his debt to Eugene Marais, for developing the idea of the insect colony as a composite animal? Even though Marais as a South African was relatively unknown in Europe in the late 1920s and early 1930s, his articles on this subject were reported in the French and Belgian press at the time of publication. In any case Maeterlinck would have been able to read the original articles, since they were published in Afrikaans and the similarity between this and Flemish to a Flemish intellectual would have made it easy to make sense of them.'

Tom shrugged: 'Scientific research is not exempt from human frailties, I admit. But it's the ideas which are interesting rather than the people behind them.'

* * *

Once Graver got the hang of setting the antennation machine up, it was easy to pass messages on. Communication was so effective among the driver ants that moments after changing the signal, a ripple of responses would go along the files travelling the pathways into the woods and out again. He was pretty well beside himself with delight about the floodlights. He leapt about his solitary shelter talking to himself like a person possessed.

'Yes, turn the lights up. Keep focusing on the nest,' he called out loud. 'The more heat you generate, the faster they can move towards their targets.'

The level of activity in the insects was positively correlated with the temperature. The hotter it was, the better. Up to the point, that is, where the increased heat caused their systems to break down. Once this happened individual ants would progress quickly from hyperactivity to death. This was the fate of an observation nest of Formica Sanguinea, slave-making ants, which he had left on a window sill in the laboratory, returning a few hours later to find the sun had come out and was shining directly on the glass over the foraging area. Virtually all the ants had emerged to sun themselves and forage, before dying in a frenzy of over-activity.

* * *

The directions had been difficult to follow, but Hugh had managed to drive there. His entire body felt weak and a fit of dizziness overtook him as he stood up. He wondered momentarily if this was what happened when people had a stroke. He stood in the large porch. His hand shook as he found the doorbell in the gloom and pressed it. Then when this apparently produced no result he used the door knocker. The sound echoed in the silent countryside and seemed to go on echoing in his head.

'So, Dr Mackintosh.'

'You know my name.'

'Everyone at the University knows you.'

Ah, thought Hugh, this was a student perhaps, or a former student. There were so many that he couldn't possibly recognise all the people who apparently knew him. The voice was muffled, through one of those voice distorters, he thought.

'You don't recognise my voice do you, Dr Mackintosh?'

'I'm afraid not.' Hugh couldn't keep the tremor in his voice under control.

'Listen carefully, Dr Mackintosh, if you want to see your wife again.'

Hugh's heart leapt. So Janie was here. He cared not at that moment for any other consequences, but only for seeing her.

'Is she safe?'

'Yes, provided you do exactly what I say.'

'I must warn you –' began Hugh.

'Shut up,' the man cut in. 'If you want to see your wife. Keep listening and keep your mouth shut.'

'I'm sorry. I –'

'In the box on the shelf to your left, you'll find a blindfold. Put it on.'

Hugh's hand trembled so much he could hardly complete this task. A wave of dizziness overcame him and he thought he'd pass out.

'Push open the door.'

Standing inside the house, Hugh jumped as a hand gripped his right arm firmly.

'Shut up and keep walking. Left here. Down two steps. Through this door. A moment, out of the way. Stand still.'

Hugh heard the man produce a key. He pushed roughly past Hugh, unlocking the door swiftly and pulling back before Hugh could think to react.

'Open it and push it open.'

As Hugh obeyed he felt an enormous blow in the small of his back which forced all the wind from his lungs and propelled him forward violently into the utter blackness of the space ahead. He was so disoriented and dazed that he hardly noticed the prick of the hypodermic.

There was very little time. Mahler's tenth symphony moved into its third movement – the allegro moderato headed Purgatorio, which lasted less than four minutes.

Graver's stomach was queazy with anticipation. He leaned forward in the near-pitch darkness and seized the shoulder of the befuddled man, pressing the hypodermic into the upper arm and pressing its syringe before the confused senses of the man enabled him to react. The drug would ensure his skin was subjected to multiple punctures – as when bitten by ten thousand ants – without him feeling the full intensity of the pain.

In the absolute darkness of moonless night, Hugh tried at the very last moment to prevent himself from falling into the deep pit, but with arms waving wildly, pitched headlong into its black depths. Across the corner of the pit was the log Graver had placed strategically to support the largest of the branches with which he had then disguised it. It was this log which the intruder had now tripped over, clutching hopelessly and bringing it down with him when he lost his balance. By a bleak coincidence, the entire nest of army ants had chosen to bivouac in a huge pear-shaped swarm half a metre wide and twice as deep on the underside of this log, around the attractive protection of its hollowed out centre. Lying semi-conscious on the damp ground, his legs hopelessly twisted and partly hidden under the ball of ants, Hugh became vaguely aware of the movements of a myriad tiny feet on his legs. The ball bubbled like a volcano. The soldiers boiled first from its hissing centre and ran blindly about as the angry workers rushed forwards in an unstoppable stream. Thousands upon thousands of them slipped under his torn trouser legs and sank their jaws into his quivering flesh.

Mercifully, by the time they reached his neck, he was already out of his mind and when the first ants bit into the tender skin inside his nostrils and lips, he had already lost consciousness. Their appetite for flesh was so keen that less than ten minutes after the first attack, when they laid part of his heart bare under his rib cage, it was still beating. Five minutes later there was no sound beyond the irrepressible rhythm of their ticking legs as they skittled back and forth, carrying chunks of grim booty from the body to their brood in the nest.

Janie wasn't aware of the faint clicking of the antennator, as its leaf like pendants flickered away inside the nest entrance. It could have operated silently, but Graver had introduced the sounds so that when it was placed out of sight inside the nest, he could confirm it was working. She couldn't see him peering at her from behind the one-way glass either, stopwatch, notepad and pen at the ready. He didn't need to use artificial antennation after the initial phase, but was keen to compare the speed of "completion", as he termed it, with the previously recorded observations using various animals' heads without its stimulus.

It was hot. She found it was impossible to exclude the craving for water from her mind. From time to time she looked towards Hugh. It was an effort twisting her head round. She tried to look solely by moving her eyes, but this made them ache. She'd given up trying to attract his attention. He didn't respond any more to her hand movements, or to her calling, and she still wasn't sure whether he'd heard her earlier.

There was a click. It gave her a shock. Not so much the loudness as the fact of a single movement from outside herself. At first she couldn't make out the direction from which it had come. But almost immediately her eye was drawn to a movement on the right edge of her sight. She knew as soon as she swivelled her eyes painfully round and saw the knot of ants bubbling from the newly opened semicircular hole, that all these events were the purposeful preparations for a drama that was now too horrible even to contemplate.

Graver retreated rapidly via a small, tight-fitting door and regained his vantage point behind the glass. He was watching and speaking into the microphone:

'The soldier form of the army ant Eciton Burchelli has reddish, sickle-shaped mandibles which would not disgrace those centimetre diameter reddish clamps brandished by the two-inch male stag beetle. These more fearless and aggressive ants rush forward ahead of the remaining army. Performing their massive biting movements, they place the first strategic markers in the larger prey, horribly disfiguring or even cutting it in two. The wounds they inflict on large animals can be truly horrendous if they happen to dig their huge jaws into a region of softer flesh, or strike a blood vessel in the process.'

Janie braced herself and clenched her teeth as the first scuttling ants reached her and sank their mandibles into the pulsating flesh of her wrists. She beat her hands wildly and shook these off whilst others ran further on towards her half-buried neck.

Graver was revisiting earlier memories, too deep and obscure to be recovered. When he saw the head with the eye sockets basically empty save for a sliver of liquid which had run down the torn cheeks, he remembered a similar appearance in an account of survivors of the atomic bomb dropped on Hiroshima.

'The first time you stuff the mouth full of formicas, it's pretty difficult.

After that, it gets easier. I used to find it was the doing which was the hurdle. Now it's more the planning, because in the nature of this method I've adopted, carrying it out follows a predictable sequence and I'm segregated from it.'

Janie thought she saw Hugh's head twitch under its thick carpet of ants, from which a straggling line emerged as individuals were already beginning to carry away indescribable chunks of booty. Weakened by the blood seeping from thousands of tiny bites, Janie's hands and arms lay helplessly pinioned by the weight of tens of thousands of bodies.

As more and more ants frothed from the hole and foamed across the sand towards her, she began to experience the unbounded terror of the paralysed victim. But as yet she was still inhibited from opening her mouth to scream, in case the horde on her face, already burrowing away at her nose and ears, crowded into her mouth.

Graver's voice had faded away. He watched, hypnotised. The entire scene was suffused with sound as the final movement of the Mahler reached its climax.

Chapter 23

Tom was about to knock on the door when he realised it was ajar. He gave it a push and looked round. The surprise was that Chris Winchester sat on the desk, crying in almost complete silence. She started at the sight of him, slid off the desk and turned away, dabbing her eyes with a tissue.

'Hey,' he said, 'I shouldn't be here.'

'No, please stay,' she said quickly enough for him to realise she meant it.

Tom was embarrassed and made for a small table on which sat a kettle, coffee and a couple of mugs.

'Let me make myself useful,' he said.

'I'll have one,' she said. 'You're not used to the iron fist of the law crumpling up.'

'We must stop meeting like this,' Tom said jovially, to hide his nervousness.

'If you say so,' said Chris, then regretted it.

He made two mugs of coffee and she seemed to relax a little.

'I wanted to say sorry,' she said, 'for the way I barged into your private life.'

'No problem,' said Tom. 'I've enjoyed the barging.' He realised as he said it how much it was true.

They were talking over the coffees.

'I wanted to take up science as a child,' he said. He stood up and stretched his legs. 'Being a research scientist isn't so glamorous when you look at the wear and tear on your body. Staring through microscopes for hours at a time is bad for the eyes, the neck and the shoulder muscles, the backbone and, for good measure, the circulation. To say nothing of the mental stress of struggling to get reports written and published, whilst between times competing with your colleagues in other universities for further research grants. My job is to keep two moves ahead of possible competitors in the grant-seeking stakes.'

'Hmm, life at the top. What a penance! You make being a professor sound like a punishment.'

'You've caught me on a mediocre day.'

'Me too and I'm sorry. I do have good days.'

'You can tell me about them some time.'

'The original purpose of Robin's unit was to examine the migration of pests. But over time what constitutes a pest has proved somewhat flexible. Basically, we follow the money. If there's a grant going, we'll consider it.'

'So now?'

'Hang on,' Tom said. He felt this questioning was too one-sided. 'I could do with finding out a little more about you.'

'You'll have to wait until your job gives you the excuse.'

'I'm not patient enough.'

'Then you'll be a frustrated old man.'

'Hey, less of the old.'

'Anyway,' Chris said, ignoring him, 'my life looks too boring and ordinary alongside your high flying career, rubbing shoulders with high profile people.'

'It doesn't feel that way under the skin,' he mused, as though thinking aloud to himself. 'A lot of the time an injection of normalcy wouldn't come amiss.'

'What about the answer to my question?' she persisted.

'Okay,' said Tom with resignation. 'We've a grant from a large honey processor, for example, to investigate the spread of varoa in bees.'

'I've heard of that. Isn't it some kind of disease?'

'It's a mite actually. Like many parasites, its main aim in life is to live off its host rather than kill it. Once it becomes established it's impossible to eradicate it without chemical means. If unchecked it weakens the hive to the point where the bees can only survive and their proneness to disease is vastly increased. Most important, no honey surplus is produced. Multiply this by several hundred beehives in an apiary, each normally producing fifty to eighty kilos per year at one pound sterling per kilo, and you're talking about an economic catastrophe for the bee farmer. My colleague Robin Lovelace supervises a team trying to understand the life cycle of the mite, to establish whether it has natural predators which could be used as a substitute for chemical controls. If we could offer the producer these, then the word "organic" could still be used on the honey jar, at an enormous premium to the producer.'

'Sounds impressive.'

'The spread of the varoa mite from central Europe to the UK since the mid-1980s has taken the bee farming industry by surprise. This has led to the current work of Robin's unit on the impact of global warming more generally on insect migration. They're doing some pretty speculative work on the possible conditions under which locust swarms might move to the present Mediterranean zone and devastate wine and sweet corn crops in the more intensively farmed parts of Spain, Portugal and southern France. Apart from that, they're carrying out studies in Europe of the movements of populations of fleas, and diseases such as rabies as well as some rather sensitive and confidential research into the migratory habits of some of the more aggressive species of bees and wasps.'

'Why confidential?'

'You wouldn't like to be mayor in a south coast or Norfolk seaside resort which advertised killer wasps and bees along with sunshine, would you?'

'Point taken.'

'Which brings us back to ants,' he added.

'Tell me how?'

'There's an open question about the minimum climatic conditions necessary to sustain, say, a species of harvester ants which formerly could only live in countries regarded as subtropical. You could say that Robin and his colleagues have without funding been examining this question informally, but in anticipation of a growing demand once certain data on insect migrations hits the mass media.'

'You're talking in riddles, I'm afraid. Decode all this for me.'

He took a deep breath. She held up her hand. 'But not now. One thing I was going to ask you. How old are ants?'

'Do you mean how long-lived are ants, or how old is the ant family in evolutionary history?'

'The latter.'

'The answer to that is being revised. Until recently, it was thought that ants were relatively young, though still millions of years before primates, apes and humans. But fossil ants have been found in Baltic amber which are fifty million years older than previous ant fossils. So when dinosaurs stomped the Cretaceous rain forests there were ants scurrying beneath their feet and on the branches of the giant trees around them.'

'Okay. That's all I've time for, sorry.'

As though to reinforce her words, a personal bleeper concealed somewhere on her person began to give out a series of insistent sounds.

'I suggest another meeting, when we've more time,' she called out, already halfway to the door. 'Byee.'

Who's in demand now, Tom mouthed as she cupped the handset against her ear.

'It's not me they want,' she whispered, 'but the uniform.'

'I should bloody well hope so,' he hissed.

'Bye,' he said to himself as she disappeared into the corridor, talking rapidly into the handset while waving towards him half over her shoulder.

* * *

E-mail Tom to Robin:

Things are hotting up here. No time to explain in detail,

but great suspicions re possible connection between former employee and unexplained murders in the area. By the way, a particular query about one of your references. Can you supply more details of Walters, .E., 1990, pp. 324-56? It's listed, but the title and journal came through as unreadable as though I'd handwritten them myself.

Regards,

Tom

Tom checked his e-mail several times over the next two hours. He didn't know how much Greenwich inter Time was ahead of Brazil. He knew Robin was capable of working straight through the night on his computer.

Chris was out of the office for a couple of hours. When she returned, Morrison had left three almost identical messages on her voicemail. She rang back.

'I wondered where you were, boss. I've been tracking e-mails.'

She considered a flippant response and was glad she hadn't, when he continued: 'It's Dr Robin Lovelace at the University. Am I right that he's on University business in Africa?'

'Basically, if that's what the list Tom Fortius supplied says, that's where he is.'

'He may be, but for the past few days at least, his e-mail messages haven't been coming from Africa, but from an address in England.'

* * *

Chris called unannounced at Tom's office. She stood half in and half out of the room. 'Sorry to burst in. Have you a minute? I must check some information with you.'

'I'm literally on my way out and am already ten minutes late for a meeting.' Tom was puzzled. Her face was sombre. This was serious.

'Two minutes,' said Tom. She closed the door behind her.

'I have to check this with you. It appears your deputy Robin isn't in Africa as we thought. I'm beginning to wonder if he ever left the country.'

'What! That's impossible.'

'We've confirmed the information. He's been in Yorkshire for at least the past three days. Furthermore, and more delicate, he's been having an affair.'

'Oh?'

'You didn't know.'

'Robin's always having relationships.'

'Tom, I'm very sorry.'

She looked down. He saw her expression and experienced one of those agonising awakenings of understanding which seem to go on for ages, but probably occupy only a few seconds. Chris stole a glance at his face. As a police officer she'd had to give many people bad news and she hated every nuance of it.

He was shaking his head. 'No, not Laura, it can't be.'

'You're positive?'

Tom was looking away. He shook his head. 'No, unfortunately, I'm not positive. The bastard.'

'I'm sorry, I assumed you'd know.'

'I didn't know about the affair, but yes, I knew what complete crap it is between Laura and me. I didn't want any of it to impinge on anything between you and me.'

'How could it? There isn't anything between us, not in that way.'

Tom saw her face and coloured up. 'Of course there isn't. It wasn't relevant. That's what I mean.'

'Let's get one thing clear. I need information. I'll decide what's relevant, but at this stage I need to know everything which might have a bearing on how you and your colleagues behave.'

'I'm sorry.' He felt a fool. He didn't know Chris and she didn't know him. He cursed himself, hardly knowing what for. Perhaps he was taking too much for granted.

She must have sensed his discomfiture. 'Look, I can see you're busy. I'll ring you again.'

She closed the door quickly and was gone. Tom didn't move for a minute of so.

'Damn,' he exclaimed out loud, driving one fist into the palm of his other hand. 'Damn, damn, damn!'

* * *

At ten in the morning Tom's door opened and Robin burst in.

'How could you?' Robin exclaimed.

'What?'

'You let them think I could kill somebody.'

'I don't know what you're talking about.'

'Somebody in this place does.' Robin turned and was on his way out.

'Before you go, please explain how you've managed to turn up here whilst e-mailing me from another continent.'

Robin looked embarrassed. 'I managed to slip away for a few days.'

'I suppose that's how you've carried on with Laura.'

You're managing to look stunned, Tom thought.

'Laura? I don't know what you're talking about.'

'I'm talking about the affair you've been conducting with my wife, the wife of your longstanding friend and colleague.'

Tom had never seen Robin change so quickly. His face seemed to collapse into unhappiness. He slumped into the office chair.

'Tom, I'm so sorry.'

'Not as sorry as I am at losing the friend I thought I had.'

'It isn't like you think.'

'Unfortunately, it is. Now clear out of my office before I do something I might regret.'

After the disastrous meeting with Robin, Tom was on the phone to Chris.

'Where is he?' she wanted to know.

'In his office I suppose. I didn't ask where he was going.'

Half an hour later Tom's phone rang. It was Helen and she was near hysterical.

'Robin's been arrested, on suspicion.'

Tom was staggered. So this was what lay behind Robin's remark. 'On suspicion of what?'

It took a while to calm Helen down. He promised to ring the police, find out what he could and call her back. He dialled Chris's direct number and within a couple of minutes wished he hadn't.

'Bradshaw's adamant. Look at it from his point of view. We have a suspect with a motive and no alibi.'

'What motive, for God's sake?'

'Come on, Tom, look at the facts. Whichever way you turn there are questions.'

'There are questions, so he's the convenient new arrival who becomes number one suspect.'

'He needs to explain his movements.'

'What possible motive could he have?' asked Tom.

'Your research unit's under threat from the management and you can ask that?'

'You believe it too.'

'I didn't say that.'

Tom's tone was harsh with anger. 'You don't have to. Actions speak louder than words.'

'There have been other killings, connected with your neck of the woods, Tom.'

'You mean my department. Serial adulterer Robin may be Multiple murderer, never.'

Part Three

Fission

Chapter 24

Tom was not a great churchgoer. Nevertheless he was moved by the funeral service for Hugh and Janie. Partly, it was the gravity of the occasion, the slow procession of the coffin down the knave of Beverley Minster, the hush over waiting rows of people in the crowded church. He couldn't imagine more than a dozen people who would attend his own funeral, yet people were waiting outside the Minster for this man's coffin to re-emerge, because every seat inside was taken. For the most part, it was the playing of a particular hymn from childhood and his mother's funeral which brought Tom close to breaking down. 'All things bright and beautiful, all creatures great and small.' Perhaps that was where he'd started with his obsession with ants. Who knows how these things work, he thought. In the depths of our minds?

Afterwards, people milled around in their hundreds outside the Minster; cars and taxis queuing for lifts to the crematorium. Tom hung around on the edge of the crush, avoiding contact with people. At one point he thought he saw Apthorpe talking to a group of research students. He had a way of attracting students. They seemed to like his avuncular manner. He was non-threatening in a kind of traditional way. Apthorpe irritated Tom in every way. He had the gift, if that's what it was, of attracting females. Tom was sure that was Naomi Waterson close to him, almost touching his arm. If anyone was a murderer, it was Apthorpe, not Robin.

Tom swivelled round to set his mind on other, more constructive thoughts. He caught sight of Chris standing across the street, staring into the crowd. He knew she'd written Robin off as a suspect and after this latest double killing was waiting for the chance to convince Bradshaw. Bradshaw, on the other hand, had to go through the ritual of adding this to the evidence of Robin's guilt. He worked with Mackintosh in the same part of the University, dammit. But then so did fifteen hundred other staff and students.

Chris was watching the black-suited men pacing to and fro, looking at the ground, mixing, exchanging a few words here and there.

What does a killer do in such circumstances, she wondered? That is, if their killer was there. Perhaps this was part of it for him. Perhaps he'd come to gloat. He could even be one of the mourners. She checked herself. That was moving in the direction of Bradshaw's thoughts. It was too obvious.

* * *

Graver couldn't sleep. The choir from the Minster echoed round the coils of his brain. The voices were growing too loud. He started shouting. Sometimes it was the only way to drown them out.

He found another way to a kind of temporary relief. The disembodied voices singing Bruckner's *Os Justi* motet wafted through the drawing room. The cadences fell gently, tone by tone into near silence. Graver was back in Palestrina's sixteenth century, where he seemed to find peace. There, all emotions were woven into abstract sounds which stretched them, pulling feelings in fine threads into infinity. Soon they became ethereal, translucent as glass and held only by gossamer to their points of origin.

His words and actions took off like music into the air, floating like clouds, dispersing as they rose towards the upper atmosphere. Even so was the mating of queens and males. The tiny bodies spiralled upwards, opposites drawn together again and again as each queen mated several times, another spent male tumbling to earth as if dead after each once-in-a-lifetime encounter.

Graver considered the pheromones produced by every queen to attract males. He had a vision of his body sweating from every orifice, but wasn't repelled by this. He wanted the smell to be strong and unavoidable. He would stop washing. He took off all his clothes.

The scraping of stridulating segments of the abdomens of the females was the final spur to the males. The accumulating excitement of the males led to females being clasped repeatedly, long after they were sated. Less a mating of equal and opposite beings than an orgy, a mass rape, near-suicide by males unable to stem their carnal urges.

Afterwards the air hummed with the gentle sound of females burring to earth, satisfied, albeit with tattered wings. That no longer mattered. As soon as they landed they would shed their wings by rubbing the joint with their shoulders against some convenient twig or pebble. They would never need to fly again.

The males would never fly again either. The ground beneath was littered already with spent and dying males, too weak to move and incapable of feeding themselves to replenish their energy. Those that weren't picked off by birds and other predators in the hours before nightfall would have little chance of surviving the cool night air.

Graver's only chance of surmounting this ritual, psychologically was to think himself into the circumstances of the queens. He was ready to multiply.

* * *

Morrison was off duty soon after lunch. He spent a couple of hours at the University library on his way home that afternoon and pored over the half dozen books he had borrowed, well into the early hours of the morning. He was already sitting at his desk when Chris walked by before 8:00 a.m. that morning, conversing with Bradshaw. Bradshaw was an early starter, usually at work well before 8:00 a.m. He lived alone. His work had long since replaced the spaces once occupied by the company of other people, including women and leisure. He worked now because there was so little else to do.

Morrison thought Bradshaw looked as pleased as Punch, no doubt because he had a suspect in custody. Morrison left his desk, heading for Chris, but at that moment a nearby phone rang and she seemed happy to be called away. He walked into the corridor and found Bradshaw staring at him.

'Can I do something?' Bradshaw asked.

'A minute of your time, please, sir.' Bradshaw was staring at Morrison as though trying to figure out whether he'd really wanted to speak to Chris. 'What is it?'

'I've been doing some work on the notes our killer sends.'

'Sent,' said Bradshaw. 'Past tense. He won't be sending any more.'

Morrison looked baffled. He was thinking this had been a mistake. He should have exercised patience.

'We've a suspect from the University, bang to rights,' Bradshaw said.

'I must speak to you about that, sir,' said Morrison.

'You should talk to your senior officer,' said Bradshaw.

'I don't think we've found the killer yet.'

'This isn't the time for theoretical speculations,' said Bradshaw to Morrison over one shoulder. 'A word of advice, Constable. Stick to the task in hand.'

Morrison found Chris half an hour later. 'We're looking for somebody with a major mental disorder, boss. Irrespective of motive or opportunity, Dr Lovelace isn't that person.'

'It isn't me you have to convince, but Superintendent Bradshaw.'

'I just tried. I can't speak to him direct, but you can.'

Chris was being pushed from two conflicting positions. Bradshaw wanted pressure put on Robin and speedy progress towards him being charged, whilst Tom was urging her to lay off Robin. He was convinced their most likely suspect was Walters. Chris knew in her heart of hearts Robin was a no-no, but it took her a while to track Bradshaw down. He was in the car park waiting for a car to take him to a reception at City Hall for a party of visiting police chiefs from the Netherlands. She was just in time. The car was coming through the car park entrance.

'We've no evidence, sir, so we've nothing to charge him with and no reason to hold him.'

'I can't discuss it now. I'll be away the rest of the day.'

'It can't wait till tomorrow, sir. We're in a tricky situation. Your visiting police are due to meet the University Vice Chancellor this evening.'

'Dr Sutherland?'

Chris knew Bradshaw was touchy about this contact. Tom had tipped her off about a large and potentially prestigious partnership deal the University was considering signing with the local police, to do with forensic work.

'I was thinking, sir. If the media get hold of the news of our investigations into Dr Lovelace, before we're ready –'

Bradshaw wasn't giving up without a struggle. 'What on earth's the sudden difficulty with Lovelace? I'm not hearing any justification for this sudden change of direction.'

'Hardly a change, sir. We're still proceeding with the trawl of all University staff, apart from our wider check on likely suspects in the region. These do rather contradict behaving as though we've found our murderer.'

'Perhaps we have.'

'Perhaps isn't proof beyond all reasonable doubt in a court of law.'

'Don't teach me my business,' said Bradshaw testily.

'Dr Lovelace's lawyer, the AUT lawyers and the University lawyers have been in touch with us, sir.'

'UCU?'

'The lecturers' union, sir. Combined with the University, they pack some punch.'

'I know what it means,' he said testily. 'I can punch as well as any two-bit academic, believe me.'

'We have no grounds on which to charge. It could be very expensive politically and financially to keep him in custody.'

Bradshaw looked at the waiting car and back at Chris.

'This is damned embarrassing. We can't afford to backtrack with the ACC. We've told him we have a strong suspect in the bag.'

You swine, thought Chris. You're talking in the plural. I bet you've implicated us all in this stupid decision. Out loud she tried to keep her patience. 'We don't lose him by holding back, sir. He isn't going to flee the country if we let him out. It could work to our advantage, quite apart from saving us from more embarrassment with the media and the University authorities.'

Bradshaw stared at the ground for a few seconds more. 'It's a bloody cock-up. Do it, but keep tabs on this man. Make it clear to your colleagues our investigation is ongoing. We don't want him slipping out of the country.'

An hour later Tom rang up the Station asking to visit Robin, and sensed some embarrassment. Apparently he was labouring under a misapprehension. Robin had recently been released without charge.

When Tom tackled Chris on the phone about it later, she was unforthcoming, except to say Robin had been asked to give further details to explain inconsistencies in his account of his movements in the past few weeks. He would be supplying them shortly.

'Does that mean he's on bail?'

'No, it doesn't.' She let Tom hear her irritation.

'So he isn't in custody, he's not on bail but he might be called in for further questioning.'

'Yes.' She was so prickly, thought Tom. 'If that's all, I need to get on.'

'Brilliant,' he said sardonically, out loud to himself. 'That gives me a marvellous basis for resuming my working relationship with my deputy.'

Five minutes later the phone rang. It was Chris.

'I'm sorry, I didn't mean to bite your head off. It's Bradshaw.'

'I kind of guessed he was standing over you.'

'Almost literally. He was fuming because we let Robin go. Bradshaw wants evidence the case is nearly resolved. For the sake of his relationship with his top brass he needs a suspect – proof his style of policing works.'

* * *

Chris knew Bradshaw was after blood and wouldn't give up. He was determined to nail somebody for the murders and to him Robin Lovelace was the most convenient suspect, even if he wasn't the most likely culprit. Robin's movements during the recent period were mysterious and this heightened questions about his trustworthiness. He had close connections with insects and with ants in particular. In respect of the latter, he had to be in a minority of one out of tens of thousands of people.

Like Tom, Chris remained unconvinced. Her team of officers were pursuing their trawl of potential suspects in the population and there was no point in trying to confront Bradshaw with her intuition about a technician employed by Tom's department at some time in the past. Bradshaw was too much driven by the facts to be swayed by intuition.

Fortunately, at that moment Morrison produced a distraction. Chris was impressed by Morrison and she guessed Bradshaw was impressed too. Bradshaw had a tacit preference for male officers over female ones, the latter in his view being too prone to emotional involvement. Morrison was what Bradshaw called "a bit airy-fairy", but undeniably showed signs of developing into a "quality detective". She had to bear all this in mind and play it carefully, keeping Bradshaw at one remove from what she was doing, without making it obvious. There was no news on the present whereabouts of Walters, but Morrison had managed to delve into his background and come up with a Mrs Blatt who had fostered him just before he left primary school. He placed a sheet of paper on the desk before Chris.

Chris laid the box file down on the desk and took a deep breath. 'That's good. Thanks, Morrison, you might try running the checks for precons and Schedule One sex offences.'

'Have done, boss. Third time I've tried. Couldn't get a result first time. There are too many John Walters. It worked today. He has a bit of a record.'

'For speeding, I suppose. Plenty of people have broken the law. So what?'

'Not a traffic offence, nor even a single offence. Our man has a catalogue of convictions to his name. On one occasion he served three years, less remission of course, for being a model prisoner.'

'Is this verified?'

'Yes, boss. Records have all the form on him. Wait till you hear what he was doing.' Morrison consulted his notepad: 'Demanding money with menaces, assault occasioning actual bodily harm.'

Chris felt considerably better. At last the tide was running her way. In this spirit she rang Tom. 'Fancy a trip to Cambridge? Walters lived in Cambridge for a while, as a young lad.'

'You did well.'

'Thank Morrison. He obtained this former home address for Walters from your Personnel department.'

'How the hell did he do that?'

'An ex-girlfriend, apparently, tipped him off. There's a filing cabinet at the University with the forms from job applications going way back.'

'Sounds dodgy. It's breaking every data protection and privacy rule in the book.'

'Dodgy maybe, but extremely useful. We can return to the moral high ground later.'

Tom still sounded surprised. 'So as far as you're concerned Walters is still in the frame?'

'We're trying to find out what we can, keeping it well away from Bradshaw.'

She didn't actually want Tom to accompany her to the interview, but thought there might be some way of their paths converging. Somewhat to her surprise, Tom snatched at the excuse to visit Cambridge, meet up with one of his former academic colleagues at his college and afterwards snoop around the bookshops.

'Bradshaw thinks I'm liaising with your forensic colleagues at the University of Peterborough,' she said. 'I feel like a schoolgirl skiving off school.'

'So you should.' He looked pious.

'At least I'm doing a job, whereas you're a worse skiver than me.'

'It's the privilege of the academic – a reflective day, away from the grind of administration.'

* * *

They made an early start and by 8:30 a.m. were on the A1 south of Peterborough, about to turn onto the A607. The traffic round the outskirts of Cambridge was horrendous. The last ten miles took as long as the previous eighty. Tom's knowledge of the less salubrious streets of Cambridge enabled him to drop her near 139 Gardenia Street before 9:30. She would find her own way back to the town centre, ring his mobile and meet him for lunch.

Chris knocked on the weathered front door of the rundown Victorian two-up, two-down fronted by a handkerchief sized garden, completely overgrown with weeds. Mrs Blatt opened the door just far enough to glimpse Chris and began to close it. Chris managed to introduce herself and the investigation.

'I'm too busy to speak to you now,' said Mrs Blatt.

'We're both busy people,' said Chris. putting her foot decisively in the doorway, 'but it's very important to me, and possibly it's important for the sake of the lives of other adults and children, that I pursue this inquiry. Twenty or thirty years ago, do you remember fostering a John Walters?'

The transformation in Mrs Blatt's face was dramatic: 'No, not children. He didn't start messing with children. Tell me he didn't do anything to children.'

'To my knowledge, he hasn't yet, Mrs Blatt. But I can't give you that reassurance for the future.'

'Thank God.'

'Why are you so anxious, Mrs Blatt. You must tell me what you know.'

'I can't.'

'Mrs Blatt, you owe it to those children.' Mrs Blatt looked past Chris, onto the street, as though it hid eavesdroppers.

Chris stood in the back parlour of the tiny but surprisingly cosy terraced house.

'Please sit down,' said Mrs Blatt. She was short and dumpy and clearly found it intimidating when people stood over her in the little room. She gave Chris the newer, less threadbare easy chair by the old-fashioned fireplace and slumped backwards into the dining chair at the table with its faded green baize cloth.

'He was always not quite right,' she sighed. 'There was a period, between six months and his second birthday. He had a hard time, many operations as a baby to try to straighten his poor little body out.'

'I didn't know he was physically disabled.'

'He was, for a long time. He still was after they'd finished, though not so you'd notice it. After they'd finished with his legs, they started on his eyes. Cosmetic they said it was. He was in and out of Moorfields in London like a car being serviced. I lost count of the operations. He was a clever boy, too. They gave him these intelligence tests and he was right up the top with the bright ones. But his eyes, they were one reason he couldn't study normally, not like the other children.'

Mrs Blatt looked at Chris, as though to verify she was still listening, before continuing.

'You had him a long time.'

'Backwards and forwards in and out of different children's homes. He came to me several times. It was the family messed him up. In the early days he was really noisy and objectionable over the periods away from home. Then later on, he accepted it. He became quiet, no trouble, but impossible to fathom. Because of his embarrassment about his appearance – the marks of the operations on his face took years to fade – he kept away from other children. He liked his own company, so it suited him really. It suited us too. We had our own problems – marital, you know, the usual – so we didn't want strange children tramping in and out of the house. It was one more thing to cope with.'

She looked at Chris and caught her eye. 'He wasn't a bad lad, you understand?'

Chris nodded. Mrs Blatt seemed reassured.

'You didn't foster him on a temporary basis then?'

'Oh yes, we wasn't responsible for him very long. I knew him before because I visited the Home, over the years. He was a quiet boy, not boisterous like the others. Some children aren't, I suppose. He wasn't affectionate, either, which suits me. I'm not that way with boys.' She caught Chris's gaze again. 'It's not as easy as with girls, is it?'

* * *

Tom was having the time of his life, delving into the second-hand bookshops he remembered so well from his time as a student in Cambridge. The time of his life lasted till a hack with a sharpened visual sense spotted him through the window of the bookshop as he browsed through a rack of dusty tomes. He looked at his watch. In five minutes Chris would be twenty yards up the road in the car, ready to pick him up at their prearranged spot. He was ready to leave, but a mob of photographers and reporters blocked his way.

'How far are you from finding the murderer?'

'I don't know,' said Tom candidly. 'I suggest you ask the police.'

He tried to push his way through. So this was the legendary rat-pack he'd seen mobbing people on the TV news.

'Are you helping the police with their enquiries?'

'I am.'

He made the mistake of stopping to engage with them. He faced it out with the patience of inexperience, thinking if he answered a few questions as candidly as possible they'd let up and go away. The opposite happened.

'You're seconded.'

'Special Constable?'

'That I'm not. I'm advising the police in my capacity as a scientist employed by the University.'

'Are these giant ants, Mr Fortius?'

'To my knowledge, no.'

'Are they man-eaters?'

'No more than any other insect is.'

'Are you scared of the ants, Mr Fortius?'

'Not particularly.'

'Professor,' said somebody. 'He's a professor, isn't that right, Professor?'

'Are you more scared of the ants than of the murderer?'

'Are these ants intelligent, Professor?'

'How does the killer control them?'

'Where do you think he'll strike next?'

'Should the government be declaring a state of emergency?'

'The problem with ants is that we don't know, we simply don't know what they can do once their capability for collective aggression is mobilised.'

There was a toot. Tom looked around. Chris was in the road, at the wheel of the car. From her gestures he gathered a hasty retreat was priority. He started to push his way towards her, but the crowd wasn't giving up easily.

'My question, Professor. You haven't answered it.'

'Yes,' said Tom. 'Let me through. I am cautious about using emotive language. But yes, some of these incidents scare me.'

Tom pushed and the scrum moved with him. He was an ace away from claustrophobia. A sea of cameras, held above head height, pointed down at him and clicked aggressively.

'Has your department been earmarked for closure?' 'Is your University benefiting from the publicity attached to this inquiry?' 'Does your University accept back-handers from the police authority for seconding you?'

He turned round and round. 'No, no, no.'

'Is your Dean a Mason?'

'Are you a Mason, Dr Fortius?'

'Is it right you're having an affair with the woman leading the police inquiry?'

He'd reached the road. There was a scrum as the car door was levered open. Chris was pushing, leaning across from the driver's side.

'DCI Winchester. Are you with Dr Fortius?'

'Professor –'

'Professor – when will you be making a full statement to the media?'

'Doctor, are you and she having an affair?'

'Did you spend last night with her?'

Tom was half in and half out of the vehicle. The door was pressing shut, but his legs were still on the road.

'Did the suspected man work for your University?'

'Why didn't you detect the suspect before he could kill anybody?'

'No comment,' he said, trying to force the door open and retrieve his trapped legs. 'Move away, I can't get into the bloody car.' No-one was listening. Photographers clicked away. Reporters scribbled on their notepads.

'Why aren't you scientists able to control the ants?'

'How can the police exterminate them?'

'Are you for or against genetic modification in insects, Doctor?'

'Have you created these genetically modified, aggressive ants to attract extra funding for your Research Centre?'

Chris jumped out of the car, raising her warrant card like a cross in the face of a host of vampires. 'Get back.' Her inflection was rising.

'Can we catch diseases from them?'

'Are they a threat to food and water supplies?'

Tom thrust the last of the microphones out of the remaining chink left by the open passenger door of the car, back into the face of the man holding it, slammed and locked the door. Chris revved up, putting several journalistic careers at risk as she drove off.

Chapter 25

'Thank God you came along when you did,' said Tom. 'I thought they were going to manhandle me.'

Chris shrugged without taking her hands off the wheel. 'I'd be more worried about what they asked you.'

'Thanks.' Tom pulled a wry face. 'There are none following us?'

'I can't see any.' She switched on the radio and smiled. 'You'll have to get used to them in this work.'

'I'm rapidly being cured of any enthusiasm for a career in it,' he said quickly. In the background the music on the radio abruptly changed to the voice of the weather forecaster.

'The weather centre has issued a severe weather warning for the East Midlands, East Anglia and the north east of England. Thunderstorms are severely affecting road conditions on the M62. Heavy downpours and surface flooding are making driving difficult. Drivers are warned to slow down and expect the hazard of slow moving or broken down vehicles. If at all possible, drivers should delay their journey or seek alternative means of travel.'

'They always make it sound so dramatic,' said Chris. 'What alternative do they propose that won't run into similar weather? Tunnelling or time travel perhaps?' The radio crackled unpleasantly loud in the confined space and she turned it down.

'Hell!' said Tom.

Chris hadn't noticed. She had enough to focus her mind on. Tom was thinking about the implications for the ants of this unusually warm, thundery weather. When thunderstorms were in the offing their response could be catastrophic. They tended to move into top gear – usually fighting and swarming. Activated to excess, with the guaranteed availability of warm, moist conditions for queens and offshoots from the parent colony to build new nests, triggered the impulse to attack linked with the instinct to procreate. The aftermath of a storm in summer weather was about as good for ants as it could get.

As Chris drove through the traffic, she related the main points from her conversation with Mrs Blatt. 'One of the advantages of being a police officer is that you can get access to less public areas of people's lives.

'Whilst I was visiting Walters' former foster home, I asked Mrs Blatt if she'd kept any of his belongings. She said she'd put them all away. I persuaded her to let me have a look through a chest full of clothes, toys and even some books and magazines, which were not of the Enid Blyton variety. His taste in literature, for want of a better word, was definitely towards 18 Certificate.'

'Didn't the adults responsible for him exercise any sort of supervision?'

'You'd better ask Mrs Blatt that.'

'All this is very interesting, but it doesn't amount to evidence of a disturbed state of mind. Even taking into account his childhood health problems and disrupted schooling, I don't see him as further off the rails than any other child of his age.'

'In which case I guess you'd like to see what I found. Open my bag and pull out the black notebook. I found it among his belongings. I don't suppose the adults in his life knew it existed, or they probably wouldn't have left it there. It's a child's notebook, hardly even a diary, but I don't recommend it as bedtime reading.'

Tom delved in her bag, produced the notebook and read the cover. 'My childhood, by John.'

'He might at least have given us his family name.'

'What's this? Date of birth 11 May 1944.'

'Perhaps he's Friday's child,' Chris offered.

'Impossible, it was a Thursday,' said Tom after a few seconds pause.

'How the hell did you know that?'

'I didn't know it. It's just a little party trick.'

'What? You can tell the day of the week from a date years ago? Some trick.'

'One of those things,' he said awkwardly. 'Everyone has one.'

'Not like that. You should be on that TV programme. What is it? The one where you bet you can successfully beat some impossible target or adversary.'

'No thanks.'

'I'm serious. You could win a holiday in Barbados.'

'Definitely not, then,' said Tom.

'Stick in the mud.'

'I'm choosy about where I spend my vacations.'

'Where would you rather be?'

'At this moment, not here with this tedious task on hand.'

'Snap, but stop avoiding the question.'

'As to preferences it's more a matter of who with than where.'

'This is where I get off.'

He held up a hand. 'Okay, I shan't say more.'

'Feel free. I didn't want to inhibit you, so long as –'

'So long as it doesn't embarrass you?'

'Something like that, yes.'

'We'll stick to the job and set the personal stuff to one side.'

It was late afternoon. Morrison was in the corridor. He'd looked for

Chris and she wasn't in her office. He could hear the blurred sounds of Bradshaw speaking on the phone and he considered waiting for him to finish before knocking on the door. In the end, he decided to take a chance and ring Tom Fortius at the University. Jean was very helpful.

'Dr Fortius is away for the day, but he can be contacted on his mobile.'

Less than a minute later, Morrison was through. 'DC Morrison here, Dr Fortius. Sorry to bother you, but do you know where DCI Winchester is?'

'She's sitting beside me in the car, two minutes from your Station,' said Tom.

'Is she calling in?'

Chris nodded. 'She certainly is.'

'Could you tell her Walters is a no-no.'

They had stopped at the traffic lights round the corner from the Station and Morrison's voice came over clearly. Chris found herself shouting past Tom. 'That's rubbish.'

Tom held the phone to Chris's ear and Morrison continued, 'I've found a death certificate. He died two years ago.'

Chris and Tom were stunned into silence.

'Hullo, are you there? Do you want me to tell Bradshaw, boss?'

'Leave it with me,' said Chris. Morrison rang off as the lights changed. She drove at speed into the car park, skidded crazily to a halt between two Panda cars and ran into the Station, leaving Tom to slide across to the driver's side and get out of the car.

Chris marched into the investigation room and with Morrison watching, picked up the phone and dialled Mrs Blatt's number. Two minutes later, she put down the receiver.

'I don't believe it,' she said.

'Why did she pretend?'

'She won't say. The only comment I can extract is that I wouldn't understand and she can't tell me over the phone.'

There was silence in the office. A phone rang in the corner. Eerily a fax machine started to print out.

'What a complete waste of time,' said Chris. 'She even pretended to be worried in case he's in trouble. All the time he's dead.' She sighed. 'This gives me a really weird feeling.'

'Fancy a hot drink?' asked Tom. Leaving Morrison to brief her on his work to check the accuracy of the report, Tom walked down the corridor and made three instant coffees. He returned just as another phone rang, near Morrison's desk this time. Morrison leaned across to pick it up. He cupped his hand over the receiver and spoke quietly. 'Are you in, boss? The Super is looking for you.'

Chris nodded with resignation. 'Tell him I'll be there immediately.' She turned to Tom. 'He probably looked out of his office window at precisely the second we drove in. Are you coming in with me?'

'I'll stay here. You know something, she spoke about him in the past tense. I remember thinking at the time it was odd.'

Chris walked towards the door and turned back. 'Hang on here for me. I shan't be long. I'll drop you back at work.' She gestured in wonderment. 'That man's nose for locating his staff never ceases to amaze me.'

Chris knocked and without waiting walked straight into Bradshaw's office. 'Walters isn't our man, sir.'

'What are you talking about? First it wasn't Martin John, then it wasn't Robin Lovelace. I've only just caught up with Morrison's latest information about Walters and now it isn't him.'

'The real Walters died two years ago from a heart complaint.'

'How the hell can you be so certain?'

'I've just come off the phone to the person you might call his maternal carer, the person who's acted almost like a stepmother to him. She was there when he died.'

'She could be lying.'

'She might be. Stepmothers may be wicked in fairy stories, they may even lie, but medical records don't.'

'Medical records?'

'Morrison's been in touch with the local hospital. Walters was in hospital at the time.'

'And you, I suppose, know who the real murderer is,' said Bradshaw sarcastically.

'I'm working on it.'

'Might be.' Bradshaw's sarcasm was unbridled. 'Put the rest of us out of our misery and tell us, Chief Inspector.'

Chris was seething, but Bradshaw's unwarranted dig made her even more determined not to approach too close to him. 'I intend to find out.'

* * *

Late the following morning the atmosphere in the investigation office was sepulchral. Chris stood in the doorway looking round at half a dozen detectives beavering away at their desks. None of their work had so far yielded a single positive lead. She had some phone calls to make and returned to her office. Between calls, there was a knock at the door. It was Morrison. She was in the middle of replacing a box file on the shelf behind her desk.

'This might be something and nothing, boss. I've just returned from a stint with the team trawling through local men. I've come across another former employee who may be worth following up. His address of origin was a children's home.'

Chris looked at him sceptically.

'In Cambridge, boss.'

He sounded weary and doubtful.

'Cambridge again.'

'He has a link with the University, as an employee.'

'Where exactly did he work?'

'He was a lab assistant in the science faculty, several years after Walters from what I can tell.'

'Would that be where Tom Fortius is based?'

'Haven't had time to check, boss, but I'll be finding out shortly.'

It took Morrison a further hour to establish that the man – his name was Thompsen – had been employed in Tom's department, though not actually in the research unit. Morrison rang the number given by Thompsen as one of his references and went straight to Chris's office.

'Boss, I've been talking to a Hilda Barker who worked as cook in the children's home where Thompsen lived before he was fostered by a Mrs Blatt. She remembers Thompsen and remembers him having a best friend – she thinks Thompsen's name was John.'

'Walters was called John. We've already seen Mrs Blatt.'

'She probably got them mixed up. Probably talking about the wrong lad. Damn.'

* * *

At three o'clock Tom received a phone call from Chris.

'Is that you, Tom? Chris here, ringing from Cambridge. I decided to drive down last evening. It's so much easier on the spot. I've spent a fascinating hour with a Mrs Barker, lovely woman, round and jolly. She should have been a parent for these kids. She used to cook at the local children's home near where Walters and Thompsen were fostered from time to time. She thinks the two boys were friends. She remembers them bringing Thompsen back from when he ran away from the children's home. It could have been the first time, she isn't sure. He was in a right state, no coat, no shoes, soaked to the skin. They put him to bed but he developed a chest infection and finished up in hospital with something, she isn't sure what. Could have been pneumonia from the sound of it. She says she can't remember whether the Sisters beat him, but says corporal punishment was the usual punishment for kids who ran away. Apparently they used to lock them in the back room upstairs with no mattress and just a night-shirt on. There was always a prayer book though.'

'Typical Christian child care,' muttered Tom.

Chris ignored this and continued: 'The same rooms in that wing served as infirmary and isolation rooms, which may be why she isn't sure what treatment he received. Normally though, she says, kids in the isolation rooms didn't see anyone except when they brought their meals up for them to eat alone.

'Apparently he ran away a few times after that. She can't remember much, except that he didn't respond to the usual methods of persuasion. On one occasion he caused a stir by visiting the gardener's outhouse in the grounds first, taking his jacket as well as a pair of boots. This was probably what kept him going a couple of days longer before being picked up.'

'Do we know any more about how and when he left that establishment?' asked Tom.

'Not much joy on that front,' said Chris. 'Apparently, after a while – it could have been about six months, she isn't sure – a woman who said she was a nanny came to collect him and take him away, without any explanation. She presumed he was either going home or to a foster home. Those were the usual options.'

'Where does that leave us?'

'I might try the local doctor,' said Chris. 'She's practised in the area for thirty years. I'm still following up the primary school. Mrs Barker mentioned which head teacher was there at the time and she lives locally in retirement.'

Tom's phone rang almost as soon as he had replaced the receiver.

'Bradshaw here, from the police.'

A less likely caller Tom couldn't have imagined.

'You're probably wondering why I'm ringing, but I can't seem to raise DCI Winchester. I wondered if you knew where about in Cambridge she might be.'

'No idea, I'm afraid.'

'By the way, Professor, what's your take on all this, now we're back to square one?'

'We aren't quite at square one,' mused Tom. He didn't want to start naming names. That would indicate he'd spoken to Chris recently. He attempted to distract Bradshaw by taking the conversation off at a tangent. 'At least we know now for certain who we're not looking for. Incidentally, as far as the insect side is concerned, I think the solution lies with communication, not predation.'

'You've lost me,' said Bradshaw.

'We've been looking at the problem from the wrong direction. It's not a question of ant predation we're addressing, but one of how ants communicate. Whoever is using them to kill people relies on their ability to communicate rapidly and attack en masse rather than simply on their aggression as hunters.'

This distinction was also apparently lost on Bradshaw, who saw it as further evidence of the total irrelevance of most if not all of what scientists think and say. 'All very interesting to academics no doubt, but I can't see how it affects our police inquiries.'

'I'm saying we shouldn't narrow the field of inquiry at the University to possible suspects within the ant predation unit, my Research Centre, or indeed within my department.'

'We haven't,' said Bradshaw stoutly. 'We're trawling across the entire institution and across the county.'

'Good, I'm delighted.'

'Did this Walters work with the insect communication unit?'

'He did,' said Tom. 'We have to allow for the possibility that we were led by the real killer to look in the wrong area. And the real killer has exploited the fact to cover his tracks. By implying that his obsession was with how ants attack, he offered false trails, hoping we'd direct our investigation towards Walters the technician. Or at me of course.'

Bradshaw was silent. He was irritated to find himself on the receiving end of these speculations. To him there was a strict boundary round police discussion of police work. Detection was not the business of this man, professor or not, or of anybody outside the Force.

* * *

It was after five when Chris rang again. Tom was still in his office.

'I did try social services,' she said, 'but they can't help. All their back records were destroyed during local government reorganisation.'

'That's illegal.'

'It happens legally to records before a certain date, but this was a fire in the office. Murphy's Law operates in some investigations.'

'Murphy?'

'If a thing can go wrong, then it will.'

Tom passed this over. 'Any news on the medical or school front?'

'Yes and no,' said Chris. 'I thought the doctor would be more reticent than the teacher, but in the event it was the other way around. Possibly that's because he became a bit of a thorn in the side of the school – disruptiveness, that sort of thing – whereas his illnesses were what the health professionals were geared up to dealing with and didn't reflect badly on them. Basically, at the age of nine – I calculate that this would be shortly after leaving the children's home – Thompsen became seriously ill and they thought for a while it was scarlet fever. The doctor at the time recalls that his temperature was so high that he went into intensive care, couldn't keep anything down, and was sick if he ate or drank more than a few mouthfuls at a time. She can't remember whether they eventually decided it was food poisoning or a virus, but from our point of view the main noteworthy item is that Thompsen had a further period of prolonged isolation from the usual domestic setting, possibly a month or six weeks, according to the doctor. It wasn't long after that when he made his first attempt at suicide.'

'What, at nine? That's terrifying.'

'I think by this time we're seeing the early signs of a withdrawal from pretty well all of what you and I would regard as normal human interaction.'

'He sounds to have boxed himself into a corner.'

'Psychiatrists might say he was well down the road towards developing some very disturbed coping mechanisms.'

'I'd hardly describe suicide attempts as coping.'

'Many serial killers hover on the edge of suicide and some eventually take that option.'

'But not soon enough for their victims, unfortunately.'

'I didn't hear that remark.'

'You seem to have an unhealthy sympathy for the murderer in this case.'

'Sympathy is the wrong word. I want to understand the motivation of our man, so we can nail him before he kills anyone else. All this is purely speculative, of course. It gives the point of view of various other people about this man and his alleged disturbances during childhood. I've known many children who have been through the care system and have suffered serious illnesses, but they don't go on to become murderers.'

'I'm a bit confused. Was he fostered or was he brought up in a children's home?'

'He was shuttled about, as far as I can tell, between the children's home and Mrs Blatt. There seem to have been behavioural problems, but we've no records, merely people's memories.'

They chatted some more, mostly about inconsequentials. In the midst of it Tom reached a decision.

'I'm thinking I could drive down now and be more constructive working with you directly than sitting here.'

'If that's what you want,' she said, and although she said nothing more Tom thought her tone lightened, as though she was pleased at the prospect.

After Chris rang off Tom left the office with the very strong feeling that they would soon be going after Thompsen as a suspect. It wasn't so much a decision as a smooth flow from frustration, anger and all the other emotions associated with the killings, to action. He wanted to take positive action, whether or not it was definitively the final stage of the inquiry, as long as he was engaged rather than sitting on the sidelines. He made preparations to leave, in haste but with the deliberation of the hunter.

'I'm coming, you bastard!' he ground through his teeth while he packed the car. 'You'd better leave them alone before I reach you, or your life won't be worth giving away.'

Tom met up with Chris in the hotel on the outskirts of Cambridge where she was staying. It was one of those hotels which feel more like a country house, with lots of intimate corners, well-upholstered sofas and small coffee tables matching the light, chestnut-coloured wood panelling. As he walked into the lounge he saw her sitting in a small nook, leafing through papers. Later he recalled this moment. The frisson of pleasure at meeting like this took him by surprise. It felt like an illicit assignment during an affair. He hurriedly suppressed the thought.

'Hi.' He stood in front of her and she looked up in surprise.

'You were quick. I didn't expect to see you for another hour.'

'We East Riding men don't mess about.'

'I didn't think you were from the East Riding.'

'I'm not, but I've worked in the county for many years. It helps to use the line sometimes.'

'You'd find it very difficult to fool anybody, apart from a blind, deaf person perhaps, into thinking you were from the East Riding.'

Chris ordered a beer for Tom and a glass of dry white wine and they sat chatting. There was a good deal of detail from her interviews which she hadn't been able to give him over the phone.

'Now if you'll excuse me, I'll go and sort out our accommodation. I assume you're staying here.'

'If they've room.'

'There's rather a lot going on in town this week, so if you don't check in here you'll be sleeping in the car, believe me. I had a huge job finding this when I came down.'

She was back from Reception in five minutes.

'Slightly tricky. They've no vacancies and their linked sister hotels and B&B addresses are all fully booked.'

'I'd better start trekking.'

'I've already told you, it's a waste of time.' She looked at her watch. 'Anyway, it's seven-fifteen. It'll be dinner soon. Are you hungry?'

'I will be once I've sorted out some accommodation.'

She looked him in the eye. 'Well, Professor, I've taken the bull by the horns, so to speak, and told them my partner will be checking in shortly. It's a large room. There's a huge sofa and enough spare bedding if you're too squeamish to squeeze in on the far edge of my super king-sized bed.'

He was speechless.

'Don't read anything into it,' she said. 'Just tell me whether or not you're staying.'

'Well ... yes.'

She smoothed the table top with one hand and poured a fresh cup of tea so she didn't have to see his expression. 'We're mature adults and I'm sure this is the lesser of many evils, so the less said about it the better.'

* * *

By the time they'd had a late dinner and speculated at length on the details of the case, it was after midnight. Tom dutifully bedded down on the sofa. In the middle of the night he had a dream in which he was being disturbed in bed by an apparition leading him to a banqueting hall in which revellers were celebrating an unknown occasion. In the morning, he came to consciousness early and was confused at first by his surroundings. An arm lay across his bare chest. He turned his head, opened his eyes and, before memory kicked in, was astonished to find he was lying in bed with Chris. She was already awake and gave him a wickedly knowing smile.

'Good morning, Professor.'
'Good morning, Chief Inspector.'
'I hope you slept well.'
'I did, thank you. And did you? I hope I didn't disturb you.'
She grinned mischievously. 'Quite the opposite. I found out professors aren't as boring in bed as they are in the office.'
He was blushing. Her directness reduced him to speechlessness.

Chapter 26

Over breakfast they considered the implications of the past few days' investigation. Chris summarised the position as she saw it.

'Our main difficulty is in deciding who these two men are, or were. Is it as simple as Walters is dead and innocent whilst Thompsen is alive and guilty? Our killer signs some of the notes G and some J. That could be either Walters or Thompsen, since they're both called John. Assuming the notes were written within the past two years, we're agreed it's not Walters, so it could be Thompsen. It could also be somebody else. They're very common initials and on their own take us nowhere. We don't know the location of Thompsen, so it's one step forward, two back.'

'I need to know how he controls the ants,' said Tom.

'You're a few jumps ahead of me. My first question is who the murderer is, and some way down the line might be a question about whether he controls ants.'

'He does something, be assured. The question is how sophisticated it is. At a basic level, he might just be manipulating temperature, light and humidity to maximise movement and response to external stimuli such as a plentiful supply of potential food.'

'You mean in the form of flesh, a body.'

'Preferably a live one, unfortunately.'

'Too macabre for me. How important are the other factors?'

'Temperature is important because it directly governs the metabolic rate of the individual – speed of movement, response to stimuli. The effect of increasing it only a few degrees can be dramatic. Watch your average comatose nest of wood ants in their conical heap come to life when the sun moves round and falls on the sloping side of the heap on a cool day in early spring. If humidity increases to some extent with temperature, it prevents ants desiccating in the increased heat.'

'I thought they flourished in dry climates.'

'Some are adapted to deserts and do quite well. But I'm talking about extremes. The entire colony can overheat if it dries out at a high temperature. Then, of course, remember different species react differently.'

'So, what device are we looking for?'

'I'm convinced he uses a mechanical device for bringing the ants to the desired pitch of excitement.'

'In effect, to use them as instruments of execution.'

'Yes.'

'Is it a box?'

'I doubt it,' said Tom. 'Some stimulus or other. A physiological trick perhaps, based on knowing what stimulates ants to act in predictable ways.'

'Trickery?'

'Yes, creating a false light source using mirrors, for instance. Ants respond to different strengths and colours of light rays. And incidentally, they perceive red light as black, which has its uses when you want to observe them inside the nest, under laboratory conditions.'

'Sounds like your experimenters have a real fun time in your red light district.'

'An absolute ball,' said Tom ironically.

Chris looked at her watch. 'It might be politic if I paid the bill.'

'Do I sense we should be setting off?'

'If I'm to head off an inquisition from Bradshaw, about half an hour ago I guess.'

* * *

The journey back to Hull was smooth and speedy. Tom arrived at work just before ten. He spent the next hour in the main office sorting out various administration matters. The phone was already ringing as he walked back into his own office and picked up the receiver.

'Chris here. How are you fixed for red wine?'

'Pardon?'

'I asked because I've some cold meat here.'

'Someone fancies herself as the reincarnated Philip Marlowe,' Tom said archly.

'Eh?'

'Raymond Chandler, you know, *The Big Sleep*.' Tom exaggerated Bogarde's drawl from the side of his mouth: 'Don't play the innocent with me, sister. After this is over maybe we can pick up on the wine tasting, when you're no longer carrying the cuffs and I'm not a scientist.'

'Okay, wise guy. I give in. Are you interested in meeting?'

'To be honest I haven't put my bags down yet. An hour ago I returned to the University from a forensic entomology meeting at Peterborough University, would you believe it?' He waited for her response and, true to expectation, she followed his lead.

'I never would believe you. Here was I thinking you were away with some scarlet woman. I hadn't thought such a thing as a flock of forensic entomologists would exist. Do you call them a swarm?'

'A convention.'

'Very good. Any other group of forensic experts is called a body,' she said with a grim snort.

Tom groaned out loud. This conversation was degenerating rapidly.

'Okay, I shouldn't have said it. What I meant was, surely a crowd like that has the potential to be pretty macabre.'

'There isn't so much of the macabre about most of them. I think you might have the wrong idea about entomology of whatever kind.'

Chris was amused by the irony: 'So here we are, a policewoman who's had enough of policing and an academic who finds detection fascinating and doesn't object to being recruited to work for the police.'

'I didn't know you were so brassed off with detective work.'

'I'm not. It's the Police Force which brasses me off.'

'There isn't that much difference between us then. It's the approaches of those fictional detectives which interests me. And their lifestyles, I suppose,' he added as an afterthought. 'I used to want to be a private detective. When I was about to take the plunge into research, I made a resolution that if ever that world crashed, I'd set up a detective agency.'

Chris giggled. 'It'll look a bit of a come down on the business card – Private Eye.'

'Private Investigator,' he corrected. 'We aren't part of the USA yet.'

'Sorry.' She paused to scribble an imaginary alteration in the air. 'Big difference.'

'Not any old investigator, though.'

'Of course not. It wouldn't be dignified, an international academic snooping on adulterous spouses.'

'I don't intend to get into that.'

'That's where the money is, sunshine. Jealous people pay well.'

'I shall set strict limits to what I get involved in.'

'High principles, unemployed, but ethically sound. Very impressive.'

'There's a whole raft of stuff with a scientific or research edge to it, equally as significant as all your adulterers. Environmental issues, industrial espionage, that kind of thing.'

'Don't pin the adultery trip on me. I never said I was interested in people who are adulterating.'

'No, not like that. I thought you said that's what your agency would be doing.'

'I never said that. I said keeping your principles intact is the way to insulate yourself against growing rich.'

'Growing rich at all?'

'You're pushing me. I'll stick at too quickly.'

'That's what I find endearing about you Chris, your flexibility.'

* * *

Bradshaw had found out a little about Chris's recent unapproved travels and was not amused. She stood in his office.

'I'm putting it down the line, Inspector Winchester, that unless you obey orders you'll be out of this office, out of plain clothes and out of the Force altogether. Do I make myself clear?'

'Perfectly clear, sir.'

'Never mind the fancy answer. Yes or no?'

'Yes.'

'Get on with it, Inspector.'

'With pleasure.'

'What did you say?'

'I said, sir, I'll be very pleased to leave this room.'

Bradshaw leaned across the desk and lowered his voice.

'This is not an ordinary room, Inspector Winchester, it is my office. And in my office, the business is done by me. I decide when it is complete and when people come in and go out. Now you will leave my office and carry out this Force's orders without further ado, or there will be serious repercussions.'

The phone was ringing as Chris walked into her own office.

'Hello, is that Chris?'

'Yes. What is it?'

'Christ!' She heard the sound as Tom slapped his forehead. 'Two things. I know the mechanism used to rouse the ants to kill and I know where Thompsen fits in.'

'Slow down, I've had my boss shouting at me. I can only take one more piece of news at a time.'

'Okay, the mechanism first. We've lost a fairly sophisticated device we named the Antennator, which was developed in my Research Centre to explore communication between ants. Now the other matter ...'

'Wait a moment. When did this device go missing?'

'I'm not sure, but I'm kicking myself. It's been missing for months, possibly longer.'

'Sounds slack to me.'

'I know, I know, but it's universities. They're very federated organisations, which means people can be left to their own devices for years, unless what they're doing or not doing infringes upon somebody else's territory.'

'Bizarre.' She was very unimpressed. 'What's your other discovery?'

'Not a discovery so much as a thought.' He paused and took a deep breath. 'I've remembered something going on at the time Walters was here. He was on sick leave after a serious accident and we'd had several temps in and were looking for a permanent replacement. He said he could find us a candidate from a local technical college who'd been employed as a technician for several years. I think I recall some discussion with our personnel department about whether relatives of staff could be employed on this basis.'

'We're talking about a relative of Walters?'

'I seem to remember something about Thompsen and Walters being brothers.'

'Right,' said Chris slowly. 'Is that all for now? I need to talk to people at this end.'

She rang off. 'Where's Morrison.' She called, 'Morrison.'

After a pause, a faint voice replied, 'Boss?'

'Morrison, where are you?'

'In the toilet.'

'I want to speak to you, urgently.'

Morrison's response indicated the problem was the curry he'd eaten last night. Chris was undaunted.

'I can't wait. If you aren't coming out, I'm coming in.'

* * *

Tom's mobile was signalling an incoming call and when he came off the phone to Chris he checked it. It was a message from his brother Basil, saying his mother had been taken ill, but was all right, and asking him to return the call. Christ, thought Tom, I can't ring back at present. I'll do it as soon as there's a space. He went through into Jean's office.

'Is everything all right?' Jean asked, thinking he looked drained.

'It never rains but it pours. My mother's ill. My brother's been on the phone, telling me the doctor's been and it's all in hand. I don't need to do anything. Let me know if he rings the office. I'll see you later.'

Strange, thought Jean, how some men live totally separate lives from their wives and families. She would have expected Tom's wife to be the one phoning with this news. It wasn't hard to pick up that Laura wasn't in Tom's universe at present.

Shortly afterwards, Chris emerged from the male toilet and rang Bradshaw. She outlined the situation, saving the punch line till the last moment.

'Morrison believes the file contains the name of a father for Walters. We need to interview him. The problem is that the only location we can trace is in the USA.'

* * *

'They talk about the victims of abuse feeling guilty,' said Tom.

'I don't know what you mean,' said Luis Deakin.

He was so quick to reply that Tom looked at him sharply. I've offended you, he thought.

'I once watched a television programme,' said Chris. 'This woman

227

was talking about the lives of people who are victims of abuse, how they need to move from experiencing it to surviving it and then dealing with it, in a therapeutic sense.'

'They ask for it,' said Luis suddenly.

'I beg your pardon.'

'I said the bastards often ask for it,' Luis repeated mechanically, as though speaking in his sleep.

'What did you say?' asked Tom. He was aware of the intensified silence from Chris's corner of the room.

Luis started as though coming out of a reverie: 'What? Sorry, I thought I was hearing a bell.'

Tom and Chris were both staring. Tom spoke. 'Are you all right, Luis?'

'Yes, yes. Why do you ask?'

'What did you think I said, Luis?'

'Did you ask me a question?'

'Actually I didn't,' said Tom. 'But you answered one.'

Luis passed his hand across his brow. 'I'm sorry.' He seemed confused. 'It's been a long day. I am overtired. I reach the stage where I imagine things.' He laughed nervously. 'Overactive brain. You know. That sort of thing.'

Tom laughed with him, slightly hesitant, but smiling nevertheless. 'Perhaps it's time to call it a day, Luis.'

'Probably it is,' Luis answered, speaking rather slowly as though surfacing from sleep. 'I'll pack up. It's been rather a long session.'

'Too true,' said Tom. 'See you tomorrow.'

'Yes, see you. Farewell.'

After he had gone there was silence for a minute or so. Chris broke it first. 'What was all that about? Presumably you knew about him being prone to hearing things.'

Tom shook his head. 'I don't know what's going on here. I honestly don't know.' He sat for a while and eventually spoke. 'Let's put it down to tiredness. We're all tired. We've all had enough.'

They sat in the car park talking. Chris left the car to go to her office and Tom drove back to work. A couple of hours passed. He was packing up when the phone rang. It was Laura.

'Where have you been? I've been ringing for ages.'

'Sitting in this office for the past few hours.'

'Tell that to whoever you like, but don't try fooling me. Anyway listen hard, your mother's critically ill.'

'How can you say that? She's been ill but she's fine.'

'How can she be fine? She's in intensive care.'

'She can't be. Basil rang and left a message saying she's fine.'

'Are you sure he said "fine" and not "dying"?'

'I didn't actually speak to him.'

'For God's sake, listen. She's in Hull Royal. In your absence we did what was necessary. It's the Infirmary.'

Tom stood up, grabbing his pen and diary and his coat from the back of his chair. 'I'm on my way. What ward is she in?'

'I'm not certain. Ask at the desk when you arrive.'

After putting the phone down, he spent a few minutes assembling the papers relating to the investigation. He crammed them into his already bulging briefcase and walked out of his office. Five minutes won't make or break it, he thought. What will be will be.

Tom raced from the hospital car park to Reception. The clerk gave him directions and he pushed past the queue for the lifts and ran up the stairs. He left the stairwell and saw the ward to his right. Just through the double doors, Laura appeared and in an instant all the haste and energy drained from his body. From her tear-stained face he knew he was too late.

'I tried,' he gasped, 'but the traffic – delayed me – the investigation – it's very important.'

'So this is what it's come to.' She shook her head, disbelieving. 'You couldn't even make it to your own mother's deathbed.'

* * *

Jean was having tea in the bay window of her lounge, on the phone to her friend Cynthia. To her great relief she had a weekday off. It wasn't that she disliked her University job, but it was good to have a break now and again.

Cynthia was sitting on a hard chair in the dining room of her bungalow in the next village. She was slowly recovering from an operation on her arthritic hips, and found it impossible at present to use the settee and easy chairs; once sitting down, she couldn't lever himself out of them.

Jean stared at the frieze of black bordering the wall, just above the skirting board. The only problem was that there hadn't been a frieze a quarter of an hour ago.

'Cynthia ...' Jean's expressive voice invested this word with full concern and a hint of anxiety.

'Be with you tomorrow, darling. Some time in the morning. I'm off to the doctor now. Having a spot of bother keeping the joints running smoothly these last few days.'

'I say, Cynthia ...'

'Yes, you're going to tell me tomorrow is too late.'

'I think – this sounds silly but I really – yes, it is. Little brats! I do believe they're stinging.'

'You'll be saying next that they're doing it deliberately.'
'They are. I've put that poison down, but it hasn't made any difference.'
'It will, darling, they'll be gone by morning. Mark my words.'
The following morning came and the ants had not disappeared. Far from succumbing to the poison, the concentration of ants was even heavier than before. They formed a black film over almost the entire carpet. Their criss-crossing of the walls in regular rectangular shapes created the effect of half timbering. Round the doorframe, the ants flowed up, across and down in a living stream.

* * *

Tom was expecting Chris to be on her own in her office, but he walked in and found Bradshaw with her, in sombre mood.
'Have a look at this,' said Bradshaw.
The note was brief. Chris scanned it and passed it to Tom.

Colleagues:

You may like to visit 4 The Leys, Lund near Beverley, the site of my latest experiment. Be careful how you gain entry. I transported some formicas to the home of my unwittingly co-operative subject, who has installed double glazing and has a fully carpeted lounge with no chimneys. Once the doors are closed and blocked, there is no way out for ant or human. As you can see, the experiment was successful, my only regret being the sacrifice of a colony of somewhat rare Formica Excecta, which you will doubtless agree with Donisthorpe, in 1927, with the right stimuli can show extreme aggression.

G

Bradshaw looked at Tom. 'You recognise the address?'
'Not offhand. It doesn't ring any bells.'
'Where does your secretary live?'
'Jean, she lives alone, somewhere out of the city. A small village. Oh my God, you don't mean –'
Bradshaw nodded. 'I'm afraid so. Forensics are there now. As you say, she lived alone. We've traced an elderly aunt who's identified the body. We'll need your help later, Doctor, with identifying and dealing with the ants.'

Chapter 27

Chris went back with Tom to the University. He ignored her hints about whether he should go home. She was concerned about his state of shock and accompanied him to Jean's office. Luis Deakin came in while Tom was trying to collect his thoughts and make temporary arrangements to cover Jean's work. Tom's head was in a whirl. He was distracted from the practicalities by thoughts about the gruesome mode of killing.

'There could be as many as 100,000 ants in a nest of Excecta. That's only a guestimate.'

Deakin agreed. 'When it comes to numbers, ants are in there with worms, beetles and Apteragota – sorry, springtails to you.' He nodded to Chris. 'Pretty primitive. You can ignore them in present circumstances. But add ability to communicate to the equation and Phwww!' His hands came together and flew up in an explosive gesture. 'Their power to succeed, overwhelm, increases exponentially. In crude mathematical terms, they must become the most powerful living force in most of the more fought over territories on this planet. Eight thousand plus species – we're still discovering new ones – and still diversifying, evolving. Their capacity for mutation based on evolutionary principles may be minimal – the so-called cousins of specimens preserved in Baltic amber still live today – but their ability to learn from experience and move on is untested and for all we know, considerable.'

Tom shrugged as Deakin reflected further. 'We're talking mega-numbers here. Approximately one sixth of the entire bio-mass of this planet is Formicidae and their cousins. Bio-mass is right.'

He still looked puzzled.

'Formicidae means ants?' interrupted Chris.

'Yes,' said Tom.

'Why choose ants as instruments of death?' Chris asked.

'There's the pathological aspect,' said Tom. 'I can't comment on that. As far as the variety of ant species is concerned, though, the choice of Excecta is a good one. They're aggressive, persistent and very social. There are ants in almost every imaginable habitat. You name it, ants attempt it. There are ants which swim. I remember hunting in Matley Bog in the New Forest as a boy, for the black bog ant, Formica Picea which lives in clumps of Tussock Grass and climbs down stalks under the water as a means of defence. They may be rare, but if you step on them or put your hand in the nest by accident, they'll give you something to yell about. There is even one species which can sew, a rare case of insects using artefacts. The most efficient and highly developed of these so-called Weaver Ants are probably Oecophylla. They live in extremely populous communities – perhaps as many as half a million. They pull together sprigs in the crowns of trees and use their larvae as shuttles to sew nests from the foliage. A large colony will occupy several trees and contains several of these nests on its periphery, as barracks for the ants, who attack any intruder to their territory. They don't sting, but have large mandibles and an extremely painful bite. They're very effective communicators, so watch out anyone who comes within their range.'

Tom paused. 'My questions are about how he managed to transport the ants to Jean's house. It seems a departure from bringing the victims to where he houses the ants, which presumably is where he carries out the killings. Obviously, it's far less complex if he brings the intended victims to where the ants are, rather than vice versa.'

'Surely you know what species from examining the bodies.'

'That's only possible when we can put our hands on one or more reasonably complete pieces of the ant concerned.'

'It seems grotesquely academic in any case. The fact is, these people have died in appalling circumstances.'

'I'll be going now,' said Luis, 'if you can manage.'

'Thanks for all your help, Luis.'

'It's nothing,' said Luis. 'If you need anything further, ring me.'

* * *

Chris was in the car on her way to work, when the car phone rang.

It was Morrison from the Station. 'There's a casualty in A and E at the hospital, ma'am, with unusual injuries.'

'I'll go down and take a look,' she said.

Chris was shocked at the woman's appearance. She could speak, though her face was a mess. She was off the critical list, though the medical staff seemed cagey about talking about recovery, due to the possibility of secondary shock. Chris decided to bring in a photographer, so they could give the media a photograph to try to identify the person.

Bradshaw called her a couple of hours later, as she walked past his office. 'DCI Winchester, I was looking for you.'

'I had to visit Forensics on my way back from the hospital.'

'Ah, I thought for a moment you'd lost your taste for the job.'

She ignored him.

'Do you want the good news or the bad news?' asked Bradshaw.

'Try both, I'm in a hurry.'

'The good news is here's your photo. The bad news is it's looking like a horror story.'

'Thank you, sir.'

Somehow Bradshaw had picked up what was going on and had intercepted the photograph. She had neither time nor energy to take this up. Nevertheless, Bradshaw wasn't mistaken to note the slight emphasis on the *sir.* He continued. 'Don't go just yet. More bad news, I'm afraid. The hospital phoned ten minutes ago. The victim of the attack died this morning.'

'What? She was recovering.'

'Secondary shock, apparently. It's even more of a risk where some unusual incident precedes the injury.'

* * *

The fact that there was no progress with apprehending a main suspect contributed to the downbeat atmosphere in the Station, despite the investigation having become higher priority. The focus was more intensely on the University. Because it had become general knowledge that Tom's secretary was the latest casualty meant academics and students were noticeably more jittery. Press and TV didn't lessen the atmosphere: interviewing on the campus, interspersing coverage with scare stories about killer insects – killer bees, killer wasps, and of course, killer ants. The Hull Arts Cinema put on a showing of a pulp classic film about army ants on the rampage. It showed to a packed audience and a second screening was organised.

'How is the search for Thompsen going?' asked Tom when he rang Chris.

Chris's voice was flat. 'Every available officer in the county is on the case. More than two hundred are combing every record, every known link.'

'Two hundred?'

'The Chief has approved it, for a short period. We have to show results.'

'How long have we got?'

Chris shrugged. 'Twenty-four hours, maybe thirty-six, or slightly more.'

Morrison and a small group of officers worked through the night pursuing more contacts with the childhood of Walters and Thompsen, in the hope of tracking down Thompsen's recent whereabouts. Nearly eight hours later Morrison gave a shout of glee. 'Yes!'

After talking to him briefly, Chris rang Tom. 'It's been something of a coup. We've been following up staff in the religious order who used to run the children's home where Thompsen was once placed. We've tracked down a former nun who used to work at the home.'

'Where does she live?'

'Somewhere near Pocklington.'

'Coincidentally near.'

'I'm not quite sure of the exact location, but we're running a check to see if she's on the phone. Whether she's ex-directory or not we should be able to trace her.'

'Not if she's married and the entry is under her married name. Don't nuns use a surname, then take a New Testament Christian name when they move from being Sister to Mother?'

'Fortunately, our informant remembered the name this woman goes by.'

* * *

When Chris drove out to interview Sister Ruth, she took Tom with her. It wasn't protocol, but she wasn't in the mood for observing that.

Sister Ruth now called herself plain Miss Ruth Craig. She was older and more frail than Chris had expected, with thin silver hair and wizened features. Chris thought it was the face of a woman who has endured, or witnessed, severe pain. The reason for her change of title wasn't clear. Apparently, several years ago she'd retired from her last job as housemother in a private boarding school, and now lived alone in a tiny maisonette in a relatively new housing development. She seemed friendly, more than willing to talk and surprisingly frank.

'I fell out with staff in the local authority soon after I met Ian – he was cook at the Home at the time – and made my application to leave the Order.'

'They made it difficult for you?'

'It wasn't the Order that raised problems. They were very accommodating. My problems arose from having admitted to a relationship with another member of staff. In the service manager's eyes, that was a major crime.'

She went through to the kitchen to make the coffee.

'Can we trust her?' Tom mouthed.

'She wants to get her own back on the employing local authority. I think it's worth talking to her.'

Miss Craig returned with three mugs of coffee on a tray, accompanied by a generous plateful of biscuits.

'I'd just returned from the shops,' she explained. 'You're lucky. I have a once-a-week binge.'

'I'd describe the regime in the Home as rigorous,' Miss Craig offered. 'I'm not saying the children were beaten or otherwise actively maltreated, but it was tough – life in dormitories I mean. I speak as a former convent pupil.'

'What about the religious side?'

'The Home was Roman Catholic if that's your question.'

'Lectures about what dreadful fate awaits sinners?' asked Tom.

Miss Craig wasn't to be drawn: 'Some would have that view,' she said softly.

'Were the children punished by the nuns?' Tom asked.

'There were punishments, but nothing out of the ordinary for a Home of that kind.'

After further questioning about Walters, Miss Craig offered the information they needed to confirm the link between the two boys.

'He had a brother,' she said. 'A half-brother, really. One of them, as you know, was John Walters, the other was John Thompsen. An unusually spelt name, as I recall. 'S-E-N at the end. Thompsen was no choir boy. When he was no more than a toddler – he was in the Home from a much earlier age than Walters – one of the councillors, a Margery Wallace, visited, bent over his push chair to say what a pretty child, or some such, and he bit her finger.'

Tom shrugged. 'You're saying he was possibly more disturbed than Walters.'

'Before he was fostered and eventually adopted, he lived in the Home for four years, till just before he started school. I remember him being brought there. He was found on some waste ground at the back of the bus station. The local media ran a big campaign to find the mother. It even made the national news. He was only a few hours old. It was raining hard. If they hadn't found him, he would only have lasted a few more hours.'

A thought struck Chris. 'You don't recall who fostered John Thompsen?' This was a long shot. To her surprise the response was immediate.

'Of course I do. The couple who fostered both boys, Mr and Mrs Blatt.'

'I don't think that's possible,' said Chris.

'It is because it's true,' said Miss Craig.

Chapter 28

Seated in the battered old rocking chair he called his mad chair, a position that gave him permission to think his thoughts without constraint, Graver looked across the empty room and addressed the invisible visitors who could now harass him constantly.

When the Inspectors came, they shut two of the kids, Louise and Ben, in rooms in the staff quarters. Everybody knew this, but nobody spoke about it. Some said they had bruises, others said it was worse. Little Margarite said she'd seen Mother Bernadette chasing Louise with a carving knife. There was a tale that Ben was taken for holidays by the driver, when the priests from the boys' college went on their summer retreat.

'One of the Inspectors – a kindly but rat-faced woman whom you couldn't trust to be in the pay of the same people that ran the Homes – stopped me when I was walking to the bath with my towel round my neck and asked if I wanted to make any complaints. I shook my head. I knew if she was genuine she'd have looked into the backs of my sad eyes and read the messages etched there. But she didn't and the moment of truth passed.'

* * *

'Did the nuns use corporal punishment?' Chris asked old Miss Craig, who seemed to become more frail and wizened as she delved deeper into her memories.

'It did take place at the Home, but I never administered or witnessed it,' she said.

'After leaving, did you communicate with any of the staff there?'

'I kept in touch with one or two.'

'Anybody in particular?'

'Father Doyle, the head.'

'Did you visit him?'

'He used to visit me at home sometimes. Of course, that stopped when I moved away from the area.'

'Were children ever beaten in the Home?' asked Tom.

'I don't know what you mean by beaten.'

A bell rang in the kitchen. It sounded like a timer on the cooker. 'Excuse me,' Miss Craig said and went into the kitchen to deal with it. When she returned, Chris looked at Tom. His face was pale and as bleak as she'd ever seen. This is getting to you, she thought.

As soon as she could, Chris diverted the line of questioning.

'Can you remember how Thompsen behaved?'

Miss Craig stared at her with suspicion. 'What do you mean?'

'Did he do anything which led to him being punished?'

'It's the school you want to be focusing on, if you want to know about punishments.'

Chris tried to show interest that was not over-zealous. 'Oh?'

Miss Craig sniffed. Chris thought she was going to cry. The old woman shook her head as though reliving the pain the boy experienced at the hands of visiting priest Father Doyle and her Mother Superior.

'I saw him go through it,' she said. 'I did nothing. Tell me you can do penance. Tell me all these years are enough.'

* * *

The knowledge that they had discovered the whereabouts of Sister Ruth meant Graver was reliving those terrible days, months, years. The dormitory smelled of sweat and slow death. Father Doyle's face in the Reverend Mother's office was in the shadows, sinister and promising the pain of Purgatory for his sins. The boy was frightened.

'Where are you from, John?'

He didn't answer.

'What are your parents?'

'I haven't no parents.'

'But you have a father and a mother.'

'Yes.'

There was a pause.

'Yes what?'

The boy didn't answer, mainly because he didn't know he had to. Without warning, the priest leaned forward and slapped him hard on the face, shouting, 'Yes, Father.'

Then, more softly, the priest asked, 'Have you heard of the Catechism?'

'Yes, Father.' The words squeezed out between sobs.

'What can you remember?'

The boy started to recite. After several minutes, Father Doyle held up his hand. 'Stop, stop.' The boy continued as though in a trance. The priest shouted 'Stop!' This time the boy stopped. The priest laughed. 'Mother Mary, it is true what they say about you.'

The boy didn't answer. No-one, least of all this priest, realised the ease with which he achieved almost total recall of most things he read.

'Do you believe in the catechism?'

'I believe in God but I'm not a cath'lic, Father.'

'You're a clever boy, John. Let me tell you what makes a good school. Not an ordinarily good school, but an extra ordinary school. You have to have a good building, yes, and playing fields, yes, to build up their bodies, and good dormitories so they can have eight hours sleep. Good food depends on a good cook and a good refectory as well, and boys whose backgrounds have the potential. But above all, yes, it is the quality of the staff, and over and above all of that it is the supreme quality of the headmaster which makes a good school into an entity which is more than good – excellence!'

He suddenly got up and lurched forward. The boy, anticipating another blow, stepped back in fear and stumbled. The priest grabbed his arm. 'I worry that my pupils won't understand what I have done, won't know I believe in it,' he muttered into the boy's ear. 'What do you hear about me?' he whispered right in the boy's face.

The boy bent his body back as far as he could, without taking an obvious step backwards. 'I know you're a strict headmaster, Father.'

'Right, right,' he intoned softly, nodding slowly at the same time. All the boy could think was: *Don't let his hand touch me. Keep him talking and pray to God to keep him away. I'll not believe in you any more, God, if you let me down this time.*

'Anything else they say about me?'

'They say to watch out not to insult the College, the Queen or the Virgin Mary.'

'Ha! That's good, very good. I like it.'

He chuckled to himself for a minute or so. 'You've told me what they tell you about me. What do you think?'

The boy did not speak.

'Nothing? Have you nothing to say?'

The boy shook his head.

'That's no answer.'

Father Doyle suddenly exploded into anger. He jumped up and banged his fist on the desk, making all the pens and papers jump. 'That's no answer either!'

For a few minutes, Father Doyle's rage was uncontainable. He picked up a cane which was leaning against the wall behind his chair, and strode about the office, ranting about the state of the boys, the staff, the school. As he shouted, he laid about him with the cane and it was all the boy could do to dodge the blows he inflicted on the bookcases, the mantelpiece, the walls and the desk itself. But he seemed not to notice the boy until he had calmed down again, when he told him to go back to his class. He was at the door when Father Doyle changed his mind. 'I think it would be better if you went back to the Home for the rest of today. Are you feeling peaky?'

The boy shrugged. He looked puzzled.

'You know, tired.'

He shook his head.

'A little sick, maybe?'

The boy realised the easier option. He shrugged again.

'Maybe. Ah. Good. Take the day off, and come back to school when you're feeling one hundred percent again.'

He hated Father Doyle. He held him responsible for everything going on in the school. Even though the priest hadn't hit him that day, he had on many other occasions. From that day the boy vowed to get him, if ever the chance arose.

* * *

As they got into the car and drove off, Chris told Tom about Mrs Blatt having looked after Thompsen, long-term.

'If it's true, I wonder why Mrs Blatt lied,' he said.

'Come to think of it, she didn't exactly lie. She just didn't tell me.'

'Perhaps she didn't want you to think she was responsible for events over a longer period in the boy's life.'

'How the other half lives,' Chris reflected. 'I felt terrible to think those biscuits were her one luxury. And you carried on eating them like there was no tomorrow. I couldn't catch your eye.'

'You take people too literally,' said Tom. 'The Church looks after its own.'

'That's where you're utterly mistaken. This woman left the safe custody of her religious order. She's probably been more disadvantaged as a consequence than if she'd never joined in the first place.'

'Spoken with feeling.'

'There's no complacency like that of the well-heeled middle class, completely insulated from any real understanding of hardship. There's no anger, rejection and punitiveness as strong as from the society when one of its members spurns it and leaves.'

'People like that who submit others to corporal punishment should be given a taste of their own sanctions,' he said.

'You've some real hang-ups about punishment,' she said.

'I have not,' he protested, but she wasn't convinced.

'To say nothing of your religious prejudices,' she added.

* * *

Graver's memories ran riot.

> *I felt near the heart of the evil of the school. I remember an incident back at the home, with Mother Bernadette.*
> *I was upstairs, sent to bed in the dormitory for rubbing my glass during supper and making it ring. I heard a*

noise along the corridor. There was a connecting door between the dormitories and the nuns' accommodation. I pushed the door. It was always locked, but on this occasion someone must have forgotten. The door swung open. I walked towards the sound. A room at the far end with the door not quite closed. I looked through the crack next to the door hinge. The music teacher, Brother Francis and a nun, with a victim. A naked girl, a Homes girl, in a room filled with blood and no cushions or anything.

The girl turned towards me, nearly unconscious, perhaps drugged or drunk. I saw brother Francis holding her while the nun forced the neck of a half bottle of whisky into her mouth. He pushed up his cassock and rubbed himself up against her legs. They were wide apart, hanging over the end of the bed.

It makes me angry to think of it. So angry I have taken action. It's time to inform you.

J

* * *

Miss Craig went to bed early that night. In her dream, she was Sister Ruth again. She heard noises outside the house and later, sounds in the kitchen. It seemed she had hardly gone to sleep when she woke to sudden terror. Her hands were pinned down and she couldn't breath. A piece of cloth was being held over her nose and mouth. She tried to move in the bed but couldn't. Then she passed out, confused as to whether she was awake or merely dreaming.

It didn't take Graver long to overpower his victim and use the anaesthetic pad to bring about a state of virtual unconsciousness.

Sister Ruth woke in pitch darkness and experienced panic as her hands fought with a soft enveloping substance which felt like fine sand. Her arms broke free and she started to pray:

'Hail Mary full of Grace, blessed are Thou –'

She panicked again and scrabbled at her hair to clear it of bits. She pulled it back from her face. When she tried to stand she realised that something was seriously affecting her power to move. An enormous weight pressed on her body, from the shoulders down. She wanted to turn and scratch her foot, in which she suddenly had become aware of an irritating tingling. Panic set in when she realised that she was, in effect, paralysed from the shoulders downwards. Her arms beat uselessly at the hard-packed substance which encased the rest of her body.

'Hail Mary full of Grace, blessed art Thou among women and blessed –'

She heard a soft grunt. It sounded some distance away. It was like a wild animal. Ruth was really scared now. What if it reached her and attacked before she had the chance to extricate herself. She redoubled the scraping with her fingers. The grunting came again. It was closer. She could hear panting now. In a panic, she imagined its hot breath fanning her cheek before it gouged at her face with its sharp tusks.

'Hail Mary full of Grace, blessed –'

A shape moved. She realised the darkness was lifting. Or was it her eyes becoming accustomed to the night? The shape was quite close, almost but not quite within reach. It was oval, not a grunting pig as she had imagined, but – she giggled – a ball, yes, one of those rugby balls, on its end, containing some kind of trick mechanism which made it move slightly from side to side.

'Hail Mary, hail Mary, hail –'

Chapter 29

Chris was standing over Morrison, who sat seemingly doodling at the keyboard of his PC.

'Here we are, boss.' He manipulated the keys and a map appeared on the screen.

'What do we know about his area of operations?' asked Chris

'Well, we know he has one. That's to say, if you put a pencil and line here on the map and draw like this around all the sites where victims have been found –'

'You get a circle. Wonderful. In other words, we know the killer operates within an area of, let's say, twenty by fifty miles on the borders of North and East Yorkshire – that's a thousand square miles. That's goodness knows how many sheep, farms and villages, to say nothing of Hull, Beverley and one or two other towns. Brilliant.'

'No, boss. Not quite as depressing. If we assume it takes the killer half an hour to set the murder scene up and a similar time to drive away, this produces a much smaller radius – say ten to twelve miles.'

* * *

The dull red light shone eerily from a bulb in a socket fixed to the wall to one side of her head. The rugby ball turned and groaned again and she stared aghast at Father Doyle's head. Puffy and discoloured, but still recognisable. Father Doyle!

'Hullo, Father, Sister Ruth here.' Could he see or hear her? Sister Ruth wasn't sure. She thought he opened one swollen eye and grunted a response. She cast her eyes from side to side as they became accustomed to the strange, subdued red light. There wasn't much to see in the arc of sand within her horizon. Apart from Father Doyle to the left of her. And a curious little semicircular shadow in the blank wall, far over on her right. Is it a painted mark or a hole? She couldn't tell.

'I intended to maintain complete darkness in the room, but installed lighting – ants cannot see red so are unaffected by it – so I could monitor my subjects. The cellar isn't ideal. It requires filling almost to the ceiling with sharp sand, poured through a pipe I've made specially to improve ventilation for the insects. I've diverted the exit though, in case any sounds from it attract attention. To overcome the problems of cold and damp conditions – anathema to ants – I've buried several separately wired heating elements. I can't risk dependence on one in case it fails.'

'I'm trying the second movement of the Bruckner for the climax of the experiment. That rhythmic power! I wish it would go on for eternity. I can't wait for the repeat after the lighter passages in between. Is it intended as a minuet and trio? After all this time I haven't found out. It's unusual, if that is the case, to put it in the position of second movement. To some extent I've overcome my disappointment at the brevity of the powerful passage by taping those first few bars over and over, so that the pounding of full orchestra goes on for about half an hour. Du,du,du,du,du,du – du,du,du,du,du,du,du. And so on. After which I'm never prepared for those rich and stretching harmonies at the start of the third movement to tear at my emotions.'

* * *

Sister Ruth panted in the heat. The perspiration ran down her face and neck, and dripped off her nose. She wiped her chin repeatedly. The liquid irritated her eyes and made her itch and shiver.

It was only when she stopped to rest that she became aware of something over and above the maze. There was silence, broken only by her calling for the children. But the something else was the silky smoothness of a quadrillion moving legs. A motion so seamless and unerring, it lapped every crevice like the incoming tide of a becalmed sea, moving upward yet almost without any movement. The slight rustling was the nearest she could get to appreciating the ticking time-bomb of attack. She knew it was plural. The sounds were many, not one compound sound. She somehow knew that, even though she couldn't guess what they were. Phalanx upon phalanx of skeletal forms, chained together by the invisible bonding of tapping antennae and interlocking legs.

When millions of them were in place, so many that they bowed every branch down and couldn't shift their places on the ground without stepping over each other, then, as if by mental powers alone, they stopped. In fact, it was the almost simultaneous waves of feelers briskly stroked on other feelers and bodies in an indescribably delicate ballet of intention, which ordered their stillness and made it absolutely inevitable. The lack of movement was complete, as devastating as the waves of motion had been. It was the silence of armies holding their breath.

Then, like a single slow transpiration, the entire horde advanced. Each occupied only the ant-space in front, and only the gap behind was filled – no less, no more. It was the merest shiver, a trickle of life. But when that slight adjustment is multiplied a billion times, and is repeated over and over again, its impact becomes gross, devastating, and irresistible.

Only then did she realise that the ants were all over her. She stood aghast, paralysed by the shock of it. Then she moved, arms flailing like sails on a windmill. But like thick streams of sticky black treacle they were pouring off the high branches which overhung her. Faster than she could brush and shake them off, fresh lumps of the black crawling masses landed on her, hissing and crackling as they dispersed to find a hold anywhere on her skin or clothing. With mandibles and hooked feet, they clung on, resisting with all means the force of her wild movements.

She screamed. She went on screaming for some minutes after she had toppled to the ground. Until they had completely filled her mouth, biting, wounding, stinging. Suffocating her.

Chapter 30

Not long after Sister Ruth stopped breathing, Tom was discussing the nature of possible links between all of the deaths.
'It's highly likely the killer is an insider to the University.'
'Or the Police Force.'
'You wouldn't countenance that,' said Tom.
'It's one of the options we should consider. The first linked death was a special constable.'
'And a university researcher.'

* * *

Graver drove the tractor with the forklift and laid the two bodies on the sacks he'd carefully placed across the trailer. It took a few minutes to reverse the tractor and connect the trailer to the towbar. He had planned where he would leave the bodies and had the envelope in its plastic cover, sealed against the elements, ready to pin onto the man's jacket.

A sudden flashback made him wince. An image blurred by many years passing. An image of himself, pressed down on those sacks in the corner of the garage, his father's garage, the palm of his hand hiding his eyes, wet with tears. I shall have to teach you a lesson, his father had said. Graver felt as though one secret part of him had never stopped weeping from that day to this.

* * *

Tom was in one of the laboratories, in deep discussion with Luis Deakin about some of the peculiar features of the current forensic investigation.
'These are by no means the most populous nests,' said Tom, enjoying the luxury of being carried away by his pet obsession. 'It's bizarre, as though our mystery entomologist has been using tropical ants for another purpose and wants to test them on this gruesome job. In a way, if speed of execution were important to him, I'd have thought the size of the colony would be his main aim. In the tropics ants can live in great communes of linked nests, colonies of several square kilometres in extent, comprising maybe a trillion individuals – who knows? No-one has ever calculated. In the average square hectare, perhaps as many as twenty million.'
Tom was speculating in response to a question from Luis about the predatory power of different species of tropical ants.

'Sheer colony size could smother a victim long before death through injuries such as haemorrhages. Take Atta, they're leaf cutters. They tend to be vegetarian. They specialise in growing fungi, which they feed on the vegetation they collect. They have fungus gardens in their nests. New colonies of Atta being established in South America, which is their usual habitat, can strip hillsides of all their growth from scratch in three years. They wouldn't be the obvious choice against out and out carnivores, but they could overwhelm by force of numbers.'

At that moment the phone rang in the office. One of the technicians called Tom to say it was the police. When he picked up the receiver Chris answered and the call turned into a detailed discussion of the latest developments in the investigation. By the time Tom returned from taking the rather lengthy call Deakin had gone.

* * *

Chris was waiting outside Tom's office, having phoned him on his mobile and agreed to wait till he arrived. Less than five minutes later she sat down gratefully in one of his easy chairs and slit open the large manilla envelope that had arrived in her post.

'I shouldn't be doing this,' she said, mostly to herself, 'but what the hell.' She put on a pair of protective gloves, passed Tom a pair and began flicking through the sheaf of A4 sheets she'd slipped from the envelope.

'This is ridiculous. Today's post, pages of the stuff. It's so self-indulgent of him to assume that we're going to have time and the motivation to read it.'

In spite of this, she sat and read. As she finished each sheet she passed it across to Tom to read. 'We have to face the fact that someone gets to know who we interview and targets them with very little time-lapse, if any. And at each stage, we're left with more autobiographical material.'

She read from the top page: 'It's easy to grow up, as the memory of each horror disappears from your life, blotted out completely.

'It was only some years later that I realised the shadows of the happenings had not gone away entirely, but still lingered at the edges of my mind. What matters now is inability as I grow older to control and curb the unpleasant feelings I'm left with in growing strength.

'I withdrew from the violence and unhappiness of the household into the more endurable world of my imagination.

'At about the same time I started to read books in earnest. I began with a few of the books on the children's shelves in the school library. I found them very unsatisfying, though I was not inclined to seek out any alternatives. Instead, I found solace in piles of books stuffed in corners and on an ill assorted collection of bookshelves in different rooms, along landings, in corridors and generally anywhere which provided a suitable surface. Many of these books were unintelligible to me. But a few claimed my attention more than the rest. Among these was a companion to music, in which summaries of the lives of great composers stirred my interest. It was some time before I discovered the lives of German and Austrian composers of the late nineteenth centuries and, because I had nobody to guide me, even longer before I found my way to the music of Bruckner and Mahler, those wonderful, complex scores – cities of sound.

'I became completely absorbed by the music and the ants. Practical circumstances tended to divide my attentions – poring over the comings and goings of the ants by day and the musical scores by night. The resonance between the complexities of the parts and the creation of a whole – the myriads of actions contributing to the grand order of the colony, the thousands of individual squiggles on the score, distributed across a hundred music stands and wrought by the conductor into a single, magnificent whole. Together, from the age at which close interaction with other people became too painful, they filled my ears and eyes, my entire consciousness. They obliterated the testing of my being against the disharmony of the household. They offered a world in which I was more and more cut off from that other world about me. I would re-engage later, but only at the most superficial level – to make the arrangements, to realise my goal of becoming the conductor.

'All this was a long time before I took the laboratory job which seemed to offer an escape from the chaotic, unreasonable, hateful domesticity which still boiled around me. I liked the idea of working in the lab, with equipment and computers rather than with people. My problems had derived from the people I knew and lived with. I had been the victim of so much from those who should have been my friends and protectors. I wanted to feel safe. Perhaps safety lay in retreating from direct interaction with people – the potential attackers.'

'He worked as lab assistant at the University,' said Tom.

'Seemingly.'

'Why doubt it?'

'There are a number of possibilities. He could have worked for a commercial company. He could be trying to put us off the scent, or to implicate someone else.'

She carried on reading.

'Outwardly of course, there was nothing. Nothing to suggest anything was different from the pictures on the wall of the sitting room. That little cluster of photographs which summed up three generations of weddings, christenings and family reunions. The sitting room they only let us use on high days and holidays. The coldest room in the house –

apart from the bedrooms, that is. In winter they needed overcoats on their beds and I still coughed every night. There was still condensation, and sometimes frost, on the inside of every window pane, encrusting each metal frame with a kind of stale, black rust which stank like that water butt at Uncle Harry's.

'From four to twelve years old, those photographs held the family together. It was the power of the camera and the power of the photographer that showed it. Grandfather and Father, who took the pictures, they were the only ones not on the wall. But they stood apart from the rest of us, invisible, somewhere else in the foreground, pushing everyone into line, insisting on a frozen smile.

'I used those photographs, and others in the pile of magazines in the cupboard under the stairs, to build up my picture of what the world was like. All those days, weeks and months, on and off, convalescing from whatever illness it was. They never named it, which made me feel even more as though I was the person in brackets, the child without a label, who for all those hours spent alone in my bedroom while the blackbirds sang outside and the street bustled with life, was away somewhere else, in suspended animation. Or in my coffin. That was the way I used to think of it. I used it to build up my picture of the world. Or rather, two pictures. One concerning everything inside my head and the other, what remained outside. The trick was to make day to day life bearable by learning to move between one and the other. I practised this trick until I had it developed to a fine art. It meant that when I was in my head nothing, no matter how bad, could get to me. The other trick was to make sure that I controlled everything. I did this by taking total charge of whatever I undertook. In my dreams I became the ruler, the generalissimo. People came and went at my orders. Anyone who didn't carry them out completely, and immediately, to my satisfaction, was punished as I thought fit.

'My head was filled with a mixture of German war films and books about crime.

'After the experience of travelling to the USA, I shunned moving from the immediate locality. I took to watching videos, not able to go to the expense of borrowing from a shop, but having no need, since I drew on an extensive collection of particularly violent and sexually explicit tapes I found stacked in bin liners in the cellar of the house, evidently forgotten about when father went abroad.

'The plots of these fed my imagination. I became a Colonel on the Eastern Front in the early 1940s. I had responsibility for punishing defaulters, boosting morale, and destroying the myth of the enemy's invincibility. I came to believe I was upholding the values of the German Wermacht. I would make promises, swear oaths of allegiance, make speeches and drink toasts. I drank on my own. I drank my own health and cursed others freely. On one occasion, I slit my right wrist, read some passages from Nietzsche's Zarathustra whilst sipping my own blood.

'Now and again, in lighter vein (I like that pun!) I found myself dreaming of summer holidays spent in a lighter world with shadowy figures and wraiths too vague and ethereal to be recognisable from my past.

'The destiny to which I aspired was beyond the world of domesticity and feelings. It lay in the world of men and action, not women and emotions.

'I returned repeatedly to the more earthy and satisfying images. This was my war and to fight it I stayed dirty. I took to living in the same battle-scarred clothes day after day until they and my body stank. After watching and living the Stalingrad campaign I learned that natural body odours and dirt keep a man waterproof. I sat for hours drinking in the details, peeling back the photo-stills and pausing, frame by frame, on the explosions, the bodies flying through the air in the wake of exploding mortars and grenades. A thousand deaths were given action replays every day. I fed on a diet of campaigns of destruction. My senses reeled after several hours of detonations. They induced a kind of drunkenness. I went into a stupor. My head ached with it. I would lie down on the carpet and close my eyes while the images catapulted across my inner vision before finally slowing down and collapsing into a daytime doze.

'Out of my room, the security of aloneness broke down. The bedsit near the railway was a tiny room and the landlady ruled with iron. I was too shy to stand up for myself at the time. I stored my resentment in the vast reservoir of anger which had accumulated for several decades.

'She told me, "I want no waste. If you have my meals, you eat them. Nothing worse than a man who won't eat."'

'I sat in front of my dinner, night after night. Night after night, when she had left the room, I fought back waves of nausea and forced myself to pick at the edges of the plate. Then I shovelled the bulk of it into a newspaper, rolled it up, hid it under the table and waited for her to return. After she'd cleared the empty plates and I'd smilingly thanked her for her marvellous cooking, I went for a walk with the packets of newspaper hidden under my coat, dreading the juices would leak out and betray me by dripping onto the carpet. Once in the street, I would head for the opposite pavement, with its succession of litter bins spaced at intervals on the street lamps, and stuff one packet down the gaping mouth of each, as casually as I could as I strolled along. Inside, I was shaking with nervousness that I might be found out, and strangely weak from hunger. It wasn't the physical hunger for food though, more a hunger of the whole body and mind for some quality absent from my life, which only the sight of the ant masses, and the Bruckner and Mahler, could begin to supply.

'I watched the ants hunting and eating. It was difficult to focus my mind on the problem of how to kill. I knew it would involve the ants, but even so, there were so many ways of doing it. I read in a magazine I picked up in the street that Mongol bandits buried their enemies up to their necks in sand and let ants eat them alive. The lucky ones, their chests compressed by the weight of sand, suffocated first. I couldn't believe in the fact of suffocation until one day walking along the beach, I watched a group of lads burying one of them almost up to his shoulders in sand. Then, ten minutes later, I returned along the same stretch of beach to a scene of frantic activity, with neighbouring adults all scrabbling away to release that very frightened boy from his sand prison. His face was purple. He gasped for breath until they freed his arms and eventually sufficient of his torso for him to lever himself out. Then he lay panting on the sand whilst they laid blankets over him and waited for medical aid. I wasn't affected by the state of the lad, but the impact on him of this brief burying did surprise me. It wasn't as though he had even been covered in sand up to his neck. I hadn't realised until that moment the claustrophobic impact on a person of even partial burying in sand. It clearly caused psychological traumas as well as being potentially fatal. Up till then I'd assumed it was similar to being ducked in a pool of water.

'I realised a person who is pinioned and subjected to additional psychological stresses, such as fear, can quite quickly succumb. Probably that's why people who fall into mud flows or quicksand lose their calm and, ignoring the objective possibility of clambering out, die quickly if rescue isn't on hand.'

* * *

'I could tell something was up,' said Chris, raising her head briefly from the papers. 'All these communications from the person we assume is our killer, they amount to a cauldron of unholy loves.'

'You're a teeny bit ahead of me there,' said Tom.

'Isn't that what St Augustine found when he reached Carthage?'

'I'll pass,' said Tom. 'Your Oxbridge education's been broader than mere science.'

* * *

I was drawn to the local University after reading about the German composers and the German Universities. I took to day dreaming about the University I walked past in my nocturnal journeying. One evening, I was out earlier than usual and I passed the science block a few minutes before the night porter locked up. I slipped into the foyer and made it down the corridor and into one of the laboratories without being seen. It wasn't long before someone in the porter's lodge picked me up on the closed circuit television and I was ejected. I pretended I had taken a wrong turning and luckily they were in a generous mood. They could see I was harmless and I escaped with nothing more than a stiff lecture on the consequences of trespass. But from my point of view it had been worth it. In the ten minutes or so before two night staff appeared with the porter, I had darted swiftly from bench to bench, peering at this experiment and that demonstration, drinking in the details of a world I felt excluded from. If life choices can be made in a moment, this was my moment of decision.

I went back to the University during the daytime. I walked into the foyer of the main hall, open to public access. I pored over the photographs of the University open day. I found out the date of the next annual open day was in three weeks' time. It was a Saturday at the beginning of June and turned out to be brilliant sunshine.

This time I could wander where I wished. I found myself in the science block. This time I gained entry to the area where they conducted experiments on insects, particularly ants. I spent more than an hour in that area. I took two reels of film.

Outside, in the corridor, I was intrigued by the noticeboards. There were postcards from staff on holiday in other places – Spain, France and Bournemouth. There were several pictures of adults and children. Were these members of staff? Which were the children of which staff?

When I reached home I found that by one of those flukes I had taken several snaps of what I assumed were academic staff explaining various experimental set-ups to visitors. I had plenty of material to feed into my search. But what was I looking for? I didn't quite know. I had a selection of the photographs enlarged. Those on which I eventually identified as the key people, through collecting brochures and prospectuses whenever I visited the University, joined the ever growing number on the big pinboard on one wall of my large farmhouse kitchen, which I dubbed HQ.

There was a time later when I used computer games to strengthen my expertise in the mass control of populations. I tried all the war games, from the ancient civilisations and the military campaigns of the Greeks and Alexander the Great through to Napoleon and the two great wars of the twentieth century. Nothing excited me like the ants, though.

While I studied the photos, I switched on the CD player. Not Mahler's First symphony. I wanted to save that for moments of consummation. I would take the third movement of the Second symphony. Every time I heard those woodwind passages, I imagined the formicidae in their convoluted tunnels, making their way up to the surface and bursting out into the sunlight. The urgency of the rhythm accentuated the frantic rush of the army. Then the fortissimo brass bursting out over the top of the strings as the soldiers advanced, their mandibles more than quadruple the size of the worker ants. Timpani and triangles now, as a small group of winged queens emerged, floating around the entrance as though in a daze before being gently coaxed back into the safety of the limitless darkness below ground. Then the restless rhythm starting again, as the urge to hunt and kill infected the host, and waves of excitement visibly moved half a million bodies in unison at the moment of advance. I did not heed the tears running down my face as the burst of sound faded into diminuendo strings and timpani, and they came to rest, sated with meat from fifty thousand insects – small mammals, injured birds and infant animals too small and slow to get out of their hunting field. As the contralto entered with the solo, I could hear nothing beyond the words Die elt ist tief *- that surely was the superiority of the ants, to penetrate the depth of the world. Deep was the suffering and the joy.* Doch alle Lust will Ewigkeit – Will tiefe, tiefe Ewigheit. *All manner of joys sought Eternity, the deep Eternity. I* *couldn't bear my own response to the words, in the face of the urge to seek to place the power of the denouement with the ants. To take the life of people back into the deep earth with them.*

J

* * *

Chris finished reading the few lines on the last sheet and tossed it down on the low table between them. Tom picked it up and scanned it. She stood up and brushed her hands down her blouse and skirt, as though trying to cleanse herself of any connection with the man they sought.

There was a faint rumble, as though deep in the distant Pennines rock strata were moving along ancient fault lines.

'Damn,' said Tom. He glanced at the ornate Edwardian brass-mounted barometer in its polished mahogany case. It hung on the wall behind Chris, curiously out of place with the modern paraphernalia of filing cabinets and bookshelves stuffed with box files and books.

'What's the matter?'

'Thunder. I've had a look at the weather reports. The main band of rain is still twenty miles away and thunderstorms are notoriously fickle in these parts. We may escape one altogether, while on the North Yorkshire Moors they're flooded out. We can't count on it, though. The pressure's down to twenty-nine and still falling.'

'Thunder doesn't bother you?'

'It's the ants I'm concerned about.'

Chris's mobile rang and she answered it. Even though she wasn't saying much, Tom could tell the call wasn't going well. She was tense when she came off the phone.

'That was Bradshaw,' she said. 'Sister Ruth's been found dead.'

All thoughts of the storm were driven from Tom's mind.

'What the hell!'

'There's a man's body as well, but they're still trying to confirm the identity of that.'

'Do we have any idea –?'

'There are insects all round the body and mouth parts buried in it.'

'Do they know what insects they are?'

She shrugged. 'It hardly matters what they think. You and I can guess.'

'How did he find her so quickly after we interviewed her?'

'Perhaps he knew we were going and had time to plan.'

'He couldn't – that would mean an insider –'

She looked serious. 'Who knew we were going? Bradshaw,

members of the team, Morrison? Bradshaw's doing his nut and wants me back immediately.'

Tom shook his head, as though he found this incredible. Chris's mobile rang again. She turned to Tom. 'We need to be at the scene of crime. Bring whatever you need to identify ants.'

'What about the University?' Chris asked, while he was gathering his things and locking up. 'Who knew where you were going?'

'Apart from me, in effect, nobody of any consequence.'

'Of any consequence,' she said. 'Thereby hangs the crucial tale.'

* * *

Ahead of them on the road from Beverley to Bainton, there were blue lights flashing. Chris's car slowed and an officer waved them off the road. She climbed out and Tom followed her. DC Morrison walked across to them,

'Boss, we found this in a canvas bag near the bodies.'

'That'll be so the ants don't get at it and destroy the paper,' said Tom. 'Leave me to read this in the car.' He didn't have the stomach for going any closer to the scene of the crime, unless she demanded it of him.

Chris saw him about to open the bag. 'Don't touch it,' she said and ran across to a group of officers in protective clothing. She returned with a pair of gloves in a packet and tossed them onto his knee. 'You'll get me shot,' she said.

Chapter 31

Colleagues: It's my privilege to let you into my secret.

The ninth symphony of Mahler occupies the high ground between individual entities and the larger reality. Through it, I enter a dream state with the entrance of the dance motif at the start of the first movement. The swinging rhythms of the violins creates a lullaby, in which I imagine being swung gently in a hammock by my mother.

Within five minutes, of course, all is loudness and disturbance. I am tipped out and the timpani with some brass and muted woodwind and strings impose their sinister echoes on my attempted relaxation. An even more subversive plot is hatched in the awesome shadow of this steadily darkening dance. The harp still accompanies, but an irresistible burst of harmonies reminiscent of Richard Strauss makes it ever less likely that the warm, sandy surface of the soil will stay quiescent.

I delicately pull the remote and the hole which forms the main entrance to the nest opens a few millimetres. A cascade of ants surges through the tiny gap, which I quickly close.

Now the music is louder as the first movement gains velocity, the few straggling themes surfacing louder than the dark accompaniment to the plot.

The foragers soon lose their extreme excitement and slow to a more deliberate quartering of their territory, criss-crossing each other's path repeatedly in their search for prey.

Suddenly there's a person there, a living body, tightly bound. A woman. I check and double check that her hands and legs are secured and that the gag is in place. Only just in time, for the second movement is beginning. I have so much to say and can't risk her interrupting.

This lyricism in the music always takes me back to a childhood which repeated itself – the dance-like motif which recurs in light and darker sound tones reminds me of the picture in my head of walking on open heathland, with sandy banks running alongside the track and isolated clumps of gorse. The heather is scattered on the banks, by no means covering them. The most striking feature to me as a young child was the brilliant orange and black colouring of the large ants darting among smaller black ones, along the length of the bank. I know now these were the workers of Formica Sanguinea, known as the slave-making ant for its habit of raiding nests of the smaller, matt-black Formica Fusca, carrying off grubs and pupae to rear as "slaves" in its own nests. In fact, these so called slaves do no more than add to the labour force of the colony, in contrast with the continental Polyergus Rufescens which still raids other nests but has degenerated to the point where it is totally dependent on being fed by the captured workers from these raids – an invidious situation to be in. It's the sharpness of the remembered emotion, though, to which I'm drawn repeatedly: a hypnotic mood, almost of exaltation in the sunlight drowning out all emotions other than rustic happiness at the complex simplicity of the unending activity and drama of the ants. It means to me the lost world of childhood, a fiction to which I feel entitled, but know I've been denied access.

The fourth movement. The victims never know, but when the movements change I respond to the change of mood. The start of the movement brings me down to the lowest point of my emotions. Underneath the slow rhapsody of strings with its modulation to darker keys, I sense the untellable story of the composer touching my own unspeakable memories. The tears run momentarily down my cheeks as I recall the tragedy of my mother dying too soon to protect me from the subsequent abuse of my body and mind. Only the music pushing onward past that awful stretching emotion saves me from weakening. A sudden jolting out of it. Sideways, into what the other adults call the real world.

You have to harden up or succumb. I won't say die

because in everything outside this music and these ants I died long ago, at the hands of those who should have cared for me.

I kill at the point of the first theme growing into its successor. This coincides in my head with the budding of the new colony from the old. It marks the establishment of the queen in the skull of the victim. I call this the temple of wisdom.

But the harmonies cripple me. They continue unstoppably, to the point of that extended pianissimo passage which for me is the eye of the storm. The music both confirms and undermines any capacity for thought, feelings and action. It reaches where no person has touched me since she left me alone, unable to defend myself. As the strings turn inward and over I'm pulled apart by my own unsatisfied love, grief and longing. I lie on the ground, motionless with emotions with no resolution. I can only wait and hope for Mahler to bring me back up, with the swelling resolution. But this time the music comes and passes unnoticed, fading into the unending pianissimo of Mahler's heaven, which for me is the silent, airless void beyond the Earth and Universe, leaving me gasping for breath, unable to rise beyond this kneeling position, racked with guilt and self-hate at what I have done. It's touch and go whether the instruments will drag me through this torture towards continuing life.

G

* * *

'Okay?' he asked, as Chris got back into the car. She was carrying a plastic bag and she tossed it onto his lap. He peered at its contents.

'Hmm, definitely ant body parts,' he mused. 'I'll let you know later more about which species.'

She looked pale. 'I don't want to talk about it at present.'

They drove some distance in silence, towards town.

'I'll drop you back home,' she said.

'Don't bother, your office will do. My car's in your car park, if you recall.'

Clouds were bubbling up.

'The sky looks a funny colour,' she said.

'An antman's Nirvana, in the normal course of events,' he said.

She gave him a puzzled glance from the driver's seat and he explained.

'Thundery weather creates the conditions for breeding. Scientists like to study the procreation of insects. It gives clues about their ability to survive natural disasters and pesticides. Unfortunately, it can also make social insects more aggressive. Ask any beekeeper whether it's safe to approach a hive in a thunderstorm.'

* * *

Chris and Tom were back in the office at Wawne Road. He hadn't driven off straight away. They sat one each side of her desk with a pile of documents between them, struggling with the gruesome reality of the latest deaths. Conversation was hard going. Neither of them wanted to focus and this made it hard to share what they already knew and discuss what to do next.

'The latest papers from our presumed killer are pretty disturbing,' he said, putting the envelope whose contents he'd read in the car down on the desk. 'Have you had much back from your forensic psychology colleagues on the previous ones?'

'They tend to talk about mental conditions and disorders.' Her voice was flat, as though it didn't interest her. 'They mention bipolar disturbance and possible intermittent psychosis. It's a very complicated way of saying he's killing people. Why does he go to such extreme lengths?' Even as she uttered the words, the question was rhetorical. She was tired of these endless intellectual discussions, the speculation which went nowhere.

Tom mused. 'The fact is, he does go to these extreme lengths. There are far simpler ways of killing a person. You just do it. Think about the time he takes, setting it all up, running with all the technical problems, maximising the part played by the ants. All the writing and associated paraphernalia. Why the complications? It's almost like junk mail.'

Chris sighed and made an effort to engage. 'I thought being an antman yourself, if anyone could make the connection between the ants and the killing, it would be you.'

'I hope that's a compliment,' said Tom.

'Perhaps there is some merit in looking at the complications. We haven't been sitting on our hands at this end.' She leaned across the desk, pointing to a box file on the low table behind him. 'Pass me that file.'

Inside the box was an Ordnance Survey map of the area, with transparent overlays. She pushed some of the papers back and laid the items flat on her desk.

'We have Morrison to thank for this,' she said. 'He's marked the location of one body on each of these.' She laid them one by one over the map. 'This top one,' she indicated a further overlay, 'is a line drawn round the perimeter of the area within which the bodies have been found. That shape is a bit irregular, more like a sausage than a circle. As you can see, it's a few miles long and about a half mile wide. The idea is to compute half an hour's driving time from the scene of each crime and search in the centre of the resulting area.'

Tom looked puzzled. He was struggling with the relevance of this. 'I've never really gone along with mechanistic theories about behaviour, insect or human.'

Chris was annoyed – with Tom, with Morrison's ridiculous theories and with herself. 'To hell with this. I've got Bradshaw on one side ridiculing every effort we make and you on the other, pouring cold water on our detection attempts. All right, he could be living anywhere. He could be a rally driver and be commuting from Lincoln or Cambridge.

'But is it likely? We have to start with what's reasonable and likely, for God's sake. People impose so many barriers to us making progress with the case!' She pushed the map with its extra sheets angrily to the far edge of the desk, crumpling them up.

Tom was unperturbed. 'I suppose it's possible.'

Chris shouted at him. 'Stop being so bloody calm!'

There was silence. She was red in the face and breathing hard. Tom was silent, pensive.

A few minutes passed and she calmed down somewhat.

'How many laboratories are there in the UK with research facilities for the study of ants?'

'That's a difficult one. On social insects in general, ten or twelve at the most.'

'Too many. How many specifically are geared up for research into communication among ants?'

'A much smaller number I'd say. London, Peterborough possibly, Hull.'

'To come back to the question as to where he's operating from. How the hell do we find out where his base is?'

'We could wait for him to reveal it, in what he sends to us.'

'That could take weeks, months even.'

'You're very pessimistic.'

'Perhaps we need to take stock. We have all this mass of disparate information. It would be helpful to put it all together and hope that a few odd jigsaw pieces will start to form a larger pattern. That's the message behind the work Morrison's done. I feel strongly we need to go back to our psychiatric colleagues.'

'Working with Bradshaw, it wouldn't be hard to feel an episode coming on,' Tom joked.

'How did you guess? Seriously, we need specialist input on the possible personality disorders this man could be suffering from.'

'Bradshaw might disagree with you. He sees the killer as bad rather than mad.'

'Then it's up to us to ensure Bradshaw doesn't have the last word.'

Chapter 32

Tom didn't expect Chris to take up his off-the-cuff suggestion that it would be useful for all those primarily involved in the murder investigation to meet on neutral territory. He had envisaged one of the University's several conference venues as suitable, but sensitivities around the University connections of both victims and suspects ruled this out.

Almost thirty people crowded into an annexe of the Eppleworth Manor Hotel on the Wolds above the sedately respectable community of Cottingham, reputedly England's largest village. It was a beautiful building, a former Victorian manor house, standing in its own grounds within sight of the preserved windmill at Skidby. The nearby car park was a forest of police cars. Caterers from the Hull Police Training Centre had been brought in for the day. A small contingent of uniformed officers patrolled outside to ensure no non-approved personnel came anywhere near the proceedings. The ACC was adamant about confidentiality and a complete media blackout, and Bradshaw willingly followed his orders to the letter.

Despite his other shortcomings, Bradshaw had a good reputation as Chair of meetings. His introduction was short and Chris took over with a detailed briefing of the stage reached. She summarised the circumstances of the deaths of the five victims associated with the case. She began with Detlev Brandt, whilst acknowledging there was some doubt about whether the cause of death fitted the pattern of the other killings.

'This is the only death not attributed primarily to insect activity. Dr Brandt's main link with the other victims is that he, like them, was employed by the University and the next victim was the clerk within days of the conclusion of his inquest. Against these links, we could argue that a considerable space of time has elapsed between this death and the others which have taken place recently, within a few weeks of each other.'

The brief pause before Chris continued was taken up by a lively debate about whether Brandt's death should form part of the current investigation.

'I'm in no doubt,' said Chris, pointing out the connection between the inquest into Brandt's death and the killing of Faith Wistow, clerk to the coroner's court.

Chris's consideration of the finding of the corpse of the pig provided some opportunities for the comedians in the room to exercise their wit. An outbreak of grunting followed. She allowed the jokers some leeway before returning to the serious business of the day.

'We'll come back later to the significance of the written material in our hands, which seems to be directly associated with these killings, beginning of course with the pig.' Chris intervened to stifle a further epidemic of pig noises. She reviewed the circumstances of the finding of the bodies of Faith Wistow and Martin John and the two latest victims, Sister Ruth Craig and Father Doyle.

'The strongest link between these victims at present appears to be the Wilberforce University. The latest two killings add an important dimension, in that they aren't associated directly with the University, but have a connection with earlier years based in the Cambridge area, in the life of one of the suspects, John Thompsen. More of this shortly. As far as the University links are concerned, the victims with direct University connections have all worked in the biological sciences.'

'Before going into detail,' said Chris, 'I want to set out the general background for the main suspects. So far we have had four main suspects in the case: 'Martin John, Robin Lovelace, John Walters and John Thompsen. The first of these can be ruled out because he was the next victim, before others were killed. We have medical evidence of Walters' death a couple of years ago. That leaves Lovelace and Thompsen in the frame at present. There are particular reasons for not taking Lovelace seriously as a suspect. This means that if our present inquiries into Thompsen don't produce results, we'll be seriously short of suspects in this case.' This comment created a ripple of reaction in the room. Bradshaw, unsmiling, sat beside Chris and unseen by her, pulled a face.

As Chris finished, Bradshaw stood up and shuffled his papers preparatory to introducing the next stage of the day. 'If you're looking for someone who knows their ants, the most likely suspect is Professor Fortius.' If Bradshaw was expecting a laugh from this attempted joke, he was disappointed. A few hesitant titters followed and he quickly moved on to introduce Mary Threadgold, Tim Rathbone and Sheila Rawlinson to talk about the profiles of the victims and the suspects.

Mary's presentation was crisp. She began with some generalities and quickly moved into the detail.

'We've been looking at the written material left with some of the victims and the very similar material we've had through the post. Quite often, killers who communicate in this way show other signs of wanting a dialogue with those looking for them. It's a paradox. They do everything they can to avoid detection, but they take the huge risk of letting us have personal details about them, which are bound to give clues and increase the likelihood they'll be caught. We've consulted our graphologist, who studies handwriting and who gives her apologies today, but agrees with our conclusions.

'We've analysed the content of the notes in detail. Whilst there are one or two which contain overlapping material, in general the notes signed J are autobiographical while those signed G deal with the current homicidal tendencies of our person. So the G documents are more worrying and signal danger. The way the J notes are written suggests an isolated and unhappy person who has been traumatised by some abusive childhood experiences. The content of the notes, taken together, form a considerable body of biographical data. There don't seem to be any significant inconsistencies. Although there are references to places and periods of time, they aren't specific enough for us to get a handle on the places where he lived or his age at particular times. We have no way of confirming the truth of statements made in the notes, but from the grammar and syntax, we guess he was either raised in the south of England – possibly Surrey, north Hampshire or South London – or had parental or teaching influences from that area. At some stage, he'll have moved to the Hull area.

'As far as the match between the two surviving suspects and these fragments of evidence is concerned, we haven't enough to draw final conclusions. There are stronger associations between Lovelace and the Home Counties than Thompsen, and the level of literacy of the written material points to a man of Lovelace's education rather than any of the others. These are superficial resemblances, but they're all we have to go on at present.'

Chris stole a glance behind her and saw Bradshaw was smiling.

Chris buttonholed Dr Rice, the acting Dean during coffee break.

'You've brought home to me the reality that our true suspect is a more formidable opponent than we realised,' he said.

'Tell me about this man Thompsen,' Chris said.

'I'm struggling. It's not easy to switch one's focus.'

'I suggest you try. Someone's life may depend on it.

Rice's defensiveness surfaced. 'I'm well aware, Inspector, of the vulnerabilities of the situation,' he said testily, 'but you must appreciate this is a large institution. With several hundred staff it would be impossible for me to keep in touch with all staff movements and know everyone personally.'

'Is there any chance of us looking at Thompsen's file later today?'

'Well, as you can see, I'm not at the University at this minute,' said Rice with a controlled sigh. 'I can ask for the file to be looked out by morning.'

'To have certain details here by lunchtime today would be more use,' said Chris. 'We've laid on an office with a phone, if you ask at Reception.'

Rice's hard stare was lost on her. 'It depends what kind of details,' he said in an extremely precise way, a mannerism those who knew him associated with moods of extreme anger which, even if he felt them, he rarely displayed.

If she noticed, she gave no sign but continued: 'Dates of employment, addresses, personal details including national insurance, birth date and any other associated facts, would be appreciated.'

* * *

Sheila Rawlinson's style was relaxed and informal, as though she was chatting to a friend rather than addressing a meeting: 'There are quite a number of diagnostic keys which would fit the present circumstances. Unfortunately, we don't have a patient to examine, so I can't try them out. Reports of gaps in the person's memory, blackouts, seizures, actions other people recall but the person doesn't. But what you've shown me is quite a good starting point. I'd hazard a guess that this person has experienced some or all of these other symptoms. Some of my colleagues might simply suggest he's suffering from schizophrenia or personality disorder and pass on to the next patient. But to me that's a cop-out. You have to appreciate no respectable psychiatrist would give a formal diagnosis on such a slight foundation, even if all the above symptoms were present. We have to satisfy a list of diagnostic criteria before considering we have enough evidence. But it's possible this man – and I'm pretty sure it is a man – is suffering from a rare and serious condition, a form of mental illness known as dissociative identity disorder, known more popularly as multiple personality disorder, or MPD. I wouldn't consider it impossible for this man to take on the personalities of key people who have had an impact on his life – such as schoolteacher, parent or whoever. We can't tell whether he'll be reinforcing a traumatic event or reconstructing the past in some ideal way.'

Chris intervened: 'So it doesn't have to be a bad experience?'

'Absolutely not. A dissociative episode can take many forms. But it's usually the bad ones psychiatrists focus on, since it is traumas or mental illness that bring people to us. The incident he recalls may be so traumatic that both the incident and his memory of it will be completely segregated from the rest of his consciousness.'

'In another personality.'

'The more traumas, situations and people involved originally, the greater the number of personalities which may be assumed by the person.'

'Is it likely that his G personality is violent, psychopathic?'

'Like Dr Jekyll and Mr Hyde?'

Chris nodded. 'Sort of.'

'It's impossible to say without interviewing the person and taking a detailed history. It could take a long time to get him to recall and explore previous traumatic experiences responsible for particular splits in his consciousness. You're crossing the boundary between diagnosis and treatment. I'm speculating now, but he could have mirrored the violence experienced by one of the significant people he encountered at one particular period of his past, and subsequent life events could have reinforced it, as an aberrant way of coping.'

'Can you translate that into a concrete example?' asked Chris.

'The Jewish teacher he refers to in the papers – Mr Regel. It's conceivable that one of the man's fragmented personalities identifies with the persecution he experienced in the school, whilst another acts out the role of oppressor, whether in the concentration camp or later. It all depends on the man's own intellectual capacity, the power of his imagination, the level of his own trauma and the extent of his own repression of memories and feelings.'

Sheila reflected for a minute or two, then continued: 'If I was this man's psychiatrist, I'd be wanting to get hold of him before the two sets of personalities – the oppressor and the victim – converge.'

'You're hinting he could become dangerous on an even larger scale. He's already a serial killer.'

'We can't tell what anger is mobilised in these destructive episodes and what he might do if at the same time he's overcome by guilt.'

'I thought you said the splits in the personality were separate.'

'If only the human psyche were that simple and mechanical. An extreme set of circumstances may provoke a rash of extremely destructive and self-destructive acts.'

'Multiple murders followed by suicide,' said Chris. 'Multiple murders yes, suicide possibly. Not good news for potential victims.' Chris turned to Mary Threadgold. 'Any comments on what Sheila has said?'

'I haven't a lot to add,' said Mary, 'except that I'm convinced Sheila is right and this is a case of MPD. My contribution to this investigation is more speculative, because that's the nature of handwriting analysis. As you no doubt all know, this man has swamped us with paper. Apart from the detail of its content, the most significant feature, I think, is the way he signs himself with different initials. So far, we've noted two – J and G. I say so far, because it is always possible in a case like this for the person to produce other aliases as well. As J he seems reflective and the diary takes on a merely autobiographical style. When he signs himself as G, watch out. That's when he's in homicidal mood.'

'You've omitted to say we're always one step behind,' said Chris. 'We get the notes after the deed.'

'True,' Mary admitted, 'but at least we know which of his multiple personalities is the more dangerous one, at present.'

'It could change?'

'It's a highly fluid situation. He's likely to be very unstable and that means unpredictable.'

'He could kill again, very soon?'

'I think that's Sheila's territory.'

Sheila spoke. 'He could kill several times more in the near future. Or he could kill only once more.'

'Why only once more? '

'The person he sees as central, and then kill himself.'

'So he is potentially suicidal,' said Chris.

'He could be. The question is whether he will reveal a crucial clue which will lead us to him before he kills again. It's probably a race between the suicide of being detected and actual, physical suicide.'

'I don't much care how quickly he kills himself.'

'Don't forget,' said Sheila, 'that last act could include any victims he's taken hostage, who are still alive.'

Mary was speaking again. 'One other thing, these fragments of writing – if I can call them that, because I'm aware some are pretty long – are so strange. The handwriting differs and the content. If the other circumstances of the murders weren't similar, I'd be tempted to assume they were written by completely different people, or that our killer wanted to put us off the scent by presenting them that way.'

'That's possible,' said Sheila, 'though on the whole people tend to mimic psychiatric symptoms successfully only in fictional stories. I'm reminded of the biographical account in the book *The Three Faces of Eve*. Eve was suffering from such fragmentation of her personality that it was difficult for other people to know who they were dealing with at any one time.'

Bradshaw was in his element during the lunch break and spared no time seeking Chris out. 'I see you've been hob-nobbing with the head-shrinks, Inspector. Next, you'll be becoming one.'

'Not much time to do that, sir, in this job.'

Bradshaw grinned and didn't let up. 'So you've been to see Dr Rawlinson about your workload.'

Chris played it straight. 'She's not that kind of consultant. I wouldn't ask a forensic psychiatrist for advice on our workloads. I'm keen to examine the implications of our murderer having MPD, multiple personality disorder.'

'I don't care if she is a forensic whatever. What good is the label anyway? No doubt it's a half-cracked scheme to excuse these bastards from taking responsibility for their crimes and get them off with mental health orders rather than serving their time in the nick. Like that Banji.'

'Kenneth Bianchi, the so-called Hillside Strangler? Actually he tried to fake MPD and claim that one of his alternative personalities had carried it out. But it was a psychiatrist who interviewed him, showed he was probably faking, clearing the way for Bianchi to be convicted of murder.'

'Rawlinson obviously primed you with the known case which shows her and her colleagues up in a good light.'

'No, sir. She did tell me, however, that contrasted with the millions of people who suffer from mental disorders such as severe depression or schizophrenia at any one time, there are probably only about two or three hundred reported cases of MPD. She did bring my attention to books written about the most well-known of these, including *The Three Faces of Eve*, *Sybil* and *The Minds of Billy Milligan*.'

'Don't get smart with me, Chief Inspector. Thank Christ some of us keep their feet on the ground in this Force. Forget your books and get your nose into catching criminals.'

'We've a pile of evidence of a man with a severe personality disorder.'

'A bad egg, that's all I see. I've seen them before. They confuse people like you and in court they use the mental health diagnosis to twist them round their little finger.'

'This man is seriously disturbed.'

'My judgement is he's bad rather than mad. This is one serial killer who won't avoid prison. You're right up a gum tree, you and your crackpot experts. Since you persuaded me to bring Fortius in, this case has gone from worse to even worse.'

After lunch, Chris brought the meeting to order with some difficulty. She stood at the front of the room, flanked by DC Morrison who looked decidedly nervous.

'It's the bloody graveyard spot, straight after lunch, boss,' he whispered.

'You'll be fine once you get going,' whispered Chris. She held up her hands but this didn't work, so she clapped them above her head and brought the meeting to order. When Morrison's fellow officers became aware he was presenting, there were whistles and catcalls. Chris spoke over the top of these while Bradshaw glared round the room, and they quietened down.

'DC Morrison has some ideas to share with us about the topography of the killings,' said Chris.

There was a guffaw from Morrison's officer colleagues in the audience. Morrison stood up, looking decidedly embarrassed. 'All right, lads.' There were muffled cries of 'Topography man, didn't know you had it in you, more, more,' followed by sniggers.

Morrison had worked hard on his material and by the time he presented his introduction he commanded a respectful silence. He walked over to the console and pressed keys. Maps of the area flashed up on the screen at the front of the room. He explained the technicalities of his analysis; there was no doubt he knew what he was talking about. The atmosphere was hot and sticky, but nobody asked for a window to be opened; Morrison had his audience's full attention. He showed how the locations of the bodies lay within a corridor of largely rural East Yorkshire, running from Beverley northwards. He overlaid transparencies of the population and travelling times from different population centres. He took the pathologists' reports on the times of death when the bodies were found and argued that since they were all left in locations where pedestrians regularly passed, it should be possible to compute the distance travelled by the killer, assuming that all the bodies were moved within the same timescale after death.

Chris had never seen her fellow officers so rapt in concentration. A pin could have been heard dropping, as Morrison placed the final transparency over the map.

'There,' he said triumphantly, 'that's the area within which the killer is most likely to have carried out the killings, based on these calculations.'

It was an extraordinary moment. Neither Chris nor Bradshaw had realised Morrison had carried his theorising this further step. Bradshaw was open-mouthed.

'You're asking us to search an area of the Wolds which consists of nothing more than a few upland farms.'

'No, sir,' said Morrison. 'I'm not asking anything. The precise area doesn't matter. There has to be a margin of error of, say, ten miles.'

Bradshaw seized on this. 'Ah, that would bring us to the outskirts of Beverley. So we're no further forward.'

'I'm just saying we'd be well advised to start with the rural locations, sir, in view of the likelihood the killer needs a good deal of space to house these ant colonies.'

Bradshaw turned to Tom Fortius. 'Is this correct?'

Tom didn't expect to be brought in at this stage. 'It sounds very plausible.'

A voice came from the officers in the audience. 'You mean the killer's living on a farm on the Wolds.'

'Nothing's for sure,' said Morrison, 'but it's the most likely working hypothesis, in my opinion.'

'So where would we start?' asked the same anonymous voice.

'We could do worse than visit estate agents and find out who's been buying and selling in this area within the past couple of years.' Morrison denoted a larger area with his finger.

'I must be missing something,' said Bradshaw. 'Why bloody estate agents for God's sake? We aren't buying property.'

Chris judged it was time to rescue Morrison, before the session became dangerously diverted. 'I'd like to thank DC Morrison for his thought-provoking analysis,' she said.

'Hear hear,' someone called and the blushing Morrison retreated to his seat among his colleagues amid an anarchic chorus of appreciation. 'The main point,' continued Chris, 'is that we need to comb through the huge mass of evidence already accumulated. We shall be following up these ideas and concentrating one of our searches on the Wolds.' She turned to Morrison. 'Incidentally, I think we may be able to short-circuit estate agents and go to the local Land Registry office to find out about recent changes in the land holdings in the area.'

'Perhaps I can come in here,' said Tom.

Chris was embarrassed. 'My apologies. I should have introduced Professor Tom Fortius from the Wilberforce University of Hull, who's acting as our forensic entomologist on this case.'

'Thanks, Chris. I've been thinking about what Mary and Sheila have been saying. There are some links between MPD and a large mass of literature written over the past century or so, about parallels between insect societies and various human societies. Some people have gone the other way and talked about the ant colony as though it was a composite animal. Others have seen it either as showing similarities with an ideal form of democracy, or as an extreme example of the fascist state.'

'With our murderer seeing himself as the fascist dictator, manipulating the masses?' Chris asked.

Sheila responded. 'It's quite common for psychotics such as schizophrenics to develop fantasies involving themselves with well-known dictators. Sometimes they identify with the dictator, at other times they report being ordered by them to carry out certain crimes.'

Tom continued, warming to his theme. 'To return to DC Morrison's thoughts about our antman using a rural location such as a farm, these are speculations, but they're not only valuable but likely. He could have a farm, literally, an ant farm. The North Yorkshire Wolds, or indeed the North Yorkshire Moors, would be ideal in some ways – secluded, large expanses of relatively flat ground and some brilliant south facing slopes where ant colonies could flourish, providing food stores were adequate. If our antman knew what he was doing, he could import food and keep it supplied fresh. Not every species would be amenable to this free-range approach, though. Wood ants and their Formica relatives such as Sanguinea – the blood red slave-maker – and Excecta, an aggressive relative of the wood ant, could cope, provided there were no human dwellings close by and few people to disturb them. They're indigenous to Britain as well, so they could cope with the rigours of the climate. In summer, especially with recent global warming, many sheltered spots could support semi-tropical species. Army ants would probably prove too nomadic and would soon be lost, unless the whole farm could be enclosed with a water-filled ditch, which would be prohibitively expensive and would make it too visible to surrounding landowners. Harvester ants would be right at the extreme of colony size and unmanageability. I can't see our killer leaving them in the wild. It would be impossible to keep tabs on one of those nests. Eight million and impossible to monitor, since there may be a thousand nest entrances. Quite difficult to keep in as well. They're mega-burrowers. You'd need to dig down eight or nine metres to insert a barrier deep enough to keep them in.'

The day wound up with a focus on the next steps in the investigation. Afterwards Bradshaw approached Chris with a few uncharacteristic compliments about how it had gone.
'We should have held this event earlier,' said Chris. 'It helps to clarify where we're up to.'
'Well and good,' said Bradshaw, 'but will a talking shop help us catch Thompsen?'
Bradshaw's mobile rang. A couple of minutes later he was hurriedly taking his leave in order to carry out the ACC's bidding at a media circus at the Hull City Hall. Chris was relieved. She was specifically addressing the core team of detectives charged with tracing Thompsen, rather than the larger group over which she had less direct authority, several dozen of whom were still present.
'We need to find out where Thompsen is. I'm going to revisit his childhood. I'll be back in the office as soon as possible. Meanwhile, Morrison, look on my desk, in the file marked University Staff. Find out what you can. If you need me, ring me on this.' She tapped her mobile. 'And don't tell Bradshaw where I am.'
At that precise moment, Chris's mobile rang and she looked disbelievingly at the screen. It was Bradshaw. She pulled a face. The officers exchanged glances as Bradshaw's voice blasted from the phone and she held it away from her ear.
'That you, Chief Inspector Winchester?'
'Sir.'
'I want you to find Thompsen, and when you find him, watch him. If you are lucky enough to locate him, don't pull him in. Find out where he's living and leave him there. And find out about him. I want to know everything about that man – what he looked like as a baby, whether he wet his pants as a child, what he did at school, what were his habits, whether he picked his nose, bullied other children or was bullied by them, whether he argued with his parents, who were his parents and what were they like for God's sake, what he did when he left school or college if he got that far and with how many certificates in his hand.'
Bradshaw rang off. Several officers pulled faces at the phone.
'The University will have a personnel file with all that stuff, boss,' said

Morrison.

'That'll be our next port of call,' said Chris. 'For now, I want you to search for everything about his background and activities. Even which girls and boys he played with, whether he went out with them, who he slept with, whether he took drugs or whatever –'

'I'll be off, boss,' said Morrison, realising that the longer he stayed the more the list would grow.

Chris pointed to the large-scale map behind her. She indicated the trio of officers near the door. 'I want all the detail collected on these items. Mullins, Todd and I'm sorry I can't remember your name?'

'Tenby, boss.'

'Tenby, you take the pig incident. You two and Morrison, the Faith Wistow killing. You two, Brandt, DC's Lounds and Moran, Mr and Mrs Mackintosh. And the rest of you by the window, Sister Ruth. I'm going to concentrate on the biographical detail in the various communications from the killer.'

There was a murmur from the back of the room. Chris picked it up.

'We should have done this before?' Her voice shook. 'Don't tell me. It's a great gift, hindsight. I know only too well. If we don't catch this bastard before anyone else is harmed –' Her voice dropped. 'We have to catch him.'

Someone asked how long they had. 'Till tonight, perhaps.' Chris looked at her watch. 'Tom Fortius tells me that in thundery weather ants' behaviour becomes more volatile and aggressive. The killer may be affected by the weather in a similar way. If one of these threatened thunderstorms breaks, that may be several hours too late.'

* * *

Bradshaw arrived back at his office at the speed of lightning. The secretaries in the office eyed him curiously as he walked in rubbing his hands up through his hair then down his face as though washing something dirty off it.

In his office he sat with his hands over his face, his forehead resting on the half-metre pile of files brought in since early that morning when he'd left for the hotel. It was a while before he responded to the insistent ringing of his telephone.

Chapter 33

Once the conference room was cleared of police, the hotel staff moved in. Chris turned to Tom, sitting in a corner and filling a notebook with his small, neat handwriting.

'We need more information about the two boys, Walters and Thompsen. Mrs Blatt knows more than she's let on.'

Tom closed the notebook and put it in his bulging jacket pocket. 'When do we start?'

* * *

Mrs Blatt peered suspiciously at her two coatless visitors standing on the exposed front doorstep, trying to protect themselves from the driving rain and wind. The door, held by a security chain, was open only a few centimetres. Chris started to explain.

'I know you,' said Mrs Blatt. 'Who's he?' She nodded towards Tom.

'His name's Tom Fortius,' said Chris. 'He's helping me.'

Mrs Blatt's eyes narrowed. 'I thought you just asked questions.'

Chris couldn't begin to guess what was going on in Mrs Blatt's mind. 'We're getting very wet. Could we talk inside?'

A gust of wind helped her argument. The door closed, then opened again with Mrs Blatt peering down at the sodden, weed-strewn path. 'I'm busy. You can come in for five minutes. He'll have to take his muddy shoes off.'

She led them through to the back parlour. 'You sit there,' she said to Tom, indicating the chair by the blazing fire. 'I like to see a man relax in an armchair.' Mrs Blatt kept glancing at him. He stretched out his legs to enable his trousers to dry and wriggled his toes in the heat from the flames.

Chris sat in the smaller chair on the far side. 'I can see there's more to pleasing you than meets the eye,' she whispered to Tom as they waited while Mrs Blatt fussed in the scullery. After a good deal of clattering and chinking of crockery, she emerged laden with a tray piled with teapot, teacups, plates, scones and Bakewell tarts.

'You caught me on a baking day,' she explained.

To say Mrs Blatt was talkative was an understatement. Chris saw a totally different side to her. It was ten minutes before she managed to slip in a few comments and eventually the question she wanted to ask.

'What puzzles me, Mrs Blatt, is why you didn't tell me about your son, and about Mr Blatt.'

Mrs Blatt was taken aback. 'You found out.'

'I was bound to,' said Chris.

Mrs Blatt sniffed, as though to announce her upset feelings. 'I thought if you found out about the father, I'd be in trouble and if you found out about the boy it would be even worse for me.'

'I'm not here to get you into trouble,' said Chris more softly. 'It happened a while ago.'

'I won't be in court for not telling you.' Mrs Blatt produced a tissue and dabbed her eyes.

'Of course not. It will save time, though, and save us bothering you or the court if you can tell us everything you remember.'

'I will, oh yes ma'am and you, sir, thank you so much.' She took an appreciative look at Tom as he tucked into his third Bakewell tart. 'I don't mind you bringing him again. I like to see a man fill his belly with good, honest food.'

'Have you an address for John?'

Mrs Blatt looked embarrassed. 'I haven't been in touch, like, recently. I did send him a Christmas card last year, or maybe the year before.' She reached across the table for a well-thumbed address book, flicked through the pages and pressed them down. She put it in front of Chris, who scribbled the details in her notebook.

'Thank you, that's very helpful,' said Chris. 'Now, the story, Mrs Blatt, if you can, please.'

'Oh yes, I saw this card in the newsagents. "Cook Wanted." At first I went once or twice a week, baked and followed the written notes he left, either putting it in the fridge or the freezer. He was a busy man, away a lot, you see. After a bit, he said he wanted a housekeeper.'

'You moved in?'

'No, he was renting. It was a poky little flat. I said why don't you lodge with me instead. I was on my own. It made sense.' She stared at the floor before continuing. 'I didn't live with him properly, not at first. He wasn't one of them, you know, men that attracts women physically. He was smart though, professional, something high at the University I think. I still had me figure then.'

She looked at Tom again, smoothing her skirt over the rippling fat where her waist had been.

'Was his son living with you?'

Mrs Blatt shook her head. 'He told me about the boy later. I didn't mind him living with us. It happened gradually.'

'Was the boy treated badly?'

Mrs Blatt's voice cracked. 'I can't swear he hit the boy.' She started to cry. 'He threatened John, though, I know he did. When I tried to stop him, he –'

Her sobs became uncontrollable and she left the room to go to the toilet. When she returned, Chris thought the conversation would be over, but she continued as though there was no interruption.

'Sometimes when it was really bad between them he'd threaten the boy with boarding school and pretend to ring the social and have him removed. He never gave his name or address though. A couple of times he locked him in the shed.'

Chris turned and looked through the window. Mrs Blatt saw her. 'Not that one, the little one for the coal. It's more of a bunker. He had to crawl in. It was very dark and cold on the concrete floor. Lionel stood there with a stick, so he had no choice.'

'We need to speak to your husband,' Mrs Blatt.

'Not about that.'

'It's a long time ago. We want other information from him.'

'That's all right then. I don't want any comeback. Anyway, he isn't my husband.'

Chris was surprised. 'What's his name then?'

'Blatt, same as me. I used his name so people wouldn't ask questions. He's still married to her, his first wife, for all I know. I suppose she was his first, the lying bastard.' She rubbed her hands. 'I'd like to see his face when you two turn up.'

'Have you an address, Mrs Blatt?'

Mrs Blatt got up as shakily as a woman twenty years her senior and crossed to the mantelpiece. She pulled a battered envelope from behind the clock and passed it to Chris.

'There you are, that's what he was like.' She motioned to Chris to look at the contents.

Chris examined the letter – a final demand from a computer company threatening court proceedings for an unpaid bill. Chris gestured towards Tom. 'May I?'

Mrs Blatt nodded.

'I rang and gave them his address. It's in Camberley, there, on the back of the envelope.'

* * *

They left after forty-five minutes, with Mrs Blatt inviting them to call again. Chris was last out of the front door and she turned at the last minute: 'Thank you for all your help, Mrs Blatt. When we contact Mr Blatt, is there any message you'd like us to pass on?'

Mrs Blatt shook her head. 'Just make sure the bastard gets what he deserves.' She had an afterthought. 'Ask him how he's supporting his other son, Gavin. Hang on.' She disappeared into the parlour and emerged with a piece of paper which she handed to Chris. 'That's Gavin's address.' She rubbed her hands. 'I wish I could see Lionel's face.'

As they bundled into the car out of the rain, Chris couldn't wait to tackle Tom. 'She took quite a fancy to you.'

'Only because I returned for more of her Bakewell tarts.'

Chris was unconvinced. 'You're a dark horse. I'm going to have to watch you with women.'

Afterwards, when she was driving along with him, sitting quietly by her side, she thought, why did I say that? It sounded as though we were a couple.

* * *

It was a long drive back to Hull. The heavy rain petered out, but the grey, overcast sky persisted. There had been no messages from Morrison while they were away. Chris dropped Tom at the University and drove to the office to follow up various matters, including the latest information about Lionel Blatt. There were several messages from Bradshaw; on her voicemail, by e-mail and a note pushed under her office door. They all pointed the same way. He'd run out of patience and wanted her back on the case, in the office, under his eye. 'Hell can freeze first,' Chris muttered to herself between gritted teeth.

At eight the following morning Chris phoned Tom. He anticipated the call was from her and pretended he'd come in early. In fact, he'd stayed through the night in his office, telling the security staff he was working on a paper and to go ahead and lock him in. It was a piece of rule-breaking they were used to. God only knew the tales which went the rounds about his eccentricities. He would never admit he was avoiding Laura and home as much as possible.

'A slight hitch,' she said. 'Blatt is no longer at the address Mrs Blatt gave us. All isn't lost, though. We've had a stroke of luck. The address turned out to be a guest house listed in the local guide, which we tracked down at the tourist information office for the area. I found the landlady's name – a Mrs Maloney – and rang her, thinking she might remember him. She remembered him all right and the upshot of it is I've a pile of gossip about the peculiarities of Dr Lionel Blatt.'

'Doctor?'

'Not the medical variety, the scientific one. More important, she gave me his forwarding address. I'm about to set off to track it down. It's a little village called Cove, on the north-west Hampshire-Surrey border.' She paused to gauge his reaction.

'Haven't heard of it,' he said.

'The problem is, I can't drive and navigate at the same time.' Tom doubted this, but wasn't arguing.

'I know a fairly indifferent navigator who will be free in half an hour.' He thought he heard her chuckle.

'That'll do me.'

* * *

Whilst she drove, Chris filled Tom in on the gossip about Lionel Blatt. 'The story is that Dr Blatt is, or was, an aeronautical scientist who was abroad and after the War came to the RAE, that's the Royal Aircraft Establishment at Farnborough in Hampshire, half a dozen miles from Camberley. The son was from his first marriage. At that time, Blatt had a high-flying research job, literally high-flying, flying round the world in a jet, doing research in a flying laboratory.'

'All of which is feasible,' said Tom. 'The 1950s and 60s were the decades when British scientists were exploring the reasons for the Comet jet airliner crashes and were contributing to debates about supersonic passenger jet traffic, six miles up.'

'Blatt became a well-known local scientist and moved with his wife to Cambridge when he took a research fellowship. Several years later, he was head-hunted for an extremely lucrative contract in California and he pushed off to the USA on his own. He returned to Camberley when things went sour for him in the USA. He's wormed his way up the ladder at work, but according to Mrs Maloney he hasn't endeared himself to the ladies, being disloyal, dishonest and untrustworthy.'

'Not a good reference.'

'Added to which, she thinks he's physically unattractive – chinless, short, fat, bald with thick glasses, can't even read a cornflake packet without them, clumsy, often knocking chairs over and dropping cups. He turned up in Camberley looking for lodgings, whilst he went through an interviewing process for employment at Pyestock, where the RAE had some extension of their work on jet propulsion. He was being head-hunted by a team who also did a deal with members of his department including a certain Miss Stanmore or Stanmere. She was the PA whose name kept cropping up a lot and who organised the entire household at one point, simply by phoning and turning up at all hours to take dictation from the great man, or whisk him off in a taxi to this or that international conference, at the drop of a hat. Throughout all of which, he grew more and more insufferable and his wife more patient and self-sacrificing.'

'Sounds like a man to avoid.'

* * *

With Tom navigating they reached Cove, which turned out not to be a village so much as a busy suburb of Farnborough. The car had developed a knocking sound. Chris wasn't an expert and could tell from Tom's reaction it could be serious. He said he wasn't an expert either. It didn't sound like a cylinder head gasket, not yet, but he thought a garage needed to confirm what was going on. He offered to drive her car to find a local garage while she did some basic research on Blatt's whereabouts.

An hour passed. Tom texted her and confirmed he was returning with a restored car. The problem wasn't serious. Apparently, the engine desperately needed oil. A rather embarrassed Chris admitted she went for months without checking the oil level.

When they met, she brought Tom up to date.

'I had a call from Hull. Morrison's been finding out more about Dr Blatt in Texas.'

'Texas is a big place.'

'Blatt isn't too common a name in nuclear physics, even when the number of universities runs into double figures. He's been at Borderville, the State University, researcher in nuclear physics. Anyway, that's another story.'

'We do need to see Dr Blatt. Your Chief Superintendent Bradshaw's going to love signing travel warrants for Texas.'

'That won't be necessary. I've also managed to find Mrs Maloney. Blatt called here at the weekend and collected some post from her. Apparently he commutes back and forth and keeps a standing arrangement with her to retain post delivered to him.'

'Seems odd. It would be straightforward to have his mail forwarded. He goes to great lengths, retaining an address here just to receive the odd letter.'

'Perhaps it isn't only an odd letter. Remember, he's commuting backwards and forwards into the bargain.'

'I read a press report of an American academic who had three wives in different States and took plane flights every week between them.'

'Mrs Blatt made a point of telling us she isn't married to him.'

'She may have her own reasons for not wanting to admit to it. Wasn't it CS Lewis who married that American woman without anyone knowing and they continued to live apart?'

'You do have a suspicious mind.'

'It's my job to be suspicious. More relevant, we need to know whether the dates of his visits correspond with the killings.'

They were halted by road works and there was a long queue at the temporary traffic lights a quarter of a mile ahead. Her fingers drummed on the steering wheel. 'He was on his way to Cambridge for an international conference at Fitzwilliam College which was due to last five days. Unless he follows the pattern of some of his more cynical colleagues and puts in a brief appearance to give his paper before disappearing, we should be able to catch him there.'

'Damn,' said Tom. 'I was looking forward to a short break. The silver lining is I know Fitzwilliam. It's part of my old stamping ground.'

'I thought it might be. Can you use the old school tie to get us into this conference?'

'I've one or two contacts there. I might even know the bursar and the conference manager. She used to have a soft spot for me.'

'You academics are dark horses.'

Tom affected to ignore this. 'Give me a few minutes to make a couple of phone calls.'

Despite busy roads, they arrived at Cambridge within half an hour of Tom's estimate. He organised parking at Fitzwilliam College and Chris was soon sitting in the lobby of the porter's lodge while Tom exchanged memories with a couple of long-term staff. They walked along the cloistered corridor and Chris gave him an envious glance.

'That envelope looks pretty authentic.'

'I picked up a spare conference package, filched by the porter from the conference office, while you were in the Ladies. According to the porter, the programme gives the delegates time off between 12:00 and 2:00 pm. Lunch isn't until 1:00 pm, so if our Dr Blatt isn't in the bar, he could be in his room.'

'Police officers on duty don't need excuses to gain access.'

Tom grinned. 'I wanted to see the papers in any case.' He flicked through the programme. 'Blatt's due to give his paper later on, so we've every chance of catching up with him in the next hour or two.'

* * *

Chris knocked at the door. There was a pause. She knocked again. A rustling sound could have come from this room or the adjacent one.

'Dr Blatt? I have an urgent message for you.'

'Just a moment.'

Chris waved Tom to stand on the other side of the door, temporarily out of the line of vision of the person in the room. There was some more rustling. Chris thought she heard whispering, but couldn't be sure. Eventually the door opened a chink and the bearded face of a man in his sixties peered round the door. Chris presumed this was Blatt. He saw the pack Chris was carrying.

'Ah.' He opened the door and held out his hand. 'Is the parcel for me? My slides for the lecture.'

'Sorry to disappoint you, Dr Blatt.' Chris held up her ID card and stepped forward, making it impossible for him to slam the door. Tom also stepped from the alcove into the line of sight. 'I'm Chief Inspector Winchester, East Yorkshire Constabulary. I need to ask you some questions.'

'The hell you do! I'm due to speak at a conference, dammit. Why don't you get the hell out of it?'

'It isn't as easy as that. We're investigating several crimes and are trying to trace a member of your family who may be able to help us.'

'I know nothing of any use to you,' Blatt asserted firmly.

'It might be easier if we had this discussion somewhere quieter.' She nodded towards the interior of the room.

'I'll talk to you out here. I don't intend to take long.'

'As you wish. I was considering your privacy as much as anyone's. It isn't always easy to explain to other people why you've been interviewed by the police as part of a homicide inquiry.'

'Homicide! Keep your voice down. You'd better come inside.'

The room was furnished in the Spartan style of student accommodation, clean but basic. There was a sprawl of women's underwear across the rumpled bedclothes, which gave it the atmosphere of a hotel where illicit liaisons took place. A young woman stood by the bed. She wore a dressing gown and looked as though she had just stepped out of the shower. Blatt looked extremely embarrassed.

'This is Martha, my PA. She's changing and preparing for this afternoon's session. She deals with the administration on these trips.'

'Good day to you, madam,' said Tom.

Martha altered her pose to look even more like the cover girl from a men's magazine: 'Hi.'

Does the name Gavin mean anything to you, Dr Blatt?'

'I know a couple of men called Gavin.'

'Try closer than that, within your family.'

Blatt looked away, shaking his head. 'Can't say it does.'

'That's interesting. My information suggests he's your son, or rather, one of your sons.'

'Is this some kind of joke?'

'So, you don't know that you have a son called Gavin.'

'Are you trying to call me a liar?'

'Isn't it a coincidence that you've come all these thousands of miles from Texas and you haven't realised that your son Gavin lives not thirty miles from Cambridge.'

Martha spoke: 'I didn't know –'

'Shut it,' Blatt snapped.

'How about your other son? John. Where is he living now? Somewhere in the north of England perhaps? Were you planning to sneak off from the conference to visit him as well as Gavin? You couldn't visit your third son though, could you, because he's dead.'

'Is this true? Why didn't you tell me?' Martha blurted out.

'All this happened years ago. There was no need to complicate our life.'

'You washed your hands of your sons. One dead, a second in a mental hospital and a third with serious behaviour problems. It makes sense for a successful academic in the USA to put that kind of family history behind him. That's what you mean.'

'I didn't say that.'

'You didn't have to. So, you've had no contact with your sons during these years.'

'That's correct.'

'Let me guess. When you used to visit Gavin, you used an assumed identity. What was it? Did you pretend to be a social worker?'

'Maybe. Look, I didn't want to disturb the young man, any more than he was already. It wasn't an offence not to disturb his little world, was it?'

'When did you last see your son Gavin?'

'Two, maybe three years ago.'

Chris looked scornful. 'You don't really have the faintest idea how Gavin is or where he's living.'

Blatt looked round the room, anywhere but back at Chris.

'Does your behaviour ever disturb you?'

'That's an offensive question. I have to ask you to leave now.'

'Then I shall have to ask you to continue this interview at the local police station.'

Blatt sighed as though realising he was out-flanked. 'Okay. Let's get this over quickly though. I have a paper to give.'

'Don't worry, Dr Blatt, I have no desire to prolong it. So your separation from your sons doesn't worry you.'

'Worry isn't the word I'd have chosen. I provided for Gavin financially. It was unfortunate that due to his mother's attitude I lost contact with him for several years, during which he had his breakdown, for reasons totally outside anyone's control.'

'You've nothing to feel guilty about?'

'No. The consultant says his state of mind is a consequence of a defective gene, a one-off, not passed down through the family.'

'That must be a great relief to you.'

'Count yourself lucky I haven't punched your face.'

'We have similar laws about assaulting police officers to those in Texas. Tell me about your other son, John.'

'Nothing to say there. I lost contact with him as well. His mother chose to take a particular line and I was left with little choice.'

'You give the impression that everything was someone else's doing and you were the victim. For a man holding such an obviously prominent professional position and wielding such power, that seems an odd statement.'

'You're twisting my words, Inspector.'

'Presumably that's also part of the reason why through all these years you have avoided taking financial responsibility and paying towards the maintenance of your sons.'
'They're old enough to take care of themselves,' muttered Blatt.
'So that absolves you from your failure to support them when they were growing up?'
'You're being unfair.'
'I'm feeding back what you tell me so you can comment further on it.'
'If you've nothing further to ask me, Inspector, I can't see the point of prolonging this interview.'
'I have a further question, if you don't mind. How do you know your third son is dead?'
'This is obscene. Of course he's dead.'
'Did you go to the funeral? Did you see the body?'
'I couldn't attend the funeral. I was at a conference in Australia.'
Blatt saw Chris looking at Martha.
'Alone, at the time.'
'How long are you in Britain?'
'I'm here for a further ten days. I have a conference in Bristol and another in Warwick, before we go to Stratford to unwind for a few days.'
'That'll be nice for you. When were you last in this country?'
'About four months ago.'
'And before that?'
'Do I have to answer?' Blatt appealed to Tom. Tom gave a slight nod, staring bleakly back.
'Maybe six or seven months earlier. That was it, I came over for the annual lecture, about ten months ago.'
'Can you prove that?' In the following silence, Chris produced a pad and pen and scribbled for a few minutes. She handed it to him.
'I'll be grateful if you'll e-mail me at my office at the address I've written down under my name, with details of your whereabouts on each of these dates. My phone number's there in case you have difficulty. I need you to notify me of your various addresses during your remaining stay. We may need to get back to you.'
'Martha will attend to it when we return to the States.'
'I must have it within twenty-four hours.'
'It'll take me three days. I'm not at home, remember.'
'I must have the information before you leave the country.'
'What if I choose to leave earlier?'
'I have to inform you that it will cause you great inconvenience if you encounter the stop I shall put on your exit through customs at any UK port or airport.'
'You bastards. You're not empowered to do this.'
'This is a homicide inquiry, Dr Blatt. Bear that in mind. Have a nice

281

day.'

* * *

'What a stink in that place,' said Chris after they'd left the college. 'Domestic violence is so cowardly. It makes me mad.'
'Mrs Blatt didn't actually accuse him of hitting her or the boys,' said Tom.
'She didn't need to. Didn't you see her body language when we interviewed her?'
Soon after the unproductive interview with Blatt, Chris plugged in the laptop and wished she'd left it forgotten in the boot of the car. There was another great mass of e-mails from Bradshaw, all of which she had to ignore if they were to pursue this stage of the investigation to the bitter end. Among them was a solitary message from Morrison. Apart from a terse preamble about Bradshaw threatening various forms of extreme action against his renegade DCI, he wrote that an American had apparently asked for the fax number of her workplace. Morrison had taken the trouble to transcribe the fax for her and finished with the cryptic 'Am working on Gavin's background.' There was one supportive detective constable, she thought, with the one grain of reassurance in this bleak, flat landscape of despair. She read the message from Blatt, as she thought.

> *Chief Inspector, my apologies for being impatient. I have a heavy work programme and not enough time for it. I'll send the information as soon as possible. The last known address I have for Gavin is 12 Menihott Road, Huntingdon. Please e-mail if you need further help or information.*
>
> *Yours,*
>
> *Lionel B.*

'How are you feeling?' Tom asked her.
'Not too bloody chuffed, as you might imagine. We seem to be several steps behind in this case.'
'You're wondering about Blatt. Do you think he's our murderer?'
'I don't know. He's not a very nice man to women. Talking of which, I've had another bucket-load of messages from Bradshaw.'
'Impatient?'
'Well past impatience. He's lost it completely with me. He knows how to deal out shit.'

'So we're on borrowed time.'
'It was borrowed time before. I'm well out of credit. Added to which, Bradshaw will want to know how we didn't find out about Gavin.'
'It can happen to anybody.'
'It's happening to me.'
'Let's catch up. We need to meet Gavin and ask him a few questions.'
'We have to reach a result, Tom. Gavin's our only lead.'
Before they set off, Chris received a phone message from Morrison. All efforts to find Thompsen had failed. The address turned out to be lodgings and the property was empty, pending demolition. The former owner was deceased.

* * *

'Have you any thoughts about this second brother?' Chris asked, as she took the A14 from Cambridge towards Peterborough.
'I'm keeping a reasonably open mind till we see him.'
'I've had some dealings with establishments in the vicinity of Cambridge before – half full of nutty academics and students with over-developed grey matter, having breakdowns.'
'Go easy on the academics. Remember you're sitting next to one.'
'Precisely.'
'Remember what Shakespeare said: "*The lunatic, the lover and the poet are of imagination all compact.*" There's a fine dividing line between the sane and the so-called mad.'
'Bulls eye.'
'You're taking me the wrong way. I mean the definition of mental illness is problematic. Any of us has the potential to go down that road.'
'Speak for yourself.'

Chapter 34

The Black Fen Unit was a small, nondescript building like a run-down motel, adjacent to a Community Mental Health Resource Centre. Chris parked in the visitors' car park while Tom went in to assess the lie of the land. By the time Chris joined him he was engaged with a trio of staff, all deeply suspicious of him and his motives for coming. The atmosphere relaxed considerably when Chris flashed her warrant card. Within five minutes they were sitting in a triangle of easy chairs, in the simply but comfortably furnished visitors' room. They introduced themselves. Chris had brought Gavin a box of chocolates and some fruit, which he seemed to appreciate. After some vain attempts to get Gavin to tell them about himself, she asked about John Thompsen.

'When did you last see your brother, Mr – er – Gavin?'

Gavin sat staring at the floor.

'Not getting us very far. He only responds if you ask a question which is directed away from himself.'

'Gavin, we want you to help us find your brother. Can you remember where he was living when you were last in touch?'

Another silence. To avoid prolonging it indefinitely, Chris changed tack. 'Can you tell us about John's life in the children's home?'

It was as if a button had been pushed. Gavin spoke like a machine, his voice a monotone.

'They picks on John. We was both fostered, then sent to the Home, then adopted. John has a better memory than me. He learns the catechism off by heart. Father stops beating him then.'

Gavin stopped.

'Who does he mean by Father?' mouthed Tom.

'The priest,' she mouthed back. Tom nodded. He wasn't as close as Chris to the whole Roman Catholic business.

The silence went on for a couple of minutes before Chris spoke, realising he wasn't going to restart spontaneously.

'Did you like the Home?'

'John didn't talk about it much.'

'You were there as well.'

'Some of the time. It was hard, being sent to the Home in them days.'

Chris shook her head: 'Please, tell us.'

'The houses was separate. They put John and me in separate houses. We never saw each other outside school. The Reverend Mother had it in for John. He called her prune face or some such. She used to take girls up to her room for punishment and do things. She never did that with the other boys, but she made him eat stuff.

Disgusting.'

'Did she do things to you?'

Silence. Gavin might never have heard the question. He sat staring at the floor. After a pause, he carried on speaking.

'She had a fall, the Reverend Mother. Nobody saw it. They said she fell down the stairs and that she'd been drinking. John never talked about it, except once, years later, when he'd been drinking, he said he never meant to do it. I wanted somebody to kill her.'

'Why didn't you tell somebody how bad it was?'

'Nobody would believe us. Some of the kids did and they got punished for lying. Nobody said anything till we were grown up. It became all right to sprag on staff. They was too old to get you. Three of the girls grassed Mother Bernadette then. It was too late because she was dead.'

'Can you remember anything about secondary school?'

'We moved back with Dad and stayed with him near his work.'

'Do you mean Farnborough?'

Gavin nodded. 'We went to the same school – a boys' boarding school run by one of those religious orders, brothers and fathers wearing cassocks and dog collars all the time. We didn't sleep there like the boarders. I was the quiet one. John had all the attention. The dormitory at the Home smelled of sweat. We was dying slow. School was escape. I worked hard at school to escape. I saw the inside of the office of Father –' Gavin paused. 'Can't remember his name, the headmaster. It was dark. He sits behind the desk. When he stands up I knows he's going to shout. He hurts my head.'

'He hit you?'

Gavin paused and eventually nodded. He continued to speak, slowly and mechanically. Tom thought, this is like drawing nails from a plank.

'There was only one teacher John liked. Mr Regel. I liked Mr Regel but he didn't talk to me. I wasn't interested in science. Once they lost some soap and toothpaste from the washroom. They searched everywhere. They found it hid under John's mattress. They had a big assembly. Father always had one. The big school in the big hall. Father give the boy one last chance to own up. He warns he'll go to Hell. My legs is shaky. He come off the stage and walks down the rows of boys. He pulls John out and starts shouting at him. He grabs him by the hair. He pulls him down the hall and shouts a lot. John was crying. I was crying. I didn't see John for ages after that. He stayed in the sick room. They didn't let us see the bruises.'

Another long silence, which Chris broke. 'Is there anything else you'd like to tell us, Gavin?'

Gavin made no movement which indicated he had heard the question.

'Some information about your family perhaps. Something you feel we should know.'

It was as though they didn't exist. Chris touched Tom's arm: 'I think we'd better be going.'

She started to walk away. 'We must be off now, Gavin. Thank you for seeing us.'

They walked slowly to the door. Gavin's silence and lack of movement was absolute. Outside the door, a member of staff was within calling distance and they were soon off the premises.

'He's shut us off,' said Chris. 'We've no way of accessing his world.'

'Correction, he's already left ours.'

* * *

Morrison rang Chris's mobile as she reached the car. She caught Tom's glance, raised her eyebrows and breathed, 'Blatt's been in touch with the Station with some dates.' She switched off. In the car, she turned to Tom.

'The good news first. You probably guessed – Blatt one, police nil. He's produced a list of venues. He was in Texas on all but one of the dates I gave him – the date of Brandt's death.'

'Yes?' Tom looked expectant.

'He was in England, yes, but reckons he was fully engaged at a meeting in Cambridge.'

'Oh.'

'Now the bad news. Bradshaw is doing his nut about my continued absence.'

She didn't answer, started the car, then changed her mind. 'To hell with it. I'm ringing Blatt to thank him for the information.'

She picked up her mobile and dialled. To her surprise, she was straight through to Blatt.

'Thanks for sending the details of your movements.'

Tom was round the other side of the vehicle and didn't hear the entire conversation. Then he heard her say, 'We're trying to trace a school teacher of one of your sons. Do you know anything about a Mr Regel?'

Chris was surprised at Blatt's positive response.

'I do actually. He was in a similar field to my own. He had an affinity with the boy.'

She tried a long shot. 'I wondered if on your visits to Cove, you kept in touch with John's former school. Assuming Mr Regel is still alive, do you know where he might be living?'

'Funny you should say that. You'll be aware, no doubt, the school wasn't far from my previous lodgings in Cove, where I visit on occasions. I did see the old boy from time to time. Last time I saw him in the street was a few years ago. He looked shaky but he was still walking to the shops.'

'You don't happen to know where he lives?'

'I'm not pouring cold water on the idea, but –' he hesitated. 'I think it's unlikely he's still alive. Sorry I can't help further.'

* * *

When Chris came off the phone, Tom was intrigued. 'I didn't know you intended to ask Blatt about the teacher,' he said.

'Neither did I. It was a spur of the moment decision.'

'It's odd, Blatt was almost too cooperative.'

'It could be a double bluff. He could still be trying to put you off,' said Tom. 'Do you trust him?'

'In an odd kind of way, yes. There's something pathetic about him, too.'

'Remember what you said about violence in the home.'

'I'm not going back on that. I'm keeping my eye on the ball, which is a multiple murder investigation.'

'Why go through the effort of chasing up the teacher?' Tom queried.

'I know it's crazy, but we've nothing to lose. It's only a couple of hours each way from Cambridge. I guess if we can reach the school before the kids and staff go home we stand a chance.'

* * *

They made it to the school gates by 3:00 pm and within ten minutes were on their way, thanks to the very cooperative school secretary, who somehow gained the impression they were relatives of Mr Regel. In the era of data protection, it was not the occasion to disillusion her. Tom held a small card with an address which apparently lay only fifteen minutes distant.

'Here we are. Leyton Gardens. What a place. He must have been desperate.'

'Past tense. You think he's gone, or dead.'

'I'm keeping an open mind on it. Number 31a, along there towards the end. Look at this metal grill on the door front. And the patching job over that hole. Someone's had a good go at kicking it in. Hullo, anybody in? Hullo.'

'I suggest we leave a note.'

'Wait. I can hear a sound. Mr Regel?'

'Who is it?'

She whispered to Tom. 'It's an old man. Sounds frail.'

'Police, sir. Can we have a few minutes of your time?'

The answer quavered after a shallow cough as though his throat had to be opened up to allow his voice to sound after a long period without use:

'I suppose so. You'll have to wait.'

There was a shuffling noise and they exchanged glances at the ponderous cacophony of bolts, chains and locks being drawn, removed and undone. Regel stood there, a cadaverous, unshaven figure in a faded blue-striped dressing gown. God, Belsen reincarnated, thought Tom. The man looked as though he wouldn't last the day. He stooped, panting with the exertion from that brief walk down the corridor to the front door.

'Tell me about teaching John Thompsen,' Chris prompted.

'Not much to tell.' Regel slumped on the chair at the battered dining table in the shabbily decorated back room. He fought to find enough breath to utter the responses. 'I never really knew him at all.'

'Okay, I want you to think back, not so much about knowing him yourself. Try to recall things about him. Perhaps you saw him getting involved in an activity. Or maybe you heard about it in the staff room, or through hearing other boys talking.'

Regel shook his head. 'I was never one for mixing with other staff. Difficult to remember anything specific.'

'Some particular misbehaviour perhaps,' interjected Tom. Chris flashed him a warning glance, but he continued. 'An offence against school discipline perhaps?'

'It doesn't have to involve the police,' interposed Chris, with a covert glare at Tom.

'Police,' said Regel. 'Only the usual stuff that all boys get up to I guess, don't they, at that age?'

'You tell me,' said Chris.

'Right,' said Regel. Then, with some embarrassment, 'You won't follow this up, will you? I can't become involved with the law.' He tapped his concave chest with his withered right arm. 'My heart. I can't have any stress.'

Tom caught a glimpse of the outlines of two narrow bands of ribs through the sagging V of the opened dressing gown. He studied Regel's raised arm. The flesh was wrinkled and grey, sinews and bones outlined as in the arm of an already dead person.

'No, Mr Regel, we aren't intending to splash you over the front pages. This is an inquiry into someone else. But our time is limited, so if you can tell us – anything at all –'

'Boys will be boys, they say,' said Regel. 'Shoplifting, buying tobacco for rollups with the profits, smoking, girls in the changing rooms, you name it.'

'Was Thompsen involved?'
Regel was speaking independently of her question. 'I was an outsider and so was he. Pupils can be cruel, but teachers as well. He may have been.'
'You can remember him being involved in trouble?'
'Not specifically. Then again, I can't recall not seeing him. He wasn't exactly one of the boys and neither was I. That's where we both went wrong.'
Regel looked at Tom.
'It is all right for you,' he said. 'You are a successful man. Nobody questions your background, your motives. They do not stare when you walk into the staff room as though you have arrived from an alien planet. You are not like her. What are you, some kind of technical, forensic person?' He stared, his eyes an intense blue, concentrating all the energy of his still alert brain, trapped inside this ageing frame. 'No, you are more than that. I am a scientist, I should know. You have the air of an intellectual. You are not a policeman. You are in research, a psychiatrist perhaps?'
Tom shook his head. He felt incredibly vulnerable under the gaze of this old man.
'I'm in a university, in insect research.'
'Of course.' Regel nodded. 'The insects, they are powerful. I take it you are a student of the social insects.'
Tom nodded.
'The ants perhaps, more than the bees. Bees are too uncontrollable. As for the wasps, the colonies die every year and only the queens survive the winter. We have to start again, from scratch.' His head rolled to the side as though the neck muscles could barely sustain its weight.
It was eerie, thought Tom, but he was transfixed by this cadaver of a man who gave off such psychic energy. 'But the ant has continuity, I showed the boys. I kept the nests in the biology lab. There were queens of Acanthomyops Niger, the common black lawn ant, ten, twelve, fifteen years old. You can do so much.'
'Tell me, Mr Regel,' said Chris, when did you arrive in this country?'
Tom couldn't believe the abrupt change in Regel's manner. The brightness in his eyes was veiled by fear.
'It's all right, Mr Regel, we aren't investigating you. It was the war, wasn't it?'
Regel nodded.
'You arrived from central Europe?'
He nodded again, never taking his eyes off Chris, as though she was the threat, the new interrogator.
'For a time you were interned. There was a period of adjustment, after the war.'

'We were the untouchables, when Hitler invaded Poland. I was in the province ruled by one of his brutes. Hitler left his barons to rule as they wished and asked no questions.'

'You are Jewish?'

'No, I am a Pole. People make the assumption I'm a Jew.'

'You had no time for the Communists.'

'We thought when Hitler's troops invaded we would be allies. We had no idea our neighbours, the ethnic Germans, would turn against us. I thought we were all one, against the Russians. Instead, Hitler made an ally of Stalin. All of us Poles who weren't ethnic Germans were all treated as one by the Germans. The Jews were sent for extermination, but according to the Nazis the rest of the Poles were the *Untermenschen*, peasants with no culture. I escaped but the rest of my family were evicted from our fine house and resettled. It was a joke. They took them in cattle trucks and dumped them in the middle of nowhere in the southern province. They had no shelter, no food. I was the only one who lived.' Tears ran down his face as he spoke, but apart from that his expression stayed unchanged. 'I ran away and lived, while my family perished.'

They waited while Regel composed himself before continuing.

'I was in a camp in Hull for a while. It was near a village overlooking the town.'

'Hessle,' said Chris. 'You were in the resettlement camp at Hessle at the end of the war.'

'Yes, I remember the name. It sounded so – Germanic. I thought at the time, the English are hostile to some of us too, how strange. Later, when I moved to the south of England and taught at the school near Farnborough after the war, somebody found out I had Jewish blood. All those years, my family hid our Jewishness. It made no difference, ultimately. They were killed. And now the pupils started on me. The other teachers, they turned a blind eye. I stayed out of the staff room. I was an outsider in Poland and an outsider in England, but I was alive. I put up with it because I was alive.'

Chris opened the folder she was carrying and carefully pulled out a long, narrow roll which she unrolled carefully.

'I'd like you to look at this,' she said, placing it on the table.

Regel took it.

'My God!' he exclaimed, showing more interest in the proceedings. 'The school photo. What an event!'

'Can you recognise him on this?'

'It is so long ago.'

'Take your time.'

Regel's gaze travelled up and down the rows of boys, cross legged at the front, kneeling, then sitting, standing and standing on forms and tables – seven lines each of about fifty boys.

'There, that could be him, no that one. That is him.'

'Are you sure?'

Regel stared and finally shook his head.

'Not really. I cannot be absolutely certain. Sorry, it is difficult at this long distance in time. I would need time to think about it.' He gave a sigh so long that Chris began to worry whether this would be his last breath. His entire body seemed to deflate and then he fought for another breath and then another. Regel was becoming so exhausted that she knew it was pointless asking any more questions.

'You could do with a holiday,' she said.

'I could, but it is getting there.'

'Would you take a holiday in Yorkshire, if there was the possibility of a lift?'

'I would, but there's little point in talking about it.'

Chris reached a decision and took a deep breath. 'Mr Regel, I can offer you a lift to Hull. You could stay a few days. You'll have to find your own hotel expenses, but one of my colleagues will run you back afterwards. While you're in Hull, we could chat more about what you remember.'

Regel's expression changed and his manner became more animated than at any time in their brief conversation.

'I would love to see Hull.'

Chapter 35

As Tom walked down the corridor to his office, he ran into Luis Deakin. Over coffee he brought Luis up to date with the latest developments. He didn't mention Regel, though. He was under strict instructions from Chris to say nothing to anybody at all about Regel. Chris had settled Regel into his hotel and arrived at Tom's office shortly afterwards. The three of them stood round awkwardly.

'I'll bring us a coffee,' said Deakin. 'The kettle's already boiled.'
They demurred but he was insistent.
'Wake up and smell the coffee,' said Chris.
Tom looked questioningly. 'You've heard the expression,' she said. He shook his head. 'Sometimes you're so quaint,' she said. She sniffed as Luis appeared, carrying a tray with cafetiere, three mugs and a jug of milk. 'Nothing appeals like the smell of fresh coffee.'
'Not fresh ground, I'm afraid,' said Luis, 'but ground anyway and at least fresh brewed.'
They sat round the low table in Tom's office.
'There must be something, some vital clue as to Thompsen's whereabouts,' said Chris.
Luis shrugged. Chris pressed one fist hard onto the palm of the other hand.
'A man as odd as this must have something distinctive about him, some quirk or habit. Tom says you have an amazing memory for people, Luis. You worked with him, I gather.'
Luis shook his head. 'I wish I could be of some help, but there's nothing I can say.'
They sipped coffee in silence for a few minutes. Luis suddenly spoke.
'I do remember something odd about Thompsen. He used to talk about his childhood, how he used to experiment on crawlies. He called them experiments. I particularly remember that, as though it was a way of justifying what he did.'
Chris leaned forward. 'What sort of crawlies?'
'Little things, insects. He was talking about his obsession with insects. He used to chop them up.'
'Why did he do that?'
'He talked about going round the garden with an oilcan from the tool shed looking for insects. He used to prefer beetles, especially ladybirds.'
'And then what?'
'He used to drop a small blob of oil on each. He used to watch them

die. I don't know how it works. There isn't enough depth for them to drown.'

'Suffocation,' said Tom. 'The oil blocks the breathing tubes. They die quite quickly.'

'Later he got hold of an old pocket watch and used the second hand to calculate how long they took to go through the various stages.'

'How many times did he do this?' Chris asked.

'He said it made him cry,' said Luis.

'Had someone hit him?'

'He said one of his friends had been killed in an accident,' Luis said reflectively. After a long pause he started to speak again. 'He said it made him throw up. He used caterpillars as well as beetles. He talked about getting onto Mussolini's wavelength with the transistor radio in his bedroom, giving the dissidents the castor oil treatment.'

Chris was silent, brooding. 'Were there any physical marks on him?'

'Such as a scar?'

'Could be. Did he – has he one then?'

'Not to my knowledge.'

'Damn! I thought you might have remembered.'

An afterthought seemed to strike Luis. 'Would a tattoo count?'

'It might. Where is it?'

'I don't know.'

'How come?'

'I don't actually know if he has one.'

'Why did you mention it?' She checked herself. 'I'm sorry, I've run out of patience.'

'He used to talk about them. There was a picture on the wall. He brought it from home. It was one of those men with tattoos completely covering their bodies.'

'So, did he go for any tattoos while he worked here?'

'I don't know.'

He glared and she hesitated.

'Let's go at it from the other direction. If he had planned to have a tattoo, what would he be likely to do?'

'You mean, love – hate, like prisoners. On his fingers. Or wet – dry on his nipples.'

'Not exactly those but yes, that sort of thing. But more appropriately, what? From what you know of him.'

'Well, I never really knew him. But in view of his job and his obsession with ants and so forth, what about, say, an ant's head – one of the soldier forms with big mandibles – on his chest?'

'How ghastly. Yes, sounds possible. The question then is how many tattoo shops are there in a square, say, between Hull, Doncaster, Hull and Scarborough.'

She turned to Tom. 'Which do you think?'

'I must confess to ignorance on this matter,' he said wryly.

'You know, I think it might be worth checking out,' said Chris. She picked up her mobile.

* * *

'Did you notice how your colleague Luis came to life when he was describing Thompsen's childhood memories?' said Chris later to Tom, as she drove him to the Station so he could pick up his car.

'I hadn't noticed.'

'Men,' she said. 'Women are so different.'

'I don't like being pigeon-holed as an insensitive male.'

'I don't think you're that. In fact –' She paused.

'You think I'm a sensitive insensitive male.'

'Not that either. In fact, I was going to ask if when you've picked up your car, you'd like to follow me and see my cottage tonight.'

* * *

It was late evening before they surfaced. Chris was surprised at how much passion was pressed into the space between them. They stood side by side on the patio to the rear of the isolated cottage, sipping a rich red wine from Bordeaux, listening to the tawny owls hooting as dusk faded to night.

'Rage, rage against the dying of the light,' said Chris.

'Which one of your poets is this?'

'Dylan Thomas. He's not my poet. I understand his anger though. It's one of those we learnt at school. O level English Lit.'

'Sounds a bit heavy. Why did you say it?'

'Something triggered off by your anger about the direction in which the world is moving – the domination by commercialism, universities becoming profit centres, the vulnerability of academic freedom, the undervaluing of intellectual traditions, the undermining of the cultural life of the people.'

'Rather a conservative view, I reckon.'

'Thomas is on about not passively accepting ageing. But it seems to me to have a wider resonance.'

'Come here,' said Tom softly. He held out his arms. They embraced and he kissed her. They sat close together on two tiny, elegant cane chairs and put their glasses on the small circular table.

'It's been a long time since we had space together,' said Chris.

'I feel I'm letting you down,' said Tom.

'I can't accuse you of that. You're determined to stay the way you

are, a stubborn old thing.'
'Hey, less of the old. You're certainly no pushover yourself.'
'You mean –'
'I would never dream of mentioning age.'
The empty Wolds lay before them, invisible in the darkness. There were faint rustlings in the shrubs at the boundary of her little garden.
'Sighs ache at nightfall falling into summer sleep,' said Tom.
'What's that?'
'I don't know. It just occurred to me. When we were kids, we used to walk around the village in our bare feet on nights like this. I was remembering the feel of sun-warmed paving stones under my toes.'
She giggled and looked down at the toes of her bare feet, wriggling as though they had lives of their own. 'You take things the wrong way. I didn't mean the poetry, but the rustling in the bushes.' She paused. 'Where did you say the quotation came from?'
'I didn't, but it's a line from a poem.'
'Who wrote it?'
'I did.'
'You?'
'You're surprised. Yes, scientists do have a life. I've known many a scientist who doubles as artist, musician, writer. There is a creative side to science, you know.'
'I'm sorry, I didn't mean to imply. Some men in science do tend to develop along rationalist lines though. I met a few at university.' She felt the heat of his questioning sideways glance and nervousness prompted her to continue. 'I was remembering the midsummer night when as students we took everything off and danced round the maypole.'
'Ah, the fecklessness of youth. Back to your friend Dylan Thomas,' said Tom. 'You young ones, passionate, fiery, impulsive and unresolved.'
'Dylan Thomas was never my kind of friend. Too feckless and alcoholic. I like my men to be sober. Anyway, he's long dead.'
'No, I mean it as a compliment. He goes on about wanting a life, not going quietly at the end.'
'Perhaps he's a Sagittarian.'
Tom pulled a face. 'I have no idea, but yes of course, that's the other possible explanation.'
'Big of you to admit it.'
Chris swung her chair back on two legs and next moment almost tipped backwards altogether. Tom leaned over quickly and supported her shoulder, preventing disaster.
'Now,' she said. 'It's good sometimes to have you to hang onto.'
'Academics do have their uses.'
'I didn't mean it like that.'

'I know you didn't,' Tom said gently and was aware suddenly that his words were heavy with more meaning than he'd intended.

She put her hand on his knee.

'You make me feel good,' she said. 'Thank you.'

'Glad to be of service in so many ways,' he replied.

'Sorry. I'm not intending to put you down.'

'I know. No offence taken.'

* * *

It was well after nine in the morning and the post was waiting for Chris in the office when she walked in with Tom. She flicked through the pile of envelopes. She quickly pulled out one letter, tore it open and scanned the single page of writing.

'Read this,' she said, handing it to Tom with a stony face. Tom read the following:

Dear colleagues,

When my son goes on campaign, he becomes strong. My view is that this is the prime of his life. Years and years of being treated as a nobody. Now at last he is in the seat of control. We have never understood how important the ants are to him. Control has always been at the heart of his dealings with the ants. He is able to link controlling the ants to his desire to exercise total control over other human beings – people he selects.

When our John wears the mask it helps him to take on his powerful identity. Fashioned from plastic and flesh coloured latex, it transforms his head into a monstrous ant form. Complete with mandibles and antennae, it is designed to induce terror and paralysis in victims of the ants. He may have told you about his list. Here's a thought for you: he may have to abandon the alphabet as his guide and fall back on the more fundamental principle of who most easily arouses his insatiable anger.

Yours,

G

'What do you make of it?'

'Who's it from?'
'Our killer.'
'But the name.'
'The signature? It's indecipherable. It's meant to be his mother, or his father. That's another of his games.'
'Or a symptom of this multiple personality disease Mary Threadgold is on about.'
'If it exists. I have my doubts.'

* * *

Tom swept up the rest of the post in one hand as he raced out of the house, slamming the door without looking behind him. What was in that formal looking envelope? At the open car door he tore it open. A very brief letter inside conveyed its stark meaning with the minimalist intensity of a laser. He slammed his fist down on the car roof.

Chris leaned across from the passenger seat: 'What is it?'

'They're withdrawing the special funding from my Centre at the University.'

'Which means precisely nothing to me.'

'It means that unless some more grants can be found from somewhere the unit will close.'

'Does that mean your work will be stopped?'

'Not future tense, but present,' said Tom. 'Like as from tomorrow, or even today, business starts to wind down.'

'I see,' she said.

'I wish I did,' Tom said slowly, staring at the letters on the page while they jumbled themselves into different patterns, like insects tumbling down a dry, sandy slope. 'Meaninglessness,' he added.

'What?'

'I was thinking what a pointless activity scientific research is, when all you've worked for, year in and year out, can be stopped in mid-flow regardless of the timescale over which you might expect the payoff – at the stroke of an administrator's pen.'

'They haven't given you any warning?'

'That's the trouble, they have. It's been on the cards for years. It's always on the cards. In fact, that's how management keep academics working night and day. They hold over their heads the permanent fear of pulling the plug if they don't come up with sufficient externally funded research. It's just that research units are particularly vulnerable to this form of intimidation, since pretty well all of their revenue funding – salaries of research staff and so on – comes from research grants.'

He sat grinding the empty envelope onto his thigh.

'That's why Hugh was so keen to second me to your Force. He

bloody well knew what was coming.'

Chapter 36

Graver abandoned his first attempt to abduct Tom and Laura's two children. It was too crude to try to win them from their mother in some direct way. He approached so far, then pulled back without speaking. He was glad afterwards; in the absence of a plan, only a half-formed set of linked ideas was not enough. Part of the problem was his head was too full of people, swimming about in the canals of his brain. Each fresh junction with reality presented him with further choices. He couldn't cope. There were too many of them.

The breakthrough came when he decided to approach the mother's friend instead; she didn't know him in any of his guises. There was always a risk with the mother that she might recognise him, or smell danger. He'd watched the children for hours on end, using his powerful binoculars. These gave him a sense of power, the external feeling of being in control, control he so lacked inside his head.

He watched them with the friend and decided they were so at home with her, it might even work better than with the nanny. What he needed now was some clarity and a sharp focus on the objective.

The second time, Graver was more lucky. Sarah played with her dolls and pram on the grass verge outside the house and Matthew rode up and down on his tricycle.

Laura rushed like a gale from room to room, hardly able to think, grabbing wildly at whatever they might need for a protracted stay elsewhere.

'Come on, darlings, we must hurry.'
'Why are we always hurrying, Mummy?'
'Sometimes mummies have to do one job after another very quickly.'
'But you aren't doing a job, Mummy. You're at home, packing.'
'When we are on holiday, where will Daddy be?'
'At work, I expect.'

Laura had it worked out. She was dropping the kids at school, Helen would pick them up this afternoon and bring them to the tea rooms in Cottingham. They could have an ice cream while waiting with Helen for her to arrive.

Laura came back to the present. 'Mummy, Mummy, you aren't answering my question. Will Daddy be coming on holiday with us when he gets home from work?'
'Daddy's busy.'
'He's always busy.'
'You're too busy as well.'
'I'm sorry. Just get ready, please.'

'Are you frightened, Mummy?'
'Of course not.'
'You look frightened. Is there a monster in the car.'
'Don't be silly. Look, you two, we must hurry to get away on time.'
'If we go slower, will we be able to see Daddy on his way home from work?'

Oh my God, this is complicated, thought Laura. 'No,' she fought to keep the impatience down, 'Daddy will be at work till very late.' I hope, she added mentally.

'I'm going to take Teddy. He'll be cold if I leave him in bed on his own. He can stay in this bag in the cloakroom till home time.'

'That's a very good idea. What about you, Matthew? What will you take? Your train?'

'I'm taking my kite and my new cricket bat,' said Matthew decisively.

'It might rain,' offered Laura tentatively.

'If it rains, I'll stay in bed.'

'Apart from school.'

'Yes, apart from school.' Laura didn't have the time to negotiate at greater length.

'Oh damn!' Laura had forgotten to collect the car. She ran back into the house and asked Helen to take the children in the van. At least they'd be off the premises before Tom arrived home. She would meet Helen and the children with the car when she'd been to the garage to collect it.

* * *

Graver realised what was happening. He had fixed it so the petrol feed pipe would fail, but he hadn't any idea how long it would be before the vibration shook the connection loose. He followed the van at a discreet distance in the fake taxi cab. Even though there was no chance that they would recognise a man they had never seen before, he didn't want to arouse any suspicion that they were being followed. If he had but known it, the fact that Laura was taking the children away was going to make it all the easier for him to intervene at this point.

'Where are we going first, Helen?'
'I have to get some petrol at the garage.'
'Are we going on the motorway, Helen?'
'Not today.'
'I'm glad. I don't like the motorway.'
'Mummy drives too fast on the motorway.'
'You don't really think so, Matthew?'
'I do. Once a policeman stopped her when she were going at sixty-three miles an hour.'

'It can't have been as fast as that. Mummy is always careful.'
'She said a naughty word when he waved at us. I heard her. But she was very quiet when he wagged his finger and told her off.'
'You have to be polite to policemen.'
I'll bet Laura curses her son's precision memory, thought Helen. Then, out loud, 'Ooops, nearly missed the turning.'

She glanced into the mirror quickly and swung into the right lane at the traffic lights on the ring road out of town. Her driving instructor always said that she under-used her wing mirror. On this occasion she would have had to be far more vigilant to have noticed the car tailing her, almost a quarter of a mile behind.

Graver lit a cigarette as he drove. This was looking good. They were beyond the edge of the built-up area now. He suffered a momentary pang of doubt about the efficiency of his tampering with her engine. But at that very moment the car in front swerved, slowed and pulled rapidly into the side of the road and then bumped up onto the verge. The hazard warning lights came on. Graver allowed his taxi to coast along and slowed as he came alongside. He called through his open window, just as Helen was easing herself out on the road side.

'Problems?'

'God knows. I'm in such a hurry and it has to cut out.'

He pulled in front and parked up on the wide verge. He glanced approvingly in both ways, but took care to shake his head. Not a car in sight in either direction.

'Just your luck eh? That's the way it goes. Are you in the AA?'

'We were. To be honest I can't tell you if the membership has lapsed. We never talk about these things. Anyway, even if it hasn't the card is at home, in my other bag. So we can forget it.'

Graver walked round to the front of her car.

'Let's have a look under the bonnet then? See what the problem is.'

Her hopes rose. 'Do you know about engines then?'

'I look after mine, if that's what you mean. He nodded back at the taxi. But mine's a diesel. Chalk and cheese, if you see what I mean.'

'Oh, right.' Her heart fell again. Possibly not so simple after all.

She fell in with his guidance, got in and released the bonnet catch. He lifted it and stared expertly, fishing around for a few minutes till he judged it right to pick up the offending connection. 'Aha!'

'What is it?'

'Fractured petrol feed, I'm afraid.'

'Oh. Can't it be fixed then?'

'Yes, it's a straightforward enough job.'

'Good, I'm in such a hurry you see.'

'Right. Only problem is, I can't do it here without the repair pack. It would start leaking again, petrol all over the engine, fire risk, that sort of thing.'

'Oh.'

How stupid I seem, thought Helen. Of course he can't fix it. He's a casual passer-by. What do you expect, she said to herself roughly. Jim'll fix it?

Ten minutes later, they were all in the taxi, three passengers in the back and Graver driving in front, speeding along towards his destination. The fog and the growing darkness helped to obscure the change of route until it was far too late and by the time they disembarked at the remote farmhouse, Helen's tiredness was overcoming everything, even her anxieties at what was happening to them.

The exception – Graver felt compelled to make an exception – to his self-imposed rule not to send any messages to victims, their families or friends, was his phone call to Laura. He had to telephone her, to assure her that there was another man in the world at least as clever as her husband, possibly even cleverer. And yes, there was another reason, which he hardly admitted to himself until he actually made the call.

'Hello.'

'Who is this?'

'Hello.'

'Who is this please?'

'Mrs F.'

'Yes. But I said –'

'Mrs F-O-R-T-I-U-S.' He spelt it out quietly, so his passengers couldn't hear. He repeated the letters slowly, rolling each sound round his mouth, because it amused him to be using them in a legitimate conversation, not a fantasy. 'You will say nothing about this conversation to anybody. Be quiet and listen.'

Silence at the other end.

'Can you hear me?'

Still silence.

'Mrs F, if you don't answer you will never see your children again.'

'Yes.'

'Yes what?'

'Yes I agree.'

'Mrs F.' There it was again, the frisson of power. It didn't happen every time, but was well worth trying for. 'Let us be clear. I am making a statement and you have to confirm. This is not a question, but a statement. You will ask nothing, you simply agree. Understand?'

'I understand.'

'You will say nothing about this conversation to anyone, not even your husband.'

Her voice almost disappeared, she was in such a nervous state. 'No.'

'No what?'
'I will say nothing.'
'Right, that's lovely. We're making progress. Now –' A sudden thought struck him. 'You are alone, aren't you?'
'Yes.'
'No other person in the house?'
'No.'
'No tape recorders, bugs or other interferences? I can tell that you know I will carry out my threat if you make any attempt whatever to –'
Laura's voice rose steadily, nearly out of control: 'Nothing, no nothing, please believe me.'
'Good, good.'
He was back to the soothing tone again: 'I take it you want to see your children again.'
'Yes.'
'And you will do anything I require in order to achieve this.'
'Yes.'
'You will drive to a place I will indicate. You will have with you in the car a recording of Bruckner. It will be Bruckner's seventh symphony.'
'That's no problem, honestly. I think we have a record of that. I'm almost positive. Something by Bruckner, anyway.'
'Mrs F, hear me clearly. I'm sorry, but "Something by Bruckner" is not good enough. You will bring with you the recording of the original scoring of the seventh symphony.'
'Oh, I don't know if we have that.' She spoke in a sudden rush. 'I suppose there's always the library, or the music shop.'
'Many people don't search diligently enough, Mrs F. But I assure you it makes a considerable difference. Sheep from goats, you know.'
'Yes, I'll do everything –'
She was talking to emptiness. He had hung up.
No directions. He had rung off without giving her directions. For a quarter of an hour – it seemed like a lifetime – she paced about, scoured the house, homed in on the record, cassette and CD collections in the lounge, in Tom's study and in their bedroom. 'Oh my God, what do I do? What if he rings before I find it? What if I don't find it? Will there be time to go to the music shop in town? Will I have to order it? Perhaps he'll kill the children before I manage to reach them.'
She collapsed on the floor, surrounded by piles of recordings, a chaos of classical, romantic, operatic, modern, folk, jazz, everything sent to taunt her except the record she was looking for. And she didn't even know whether they had it.
Brr brrr. Brr brrr. The phone rang, double rings, insistently.
Laura flew to answer it. Quick, before it stops!
'Yes?'

'Is that the lady of the house, Mrs Fortius? I'll introduce myself. I'm not trying to sell you anything. Quite to the contrary, you may be able to help us and benefit yourself.'
'Who is this?'
'Have you had heating problems in the cold snap last winter?'
'Who is speaking please?'
'Howard of Double Glazing Consultants speaking.'
She slammed the phone down. It rang again. Brr brrr.
'Hello.'
'Oh, Howard here again Mrs B. I forgot to add details of our special bonus –'
'Get off the phone,' she shouted. 'I'm expecting an important call. If you ring me again I'll kill you.'
'Mrs B, did I mishear? I only –'
'You did, I'm sorry.' She was so confused. 'The dog made me spill my coffee and I was shouting at him. I've burned my hand. So if you'll ring back some other time.'
'Of course, and remember we're only a phone call away. Byee.'
Graver had one more call to make. He would enjoy making this before anybody else and very carefully placed a muffler over the mouthpiece of the receiver before dialling.
'Mr F?' He put a slight emphasis on the Mr. He'd planned this detail of misdirection and was particularly proud of it. 'I'm ringing about your children. Are you sure you know who is looking after them?'
He rang off immediately. He liked the idea of this. This was turning out to be one of his particularly focused days.
'The children,' Laura shouted and there was nobody to hear. 'The children. How could I forget? Helen was taking them. She's picking them up later and taking them to play at friends this morning, with Mum. I must get through to Mum.' She picked up the phone. 'No, what am I thinking of? They'll be at school. Helen's collecting them later.' Her hand was shaking so much she dropped the receiver. There was a cracking sound and it lay on the tiled floor buzzing like a dying bee, the plastic cover on one side, the intricate interior wiring on the other. 'My God, another phone. I must find one. Tom's study.' She raced for the stairs.
In the study she was reminded of Tom. She'd ring him first.
It wasn't surprising that Tom's direct number was engaged. Graver's neat contrivance ensured their panic was mutual and simultaneous. It was several minutes before one of them put the receiver down long enough for the other to get through.

Part Four

Inside the Labyrinth

Chapter 37

Laura was distraught. She should never have let the children out of her sight. She had a strong premonition that a disaster had occurred. Thunder rolled like a distant drum. She ran to the window and looking out saw a massive storm cloud piling up to westward. Had they taken their coats? In such a serious situation, it was as though the only way she could cope was to think of such unimportant details.

* * *

The children went off happily into the man's garden. They didn't know his name but Matthew thought he recognised his voice from visits to Daddy's work.
'I met you once,' he said.
'I don't think so,' said the man.
'Are you Daddy's friend?' asked Matthew.
'You could say that,' said the man.
'Helen says to go and play. She's coming in a minute,' said the man. 'You can go and play in the maze.'
'He thinks Helen's a real nanny,' said Sarah.
'A maze. Gosh how exciting!' exclaimed Matthew, all thoughts of where Helen had gone set aside. The two children ran off into the maze, to engage in that most delightful of childhood games – hide and seek.
'You can't find me,' called Matthew.
'Yes I can,' Sarah shouted.
But try as she might, she could not reach him. The tall hedges with their close-cropped foliage baffled her. It was particularly confusing to hear him so close and change direction, only to find her way blocked by a barrier. It was a thick matting of hop poles, netting, hedging and creepers, which in the half light formed as effective a screen as any solid wooden fence.
'Where are you, Matthew?' Her voice had an edge to it now. She was beginning to feel anxious.
Thunder rumbled in the distance and Sarah trembled. She was frightened and she'd seen many times Matthew's terror in thunderstorms. She desperately hoped it would go away.
'Here. Come this way.'
'Matthew, I want to find you.'
'You can't yet. You have to go round the other way.'
Sarah's voice rose as the anxiety steadily grew.
'I want this game to end.'

'It can't end till you find me,' he called tantalisingly.

Sarah started to run. She hurried towards his voice, only to find her way completely barred by a wall of branches. She heard him but couldn't see. She couldn't breathe properly. Tears and panic flooded her.

The man couldn't be Daddy's friend if he let her become lost. Unless it was an accident.

'Matthew,' she called. 'Is the man really Daddy's friend?'

'Of course,' said Matthew.

'He shouldn't let you be horrid to me.'

'He isn't.'

'I'll tell Daddy if you don't play with me properly.'

'I am.'

There was an unmistakable clap of thunder. Matthew heard it. 'That's thunder.'

'It isn't, stupid,' she said. 'It's a plane in the distance.'

'Are you sure?'

'Cross my heart,' she said.

Unseen by Matthew, Sarah sniffed and quietly started to cry.

'Coming now,' called Matthew, running to the end of the avenue of hedging and turning left to bring him to her.

Sarah wasn't there. He turned left and ran again. She wasn't at the end of that row either. Matthew's stomach tightened as he heard Sarah calling, further away this time.

'Matthew, Matthew where are you?'

'I'm here,' he shouted, a dreadful panic seizing him and raising the pitch of his voice.

'Matthew, you said you were coming.'

'I am,' called Matthew. 'Tell me how to reach you.'

'I can't,' Sarah cried and kept on crying.

Matthew sat down.

'I'm think I'm nearly crying,' he said with a sniffle, holding tightly onto the tissue in his trouser pocket.

* * *

It gave Graver so much pleasure to watch the little workers running round the labyrinthine passages of the observation nest with its two vertical glass plates and the finger-thin plug of soil between. In the end, he narrowed the space because if he allowed any other than light from the red bulb to penetrate – ants couldn't see red, because to them light at that end of the spectrum was indistinguishable from darkness – they would smear soil and saliva over the inner surface of the glass so he could no longer see in. The optimum width for the observation nest, he decided, was one ant's width plus two millimetres.

Staring for so many hours a day at the workers scurrying through the maze of underground passages gave him that pleasurable sensation in his groin, but made his head hurt. It was all becoming muddled in his head. He so much wanted those neuro-receptors he imagined sparking with micro-volts to combine these stimuli now with a few millenia of his inheritance from different species, right back to these prehistoric ants. He wanted to become part of the colony. He wanted the colony to become him, to take him over.

'Second by second, the hand on the clock ticks off the lifetimes which remain. He told you they're taking over.'

'Taking over?'

'Yes, removing the repulsive genes and replacing them.'

'He's telling you. He has to endure the invasion of the brain's most intimate and pain-contorted corridors by foreign agents. That's madness.'

He knew that while he was able to separate his sensations of what happened in the endless corridors and coils of his brain from those he stared at, he could prove to himself he was not mad.

'Of course I'm not mad. I discovered the ants. I waited. I'm still capable of rational thought. I planned. The queen was an egg, at the moment of genesis. She matured, mated and began to lay eggs herself. This was the period of generation. The workers developed. They sought food on an increasing, a massive, scale. This was the moment of fission. The colony reached its optimum size. Young queens and males were reared.'

'I told you.'

'He told you they issued forth from his ears and nose while he slept. You used to laugh when at the age of nine he wouldn't allow you near his face with the flannel at bath time, and refused to blow his nose and clear the thick snot which dribbled and formed a green crust. He feared the insects pouring out, but he feared them crawling up at night as well. It was worth them shouting 'snot-rag' at school. This barrier of repulsiveness to others suited him. It kept them at a distance.'

They dug a way out of his head, created and occupied the maze of tunnels and chambers, which rivals the complexity of the labyrinthine channels and corridors of the brain.

> *We have made the crucial leap of the imagination, by creating this maze, the labyrinth outside my cranium, thus fusing the external and internal worlds. This is difficult to grasp, without an understanding of the ant colony as a composite being, at its apotheosis represented in the spreading city of millions of*

individuals of Atta Vollenweideri, the leaf cutter ant, a single presence spreading over several fields, across the trees and bushes of half a copse and deep into several surrounding acres of soil.

The programme and the major themes of the first symphony of Gustav Mahler continue to resonate through my head all day long. We live and move with Mahler's and Bruckner's music, replayed from memory and insinuated into this body, seeping into all its everyday activities. The maze-like complexity of their musical scores fascinates us. We want to go behind the printed versions to the handwritten scores. In the reading room of the British Library at Boston Spa, the one called 'I' searched books and manuscripts, looking for photographs of pages of the original manuscripts in biographies of the composers. When this proved fruitless, 'I' tried to find out where the scores were held and planned various imaginary journeys to view them, as a pilgrim visiting a shrine. The first symphony of Mahler at that early point became my own programme. 'I' was the Titan of Mahler's imagination; the first two movements became the idealisation of my own unhappy childhood. The third and fourth took on the qualities 'I' associated with the Hell of existence, with death and whatever lay after death, if anything.

It has taken much effort to grow what we planned so meticulously on paper.

THE LABYRINTH is labyrinthine. It's a joke, so laugh if you please. Don't ever accuse me of having no humour. A labyrinthine labyrinth. I repeat the word labyrinth labyrinth labyrinth until it loses meaning and becomes a succession of vowels and consonants.

Labyrinth: By using hop poles and netting and planting Russian vines and other fast-growing creepers, in less than three years we have created the effect of vast rows of impenetrable living barriers – a fraction of the decades it takes to grow a conventional maze, using traditional hedging such as box or other evergreens.

Planning and finalising the design, that was the first

problem. We couldn't settle on it. We'd sit and draw for hours. Symmetrical layouts with many open spaces and blind alleys in the corners; spirals with narrower passages, with alternatives leading from an initial point near the entrance; a random arrangement of passages, with the farmhouse near one edge. Eventually we have settled for the last of these. There are several advantages of this approach. It is more likely to baffle the players and it is simpler to arrange. We don't have to meet some totally predefined goal. We can change it if we encounter obstacles on the way.

G

* * *

For a while, Helen couldn't place this man who was entertaining them and promising them that Tom would arrive any minute. The uncertainty was enough to prevent her running away with the children.

When she heard that radio news item about the former technician at the University being wanted to help police with their enquiries, she put two and two together and her panic knew no limits. By the time she realised, they were captive, locked up in the cellar. It was ages later before she remembered the mobile in her bag. It was so stupid, a detail which could have saved any further hassle. She could have phoned Laura, Robin, the police, anybody.

* * *

How Helen escaped, she couldn't remember. Perhaps she ran up the steps and through the door which the man hadn't intended to leave unlocked and unguarded. Perhaps there were other steps and a trapdoor leading directly to the outside. Had he done this deliberately? Helen was muddled. She wasn't where the man said. She was in another part of the garden, her head still fuddled. She felt drugged, but couldn't recall how it could have happened. She wanted desperately to find her way to the children. Where were they? She called their names, softly at first, then louder and more anxiously. There was no reply. She ran this way and that, calling their names repeatedly. After what seemed like eternity, she heard their sobbing. Somehow, she found herself next to the outer passage of the maze, calling 'Sarah, Matthew!'

The almost total darkness made it impossible to make out anything beyond the faint outline of the hedging. Strange shapes and outlines like gargoyles rose from the creepers and bushes all around. The huge creepers created a monstrous topiary, huge and overhanging, like ghosts crowding in, dark and silent at every turn she took.

Helen heard a totally different sound, the sound of children screaming. The screaming went on for a long time. The screaming was coming from inside her head. Then she realised it was her own voice. She was screaming again and again and again.

* * *

The wind was starting to blow, hard enough to agitate the tops of the trees and shake the lower branches. Tom was in a panic. He looked out of his window, his guts in turmoil as though he'd swallowed the most nauseating potion. Below him in the campus grounds, the contrast was incredible. Ducks swam quietly across the placid waters of the sheltered lake to the rear of the building. Its surface rippled slightly in response to the gathering wind. The sun was low in the sky, visible through the cloud as a glowering purple globe.

There was a knock at Tom's half-open office door.

'Mr Fortius?'

'Yes?'

A young man with short cropped hair wearing a smart jacket and immaculately pressed trousers pushed the door open and stood hesitantly just inside. 'Sorry, sir, the door was open. I came straight along the corridor.'

Tom's stomach gave a sickening lurch. Detectives wore the unmistakable uniform of police officers despite their plain clothes.

'What is it?'

DC Moran stepped forward, held out his identification card and another officer appeared behind him. 'Detective Constables Moran and Lounds, sir. I think we've met when you visited DCI Winchester.'

His stomach still churning, Tom waved them inside and closed the door behind them. He recognised them from his visits to the Station. They walked with that terrible inevitability policemen in particular have of placing their boots on soft carpeting when bearing bad news. He had a terrible premonition it was more bad news about the children. He stood by his desk and tried to keep control as he faced them.

'No sign of your children yet, sir, but we're doing everything we can.'

Tom couldn't stop himself exploding. 'Everything you can is no bloody good if you haven't found them.'

'No, sir. They aren't at home or at school,' continued the imperturbable Moran. 'We've been in constant touch with Mrs Fortius. She hasn't seen them today. They may have simply gone on an outing.

'We have no reason at the moment to believe they have come to any harm.'

'No reason to believe?' Tom's thoughts spun wildly out of control. 'They should have been safe. They were with the nanny.'

'Your nanny wasn't in the picture, sir. Your friend Mrs Lovelace has disappeared as well. She may have gone with them, or she may have gone somewhere else, but she may have a clue as to their whereabouts.

'We don't know at this stage. We are considering the hypothesis she may be implicated in their disappearance.'

'Hypothesis? Implicated? She's Laura's best friend for God's sake. What is this, a bloody Agatha Christie guessing game? My children's lives are at stake.'

'I'm sorry, sir.'

'Sorry! It's absurd. Helen would never do anything like that. She'd have no reason to.'

Moran shrugged. 'Let's say we have an open mind at present.'

'I've had a call from a man claiming to be responsible, and so has my wife,' said Tom.

Moran's manner changed. 'You what, sir? Who did you tell?'

'I haven't told anybody,' said Tom belligerently. 'It would be a calamity if it reached this man that I've told the police.'

Moran looked worried. 'With respect, sir, you should have got straight onto DCI Winchester.'

'With respect, you should have found my children by now.'

'Just a minute, sir.' Moran fumbled for his mobile. Tom paced about while Moran stepped to a corner of the office and dealt with the call. When he'd finished, Tom had more questions.

'We're doing all we can,' said Moran. 'Sorry, sir. I know this has come as a shock.'

'Never mind wasting time consoling me. How long have the police known?'

Moran didn't know where to put himself. 'I can't say for sure, sir.'

Tom saw he was up against the solid wall of the man's ignorance of the wider situation.

'Okay, how long have you personally known?'

'Me, sir, only since I came on duty.'

'When was that?'

'Last night.'

Tom clenched both fists. Chris had known at least since last evening and hadn't rung him.

'Carry on with the search and don't come back till you've found them.'

'If you're all right, sir, I'll be off now. Goodbye.'

'No, hang on. Where is Chief Inspector Winchester?'

'She'll be at HQ I expect, sir.'

'Are you returning there, Sergeant?'

'I expect so, sir.'

'I'll come with you. No, dammit, I can't. I'll have no transport. A taxi.' Tom felt in his pockets to see what loose change he had. 'It's okay, Sergeant. Car's broken down, you carry on.'

The two officers turned back towards the office and Moran spoke. 'Sir. If you want me to pass on a message to DCI Winchester –'

'No message,' he called. And then, when they were out of the door, he said to himself, 'Tell the Chief Inspector to go to hell.'

He watched from the office window as the sergeant's car coasted slowly out of the car park towards the main entrance at the junction with the main road.

'They say the police look after their own,' he mouthed. 'Carry on doing it in your way, and I will in mine.'

* * *

The temporary secretary from the agency wouldn't be in yet. Tom went through the stack of mail, as yet unsorted. He was in such a state that he knocked the entire pile onto the floor, together with his desk diary. He bent down, picked up his diary which he wanted to take with him, and as he scrabbled to pick up the letters and packages, flicking through them for anything urgent, a small envelope fell out from among the large brown packages. A distinctive collage of newspaper fonts composed his name and address. He tore the envelope open.

Dear Professor Fortius.

'Fucking bastard!' Tom shouted, clenching his fist. He read on.

First, let me thank you for the information about the nun. She had a lot to answer for. You should have seen her face. I got through to her. A hundred thousand ants achieved more contrition in a few hours than all those years of Hail Mary's.

Now to the major point of this letter. It was so easy. I had time to plan it so carefully.

And so on. There was much more in similar vein. Tom felt physically sick. Who hated him at work? The one person he hadn't considered yet: Apthorpe. He had a sudden urge to confront Apthorpe and see how he reacted. Events took over for the next few hours and his suspicion had to stay on the back burner.

* * *

When Chris reached Wawne Road Police Station there was a message from Sheila. She dialled Sheila's direct line. 'How busy are you?' Sheila asked.

'Averagely at my wit's end, I guess.' Chris's voice was flat. She felt completely at sea with the case. To make matters worse, her personal life was in a mess. She knew things were all wrong between her and Tom, but hadn't time to sort that out at present. 'To be frank, I don't know where we're going on this case. What can you offer?'

'I've been looking back at all the material he's written. There are at least two, possibly three, personalities involved. Given what we have, we can try to predict the nature of the fragmentation of his personality which may be occurring. There's a chance we can guess his next move from whichever persona seems most of the time to be dominant or uppermost.'

Sheila knew this was highly speculative. She hoped she could reassure Chris, offer a lifebelt.

'We can guess from the written material what stage he's reached in the projection of his fantasies. I judge he's reaching, or has reached, a crisis of some kind. It's represented for him in an externalisation of the labyrinth of his brain, which he can't fathom, and from the inside of his head, in his fantasies about the mass of insects populating it and threatening to overwhelm him.'

Chris sighed and didn't say a word.

'You're wondering where this connects with the need to apprehend him.'

'I am.' Chris sounded tired. She felt wrung out. She didn't believe in God. But she found herself praying out loud, as a last resort, to the only person outside herself she could think of as remotely able to help: 'Please don't let me be wrong.'

'Bear with me a moment. I've been thinking about masks. I think our killer is adept at using them.'

'You don't mean literally?'

'Metaphorically. He's probably good at disguising himself. In a particular personality, he assumes what we would call a disguise. He would regard it at that point as simply himself.'

There was a sound in the background. Sheila was distracted momentarily.

'Just a moment,' she said. 'Someone at the door. I'll send them away.'

She was back in a few moments.

'You've come across the mask of Demetrios?'

'Remind me,' said Chris, who had only a vague memory of this.

'It's the Janus-faced or two-faced mask widely used as a symbol for dramatic performance.'

'I remember, we printed it on the front of the programmes for our school drama productions.'

'It's very likely widely used by drama groups. We discussed this on the recent away-day. Think of the characters of the play, with our murderer playing many, possibly all of the parts. Inside the mask there may be not two but any number of different characters. I've seen case studies of more than a dozen. The psychiatrist may try to penetrate the fragmented personae presented by a patient suffering from MPD, without encouraging it. The difficulty often reported is that by recognising and engaging with the symptoms, the questioner reinforces the existence of a particular personality, or encourages new ones to form. Imagine trying to hold a conversation with up to a dozen people at once, possibly more.'

'It sounds a nightmare,' Chris reflected. 'Walters, Thompsen, or someone else. I'm uncertain which of these is or was our man.'

Sheila took a deep breath. 'That's it, that's MPD. You switch from one identity to the next, sometimes so fast you don't just confuse other people but yourself as well. It's complicated. He's putting the record straight, emotionally speaking. Different fragments from his past and present are triggered by, or trigger, different responses. We're dealing with all these personalities in one. Walters is dead. Part of the time – whether he's Thomsen or somebody else – he wants to communicate with us. He may display other personae, of which we know nothing because they don't have that need, that urge. You're wondering where this leaves us.'

'It does seem pretty hopeless.'

'We have to assemble all the information we possibly can, cross-referencing the incidents and constructing the fullest life story.'

'You're joking. There isn't time. We must find the latest people he's abducted, before they – before he –' She couldn't say it.

'We must have this information, to maximise the chance of predicting where he is.'

Chris took a deep breath. She had to calm down. 'You mean the killings and,' she hesitated, 'the latest abductions of the two children of Professor Fortius.'

'Yes. It's like identifying a spot on a map, using grid references. We must see where the lines cross and whether there are points of convergence. The next stage –'

Chris clenched her fists. 'We haven't time. There'll be more victims. He's becoming more desperate. He's accelerating. His personality is fragmenting.'

Sheila spoke with greater emphasis.

'It's the only way to find him. The next stage is to cross-check through the people at that point. We have to be particularly careful over identities. Remember, we're looking for somebody playing more than one role. We may find the person is known by different names in different reference groups. Third, if possible we must avoid interacting with him. That might only lead to further fragmentation of his personality.'

Chris's nerves were worn to the wire. There was no alternative. She wasn't sure she understood, but she knew what she had to do. First she rang Tom's number, intending to ask how the letter was signed. There was no reply, so she left a message on his voicemail.

I need some space, Chris thought. Some time with Regel was overdue. It had saved time to offer to bring him to Hull, but she couldn't keep the situation going much longer, even though she still hadn't a clear idea how he could help, beyond filling in background details. Well aware that this elderly frail man couldn't be left alone in that strange hotel she had sent Morrison to sit with him. Morrison would be able to chat and might even elicit some useful information.

She rang Morrison. Regel was coping, and according to Morrison had been talking, almost to the point of chattiness. It was as though he was fed up with being on his own and welcomed the stimulus of the stay in the hotel and the investigation going on around him. She instructed Morrison to spend time with Regel, take him out if it would help, and build up a picture of his life from the point where he'd first come into contact with Blatt and his sons.

Having settled Mr Regel into his hotel near the railway station, Morrison became aware of how pent up the old man was about his former stay in the resettlement camp at Hessle, and offered to drive him up there immediately.

'It'll only take us an hour or so,' said Morrison. He would make sure he stopped for a cool drink and sandwich.

'Ooh, I don't think I could stand an hour's driving.'

Morrison laughed. 'Five minutes each way, if it's busy. The rest will be you and me nosing around. You can show me your old haunts.'

They made an incongruous pair, Morrison, youthful and upright, Regel frail and stooping, walking with difficulty, stopping every few paces to catch his breath. An onlooker would have surmised they were grandfather and grandson.

In contrast with his appearance, Regel was becoming more animated by the minute. They walked up the track off Heads Lane in the rural district of Hessle, overlooking the town of Hull three or four miles away.

'This was the entrance to the camp,' said Regel. 'These beech and larch trees look as though they've been here forever, but they must have planted them after we left and they demolished the buildings.'

They walked up the lane and Regel dived into the wood, nearly tripping over some brambles. Morrison lurched forward and rescued him. Regel bent and started scratching with his fingers at a patch of bare soil.

'Hang on,' said Morrison, looking around for an implement. A chunk of metal was lying on the verge. He used this to scrape away the surface material. It was surprisingly loose, composed of rubble and a coarse mixture of grit and soil.

Regel was watching as a flat block of concrete came into view.

'This was the cookhouse.' He brushed his sleeve across his eyes. 'There's one of the hearthstones. Over there were the rows of huts where we lived and slept. They took people from here straight to the docks for repatriation. At about the same time, some of us were discharged for other destinations. You needed documentation to support an application to stay. I travelled south. My longstanding friend Marko offered to put me up and organised an interview for a teaching post. I was successful but a dreadful calamity occurred the day after I gained the position. Marko died of a heart attack. I found out he had no relatives and had left the house and all his personal effects to me. It was only after I began to teach at the school that I found out the war had vanquished the Nazis but not prejudice against Poles resembling German Jews.'

Later, Morrison dropped him back at the hotel. Regel was very excited at the prospect of exploring the town and gentrified docks district.

'He's eaten his way through two brunches and I left him planning his evening meal,' said Morrison when he reached Wawne Road Police Station.

There were smiles all round at this. 'He'll be putting on a couple of stone,' said Chris, 'after years of catering for himself.'

Morrison was moving his balance from one leg to the other. 'I've a problem, boss. I need some information, possibly from the town archives in Hull and certainly from the Imperial War Museum. It's very urgent. Some of the information may be accessible from the Internet. Can I see you in your office?'

When Morrison and Chris emerged, Morrison had three officers to help him with the task.

* * *

Graver was busy indoors, quite distracted by the number and complexity of tasks facing him. Sweat bubbled from his brow and ran in copious streams down his blubbery flesh. There was much to do before the police inquiries either intensified, or reached him in the routine course of events.

The police had made a half-baked attempt to find him, to intervene. He judged it pathetic, as pathetic as all police are. His mouth opened and conversation flowed between the beings inhabiting the darker regions of his mind. Many of them were shadowy, too vague and horror-filled to contemplate full-on. He was grateful for the chance to retreat from these.

'It isn't surprising.'

'Why is that?'

'Didn't you know, they draw their recruits from the same lower social class as that from which criminals spring. If we're crap, they're the same crap.'

Once, recently, the head officer sent a constable to the farm, on the back of a tip-off, or a whim. The result was a complete farce. Graver was able to hide everything before the fellow arrived. He was able to disguise himself and let the officer search to his heart's content.

He spoke with disdain to the blank wall. 'It proves you're right, they're crap.'

And then, in a different voice: 'They'll never find anything, looking that way.'

He put it down as a near miss. Even though the police did not find any tangible evidence in the house linking him to the murders, the circumstantial evidence was strong. They visited the farmhouse three times, taking him in for questioning twice, the second time holding him for several days on suspicion of abducting someone who'd disappeared. This was all as a result of that stupid bitch. He put her number one on his list for fixing at the next stage.

'Are you on a programme?'

'You have to be. It's the scientist in us. Part of our genetic inheritance. How we learn from the larva through the pupa to the hatched stage, is by experimenting through our senses. We receive information through our seven senses: from our eyes, ears, touch, taste, smell, the proprioceptor system which tells us how our parts relate to each other in the nest and our vestibular system which signals which way up we are in its total underground darkness. All these sources of data are processed in the utter darkness of our brains.'

* * *

The truth was that a clash had always been inevitable between Chief Superintendent Bradshaw and Chief Inspector Winchester. It was more than a personality clash. Bradshaw was totally at odds with the style of investigation Chris was used to carrying out. She could live with the constant uncertainty of pursuing several parallel lines of inquiry simultaneously. He needed constant reassurance that resources were being managed, time wasn't being wasted. Over and above this, he would cave in now and again under pressure from top management and on occasions could react off the cuff to the usual probing by the media. This was always going to be dangerous.

Bradshaw was going through one of his bad patches. Today he dilly-dallied around in his office, sitting down to open the mail, standing up, putting on his coat to go out, returning to his desk and folding the coat over his chair. He smacked his fist into the palm of his other hand. 'So close,' he said out loud. 'We're so damn close.' They might just as well have been in Antarctica for all the difference it made. His head would still be on the block if this investigation stayed unresolved much longer. So many deaths and so many unanswered questions. In the end, he decided to go into the office and press the team for an update on the briefing he'd had an hour ago.

* * *

The police questioned Laura closely, asking her if she knew Thompsen the technician. She had quite a clear recollection of him from the few times she had seen him in the department, when she used to hang onto the car and pick Tom up late after he'd had a long day in the lab. There was the college staff party and that after-party binge at Hugh Mackintosh's house, at which most of them had let their hair down and finished up quite drunk without worrying about who was there and what the consequences might be. That was before Thompsen's accident. This was and yet wasn't the Thompsen she had known. Without the trigger memory, she'd never have recognised him at all. Of course, Thompsen had been off sick for ages and she hadn't seen him again. He never returned to work, as far as she knew, though she'd never asked Tom and she couldn't be sure. To think she had sort of fancied him, when things had first been bad between her and Tom. She hardly dared to admit this now. The mere thought of him caused her intense revulsion. That this man could at this moment be near her children, let alone touching them in any way, was too awful a possibility to contemplate. A surge of anger welled up from deep inside her. 'I'll kill you if you harm them at all,' she thought, recoiling at the words. She thought she heard someone else saying them and then realised she had spoken out loud.

* * *

It was one of those thundery days when without the relief of the thunderstorm breaking, the closeness of the atmosphere grows. Helen was perspiring in the humid heat. When she reached the woodland area, it was growing dark, not too dark though, to see the carpet of ants, with ribbons of advanced foragers and scouts moving out in front.

The trees looked to her like birches. Somehow this distraction of what species they were helped to calm her. They weren't thickly planted and had a good spread of sturdy branches near ground level.

How could the children get out of the maze? Where were they? She called their names, softly at first, then louder and more anxiously when there was no reply.

Helen didn't know how long she wandered around, distracted and in the end completely distraught, though trying not to lose control. She was almost completely exhausted by the heat and stress of it. Then, almost inaudible, she heard Matthew's voice. It was very faint as though he was small and distant.

Somehow Helen found her way to Matthew. Sarah wasn't with him. But Helen could hear her crying quietly, not far away.

'Crawl under here,' she whispered to Matthew. 'There's a gap. Follow me.'

A brief frisson of elation swept through Helen as she realised how to beat the maze; keeping low on the ground, looking for gaps where the netting wasn't pegged tightly and where the foliage hadn't reached ground level. They found Sarah sitting in a corner where the hedging ended in a blind alley.

'Quickly,' said Helen. 'We must crawl through.' She saw Sarah looking down at the muddy ground. Please don't mention creepy crawlies, she thought and focused on the manageable aspect.

'It's muddy. Daddy bought us these smart jeans. He'll be really really cross.'

'Don't worry about the mud on your clothes. I'll explain to Daddy.'

Helen's terror grew. In the darkness, shapes merged and transmogrified. Her imagination fed on the few details she could make out. Every fragment of her childhood terrors rose up to haunt her. Her hands and legs trembled. The sensation spread to her body.

'Matthew, Sarah, climb the tree.'

It was an intuitive response.

The children climbed. Matthew hauled himself up one almost vertical branch. Sarah scrambled up the more gently sloping adjacent one. Helen hadn't the strength to climb higher. She hoped the children would be high enough to avoid attracting the attention of the ants. She stayed at the first fork, where the main trunk split into three thick branches, about ten feet above the ground.

'Matthew, will you come here?'

There was a desperate note in Helen's voice, but the only sound from the other tree was a whimpering. Helen looked down with trepidation at the undergrowth beneath. Brambles and nettles grew shoulder high. When the breeze paused she thought she could hear a soft, insistent rustling, like the patter of rain on leaves – a warm, reassuring sound in any circumstances but these. The warmth of the humid air with its full charge of electrical energy before the storm broke, stimulated the ants to even quicker movements. They darted in scores, hundreds, thousands over the surface of the bark. The speed of their advance was unprecedented.

'Keep away!' screamed Helen, unable to see the children above her. 'Climb as high as you can and stay there till help comes. They'll be searching for you. They'll find you soon. Don't worry about me. I'll be g-'

With these last words, Helen's voice petered out in a choking sound as the ants on her face moved purposefully towards the nearest orifices. Those on her upturned hands presented as blotches, like the dark buboes of some ghastly plague. She spat desperately, clawing at her blocked nostrils and lips bleeding from a dozen nips of tearing mandibles.

Little Sarah saw the dark shape of the bivouac of ants unfold like the hood of a cloak, as a treacle-black stream issued forth from the front of it and flowed up the trunk of the tree in which Helen was scrambling for safety.

Helen screamed again.

'Don't look down, Matthew!' Sarah shouted.

She heard Helen scream yet again, hoped Matthew couldn't hear that bubbling cadence as it died away, and couldn't stop herself from taking a quick glance below.

At that instant, Helen's ravaged head turned upwards, eyes and ears completely blotted out and ants in great brown clumps on her face and neck, a pulsating mass where her mouth and nostrils had been. Her arms shot into the air, streaming with long skeins of ants. She gave a last shriek as she forced air from her lungs past her tortured lips and expelled from her mouth a gory gobbit of torn flesh and ants. Her arms flailed uselessly. The insects clung to her, biting ferociously, with hundreds more clinging to their bodies and legs, struggling to gain a foothold and sink their mandibles into her flesh. As she sank to the ground the small stains of ants on her head converged again on her mouth, stifling her last gasps for breath. The huge masses milling around on the woodland floor mounted her prostrate body in growing excitement and within seconds blotted the last uncovered areas of skin from sight.

A mock silence returned to the woods, then sounds of sobbing emanated from the tree where Sarah was. From Matthew's tree there was a different sort of silence – the silence of terror.

Chapter 38

Morning came and there was still no relief from the close atmosphere and unseasonal warmth. The birds sang in subdued voice over the wood. They would break out into full song once the rain had refreshed their territory. The quiet voices of Matthew and Sarah could be made out amidst the birdsong.

'If you can reach the fork of your tree, I can bend this branch down so you can cross it.'
'I can't move.'
'Don't be silly, Matthew. Of course you can.'
'I can't. I can't do anything.'
'You can use the ropes.'
'They're only for playing.'
'Silly Matthew, I'll have to come and get you.'

* * *

Just over twenty-four hours later, DC Morrison was back from the War Museum, looking as pleased as Punch. Chris was surprised, but didn't have time to question him. She was with Sheila in the investigation room, poring over a row of Ordnance Survey maps spread over four tables down one side of the room. Morrison was there too with DC Moran, accessing large scale maps on conveniently placed computers.

'Let's listen to the message from Helen.'
It was just four words, then the crackling as the battery went and the signal broke up. Then the awesome silence. They might as well have been in the Antarctic, thought Chris.
'Zzzzz hxlp zzzzz zzzzz aich.'
That was all they had to go on.
Sheila played it over and over, slower, faster, turning up the lower then the higher frequencies.
'That second word, it's help,' she said.
Chris nodded.
'What if that last word ends in the sibilant s?'
'Ace, mace, face.' Chris was fumbling for meaning.
'What if it's a harder sound at the end. More of a 'z'. Craze. No, the initial consonant is different. Let's see the possibilities. They are limited. Baize, faize, g, h, j, k, l, maize, naize, paize.'
'It could be an m, boss,' said Morrison. 'Maze. They could be where there's a maze. Perhaps it's a way of telling us where to look.'
'Maze, maze.' Sheila considered this, letting the words hang

between the officers in the room.

'It could be more than an ornament, boss,' Morrison added. 'It's regularly used in animal and insect experiments. Rats and ants in mazes. It's an ancient idea, back to the myths of Ancient Greece. Theseus, the Greek hero, went with a tribute of seven boys and seven girls to be paid by the Athenians to Minos, the king of Crete. They were to be fed to the Minotaur, a monster – half man and half bull – kept by Minos in the Labyrinth, an underground maze. Theseus used a ball of twine given him by his new lover Ariadne, the daughter of Minos, to escape with the children from the Labyrinth once he'd killed the Minotaur. I'm wondering if our killer plays the role of Daedalus.'

'You've lost me,' said Chris. 'Where do you find this information?'

'The public library and the internet, boss,' said the unstoppable Morrison. 'I haven't a PC at home. The Greeks respected Daedalus as the prime human craftsman. But he played a kind of traitorous role. He'd already thrown his nephew over a cliff for inventing the saw by copying the spine of a fish and he went on to be employed by Minos and the designer of the Labyrinth.'

'So Daedalus is a helpful friend and a betrayer.'

'Precisely, boss. Daedalus could be the key to this entire investigation. We're looking for someone who is trusted enough by the authorities to be close to the information we have at each stage, close enough to identify a succession of victims, sometimes before it would be apparent to a member of the general public that they had some connection with the University's Insect Research Centre.'

'I don't see. We've searched locally, at the University, in the region.'

'Like Daedalus, the person could be right under our nose.'

'A police officer?'

Sheila intervened. 'We should keep a totally open mind. It's like the traditional method of research by RCT.'

'RCT?'

'Random Controlled Trial. Where you give half the group the pill you're testing and the other half an identically shaped placebo made from nothing chemically significant. It's the traditional way to conduct thorough scientific research. We'll have to start again, and work thoroughly through everyone.'

'We can't,' said Chris. 'It's already taken months.'

'But we've got nobody at the end of it.'

'It must be an outsider.'

At that moment the phone rang and Morrison left them to answer it. The discussion continued as though he were still present.

'Impossible. All the killings are in a corridor between Hull and Lund, about a dozen miles north of Beverley.'

'That's a classic ploy. From Jack the Ripper to the Yorkshire Ripper, every intelligent murderer knows about zones of murder victims. Our killer is smart. He could be zooming in and out. He could be living in Doncaster, Sheffield, even London.'

'We've checked the trains.'

'He could be driving, or flying.'

'By hot air balloon or hang-glider?' Chris's tone was sardonic. 'The nearest airport is Leeds-Bradford, twenty miles away.'

'There are airstrips near Hull. Pocklington for instance.'

'He'd still have to drive,' said Chris. 'He'd be noticed. We've checked there, and at Breighton, Elvington and Sherburn in Elmet, all the way round. You name the airfield, however small, we've checked it. Nobody strange who can't be accounted for has been seen landing or taking off in the duration of these murders.'

'Find somebody who knows all the country houses in East Yorkshire where they're likely to have a maze. Or where the local eccentric farmer has built one.'

'I know somebody who'll tell us,' said Chris. 'He owes me a favour.'

'A journalist?'

'No, but you're getting warmer. An ex-boyfriend journalist named Jonah, who's written a book about the mazes of England.' She consulted the little address book in her handbag. As she picked up the phone Sheila made a discreet exit.

Five minutes later, Sheila came back from the toilet. 'Any luck with your Jonah?'

Chris shook her head. 'He can't help, apart from a turf maze overlooking the confluence between the Trent and the Ouse.'

'Won't that do?'

'It's on the south bank, about thirty miles away. Julian's Bower they call it.'

'Never mind, it was a good thought. Send a car. No, on second thoughts, send a helicopter to check it out, just in case. Ask around, local historians, writers, tourist information offices, anybody who's likely to know about a maze within a 30 mile radius of Hull.'

* * *

Tom was in a state. He knew he wouldn't rest night or day till he had found his children. He'd decided to hand over his day to day responsibilities as far as possible, so he could devote himself to the search for them. He parked in the faculty car park at the University, scrambled quickly from the car and ran to the porters' lodge:

'Where's Luis Deakin, please Len?'

Len looked up from a counter-top piled with paperwork. His efficiency and memory were legendary. He dealt with busy academics and frantic students equally imperturbably.

'Afternoon, Tom. Dr Deakin left some time ago.'

'Some time, you say?'

'Len consulted the book in the centre of the desk.

'Two thirty-five to be precise.'

'Two-thirty. Five hours ago.'

'Do you want to get in touch with him?'

'No, I wouldn't do that.'

'Righto.'

'He's probably at home.'

'When he gets back from his mother in East Yorkshire he will be, yes.'

'Okay,' said Tom absently, his mind on a dozen other things. Then it hit him.

'Did you say mother?'

'Yes.'

'Mother? You're sure about that.'

'Dr Deakin visits her regularly, since her illness.'

'Thanks, Len. You've done a fantastic job. Very helpful.'

Len looked puzzled. 'Thank you.'

'Hang on a moment. There is something else. When people – er, any of us – go off, do you record in the desk diary the telephone numbers we – er – give you?'

'I can't speak for my colleagues, sir, but I do, without fail.'

Tom could imagine what a difference a systematic person like Len would make to the average academic's office chaos. When he said he'd organise something he did it.

'Len, have you space at the back there for me to have a quick browse through the diary? No, I'll go and get a coffee from the machine first. I'm absolutely dying of thirst.'

'I can do better than that, Tom. Sit yourself down over here while I brew up. I was about to do myself a mug and there's a spare one. It helps to keep the chill off these draughty shifts.'

'You're a winner, Len.'

As he busied himself, Len recalled the nights when Tom had persuaded him not to make the long, largely unlit cycle ride home, and had given him a lift, picking him up very early the following morning and dropping him in college in time for a 6:30 a.m. start.

'If there's anything else you want to look at, Tom, let me know.'

'One thing only, Len.'

'And what's that?'

'Can you give me that phone number for Luis?'

Chapter 39

Chris stood in the investigation room, going back and forth over the map. The response from queries about mazes had been nil. I don't even know what I'm looking for, she thought.

Officers were arriving and the office was filling up. Chris hesitated to admit it to herself, but this sense of solidarity was normally one aspect of police work she found reassuring. A prison governor she'd been out with had once told her that prison officers rely on this sense of numbers to carry them through a typical working day, when they're outnumbered by inmates all the time by at least thirty to one: in the exercise yard, on the landing, in the workshop. 'That's why in the old radial prisons, when an officer used to press the panic button and it flashed up on the Centre, everybody, even officers on desk jobs or in the toilet, everybody ran to that place.'

Today solidarity wasn't working for Chris. The downbeat meeting wound to its end. She'd given a report on the probable abduction of Tom's children and Sheila had summarised her analysis.

'We could be looking for a maze,' Chris said, 'but so far we've drawn a blank. Any other ideas?'

'Haven't any of these posh country houses got mazes?' asked Moran.

'None of those within fifty-odd miles. The one maze within reasonable distance is Julian's Bower at Alkborough on the south bank of the Humber. It's a miniature turf maze about so high.' Chris held her hand slightly above the table. 'Our helicopter picked up nothing untoward in that area.'

Morrison was chewing reflectively on his pencil. 'Our killer won't use a public maze to fulfil whatever crazy fantasies he has. He's not looking for a place in the tourists' guide. Whatever he's doing will be tucked away near the property or other buildings he uses to house the ants. It must be a fairly large building, considering what he's done so far. I'd go for a disused farm with barns and other outbuildings.'

Chris looked around the room at the blank faces. There was no optimism here. She wanted to conclude on a positive note.

'So, to summarise, boss,' said Morrison, 'we're looking for a farm-sized property, possibly with a shrubbery or copse adjacent which could serve as a maze, within an hour's drive of Beverley.'

'We've less than a day,' added Chris, 'or maybe less than that.'

'Could be worse,' said a voice.

'Try me,' said another.

The meeting broke up amid the ripple of ironic laughter which spread out from these comments.

* * *

Tom picked up his diary in which he kept many of the notes forming his records, gratefully left the untidy mess of unfinished work in his office and made his way across to the porters' lodge. There, it took him about half an hour to collate the two sets of records: his own and the records there. At the end of it, he rubbed his hands over his face and up into his thick mop of hair, stretching his legs and leaning back in the creaking office chair.

'Hey, don't put too much pressure on that chair,' said Len. 'I don't know if it will take it.'

Tom relaxed. 'Sorry.'

He recalled all those adults who had said the same words to him over the decades since he was a little boy. 'Don't swing back on that chair. You'll hurt your back if you fall.'

'Is there anything else, Tom?'

'No, Len, you've done me proud.'

'Another coffee perhaps?'

'I could easily, but I must be going.'

'Okay, you never were one for sitting about.'

'That's the way it goes.'

'I guess it is.'

* * *

Chris had already come near – too damned near to ignore – to filling the chasm in Tom's life left by Laura's absence, however temporary that might turn out to be. She reverted to thinking of herself and Tom as two independent people who happened to be working together. Yes, their individuality struck similar sparks off each other, but they remained very different people.

Am I in the middle of a crisis, or what, thought Tom? He knew what they said about crisis. It's a traditional Chinese concept meaning change. Change brings danger but also opportunities. He faced the opportunities posed by not knowing yet where the kidnapper of his children was hiding. This was about as unpalatable a crisis as he could imagine. He needed to go through the staff files in the University's human resources department. There might be a clue somewhere. He didn't feel they'd struck the University connection yet.

* * *

It was five o'clock. Tom's arrival with sheets of notes stuffed into his bulging diary, put noses out of joint in Human Resources and it took several phone calls back and forth between that department and Tom's department before he could start. Six o'clock came; there was nobody else staying behind in the office and the security staff wanted to lock up. Apparently, somebody apart from Tom needed to supervise the files and ensure the confidentiality of their content at all times. After bad-humoured consultation with the Vice Chancellor's office, one of the senior staff agreed to stay on for an unspecified period. At seven o'clock Tom was still reading slowly through the files. The phone calls started again. This time, the deputy head of Human Resources agreed to return to the office.

At half past eight, with the deputy head of Human Resources pacing up and down in front of him, Tom finished going through the material. He didn't know whether the details he'd copied down were useful or not. Among other nuggets, he'd found out that John Thompsen had previously worked in a slaughterhouse. He also had a couple of duplicate passport photographs secreted in his pocket.

Tom rushed to Luis Deakin's office. He had to find something he remembered. A file he'd seen with Thompsen's name on it ages ago, gathering dust. It was so absurd. He scrabbled frantically along the bookshelves, pulling books out, causing piles of papers to fall onto the floor. He opened drawer upon drawer, emptying out their contents. Eventually he came to a drawer which was locked. He looked around and saw a stout pair of scissors. Using it as a lever, he yanked up and down till the wooden frame split. He pulled it open and sifted through the pile of papers. He found a bulky notebook and balanced it on the edge of the drawer while he flicked through it. Clumsily, he knocked it and it fell, lying open at a loose page near the end. There were only three lines at the top, in large print. The rest was taken up with the kind of scribble in bright colours a young child might do. He read out loud:

'My anger may explode occasionally, but never in full. I am in control. I will never recover from losing people.'

He turned the page and read on, peering between the intensity of the violently coloured scribbles.

'I grew up, but outwardly, in body, not in my feelings. How could I when the injuries were so extensive and damaging. Meanwhile, as if to rub in the injustice of losing a brother and a parent, the teachers and the caretaker especially, blamed me whenever there were ants in the buildings at school, or at home. I could not let anybody see it fully. I held it inside. The hurt also stayed deep down, where Nanny and other adults would never find it, or hurt that vulnerable part of me any further. Then, magically, I found a way to massage the hurt without losing control. Or rather, I passed it over to the others. The people I'd lost came and took me over, sometimes alone and sometimes together. At first only the people I'd lost, then others as well. Through this I stayed whole. I preserved – yes, I preserved my mind, by appearing as someone else.'

Tom had the passing thought, wondering whether this meant Thompsen was upset at the death of Walters. Or whether, in addition to them, there was another brother? He put the thought from his head.

* * *

Chris was on the phone and Morrison was trying to catch her attention and draw her away from where he could be overheard.

'When you've a moment, boss,' he mouthed.

Chris came off the phone and followed him to a space between desks, next to a window.

'A message from our helicopter,' said Morrison. 'They may have found something. They've e-mailed some photos direct from the air. I've printed them out.' He handed Chris half a dozen stills.

'The wonders of modern technology.' She flicked through them and scanned one of them. 'Where's this?'

'The map reference is on the back, boss. It's approximate, but near enough. If we go to the map ...' He led her across to the table where the maps were laid out. 'It's about here.' He put his finger on an open area of farmland adjacent to a village, with what looked like small farms dotted about, each clustered round farmhouses and outbuildings.

'Where's Bradshaw?' Chris's voice was urgent. 'Great work, we're in business.' She realised she needed authorisation as quickly as possible. She spotted Bradshaw disappearing along the corridor and made a beeline for him.

Her voice rose. 'Do everything you can to contact Tom Fortius. Phone him, e-mail him, call on him. Give him the name of the nearest village. Tell him to be there with whatever equipment he uses to identify ants.'

In less than five minutes Chris had the authorisation she needed; every available uniformed and CID officer could be mobilised.

'Boss, there's a lot more from the War Museum I need to tell you. We've been having some success.'

'Tell me,' said Chris. 'Why did Thompsen leave?'

'An accident of some sort. I can't recall the details. A car crash. Yes that's it, smashed his leg and his face pretty badly. He was able to recover the use of his leg. The surgery on his face gave him the opportunity to develop a new identity. It reduced the likelihood of anyone recognising him.'

All the shades were off. There was no longer a news blackout. The warnings could be broadcast. Details of the police searches and public appeals were cleared to go out on the national, regional and local TV and radio. Radios Leeds, Humberside and York as well as the commercial stations ran special news features and Calendar North and BBC TV local news ran stories as well. The Yorkshire Post, Hull Daily Mail and Yorkshire Evening Press gave the murders and the investigations priority. A daily headline and page of news about the progress of the investigation became pretty well standard in all these papers, fed by regular bulletins from the police press office.

Police toured Pocklington, Malton, Driffield, Beverley and Market Breighton with loudspeakers warning people to keep their children indoors. It wasn't hard to persuade people to heed the warnings. The atmosphere locally could best be described as panicky. Helicopters patrolled overhead. Ant experts arrived from the Entomological Section of the Natural History Museum in South Kensington to consult with Tom about taxonomical aspects of the species used for the killings.

Bradshaw was fuming, partly because he'd received an invoice from the University. He called Chris in to explain why she'd hired a graphologist and more than one psychiatrist. What was wrong with using as few of these professionals as possible, he wanted to know.

'Nothing,' said Chris, 'unless you want to solve crimes.'

'This is costing me a fortune.'

'You make it sound as though you're meeting the bill personally.'

'I may have to if this goes on.'

'Murder investigations cost money.'

'The bills for this one are sky high. The Committee will go mad.'

'Let me attend the next meeting. I'll give them some figures about the real costs of some recent murder investigations and I'll point out how we need resources to carry out a large-scale, complex investigation into high profile cases such as this.'

Later Chris was talking to Sheila Rawlinson.

'How long is it since we last had a communication from the killer?' Sheila asked.

'Two days, three days. It's difficult to say, with the post being rather erratic.'

'The last note wasn't left on a body.'

'No, but don't say that. We're counting ourselves lucky we haven't had a body for several days.'

'There will be a crisis coming, given his psychological state,' said Sheila. 'How many hostages has he had so far?'

'It's impossible to tell. We only have the bodies.'

'He could be holding further victims while he prepares himself. There could be a succession of people.'

'What time-scale are we talking about?'

'It's impossible to predict. It depends on a number of factors. We don't know this man's circumstances, where he's coming from, where he's going. He may be acutely paranoid. The delusion could hold the key. He may imagine some gross disaster is about to engulf him, and us.'

'We must find him,' said Chris, who was feeling increasingly desperate.

'One certainty is that the frequency of killings so far indicates he's on a short fuse,' said Sheila. ' Whatever is driving him, he doesn't believe in hanging about.' She paced around the office. 'There's another aspect of it. The whole issue of MPD. If you've ever tried to interview a severe case you'll realise the problem. At the least stimulus he'll be likely to jump from one personality to another. It could be quite random. He could arrive at a personality poised to commit a further murder, or series of murders. Finally, of course, there's the cumulative impact of all this on a seriously unstable and depressed person. The inevitable conclusion of many multiple murders is that the murderer makes a final, dramatic murderous gesture, then commits suicide. We have no way of knowing how soon he'll feel so boxed into a corner that he has to start mass killings and then kill himself.'

Tom was still alienated from Chris. His mood was sombre. At present he didn't care if he never saw Chris again. Tom took the quick decision to stick with the task at the University while Chris went off to the Wolds.

The phone rang. When Tom picked it up he heard Regel's voice, weak but assertive. I take my hat off to you, old man, thought Tom, you have so much *go* in you.

'I want to know what's happening. If there's no need for me to stay, I'd like to go home as soon as is convenient.'

Tom explained about the search for Thompsen's house and Regel took him by surprise.

'Anything I can do to help?'

On the spur of the moment, Tom said, 'I'm on my way to catch up with what the police are doing.'

He didn't mention about falling out with Chris. Regel's response was immediate.

'Can I come along?'

Tom couldn't think of a reason why not.

Less than an hour later, Tom picked Regel up from the hotel. He'd checked out so had all his bags with him. Tom had first to call back at the University. He rang Morrison to find out what was happening.

'Sorry, sir,' said Morrison, 'you must have been left out of the loop by mistake. We're up at Napperton, the other side of Beverley just off the B1248, the back road to Malton, about five miles from the junction with the road from Middleton on the Wolds. At Tibthorpe take a left turn towards Huggate. You'll see a sign for Pickthorpe. Turn left and it's about three miles back towards Middleton.'

While Tom cleared his office desk Regel sat in the easy chair opposite him, nursing a mug of milky coffee. Glancing up, he caught a glimpse of a photo on the wall. It was the staff contribution to the concert celebrating the fiftieth anniversary of the founding of the University. They were all disguised in fancy dress costume.

Regel pointed to one of the figures.

'That's John.'

Tom knew without looking it couldn't be, because the event had only happened last year and only involved academic staff. 'No, you must be mistaken.'

'I tell you, that's him.'

'Who do you mean?'

Regel rose and jabbed his finger aggressively onto the photo. Tom laughed at the sight of Luis dressed imposingly as an upper class Edwardian with boater and handlebar moustache. 'Impossible, that's Luis Deakin, one of the research staff in my unit. I'm afraid he doesn't look anything like that in real life.'

Tom was in a hurry. He couldn't put Matthew and Sarah out of his mind. He left Regel to finish his drink and left one or two items for his temporary secretary to deal with. When he returned, Regel was finished and ready to go.

'Now,' said Tom, 'there's the question of what we do next. I have to follow the search up and find my children before –'

Regel nodded and stood up. 'I'll go with you.'

'You can't. It's a police operation.'

'I'm a police informant, escorted from my home two hundred miles away to stay in Hull and help them with their inquiries.'

'According to DC Morrison, you're on holiday.'

'We won't talk about that.'

'Are you sure you're up to this?'

'I can stay in the car. I've picked up a little of what's going on. I feel in some way involved. I don't want to miss the ending. I won't hinder you and I'll keep quiet.'

Tom stopped objecting. Suddenly, taking Regel seemed to him the next most logical step.

Chapter 40

It was a race against time for the police to set up road blocks round Pickthorpe and further barriers near the remote farm.

* * *

Tom was desperate for the case to move forward. Following the directions he had received from Morrison, he was on his way to the location identified. On the road, he questioned Regel.

'You know more about them all than you've let on, Mr Regel. It's time you let the rest of us into the secret. People are being killed. My children have been kidnapped by this man. They could be his next victims, dammit.'

A hundred yards ahead, a rabbit hopped out from the left hand verge, then another. Tom swerved to avoid them, almost ditching the car in the soft soil beyond the offside verge. Regel clutched at the car seat. He looked frightened.

'I will tell,' he said. 'Lionel Blatt was not Blatt when we lived in Poland, but Lionel Regel.'

'So you're brothers. Detlev Brandt was German,' Tom added, half to himself.

'Brandt,' said Regel. 'You know the name. Brandt was the name Lionel used when he moved through Poland to make a new life for himself after the war. That was before he became Blatt.'

Tom's mind was racing. 'Was there anyone else in Lionel's life at that time called Brandt?'

Regel mused. 'I don't know. I can't think. I didn't know all his activities. He was quite secretive and we weren't exactly on the same wavelength, so to speak.'

Before Tom reached the outskirts of the village, there were indications of out-of-the-ordinary activity. A Special Operations police transit van and two police patrol cars stood in the lay-by adjacent to the bus shelter. Three uniformed officers stood by an improvised barrier, a pole slung across two oil drums. One of the men stepped forward as Tom pulled up at the barrier.

'I'm part of the team,' Tom explained as the more senior police officer – to judge from the pips on his shoulders – leaned towards his open car window on the driver's side.

'And what team might that be, sir?'

Tom thought he heard one of the other officers mutter 'Oinks from Surrey'. There was a muffled guffaw.

'A moment please, sir. These officers will stay with your car.'

'I've been asked to advise Chief Superintendent Bradshaw of any newcomers to the scene. Who shall I say it is?'

Tom informed him and the man's manner changed immediately.

'Professor Fortius, is it?'

Tom was feeling pretty raw with worry. 'If the title makes a difference to you, yes it is.'

'My apologies, sir. We have to check all visitors with Chief Superintendent Bradshaw, Wawne Road Police. I'll have the barrier lifted and if you'd like to drive through there, sir, we'll soon have you sorted.'

He held a brief conversation on his crackling handset. 'Right. Over and out,' he called briskly and turned back to Tom. 'When you reach the main street, go to the far end and take the first left. Our checkpoint is a couple of hundred yards along on the left. A police officer will be waiting there and will accompany you to our command HQ.'

It was strange, passing through the barrier, then having the freedom of the village. Tom's stomach cramped painfully with hunger as he drove into the village centre. He realised he'd have to eat, and so would Regel. Hunger and the mental strain were taking their toll. He glanced about. He couldn't believe how quiet and untouched by the drama the scene looked. There was the village shop, halfway along the main street. The archetypal village shop, he thought as he scanned the tiny converted ground floor area of the old cottage. They would pay a fortune to dismantle and remove this, lock, stock and barrel, and transport and reconstruct it, stone by stone, in some fanatic's heritage museum in anywhere – Surrey, California or, these days, Yorkshire.

The proprietor didn't conform to the stereotype of the village shopkeeper, being a tall young woman whose manner and voice when she spoke indicated that she, like himself, was born and bred a couple of hundred miles south of this remote part of East Yorkshire.

'Can I fetch you something?'

'Please, I'm in a hurry. A loaf of bread and some cheese.'

'Wholemeal or white, sliced or unsliced. There's quite a variety.' She looked at him and waited.

'I don't mind.'

'Cob, nutty cob, granary, or tin, for sandwiches.'

'Er, a couple of rolls please.'

'Did you say cheese with it, sir?'

'No, this is fine.'

'What sort would you like?'

'Oh, any, whatever is quickest.'

He was sorely regretting even mentioning anything but the bread. It seemed quicker not to argue, though, in the face of her punctiliousness.

'We've quite a selection.'

'Er, Wensleydale will be fine, please.'

'We've four or five different cheeses from Wensleydale – goats' cheese, pasteurised or unpasteurised, you can have sheeps' cheese, and then there's ordinary farmhouse, waxed whole cheeses or blue.'

A faint smile of superiority hovered at the corners of her lips.

'Blue please.'

He was well past caring, but she persisted. 'How much?'

'That piece.'

She took an age, wrapping the cheese carefully in heavy paper. Tom remembered from his childhood visits to the old-fashioned grocer in town how the man had pencilled the price of the cheese and the bread carefully onto one side.

Why the hell did I ask for this, Tom thought. All he wanted was to stuff the bread into his mouth, stop the incipient ulcer he was fairly sure he was nurturing deep inside, and drive to the scene of the action.

'Anything else?'

'No, thank you,' he said as he rummaged in his pocket for some money. Then he responded to a quite extraordinary impulse which afterwards he couldn't explain.

He pulled the passport photo from his top pocket.

'Yes, there is,' he said. 'I wonder if you have seen this colleague of mine. I'm trying to find his house and I left my map at home.'

'Oh yes, that's Mr Thompsen from Coldharbour Farm. Go out of the village, turn left on the Driffield Road, about half a mile up on the right. Are you a friend of his?'

'Thompsen? No, hang on, I've given you the wrong photo.' He reached over and half snatched, half pulled the picture from her grip. One glance told him he hadn't made a mistake.

'Deakin, it's Deakin. Oh my God!' he exclaimed and rushed from the shop. He was already in the car turning the key in the ignition when there was a knock at the window on the passenger side.

He leaned across and opened the door.

She pulled it further open and offered him a carrier bag.

'You forgot your groceries,' she said.

'Thank you, I'm sorry,' said Tom. 'I've remembered something. I had to dash.'

'The whole world's in a hurry,' said the woman. 'Enjoy your picnic.'

'Thanks,' said Tom as she slammed the door. But she had already turned away.

He had nodded at Regel who was still reclining patiently on the back seat, and was about to turn round when a sudden sharp knock on the window made him jump. It was the shopkeeper again. He wound down the window.

'I made a mistake,' she said. 'Coldharbour isn't that way. Don't waste time turning round. You're facing the right way. First left past these houses, then first left again.'

* * *

Tom was down the first road to the left before he reconsidered. There was something amiss. The shopkeeper had said left, then right. Then she'd changed her mind to left and left again. The problem was, neither of these instructions corresponded with what the police had told him. She's probably confused, he said out loud as he drove, ignoring both the subsequent left and right turnings. He stuck to the improvised scribbled note he'd stuck on the shelf below the dashboard.

* * *

The scene of operations was about a mile out of the village. While trying to phone Chris on his mobile with one hand and steering and changing gear with the other, Tom nearly crashed. Here we are, he said to Regel as he reached the barrier. Thank goodness he'd stuck to the first instructions. DC Morrison advanced and put up a warning hand.

'Morning, sir, I thought you'd got lost. Glad you made it, with Mr Regel, I see.' Morrison greeted Regel, who nodded politely.

'I had to eat,' Tom muttered through the last chunk of bread roll he'd just stuffed into his mouth. Morrison came round to the passenger side and got in. Tom revved and crashed into gear before Morrison had the door closed.

'We must hurry,' Tom said and put his foot down. They swerved crazily across cart ruts and he fought to control the steering.

Morrison clicked his belt on. He guessed the professor was worried about his children and knew when not to ask questions. 'Straight on, sir. Right up that track, as far as you can see, till that bend. Till I say stop. I'll show you where to park.'

'You don't seem surprised we're here,' said Tom.

'We phoned the University and the hotel,' said Morrison with a grin. 'Keeping tabs on the opposition.'

Tom caught a glimpse of a valley to the right of the road. A wide expanse of open grassland up the hill slopes and, he guessed, somewhere at the far end, a distance away, an isolated farmhouse adjacent to a few acres of woodland. Morrison saw him looking.

'The farm's that way, sir. You can't see it from here, but we turn left.'

Obediently Tom followed his directions. Driving through a wooded area deep in trees, they reached a clearing which couldn't have contrasted more greatly with what he'd seen so far. Grouped round the edges of the clearing were three police vans, a fire engine, three ambulances and half a dozen other police cars.

Tom skidded to a halt. He buzzed down his window and tried to pick up what was going on. He quickly ascertained that Chris was somewhere nearby, setting up and checking, and would be back shortly.

A moment later he saw her and leaned out of the window. He had to clear it up straight away.

'Why didn't you let me know that evening about the children being kidnapped?'

To his surprise she was apologetic, but not in the sense he'd anticipated. She clearly didn't perceive either the police or herself to be in error.

'We spent an hour trying to contact you, by phone at home, at the University, on your mobile. In the end, I drove past the University on my way home late at night and dropped a note in at the administration building.

'Oh.' He didn't know what to say. All those messages and, of course, he'd been out of contact, deliberately so. He hadn't checked his office phone and he'd been out on the road, desperately searching for several hours late into the night, having forgotten to take his mobile with him. As for the note, he hardly dared ask how she'd addressed it.

'I pushed it into an envelope before I left the office,' she said, 'hoping I'd see you and wouldn't have to leave it.'

Tom had a sudden thought, picked up his desk diary off the back seat of the car and shook it. There it was, a small manilla envelope, near the bottom. He picked it up, slid his finger along the sealed flap and unfolded the small piece of paper inside.

Dear Tom,

I'm terribly sorry to have to write, but we've been trying all means to reach you by phone all evening and you must be incommunicado.

It ran onto the back, explaining about Matthew and Sarah and assuring him everything humanly possible was being done and he was to phone her at any time, day or night. There was a little scribbled phrase at the end, in French.

Je t'embrasse

Chris

Tom was mortified. Chris was walking away. He got out of the car and followed her, leaving Regel still on the back seat. 'What can I say? You did try and I thought you didn't. I'm so terribly sorry.'

'Forget it. You're the parent. The pain is yours.'

His voice was quiet. 'I really regret this, Chris.'

'Say no more.'

'Chris, I must have my children back. I don't care what the cost is. I'll pay any ransom.'

Chris watched him clench his fists and thrust them into the air. 'I don't think this man's motive is money,' she said gently. 'We'll let you know as soon as we hear anything.'

He knew by the use of the word *we* that the chasm between them was real. Before, they were colleagues, now he was a victim, a member of the public. It should make no difference. In some indefinable way, it made all the difference in the world.

'I don't care.' He hardly knew what he was saying. 'Find that man before he harms them. If he so much as lays a finger on them, I swear I'll – Oh, forget it.'

His aggression dissolved and he crumpled.

'Is that it?'

'Yes.'

'We are doing everything we can. I want to say I'm a woman and – I can imagine how you feel.'

'We must get my children out. That's my priority above everything else.'

'It's ours as well. Unfortunately we have to catch this man in order to guarantee their safety and the safety of other possible future victims.'

'I agree,' said Tom. He opened his diary at the back, where he'd stuffed a few sheets. 'Have a look at these. I found them in Thompsen's file.'

She glanced quickly at them. 'God, this ties up with what we've been doing. I'll bring Morrison over.'

She was holding a large Ordnance Survey map and didn't give Tom her full attention at first. She was puzzled. 'I'm trying to figure this out,' she said.

'Show me the farm on the map,' said Tom.

She looked at him curiously. 'What's the problem?' He seemed stressed but she put that down to anxiety about Sarah and Matthew.

Chris was poring over the map, turning it to correspond with the direction they were facing. Tom couldn't wait.

'Which farm are you watching?'

She found the spot on the map, indicated by a neat circle in black ink. 'There we are.'

'Whose house is it?'

'What's the panic Tom? Have we made a mistake?'

'At this stage I don't know, but frankly there is a chance.' Tom paused. 'I think Thompsen and Deakin could be twins.'

'That's impossible,' she said.

'I'm talking about personal details – date and place of birth and so on – not physical appearance.'

'No, they don't even look similar.'

'There's an even more awesome possibility, that they're one and the same person.'

'Christ!' Chris clapped her hand to her head.

'The two houses are near each other,' said Tom. 'Let me explain. Deakin has been living in a farmhouse near here, bequeathed to him by his aunt. I haven't any knowledge of how she died. Quite coincidentally, or perhaps not, Thompsen had a house nearby. I assume you're staking out Thompsen's place.'

'We were rather congratulating ourselves on tracking it down.' Chris groaned.

Tom nodded grimly. 'He's pulled a clever stroke.'

'You're implying our murderer has slid rather neatly from one identity to another.'

More than that. Perhaps he's done it more than once. He does it now, as and when it suits.'

'How the hell could anyone who's worked in your University reappear as somebody else?'

'Remember Thompsen had a serious car accident a few years ago. Who knows what facial reconstruction was needed?'

'Whoever we're dealing with appears to have moved from student to staff researcher over a ten-year period. There's little likelihood anyone would have noticed if he had bothered to change certain personal details, when he changed from being Thompsen to Deakin.'

Chris ruminated. 'Or Deakin to Thompsen.'

Tom was running for his car.

'The woman in the village gave me some directions and I ignored them. I think that's where Deakin's aunt lived.'

'Hang on,' called Chris.

'You stay here and organise your people,' said Tom. 'I'll go on ahead.'

She followed him towards the car. 'No way. I'll organise them in one minute. I don't trust you not to do something daft.' She looked towards a group of uniformed and plain clothes officers. 'Has anyone seen Chief Superintendent Bradshaw?'

Chapter 41

'It's incredible. Luis Deakin. He's so normal. No other word for it. Given all this, I find it amazing that when he applied for the post his background seemed so impeccable. Thinking back to his interview, his application form, his CV, it doesn't add up.'

'Let's have a look.'

'We can't. Personnel have all the details.'

'He'll have glossed over crucial details which could have given you clues as to his real nature. Or he'll have lied.'

'I realise he can't be exactly what he seems. But tell me this: if a person is able to hold down a highly responsible job at one level, surely that tells you something about their abilities.'

'About abilities, yes. But when that same person is living an altogether criminal existence in secrecy at the same time, it confirms the fundamental nature of the disturbance in their personality.'

'Things can only get better,' said Chris and was immediately proved wrong.

Tom jumped as though struck by a physical blow. 'What am I thinking about? We've no time for this.' He started to run towards the large barn on the far side of the farmyard and, before she knew it, Chris was following him. Before she'd even had time to think about picking up the mobile or the radio set she'd put down a few moments before, they were entering the barn through a small side door.

'I don't believe it,' said Tom.

The greatest part of the space was taken up with a row of large aquarium tanks on either side of the gangways running the length of the barn. Most of them were filled with colonies of ants, some in single tanks, others linked together in series. There were temperature controls, lights, humidity measures and thermometers everywhere. The atmosphere was warm, overpowering, with a palpable sensation of evil emanating from millions of scurrying bodies, massed together for no good purpose.

'My equipment budget,' said Tom, half to himself, shaking his head in disbelief.

They reached the door halfway along on the far side of the barn, and behind it the steps to the cellar. Chris led the way. She took a deep breath as she stepped hesitantly down each step into the darkness below. Suddenly, as she reached the foot of the steps, a small electric light flicked on above her. As they walked forward, a chain of similar lights came on and those behind turned off, creating a series of eerie shadows mirroring their progress on the walls bearing in on them on each side.

Ahead was an open door at the end of the corridor. Chris peered into the room, lit only by a dull red glow. Across the far side she could make out a shape, a disfigured outline as though a body was moving inside a sack. She shone the torch across the intervening space and saw it was a man. At first she thought he was covered in tar. She steadied the torch with both hands and made out the contours of the face, but it was the skull that held her attention. The wide bony cavity and empty eye sockets filled with a pulsating mass of ants. Every now and again, the cluster thinned in one part or another. Through the gap she caught glimpses of an enormous swollen form beneath. Right there in the location of the original brain the queen ant lay, hub of the nest and subject to the ministrations of ten thousand workers at a time.

A sound behind Chris distracted her attention. She looked round quickly and caught a glimpse of movement. The door was slowly closing, apparently propelled by a lever set into the wall. She didn't connect this at first with the mass in front of her. By the time she moved towards the door, it was too late. It clicked shut just before her shoe wedged in the remaining gap. Intuitively, she reached down for the handle, but met only the smooth surface in every direction. She looked down and saw there was no projection of any kind on the inside of the door. Somebody wanted to ensure there was no escape.

In front of her the antennation machine began to click threateningly. Although she'd never heard it, from Tom's description of the machine she had an inkling of the significance of those clicks. Already she could see a stirring on the far side of the room. The dark mass began to move.

Chris heard another sound, incredible to her in this strange prison. The first time, she couldn't believe it. A child's voice, softly spoken, reassuring someone unknown, as though grooming a pet, or –. There was another child, whimpering. Chris knew.

'Matthew, Sarah, is that you?' she called. 'I'm your father's friend, Chris, a detective from the local police.'

They were almost within arm's length, in a small lobby to one side of her, piniioned shut by a metal grill held in place by four metal pegs through rings protruding from the wall. In a matter of seconds, Chris had the grill down. They knew her name from conversations they'd overheard at home. There was no hesitation on their part and she was suddenly cuddling two very frightened children.

Tom ran down the corridor seconds later to find the door closing in his face. He beat his clenched fists on it ineffectually, before looking round for another way in. The door was solid. In the dim light he could make out rivets round the edge of the metal surface and imagined it had been cut to fit over a heavy wooden door. There was a metal handle, but it refused to move and had been locked by some means. At waist height a sturdy horizontal metal bar was fixed across the door.

He stood back and scanned the area round the door. A small square panel above it caught his attention. A ventilation grill, perhaps. If this was in some way connected to the maintenance of ant colonies a steady supply of air was essential. He needed some way to lift himself. Summoning up skills set aside since schooldays in the gym, he put a foot on the metal bar and, grasping the door handle, levered his body up. He hoped the handle would be strong enough. He stretched his other hand and managed to secure a grip on the lower edge of the ventilation grill. He straightened up and found he could see through the metal grill into the semi-darkened chamber.

'Chris, are you there?'

Next moment, he nearly lost his balance as the three voices responded. There followed an emotional few seconds.

'Chris, have you any deodorant or scent sprays?'

It was a long shot, but in a miniature handbag she was carrying a small plastic bottle in a pocket of her jacket. He gave precise instructions.

'Stay within a small semi-circle, immediately to one side of the opening edge of the door. Keep the spray in front of you. Spray the floor in short bursts. Every time ants cross, stamp on them and spray again where they've been. It should keep you clear for long enough. Meantime, hang on, I'll be back shortly and we'll have you out.'

As he jumped down clumsily he thought at first he'd sprained his ankle as it cockled over, but he stood up, uncomfortable but not in significant pain. He ran back down the corridor, up the stairs, along the length of the barn and met the first of the officers coming towards him.

Chapter 42

Laura was distraught, almost hysterical as she drove up to the farm and saw Tom and Chris leading Matthew and Sarah across the farmyard towards the barrier and the other officers. In a moment of high emotion she screeched to a halt, leapt from the car and hugged the two children she had wondered if she would ever see again. Then she looked up, saw Chris first and then Tom.

'Mummy, this is Chris. She rescued us with Daddy,' said Sarah.

Laura didn't know what to say. The first words to occur to her tumbled out, meaningless. 'Oh, it's you.'

She was still in shock from Helen's death. She couldn't get her head round what was going on, let alone grasp whether the police or Tom even knew. She didn't know if she was surprised or upset to see Chris. Nothing mattered now she had her arms round her children. Sometimes emotion freezes speech out.

Tom also wanted to speak but no words were powerful enough to thaw out his vocal chords.

The children were in the back of the car now. As Laura was reversing and turning, Matthew pushed his way across the rear seat, wound the window down and, clutching his Teddy, stuck his head out.

'Are you coming back to live with us, Daddy?'

'I'm very busy at work,' Tom managed to say.

'You can be busy and still stay with us in between.'

'It's difficult, Matthew.'

'Not difficult for me,' said Matthew.

Sarah crawled over and leaned across Matthew's shoulder. 'Nor me,' she said tearfully.

'I can't come home. Sometimes mummies and daddies can't live together.'

'Sometimes they're stupid and fight all the time.'

'It would be bad if I came back and we argued all the time.'

'I wouldn't mind you fighting if you'd just come home,' said Sarah.

'Me too,' said Matthew.

Laura shuffled nervously, not knowing how to close the situation off. She felt as though a bad ending was inevitable. She turned round and put her hand on Matthew's head. 'It's all right, darling. Daddy's got a job to do, but you'll still see him lots.' She looked at Tom. 'Won't they, Tom?'

'Mum's right, Matt. Be good for Mum. Daddy will be away some time. But I'll be back to see you – so don't be naughty.'

Matthew stretched his arm out of the open window, tears running down his cheeks. Tom stooped and gripped his son's shoulder through

the window. 'You promise to be good while I'm away. Promise?'
'Yes.'
'Good chap.'
He leaned forward and kissed his son. He walked round to the other side of the car, opened the door and gave Sarah a hug and a kiss.
'I love you both. Bye.'
Laura revved up the engine. Neither child was able to look as he stood back. Tom's heart felt like a stone as he watched the car disappear down the lane.

* * *

Gusts of wind tossed the branches of surrounding trees back and forth, like the long arms of prisoners trying to break free. Tom glanced anxiously towards the dark clouds advancing. 'It's time we had a word with Mr Regel. A few things need straightening out.'
He walked across towards Regel, who still sat in the back seat of the car, staring sightlessly ahead. He opened the car door. The most striking feature of Regel's pose was his hands. They contorted and writhed, grasping and loosening each other like two intertwined serpents in their death throes. Chris stood behind Tom while he stooped down and faced Regel, placing a hand on his shoulder.
'There's more, isn't there, Mr Regel?'
Regel nodded, tears coursing down his face.
'Will you tell me?' Tom produced a tissue and Regel took it, nodding slowly.
'Graver isn't Dr Blatt's missing son, is he?'
Regel shook his head.
'He's your son.'
Regel sobbed silently, his face now buried in his hands.
'What's his name?'
'Gravek.' Regel's voice was no more than a whisper. 'I had a nickname for him, Graver.'
'You recognised your own son in my office at the University.'
Regel nodded.
Tom spoke to Chris. 'Mr Regel isn't quite the person we thought.'
'Very true,' said Chris. 'Morrison's been doing some family history research. It's a very popular pastime in England, Herr Regel. You were trying to protect your son's identity when you killed Brandt last year. Am I right?'
Regel gave a loud cry. 'No, no.'
'It's no good, Herr Regel. Brandt's father was in Poland and recognised you when he visited you. You weren't a victim, but one of the ethnic Germans recruited to the side of the SS. You needed job

security and somewhere to live, so you tricked Marko into offering hospitality and killed him.'

'I never killed Marko. He was dying.'

'Okay, so you waited until Marko died, ensuring he thought you were his saviour and nurse. In gratitude he left you the house. You probably hoped you'd buried the past with Marko, but we know quite a lot about it, because we found Marko's diary in the War Museum. It was in the attic after you left the house. You weren't too steady on your feet, even in those days and you didn't look in the attic for any of his private papers. You knew he had a son named Detlev and that he'd moved out but kept in touch with dad and probably knew all about you. All those years you lived and worked in fear of being exposed. Forty years on, your son was working in Hull. You visited him. You'd already been to Hessle. It was all a sham with Morrison a few days ago. You travelled back last year and killed Detlev Brandt.'

Regel gave no reaction to all of this and Chris showed irritation.

'Tell me, how did you manage it with your heart condition? Or is your heart condition a sham as well?'

After a long pause, Regel responded. 'My heart is bad. The doctor says I have to avoid stress. I came to Hull by train. It was not how you think. I had to put the past to rights. You do not know how it is to live with fear for fifty years, that my son might be revealed as the son of a – well, a war criminal. It was a terrible coincidence that Brandt came to work at the same university. I knew one day he would recognise my son. I did not kill him. I paid a man to do it.' Regel's words came out in short phrases and he gasped several times to take a breath between each.

'You didn't avoid stress last year when Brandt was killed. You were there. Well, well, that was brave. We can tell. It's the details that give us away, Herr Regel. You're a ritualist. You haven't quite equalled the obsession of your son for ants, but you know about it. You made Detlev Brandt pay for the past by forcing him to chew and swallow a live ant before he died. Pay for the past which had nothing to do with him, or the deep disturbance of your own son which had everything to do with your treatment of him. Nobody else but you would have bothered to go to those lengths. Your murderous background knowledge came in useful. You made it look like suicide. They say an SS officer never forgets his skills.'

'I was never an SS officer.' Regel was panting, as though under severe stress.

'It wasn't as though you didn't try. You were a sympathiser.'

'We were all indoctrinated into the Hitler Youth. We had no knowledge outside it. We were brainwashed.'

'The difference was you took to it like a duck to water. You worshipped Himmler. When he visited you couldn't get enough attention. My colleague DC Morrison has recovered some useful footage from the Imperial War Museum archives. You were Artur Greise's right hand man. He was in charge of your region of Poland.'

'I had to survive, for my family's sake.'

'Oh, your family. All this was for your family. We forgot them.'

'While you were clambering up over junior staff in the SS, your parents were receiving short shrift at the hands of the SS in Berlin. You had to distance yourself from them, didn't you, because your father didn't like Hitler. He was a printer and he became mixed up in a group wanting him to print a newsletter detailing the nasty things Hitler and his cronies were doing. So what did you do? You didn't try to persuade him to stop. Instead, you made sure the SS knew about him and that you had cut yourself off from the family. They didn't bother to distinguish the rest of the family. They strung up your mother as well, your younger sister, your aunt and uncle and your grandmother, all living at the same address. It was a bit tricky, though, at the end of the war. You had to do a quick disappearing act and re-invent yourself as a persecuted Pole, possibly a Polish Jew, if you could get away with it.'

'Many of us suffered under the Nazis and we did not want to suffer again under the Allies.'

'Except that you didn't suffer under the Nazis. You rose through the ranks and did rather well. In fact, you did so well that your name was mud among Poles and other victims after the war. Fortunately, you were well practised in changing your identity.'

Regel nodded. He was straining for breath.

Chris called Sergeant Brill over. 'Make sure Mr Regel doesn't come to any harm. Use whatever means you need to protect him. Keep two officers with him at all times.'

Brill smiled. 'It'll be a pleasure.' Tom turned his attention to a little group of officers who stood round a figure of authority who had appeared from nowhere, so it seemed.

'Apthorpe,' said Tom. 'What an amazing coincidence you've turned up.'

'At the invitation of Chief Superintendent Bradshaw,' said Apthorpe with a smug smile.

'No less.' Tom glanced around at the equipment on the ground.

'You're in time to see us blast the formicas out of the ground,' said Apthorpe, 'once we've confirmed there are no people left in the buildings.'

'All accounted for,' said Bradshaw.

'What about our killer?' asked Tom.

'Confirmed dead by our officers. The body has been removed for forensic analysis. He seems to have decided to offer himself to his own ants for dinner.'

There were signs of pleasure among those standing round and one or two muttered remarks which provoked sniggers. Bradshaw appeared unaware and turned to Apthorpe. 'You were saying?'

Tom interrupted. 'Without wishing to spread despondency, I have to say that the very last strategy for dealing with ants of this type is any kind of explosive.'

'Fine,' said Apthorpe who, Tom realised now, was the self-appointed expert in this group. He squinted his piggy eyes at Tom through a pair of diminutive half lens spectacles. 'Then how do you suggest we contain them, Fortius? Invite them to a seminar?'

'It would be preferable,' said Bradshaw in a rare moment of conciliation, 'if we weren't at loggerheads in the command team at the start of this operation.'

'Also,' said Tom, 'I can't see how gas will be effective, for three reasons. It risks affecting any civilians in the area. Its penetrating strength is limited as at least some colonies in the woodland enclosure are likely to be dug in anything up to three metres in depth. And finally, the metabolism of ants is such that they are only likely to ingest it slowly.'

'Little beggars,' said Bradshaw, whose moment of conciliation had passed. 'Carry spades, do they?'

'Or pneumatic drills presumably, on this rock,' said Apthorpe sarcastically.

'Something like that,' said Tom. 'Or more simply, where the soil overlies loose aggregates of a tip, ants are as capable as people of finding passages to underground cavities, only more easily because they're so small.'

He could see from Bradshaw's face that the point had gone home.

'What's the weather doing to windward?' asked Tom, his voice trembling slightly. 'The thunderstorm is imminent.'

'Weather? Why worry at a time like this.'

Tom's impatience showed. 'I thought I had explained the tight correlation between temperature, humidity and the metabolism of the ant. Our killer will ride on the back of it.'

'Balderdash!'

'Not only through the trees,' said Tom. 'There must be tunnels all over this area. Our antman probably triggered some automatic timing device to let the remainder of the colonies of marauding ants loose after he was dead.'

Bradshaw turned to Apthorpe. 'Now then, what have you to make of all this?'

'Not a lot.'

'In what way?'

'Well, from my experience with rodents, I would predict that you can use flamethrowers to clear the bulk of them from surface vegetation, a couple of stun grenades to destroy the brood nest and then a whiff of gas to snuff out any underground survivors.'

'Ridiculous!' exclaimed Tom.

Bradshaw glanced at Apthorpe then fixed his stare on Tom.

'You were about to say?'

'That's a prescription for total disaster,' said Tom.

'The man's an eccentric, right up his own arse,' said Apthorpe quickly.

'Hang on,' said Bradshaw. 'Before we go any further, let's have this clarified one way or the other. What is your view, Professor?'

Tom took a deep breath. 'My view is that irrespective of the method of extermination adopted, it's absolutely essential that I go in first, to try to identify which species we're dealing with, in the singular or the plural. Only then can we begin to guess how they might respond to the changed conditions we create. We should bear in mind that ants can survive environmental extremes partly through their enormous capacity for adaptation in the face of adversity.'

'For more delays, call on Professor Muddle,' Apthorpe interposed.

'You're wrong,' said Tom. 'By using explosives, you won't eliminate the problem; you'll simply spread it out.'

'Rubbish,' retorted Apthorpe. 'The pressure waves will blanket and kill every living thing within a fifty metre radius.'

Tom shook his head in disbelief. 'Fine if we're talking about human beings. But ants are different, particularly in this case, with ants living many metres underground.'

'All this fuss over a pile of insects which have dug out a few bucketfuls of soil.'

'Hardly bucketfuls. Lorry loads more like. You'll find their nest extends a good few metres further down than your explosives can reach. They're extremely resilient. Short of direct exposure to heat such as flames, they can resist most forms of military attack, including nuclear bombs. They're immune to radiation, although they're as liable to mutate subsequently as any other living beings.'

'Scientific claptrap,' snorted Apthorpe.

Tom leaned forward. 'You'd stand a chance if there was only one queen and you scored a direct hit on the heart of the nest. But some of these will be in a composite colony. There will be many federated nest sites, which means hundreds of thousands of brood chambers, thousands of fertilized queens already laying and probably tens of thousands of alates – winged queens and males ready to be transported in a blast wave to mate miles away and found further nests, God knows where.'

Apthorpe looked taken aback, but only momentarily. 'The pressure wave from the explosion will kill them.'

'If only,' said Tom. 'We don't know how much pressure an ant's body will need to withstand, given the muffling effect of many metres of soil between it and the blast. The stuff you're using – remember it's a quick blast rather than a blanket – will probably create a hurricane effect at ground level and up to a few metres. But from, say, three metres in depth, you'll suck up like a vacuum cleaner bucketfuls of soil, nest materials and ants, and redistribute them over as wide an area as you can see the clouds in the sky. Except for the winged ants, as I've said. Once liberated and blown to a sufficient height to catch some decent thermals, there's no telling where they will eventually land.'

Bradshaw saw this was going nowhere. He held up his hand. 'Can you summarise the implications of this for me, Professor?'

'For pity's sake don't detonate anything at this stage. The brood nest in the area of primary detonation will be destroyed, but from the peripheral chambers and passages you'll have thousands of newly mated queens scattered over half the country.'

'It's what I told you,' said Apthorpe. 'Remember, I'm not just an academic, but a major in the Territorials. It's horses for courses, Fortius. I've never met a pure academic yet who has an accurate idea of the damage scientifically calculated explosives can inflict. There isn't much time though. We can agree about that, can't we?'

Tom nodded wearily. Apthorpe's naivety was astonishing. He wasn't motivated to push it further.

'Yes,' he said. 'I can vouch for that.'

Almost simultaneously, there was a streak of lightning and a second later an enormous clap of thunder. Rain deluged from the clouds overhead. For a few seconds, it was like a wall of water falling from the sky. Then, as quickly as it had started, the cloudburst ended and gentle rain fell.

The explosion resulting from Apthorpe's efforts couldn't be heard above the thunder. The roof of the barn seemed to lift then settle back and fire spurted from the windows. Regel saw the flames and in his mind's eye could see only the flames which consumed so many of his generation in the Third Reich. He stood up, his clothes hanging off his fleshless frame like garments on a scarecrow whose arms and legs were no more than broom handles.

'My son!'

Regel's voice rose to a scream of pain. 'Red!' he screeched. 'The colour of fire. Forgive me, my son. I did not mean to hurt you.' His arms were stretched out towards the origin of the blast. His mouth opened. He appeared to be trying to speak again, but there was no breath left in him; his throat was a dry box of rattling bones. His skin turned purple, then blue. He seemed to shrivel and collapse, and where he had stood there was only an untidy pile of clothing. Uniformed officers wearing body armour, combat trousers and heavy boots stepped over the pile of clothing that moved no more of its own volition. Nobody paid any attention.

Apthorpe turned his back on the conflagration. 'There, gentlemen,' he said smugly. 'I think we can congratulate ourselves that we've given the enemy a royal rocket up the rectum.'

Bradshaw watched in silence for a few moments.

'Don't do any more, idiot!' Tom shouted. 'You'll start a nightmare.'

Apthorpe stepped aside, temporarily taken aback. Then he moved forward again. 'It's all right. It's only Fortius. Carry on blasting.'

Bradshaw deliberately turned his back on Tom, who shook his head.

'You're living in an unreal world,' Tom muttered to himself, 'where the baddie gets his comeuppance and everyone else is happy.'

* * *

There was a prolonged period of checking before the officers were called back. The general view was that the site had been secured for the night. A guard was to be set up at the far end of the lane, where it met the main road. The media and police transits moved off. One by one the other cars drove off and soon the clearing was virtually empty.

As the last of the police cleared up, Chris sought out Tom. 'You aren't leaving yet?'

'I don't know what I'm doing,' he said.

'I wanted you to know before some friendly person leaks it,' said Chris. 'I almost handed in my resignation this morning.'

Tom looked astounded. 'I thought you were one of the –'

'Boys? Think yourself lucky I'm still at work, let alone still at the driving wheel.'

'I was actually going to say team.'

'Okay.' She seemed slightly mollified.

'You can't leave this investigation in mid-course.'

'I am going to stay till the crime is solved.'

The panic left his face. 'Tell me what's brought this on.'

'No single factor.'

'Beginning with Bradshaw.'

'It goes back long before Bradshaw, a combination of things. I'm fed up with being treated as less than a full person.'

'I thought the police were beyond all that sort of crude sexism.'

'They are. Well, that's the irony. They have moved beyond the crude bit to a more subtle version which is more difficult to spot and therefore to tackle.'

'But there are compensations. All that pension.'

'You must be joking. At my age? Anyway, that's part of the other reason. Most of the men I work with – even more so the over thirties – are pension watchers. Apart from their cars and caravans and football and women of course in that order, almost the only conversation point is their pensions. I am definitely not cut out to be a policewoman.'

'I must admit the way you describe it is rather a horror story,' admitted Tom.

'So,' said Chris, 'I've shocked you.'

'Yes, you have,' he said slowly. 'And now, like a true equation, I have some news on my own behalf.'

'You've applied for a job. You're taking a research appointment overseas.'

'Not quite,' said Tom. 'I too am thinking about chucking it in.'

'What? This really is unbelievable. You can't be serious.'

'Never more.'

'Why?'

'Oddly similar reasons to your own, in most respects. What is it they say these days – Get a life? In my case, I've been thinking of working independently, as a consultant. I could go back to the research I love, carry out the odd overseas project. I'd be free to take on what appeals to me, rather than jumping to the tune or this or that university.'

'Yes, but what about mortgages and family commitments. What will you do about that?'

'I have none. Well, soon I won't have a mortgage anyway.'

'What a fool I am. Sorry. I didn't want to pry by asking about Laura and the children.'

He held up a hand. 'It's okay. I'm getting used to it. Since you didn't ask I'll tell you. It looks as though Laura will be going with her mother to her sister's in Sydney. In which case the kids are going with her. They aren't emigrating exactly. It's more of a trial. If it doesn't work out, they can come straight back. If it looks promising, then they'll probably stay.'

'I suppose it depends on the availability of work and schools and suchlike.'

'That's the least of my problems. I may not see them again.'

'Oh God, I'm so insensitive, but surely it's not as bad as that.'

'That is the extreme, I admit. But they aren't exactly within regular travelling distance for access visits. They would cost an arm and a leg. On the practical side, work isn't so much of a problem, in the short term at least. We lived there before, you see. I was in research at the University in Sydney for a couple of years. Laura still has a lot of friends there. I think she's exploring a request from one of her former colleagues to do some editorial work for one of the international academic journals. It's not full-time but it will give her the necessary foothold should she want to make a life there with the children.'

'And how would you feel about losing your family?'

Tom shrugged and said nothing.

Chris nodded slowly. 'Words fail you, eh?'

'Something like that.'

'I can't imagine you as a private researcher. You're much more at home with the laboratory and your research students.

'I don't see you as a senior policewoman, among all those hunky coppers, working out in the gym and talking about cars and pensions.'

'Touché.'

'I'll take your new image seriously if you'll believe me.'

She nodded.

A little later, Tom caught a glimpse of someone wearing an anorak of the same distinctive green and blue of Chris's, disappearing round the far side of a police car.

'Hang on!'

He broke into a run and she turned round.

'I thought you'd gone.'

'I could say the same.'

'I wouldn't go willingly without you.'

'That's not very original.'

'It's not a very original feeling. Rather deep and traditional in fact.'

'Don't embarrass us both, Tom.'

'I'm not intending to, merely describing and giving a compliment.'

'I don't mean to offend you, but I can't accept it. The time's not right.'

'When is the right time?'

'I don't know, but this is the end of the journey for us.'

'Does that mean forever?'

'Forever's a long time. I can't answer that.'

'It's very presumptuous of you to decide on our behalf.'

'I'm being practical. You've got your life here, your – your family. Me, well, things change all the time.'

'What sort of change?' Tom was groping for a foothold on where she was at. There was something new here he had to grasp, before over-reacting, which he knew he was about to do.

'I'm leaving the office.'

'Leaving?' Listen to me, he thought weakly. God, I sound like an overwrought teenager.

'Leaving the town, leaving Yorkshire, leaving this country.'

Tom felt dizzy. He wanted to sit down, but there was nowhere. He reached out for the wall and it held him up while his head swam and his eyes slowly came back into focus.

'Leaving the country.'

'Yes, a trip abroad. Well, more like a secondment, or unpaid leave to be more precise.'

'Where for God's sake?' It's probably Calais or Brussels, he thought. Only down the road in these days of rapid transport and electronic mail.

'Japan.'

'What the – what the hell are you going to do in Japan of all places?'

'Thanks for the vote of confidence. I'll file it.'

'Sorry, it's a shock I guess. How long for? Three, six, nine months?'

'It's not like that. More or less open-ended, I suppose.'

'You mean you won't be back, ever?'

'I mean I don't know yet when I will be back. And no, I might never return. It all depends, as they say.'

He was still struggling along behind her, speaking now to fill in time while he caught up. 'And what are you going to do?'

'Something I've already started. Some work with Japanese Police Forces on interrogation techniques. They want to develop more softness and sophistication, Western-style. I've got the skills to facilitate this.'

'So it's goodbye, then.'

'Yes.'

'You seem pleased.'

'I am pleased this case is over and I'm pleased to be going to Japan. But let's be clear, Tom, I definitely am not pleased to be leaving you here. Understand?'

'I can see that.'

'You're letting me go then? Without guilt?'

'I am.'

'And you can go back to Laura and the kids?'

'The kids yes, Laura, maybe.'

'You'll come round to the idea.'

'I said maybe.'

Chris suddenly walked back round the front of the vehicle and leaned against him, pressing him back against the bonnet.

'It's been good, Tom, very good,' she said.

'It has been good.'

'Let's take that away, without any surplus baggage.'

'If ever you change your mind, and need a porter –'

'I'll keep you in mind,' she said, her upper lip quivering in that distinctive way he'd come to know so well.

'I'll damn well keep you in mind as well,' he said as he watched her walk to the vehicle and slide in. Like Venus, he thought distractedly as she drove away.

The edge of the storm was moving rapidly eastwards in the stiff wind, away from the Wolds. The rain ceased suddenly, like a tap being turned off, leaving the ground steaming in the glowering light of the over bright evening sun. Humidity and heat together sank into the earth, fomenting energy. It could only be a matter of time before an eruption took place, through any accessible aperture to the surface.

Ten yards away, in the middle of the clearing was an exit hole, about half a metre across. A dark red stain several metres in diameter spread in a rough circle around it. It flickered and danced in the late sunlight. It resolved itself into thousands of milling bodies.

Chapter 43

Graver turned up the volume to shut out the sound of his own heart beating. He sat in his cellar and peeled off the mask, shaking his head and wiping his face with a towel he'd placed ready. He was pleased the police had taken away the body of the druggie he'd picked up from a bench in Queen's Gardens near the town centre of Hull the other night. The ants had already dined on the face, so it would take time for the police to put two and two together. There would be DNA analysis, of course, but by then he'd be out of the country. He preened himself on his skilful disguises, first as John Thompsen, then as Luis Deakin. From the control centre he could see through to the adjacent underground storage areas where the vats stood, with their sealed feeder entrances strapped to the sides and plastic reinforced hoses disappearing towards the surface. He adjusted one of the underground cameras, training it and focusing on the nest in vat number four, to check that all was as it should be. The camera was set high in the side on a bracket, with the infra red light directly behind it and the white light on a timer over the other side, to sustain the pattern of night and day. The other tubes and apparatuses regulated the supply of air and cleaned out excess carbon dioxide, as well as offering supplies of synthetic food. In this way, the breeder colonies could survive more or less indefinitely.

He trained one of his two surviving cameras – perched high on the tree-lined slopes of the far valley side – on the scene and zoomed in. He nodded as he watched the officers poring over what they imagined to be his remains. Not that it didn't have some attractions. He'd noted with approval the element of affection in rituals involving the members of the tribe eating the remains of newly deceased relatives. He smiled to himself at the thought that one day, but hopefully a long time in the future, at the last he would offer his body to the ants.

'The problem is how to ensure you die at the right time,' he said out loud to himself. There was much to do but he must be patient. He switched on the emergency gas supply and put the kettle on the little cooker. But first, a cup of coffee.

Apthorpe had driven back to the farm in his Land Rover and sat in the clearing beyond the farmyard in that sole remaining vehicle, staring forward vacantly.

The colour of the ground changed dramatically as the ants swarmed from the hole as swiftly as an unfolding carpet. Within seconds the mass braided into many columns which snaked quickly forward. A close-up of each column revealed that its rapid progress was due to ants from the rear running over the still bodies of those in front, thus forming a living causeway.

Several metres from the hole a change was visible in the columns. They were broadening at their furthest extremities from the hole. As each assumed the shape of a huge goblet, their edges touched each other and a single army of ants coalesced and sped towards its target – the vehicle parked in the clearing.

'Sorry, comrade,' muttered Graver almost wistfully. 'It's a hard world.'

* * *

After a few minutes, Apthorpe felt the desire to go and have one last look at the nearest crater, fresh from his subterranean explosions. He opened the door and climbed down awkwardly, the jeep not particularly friendly towards the mobility of his considerable bulk. He waddled over to the fringe of trees at the edge of the clearing and peered into the gloom. He could just make out the circle of black against the lighter background of the surrounding thickets which prevented him getting any closer.

The strains of Mahler's symphony no. 10 filled the farmyard. Odd, thought Apthorpe, where was the music coming from? At first, he thought he saw a ripple of movement on one side of the hole, but as he stared the effect seemed to stabilise and dissolve. The silence in this place was pretty well absolute, save for the usual tiny forest sounds of the night. Apthorpe turned round, went back and levered himself up into the driving seat again. He reached forward to turn the key in the ignition. He felt a tickling sensation on his leg. Without thinking he put his hand down and scratched it. He jerked his hand up in a reflex action at the stabbing in his finger. He shook his hand wildly at the shock of seeing a huge Sauba soldier ant hanging there, mandibles firmly embedded in the soft flesh of the fat mound below his thumb. But it only released its grip in death, when he had virtually scraped its body into sticky fragments against the door of the jeep. By then, of course, the shadow between his legs had resolved itself into a solid mass of ants, climbing up over each other, completely covering his legs and thighs in a matter of seconds. If it hadn't been for the overwhelming pain at thousands of almost simultaneous bites, and the terror as ants started to drop from the roof onto his bald head and scurry down his neck, Apthorpe would have been quicker off the mark. He got the vehicle started and pushed it into gear. It rolled clear of the carpet of ants. Slowly, it ground up the mound at the edge of the clearing.

A huge, dripping canopy of ants wafted across the treetops, along nets attached to the highest branches projecting beneath. As if at a signal, they cascaded down the tree trunks all round the vehicle and hung in living chains and curtains across the track. Several of these smacked into the windscreen and dissolved into thousands of scurrying ants at each flail. Apthorpe couldn't see where he was going. He drove ahead, the wheel spun under his shaking hands and he jolted across a shallow ditch and up against a tree. Steam rose from the buckled bonnet. It was journey's end for the Land Rover.

If Apthorpe hadn't flailed about wildly he might have left the vehicle and propelled himself towards the boundary moat. As it was, he lost consciousness just at the moment of realisation that they had got into his trousers and were beginning to tear away at the folds of fat on his huge paunch.

Graver emerged from his observation chamber in time to witness the last groups of ants skirmishing round the feast. Morsels of brain were being sawn off by the workers and dropped from the well-cleaned skull. A dozen of the small workers clamped their mandibles into each juicy fragment and struggled to carry it away. The gruesome feast was nearly finished.

Chapter 44

At Chris's home, the phone was ringing. She lay in the bath, waiting for it to stop. It went on and on, stopped, then started again. Eventually, she levered herself out, wiped her feet on the bathmat, gave herself a quick rub with the bath towel, threw on a bathrobe and padded to the phone.

'Hullo?'

'Chris? This is Tom.'

'I know.' She sighed. 'I thought we'd agreed. No more calls.'

'It's not any old call. I'm outside. Are you going to let me in?'

'You stupid man.'

'I understand.'

'I don't mean that. Wait while I find the key.'

She scrabbled around with a hairbrush to make her hair decent and checked her face quickly in a mirror. She let him in and gave him a quick peck on the cheek.

'I have to say this. That other life we were discussing three months ago. I thought I should let you know, there's been a change. I think it's beginning.'

'That's good, Tom, very, very good.'

'There is – there can be a future for people like us, Chris.'

'Lots of things can be, for people like us.'

'You know what I mean.'

'I know what you mean.'

'Can we keep in touch?'

She took a deep breath. 'Perhaps. I think you should go now. Here's my card.'

'Au revoir, ma cherie.'

'I'll write and keep you posted.'

She watched him as he turned and walked away. The phone was ringing. She closed the door and picked up the receiver.

'DCI Winchester here. Right, yes. I'll be there in less than an hour.'

She walked into the bedroom and reached across the dressing table for a tissue to wipe her eyes. It was time to get ready for work.

The End

Acknowledgements

This book owes everything to my obsession with ants over more than half a century. The killing power of ants has fascinated me for many years. If we extend the idea of killing other beings to include the rest of the human and non-human living beings in the world – ants not least among them. We all have the potential in us to become killers. I wanted to explore in this book how ants can be used as murder weapons.

I've lived with the two antmen in this book – Fortius and Graver – for more than fifty years. Fortius has grown out of me. Hopefully, whatever is grotesque and monstrous belongs exclusively to Graver. The dark side of the vast majority of us will never reach the extremes portrayed in this book. But we dip into that dark world from time and return with relief to the light.

I also wish to acknowledge my debt to the following:

- my late parents and other household members, for putting up with the permanent presence of ants in the 'ant shed', in the garden, as well as in the bedroom;

- my biology teacher Mr E G Jones, at Farnborough Grammar School, for being patient with my childhood obsession with keeping ants, for turning over the school biology laboratory to them at one point and for introducing me to the Schools Natural History Society, which made it possible in my mid-teens to trek to London and exhibit my observation colonies at the Burlington House premises of the Linnaean Society, Piccadilly, London;

- the distinguished myrmecologist and author Derek Wragge Morley, whom I met as a young teenager and who had a great impact on my preoccupation with the longitudinal study of ant societies;

- many colleagues who have tried to be patient with my no doubt irritating tendency to engage them in unscientific, but fascinating debates, beyond behaviourism and socio-biology, about how ants communicate.

RVA